Presented t

From

Date

# The Baker Bible Dictionary For Kids

Baker Bible Dictionary for Kids



Produced with the assistance of The Livingstone Corporation.
Bruce B. Barton, James C. Galvin, Shawn A.Harrison, Daryl J. Lucas, Carol J. Smith, David R. Veerman, project staff.



Published in Grand Rapids, Michigan by Baker Book House.

ISBN 0-8010-4345-x

Printed in the United States of America.

3 4 5 6 7 — 00 99 98 97

The Baker

# Bible Dictionary For Kids

Daryl J. Lucas

*Contributing Editors*
Bruce B. Barton, D. Min.
James C. Galvin, Ed.D.
David R. Veerman, M. Div.

BAKER BOOK HOUSE
Grand Rapids, Michigan

New Kids Media

# *How to Use*
# *the Baker Bible Dictionary for Kids*

This dictionary has tons and tons of Bible words, and nothing but Bible words. If you find a word in the Bible that you don't understand, grab this dictionary. It has just about every Bible word that your regular dictionary leaves out or doesn't tell enough about.

It also has some of the high-voltage words that you may hear in church. What is "propitiation," you ask? Look it up! You'll find a definition for it and other slippery church words in here, including "redemption," "sanctification," "Trinity," and many others.

And since this is a Bible dictionary, every definition tells you where you can find that word in the Bible. For example, the definition for the mysterious Melchizedek will tell you not only who he was, but also three key places where you can find his name in the Bible.

## Finding the words

All the words appear the way they would in any other dictionary. If you want to know what an **ephod** is, go to the **E** section. It'll be after "Easter" and before "eternal life." You know the drill.

If you can't find the word you're looking for, think about how else it might be spelled. Some Bible words can be spelled more than one way because the Bible was first written in Hebrew and Greek, and the translators got to make up their own spellings. (Pretty nice for the translators, huh?) For example, some of the men and women who translated the word "Chorazin" noticed that it started with a hard K sound, so they spelled it "Korazin." Others said "Chorazin" is better because it looks more like the way the Greek word looks. Who's right? Nobody. You just have to know that Bible words drive teachers nuts at spelling test time. It may pay off to have another Bible handy that spells words a little differently.

## Pronouncing the words

Don't feel bad if you don't know how to pronounce a new word. Just look at the part in parentheses. Here's an example from the word Jashobeam:

**Jashobeam** (juh-**shoh**-bee-uhm)

The part in parentheses tells you how it sounds. Say the bold part loudest.

**Learning more about the words**

This dictionary even has hyperlinks. The definition of **scribe**, for example, has three of them; see if you can find them in this sample:

scribe **(skribe)**
* A person who wrote and copied important documents. In Old Testament times, kings often had scribes write letters, record histories, and take notes on legal matters. Scribes also copied the Scriptures.
Jeremiah 36:32
* An older word for teacher of the law.
Nehemiah 8:13
See also Pharisees

The italic type tips you off to other words in this dictionary. If you don't know what "Scriptures," "teacher of the law," or "Pharisees" means, you can put a bookmark at **scribe** and look them up.

**Surfing the themes**

One more thing you should know about is the themes. This dictionary calls special attention to three kinds of words:

| | |
|---|---|
| Words about Sin and Salvation | Yellow Highlighting |
| Words about God and Jesus | Green Highlighting |
| Words about the Christian Life | Pink Highlighting |

Each time you see a word and definition highlighted with one of these colors, you know that word belongs to that group of words. It's a handy way to find words about those important topics.

That's it! The Baker Bible Dictionary for Kids isn't hard to use, just fun and packed with information. It's here for you any time you need to look up a Bible word or phrase. I hope you like it.

May God bless you as you study his Word.

Daryl J. Lucas

Exodus 7:1-2, 9
Exodus 30:30

**Aaron** (**air**-uhn)
*Moses*' older brother and one of the men who led Israel out of slavery in Egypt.
See also *Exodus, the; priest*

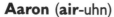

**Ab** (**ahb**)
Fifth *month* of the Israelite year, overlapping July and August. Ab is not mentioned in the Bible.

Revelation 9:11
Job 31:12
Proverbs 15:11

**Abaddon** (uh-**bad**-uhn)
A word that means "destruction." It is used to describe death.

Mark 14:36
Romans 8:15
Galatians 4:6

**abba** (**ah**-buh)
An Aramaic word for father. Children used it to address their fathers, and students used it to address their teachers.

**Abdon** (**ab**-don)

Judges 12:13-15

• Son of Hillel and eleventh *judge* of Israel after *Elon*. Abdon judged Israel eight years.
• Three other Israelites mentioned only once.

Joshua 21:30

• A *Levitical city* in the territory allotted to *Asher*, about 13 kilometers north-northeast of Acco.

**Abednego**
(uh-**bed**-nuh-goh)
One of the three Hebrew men thrown into the fiery furnace for refusing to bow down to the statue that King *Nebuchadnezzar* made. Abednego was the name given to him by the Babylonians. His Hebrew name was Azariah.

*Daniel 1:7*
*Daniel 2:49*
*Daniel 3:28*

**Abel** (**ay**-bul)
The second son born to Adam and Eve; Cain's younger brother.

*Genesis 4:2, 8*
*Hebrews 11:4*

**Abel Beth Maacah** (**ay**-buhl **beth may**-uh-kuh)
A *fortified city* in the territory allotted to Naphtali famous for its part in Sheba's revolt against David. *Sheba* tried to hide in Abel Beth Maacah, but the *elders* of the city decided not to resist Joab's forces.

*2 Samuel 20:14-22*

**Abiathar** (uh-**bye**-uh-thar)
A priest at Nob when King Saul tried to kill all of the priests there. Abiathar escaped to become one of King David's counselors.

*1 Samuel 22:20-21*
*2 Samuel 15:24*
*1 Kings 2:27*

**Abib** (**ay**-bib)
The first *month* of the Israelite year, overlapping March and April. Abib is called Nisan in Nehemiah 2:1.

*Exodus 13:3-4*
*Deuteronomy 16:1*

**Abiezer** (ah-bee-**ay**-zur)

A name that means "my father is help."

• A clan in the tribe of Mannaseh. *Gideon* was a member of this clan.

*Joshua 17:2*
*Judges 6:34*

• One of David's *mighty men*. He had command of 24,000 men in David's militia.

*2 Samuel 23:27*
*1 Chronicles 27:12*

**Abigail** (**ab**-i-gale)

• One of David's wives and mother of David's second son Daniel. Before marrying David, she was a widow of *Nabal*, a wealthy man who refused to help David while David was on the run from King Saul.

*1 Samuel 25:3, 23*
*1 Samuel 25:39*

• One of David's sisters.

*2 Samuel 17:25*
*1 Chronicles 2:13-17*

**Abihu** (uh-**bye**-hoo)

One of Aaron's sons, a priest. Abihu and his brother *Nadab* were killed for disobeying the laws for sacrifices. His name means "he is my father."

*Exodus 6:23*
*Exodus 28:1*
*Leviticus 10:1-2*

**Abijah** (uh-**bye**-juh)

At least five people:

• Son of *Reheboam* and second king of Judah after his father; also known as Abijam. Abijah declared war on the northern kingdom of Israel for rebelling against

*1 Chronicles 3:10*
*2 Chronicles 12:16*
*1 Kings 15:6-8*

his father. He reigned three years and was succeeded by his son *Asa*.

• *Samuel's* second son. — 1 Chronicles 6:28

• A descendant of Aaron, appointed by David to be a priest. — 1 Chronicles 24:5-10

• A son of *Jeroboam* I. — 1 Kings 14:1-4

• One of the family heads at the time of Zerubbabel. — Nehemiah 10:1-7; Nehemiah 12:1-4

• King *Hezekiah's* mother. — 2 Chronicles 29:1-2; 2 Kings 18:1-2

A

**Abijam** (uh-**bye**-juhm)

Another name for King *Abijah*.

**Abimelech** (uh-**bim**-uh-lek)

Three *Philistine* kings and one *Israelite*:

• A king of *Philistia* in Abraham's time. — Genesis 20:1-7; Genesis 21:22-34

• A king of Philistia in Isaac's time. — Genesis 26:1-6; Genesis 26:26-29

• A king of Philistia in David's time. — 1 Chronicles 18:16; 2 Samuel 8:17

It is possible that in Philistia "Abimilech" was a title, like "king" rather than a personal name.

• Illegitimate son of *Gideon* who murdered 69 of his half-brothers. — Judges 9:1-6

**Abiram** (uh-**bye**-ruhm)

• Brother of *Dathan* and one of the rebels in league with Korah. — Numbers 16:1-2; Deuteronomy 11:5-7

• A son of Hiel who died while Hiel was rebuilding Jericho. — 1 Kings 16:34

1 Kings 1:1-4

**Abishag** (**ab**-i-shag)
A woman who took care of *David* in his old age.

1 Samuel 26:6-9
2 Samuel 2:24
1 Chronicles 2:16

**Abishai** (**ab**-i-shye)
David's nephew and a very high-ranking officer in David's army. Abishai commanded one of the elite groups of *Three* among David's *mighty men*.

1 Samuel 14:50-51
2 Samuel 3:26-27

**Abner** (**ab**-nur)
A relative of Saul who commanded Saul's army. He was murdered by *Joab* after Saul's death.

Proverbs 6:16-19
Luke 16:15

**abomination** (uh-**bah**-mi-**nay**-shuhn)
Something God hates.

Genesis 12:4
Genesis 15:5-6
Hebrews 11:8-12

**Abraham**
(**ay**-bruh-ham)
Father of the Hebrew nation, first called *Abram*. God called Abram out of *Ur of the Chaldeans* and told him to go to "a land I will show you." Abram obeyed. God promised to make him into a great nation and changed his name to Abraham, "father of many." All semitic peoples trace their roots to Abraham; the Jews through his son Isaac, the Arabs through his son Ishmael.

**Abraham's bosom** (**ay**-bruh-hamz **bu**-zuhm)
A figure of speech that means "close to Abraham." Jesus used this expression to describe the place of comfort where *Lazarus* went after he died.

*Luke 16:22-23*

**Abram** (**ay**-bruhm)
The name that *Abraham* had before God changed it; the name Abraham had when God first called him out of *Ur of the Chaldeans*.

*Genesis 17:3-7*

**Absalom** (**ab**-suh-luhm)
Third son of King *David* who once led a rebellion against his father. King *Rehoboam* married Absalom's daughter, *Maacah*.

*2 Samuel 13:20-22*
*2 Samuel 15:-7-11*
*2 Chronicles 11: 20-21*

**Abyss** (uh-**biss**)
A place of torment reserved for Satan and his demons. This is not the same as the *lake of fire*.

*Luke 8:30-31*
*Revelation 9:1-2*

**Achaia** (uh-**kay**-uh)

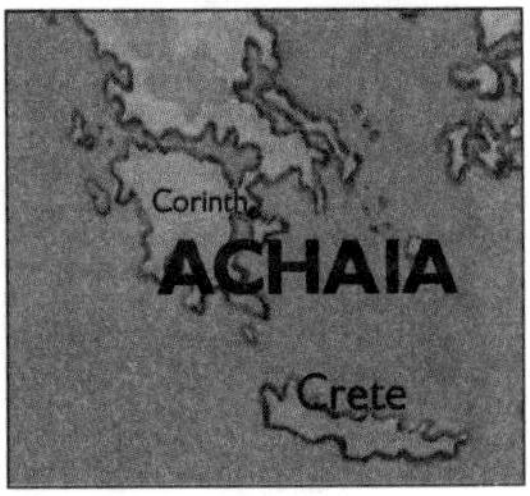


A Roman province and the smallest region of Greece on the *Peloponnesus* at the time of Christ, directly south of Macedonia. Its most famous biblical city was *Corinth*.

*2 Corinthians 1:1*
*Acts 18:27*

A

Joshua 7:1
Joshua 7:20-21

**Achan** (**ay**-kuhn)

An Israelite from the tribe of Judah who stole some of the spoils from the attack on *Jericho*. God had told the people not to take any of the spoils for themselves.

1 Samuel 21:10-15
1 Samuel 27:2-7

**Achish** (**ay**-kish)

The king of *Gath* while David was running from King Saul. Achish's reign lasted until the time of Solomon.

**Acropolis** (uh-**crah**-puh-liss)

A very large hill in *Athens* where the temple of Athena (the Parthenon) stands.

Acts 2:1-4

**Acts, book of**

The fifth book of the New Testament, after John. Acts records "the acts of the apostles," the leaders of Christianity after Christ returned to heaven. The book tells of the spread of Christianity from Jerusalem to the Roman world, and from the Jews to the *Gentiles*. It was written by Luke, the same man who wrote the Gospel of Luke, sometime between A.D. 62 and 70.

Genesis 2:7
Genesis 4:1-2
Luke 3:38

**Adam** (**ad**-uhm)

• The first man God created. Adam was created perfect. But Adam's decision to disobey God's instructions brought *sin*

into the world. From that day on, all people ever born would be *sinners*. That is why God required the Israelites to make *offerings*, and why he sent his Son *Jesus Christ*.

• A city on the banks of the Jordan River 28 kilometers north of Jericho, just south of where the *Jabbok* River meets the Jordan. *Joshua 3:14-17*

See also *born again; death; forgiveness; make atonement*

**Adar** (**ay**-dar)

The twelfth *month* of the Israelite year, overlapping February and March. *Ezra 6:15; Esther 3:7; Esther 9:15*

**Adnah** (**ad**-nuh)

• A commander in Saul's army who defected to David along with several others from the tribe of Manasseh. Adnah became a commander in David's army. *1 Chronicles 12:20*

• Commander over 300,000 men in *Jehoshaphat's* army. *2 Chronicles 17:14*

**Adonijah** (ad-uh-**nye**-juh)

• David's fourth son by his wife Haggith. Adonijah laid claim to the throne after David, but David had already promised it to Solomon. *2 Samuel 3:4; 1 Kings 1:5-7, 53; 1 Kings 2:23-25*

• A Levite sent by *Jehoshaphat* to teach in Judah. *2 Chronicles 17:8-9*

• One of the Israelite leaders who agreed to Nehemiah's covenant. *Nehemiah 10:1, 14, 16*

A

**Adrammelech** (uh-**dram**-uh-lek)

*2 Kings 17:31*

• One of the false gods that the Assyrians brought into *Samaria* after taking control of the area. Worship of this god involved child sacrifice.

*2 Kings 19:36-37*
*Isaiah 37:38*

• One of two Assyrian brothers (the other was *Sharezer*) who murdered their father *Sennachrib*, king of Assyria.

*Exodus 20:14*
*Matthew 19:3-9*

**adultery** (uh-**duhl**-tur-ee)

To have sex with a person who is not your wife or husband. Adultery is forbidden in the *Ten Commandments*.

*John 3:23*

**Aenon** (**ee**-non)

One of the places where *John the Baptist* baptized people because it had so much water. Aenon was on the west bank of the Jordan near *Salim*, but its exact location is unknown.

*Acts 11:28-30*
*Acts 21:10-12*

**Agabus** (**ag**-uh-buhss)

A Christian prophet from Jerusalem who lived during the church's earliest days. He predicted a famine and the imprisonment of Paul.

*John 13:34*
*2 Corinthians 2:4*
*Galatians 5:14*

**agape** (uh-**gah**-pay)

A Greek word for *love* that implies selfless giving. One of the most famous examples is in John 3:16, "For God so *loved* the world that he gave his only Son, so that everyone who belives in him will not perish but have eternal life."

**Agrippa**
See *Herod Agrippa*

**Ahab** (**ay**-hab)

• Seventh king of Israel and husband of *Jezebel*. Ahab promoted the worship of Baal. Elijah defeated Ahab's prophets of Baal in a showdown at Mount Carmel. *1 Kings 16:29-33* *1 Kings 22:39*

• A false prophet during the time of Jeremiah. *Jeremiah 29:21-22*

**Ahasuerus** (ah-hah-zhoo-**air**-uhss) *Ezra 4:6* *Esther 1:1* *Daniel 9:1*

The Hebrew name for *Xerxes* I, king of Persia and Babylonia during Daniel and Esther's time.

See also *Cyrus; Darius*

**Ahaz** (**ay**-haz)

• Twelfth king of Judah who promoted the worship of false gods. *2 Kings 16:1-4* *2 Chronicles 28:24-25*

• One of King Saul's great-great-grandsons. *1 Chronicles 8:35-36*

A

**Ahaziah** (ay-huh-**zye**-uh)

*1 Kings 22:51-53*
*2 Kings 1:1-2*
• Son of *Ahab* and eighth king of Israel.

*2 Chronicles 22:1-5*
• Son of Jehoram and sixth king of Judah (also called Jehoahaz).

See also *Kings of Israel; Kings of Judah*

*Numbers 34:27*
**Ahihud** (uh-**hye**-hud)
The family leader of Asher chosen by God to help divide up the land after the conquest of Canaan.

**Ahijah** (uh-**hye**-juh)
At least nine people held this name, the most important of whom were these two:

*1 Kings 11:29-31*
• A prophet from *Shiloh* who told Solomon that his kingdom would be divided, with 10 of the tribes going to *Jeroboam I*.

*1 Chronicles 11:36*
• One of David's *mighty men*.

*2 Samuel 16:23*
*2 Samuel 15:12*
*2 Samuel 17:23*
**Ahithophel** (uh-**hith**-uh-fel)
One of David's most trusted counselors. Ahithophel betrayed David and joined *Absalom's rebellion*. He committed suicide after his plans failed.

**Ahitub** (uh-**hye**-tub)

*1 Samuel 14:3*
• A son of Phinehas and grandson of Eli.

*1 Chronicles 9:11*
*2 Samuel 8:17*
• Zadok's grandfather.

**Ai** (**ay**-eye)

A fortified city in Canaan just east of *Bethel*, one of the cities that God told the Israelites to destroy. The name means "heap" or "ruin." The Israelites took the city only after *Achan* had been punished for stealing some of the plunder from Jericho.

*Genesis 12:8*
*Joshua 7:2-5*

**Aijalon** (**ay**-juh-lon)

- An *Amorite* town in the territory allotted to Dan. The Amorites of Aijalon and *Shaalbim* stayed and became slaves of the Israelites rather than leave. *Judges 1:35*
- The *Valley of Aijalon* featured in Joshua's battle of Gibeon. *Joshua 10:12-13*
- The unknown place of *Elon's* burial in Zebulun. *Judges 12:12*

**alleluia** (ah-le-**loo**-yuh)

See *halleluia*

**alms, almsgiving** (**ahlmz**, **ahlmz**-giv-ing)

Gifts to the poor. God required the Israelites to share with the poor and to make sure they had some means of survival. Jesus added that alms should be given without noisy display.

*Matthew 6:1-4*
*Acts 10:2*

Revelation 1:8
Isaiah 44:6

**Alpha and Omega** (**al**-fuh, oh-**may**-guh)

A term for both God and Jesus found only in the book of Revelation. Alpha and omega are the first and last letters of the Greek alphabet. The term means that God is eternal and over all.

See also *God; Jesus Christ*

A

**Alphaeus** (**al**-fee-uhss)

Mark 2:14

- *Matthew's* grandfather.

Matthew 10:3
Acts 1:13

- The father of *James*, one of Jesus' disciples (to distinguish him from James son of Zebedee).

Genesis 8:20
Exodus 17:15
Acts 17:23

**altar** (**ahl**-tur)

A place of *sacrifice* or *worship*. An altar could be as simple as a pile of stones or as elaborate as the bronze table that the Israelites built at God's instructions to Moses. Burnt offerings were always to be made on the altar.

Genesis 36:12, 16

**Amalek** (**am**-uh-lek)

Esau's grandson and father of the Amalekite clan.

1 Chronicles 4:43
1 Samuel 30:18
Numbers 14:45

**Amalekites** (uh-**mal**-uh-kites)

People descended from *Amalek*; the Amalekite clan. They lived in the *Negev*. God told the Israelites to destroy the Amalekites, but Israel failed to do this. They were Israel's bitter enemies from the time of the Exodus to the time of Hezekiah.

**Amariah** (am-uh-**rye**-uh)

A common name among the Israelites:

- One of the leaders of Israel who sponsored *Ezra's reform*. — Nehemiah 10:3
- *Chief priest* during the time of *Jehoshaphat*. — 2 Chronicles 19:11
- Several others mentioned only by name.

A

**Amasa** (uh-**may**-suh)

- One of four leaders in the northern kingdom of Israel, together with *Azariah*, *Berekiah*, and *Jehizkiah*, who spoke out against making slaves of 200,000 prisoners of war. The prisoners were all fellow Israelites from the southern kingdom of Judah, captured after the defeat of *Ahaz's* forces. — 2 Chronicles 28:12
- David's nephew and Absalom's cousin. Amasa joined with *Absalom* in rebelling against David and commanded the rebel forces. After Absalom's defeat, David promised him Joab's position. But *Joab* murdered Amasa instead. — 2 Samuel 20:8-10

**Amaziah** (am-uh-**zye**-uh)

Four people had this name, the most important of which were these two:

- Son of King *Joash* and ninth king of Judah after his father. Amaziah was known as a good man who did not go as far as he could have in clear- — 1 Chronicles 3:12; 2 Chronicles 25:14-16

ing the land of pagan *high places* and *shrines*. He was assassinated by his own people after 29 years of rule.

Amos 7:10-17 • A priest in Israel who accused the prophet *Amos* of treason against *Jeroboam* II.

See also *kings of Judah*

A

Nehemiah 8:6

**Amen** (ay-**men** or ah-**men**)

An expression that means "so be it." It comes from the word's root meaning of "surely" or "truth."

**Ammiel** (**am**-ee-uhl)

Numbers 13:3,12 • One of the 12 men chosen by *Moses* at *Kadesh Barnea* to spy out the land of Canaan; a leader of the tribe of Dan; son of Gemalli.

1 Chronicles 3:5 • *Bathsheba's* father.

2 Samuel 9:4 • *Makir's* father.

1 Chronicles 26:5 • One of the temple *gatekeepers* during the time of David; son of *Obed-Edom*.

**Ammon** (**am**-uhn)

2 Chronicles 20: 10-12 • Another word for *Ammonites*

Amos 1:13-15

Judges 11:28-33

• The territory in which the *Ammonites* lived, a small region east of the Jordan River that was heavily protected by foritified cities. *Rabbah* served as Ammon's capital.

**Ammonites** (**am**-uhn-ites)

The people descended from Ben-Ammi, the son born to Lot's daughter. God told the Israelites to be kind to the Ammonites. Sadly, the Ammonites abused this kindness during the reign of *Jehoshaphat* in Jerusalem.

See also *Molech*

*Genesis 19:38*
*Deuteronomy 2:19-23*
*2 Chronicles 20:1-4*

A

**Amon** (**ay**-muhn)

Son of *Manasseh* and fifteenth king of Judah after his father. Amon was known as an evil king. He was assassinated by his own servants after only two years of rule.

See also *kings of Judah*

*2 Kings 21:19-24*

**Amorites** (**am**-ur-ites)

A common name for the people who inhabited Canaan before the Israelites; the Canaanites. It often referred to groups that lived in the hills as opposed to the plains.

*Numbers 21:13*
*Genesis 14:7*
*1 Samuel 7:14*

**Amos** (**ay**-muhss)

A prophet from *Tekoa* in Judah whom God called to preach to the northern kingdom of Israel.

See also *Amos, book of*

*Amos 1:1*

Amos 1:1

**Amos, book of**

(**ay**-muhss, **buk** uhv)

Thirtieth book of the Old Testament and third of the *minor prophets*. The book of Amos condemns the northern kingdom of Israel for its *idolatry* and neglect of the poor. It was written by the prophet *Amos* during the reign of *Jereboam* II.

A

**Amram** (**am**-ruhm)

Exodus 6:18-20

• *Moses'* father.

Ezra 10:18, 34

• One of those involved in the reform led by Ezra.

**Ananias** (an-uh-**nye**-uhss)

Acts 5:1-3

• Husband of *Sapphira* who lied to church leaders about the money that he and his wife had given to the church.

Acts 9:10-19

• The Christian living in *Damascus* who welcomed *Saul* of Tarsus right after Saul's conversion.

Acts 23:1-5

• *High priest* in Jerusalem whom Paul called a "whitewashed wall."

**Anathoth** (**an**-uh-thoth)

Joshua 21:18
Jeremiah 1:1

A town in the territory of Benjamin, about five kilometers northeast of Jerusalem. Anathoth was Jeremiah's hometown.

**Ancient of Days** (**ayn**-shuhnt uhv **dayz**)
A name for God found only in the *book of Daniel.*

*Daniel 7:9, 13, 22*

**Andrew** (**an**-droo)
One of Jesus' *Twelve* disciples. He was Simon Peter's brother and a fisherman when Jesus called him.
See also *Twelve, the*

*Mark 1:29*
*John 12:22*

**angel** (**ayn**-juhl)

A spiritual being much like a *cherub* but with a different job. The main job of an angel is to serve people and deliver messages to them. God created angels to do his will and serve people.

*Psalm 148:2-5*
*Colossians 1:16*

**Anna** (**an**-uh)
A prophetess who lived when Jesus was dedicated at the temple. She was one of the first to recognize Jesus as the *Messiah.*

*Luke 2:36-38*

**Annas** (**an**-uhss)
*High priest* of Israel during Jesus' childhood, from A.D. 6 to A.D. 15. Later in life he served as an advisor to his son-in-law Caiaphas.

*John 18:13*
*Acts 4:6*

A

Exodus 40:15
Luke 7:46
Mark 14:8

**anoint** (uh-**noint**)

To pour a special oil on a person or thing and set apart that person or thing as *holy*. When a priest anointed a person, it meant that the person had God's favor or blessing. Being anointed meant being dedicated to God's service. God required that *anointing oil* be made in a certain way (Exodus 30:22-33).

A

**anointed** (uh-**noint**-uhd)
See *anoint*

Exodus 40:9

**anointing oil** (uh-**noint**-een oil)

Oil made according to the instructions of Exodus 30:22-33.

See also *anoint*

**antichrist** (**an**-tye-kriste)

1 John 2:18
1 John 2:22

• Any person who is against Christ and tries to lead people away from him.

1 John 2:18
1 John 4:3

• One person who will lead the entire world away from Christ right before Jesus returns; "the antichrist."

Acts 11:25-26
Acts 15:35

**Antioch** (**an**-tee-ok)

A major city in *Syria* about 500 kilometers north of Jerusalem. Believers in Christ were

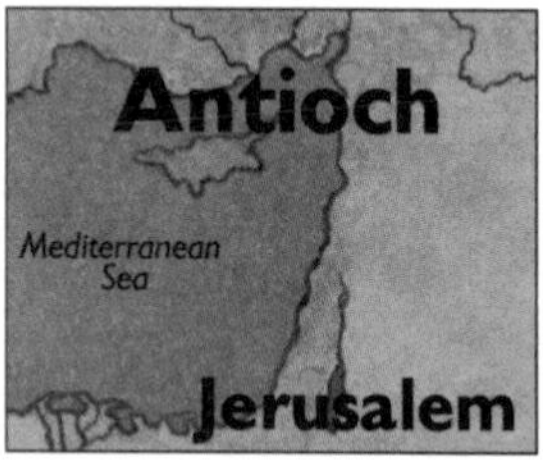

first called Christians there. Paul used it as a base of his ministry.

**Antioch, Pisidian** (**an**-tee-ahk, pi-**sid**-ee-uhn)
See *Pisidian Antioch*

**Antipas, Herod** (an-**tip**-uhss, **hair**-uhd)
See *Herod Antipas*

A

**Aphek** (**ay**-fek)
The name of at least four different places in *Palestine*:
• A city northeast of Joppa where the Philistines drew battle lines against Israel. *Joshua 12:18* *1 Samuel 4:1-2*
• One of the northern cities that Joshua did not capture. *Judges 1:31*
• One of the towns given to the tribe of Asher. *Joshua 19:30*
• A city east of the Sea of Galilee. *1 Kings 20:26*

**Apocalypse, the** (uh-**pah**-kuh-lipss, the) *Revelation 1:1*
Another name for the *book of Revelation*. "Apocalypse" means *revelation*. The word translated as "revelation" in Revelation 1:1 is the Greek word from which we get the word "apocalypse."

**Apollos** (uh-**pahl**-uhss) *Acts 18:24-25* *1 Corinthians 3:4*
A Jewish Christian who taught and led others in the church when Christianity was still very new. He met the apostle Paul in

Ephesus during Paul's third missionary journey. Apollos had been teaching the Christians there.

*Job 31:12*
*Proverbs 15:11*

**Apollyon** (uh-**pahl**-ee-on)
A Greek form of the Hebrew word Abaddon. It is used in Revelation 9:11 as a name for *Satan*.

A

*Acts 1:21-22*
*Acts 4:35-37*

**apostle** (uh-**pah**-suhl)
A person who received instructions from the risen Christ to lead and teach others about Christ. The word means *one who is sent*. It usually refers to the first group of those who began telling others about Christ. The most important of these were the *Twelve* and *Paul*.
See also *evangelist; prophet*

*Acts 18:1-3*
*1 Corinthians 16:19*

**Aquila and Priscilla** (uh-**kwil**-uh and pri-**sil**-uh)
A husband and wife pair of Christians who were friends of Paul. They lived in *Corinth* when Paul came there on his second missionary journey. Aquila had the same kind of job Paul had; he made tents.

*Numbers 21:13-15*
*Deuteronomy 2:9*

**Ar** (**ar**)
A main city of *Moab* during the time of the Exodus. It was located east of the Dead Sea, but no one knows exactly where.

**Arabah** (**ar**-uh-buh)

*Joshua 3:15-16*
*Mark 1:4-5*

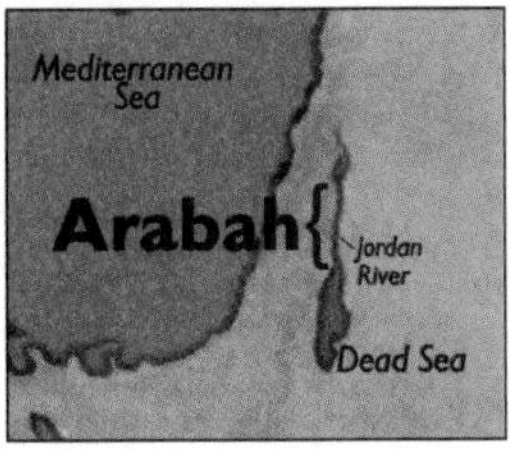


The rift valley that runs north-south from the Sea of Galilee to the Dead Sea to the Gulf of Aqabah. The Jordan River flows through the middle of Arabah.

**Arabia** (uh-**ray**-bee-uh)

*2 Chronicles 9:13-14*
*Isaiah 21:13*

The Arabian peninsula southeast of Palestine. The countries of Saudi Arabia, Yemen, Bahrain, Oman, the United Arab Emirates, Qatar, and Kuwait occupy this land today.

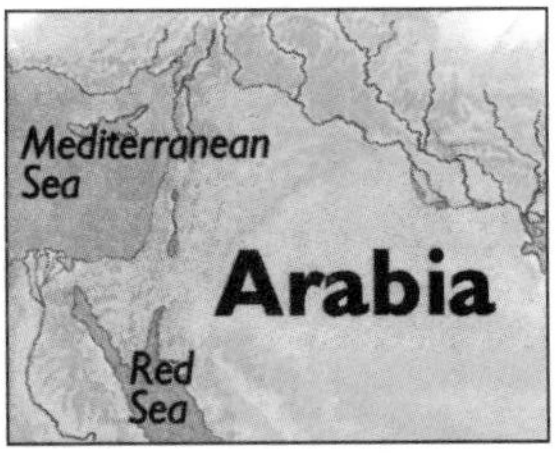


**Arad** (**air**-ad)

*Numbers 21:1*
*Judges 1:16*

One of the Canaanite cities conquered by the Israelites on their way to the promised land during the Exodus. It was located in the Negev south of Hebron.

**Aram** (**air**-uhm)

- A son of Shem and father of the Aramean people. *Genesis 10:22-23*
- A very large area northeast of Palestine settled by people descended from Aram, Noah's grandson. This area was sometimes called Syria, but *Genesis 24:10*

it occupies a much larger area than modern Syria.

*Ezra 4:7*
*Daniel 2:4*

**Aramaic** (air-uh-**may**-ik)
The language of the *Arameans*. Aramaic was a lot like Hebrew, and some people of the Bible used it. It was the main language in use during the time of Ezra, Nehemiah, and Daniel.

*Deuteronomy 26:5*

**Arameans** (air-uh-**mee**-uhnz)
People descended from Aram, the grandson of Noah. They lived in the land of Aram and included the Syrians and the Assyrians. They were a major part of Israel's history for hundreds of years. They harassed and oppressed Israel during the time of the judges, resisted David and Solomon's rule, and by the eighth century B.C. had captured most of the northern tribes of Israel.

*Genesis 8:4*
*Jeremiah 51:27*

**Ararat** (**air**-uh-rat)
The mountain on which Noah's *ark* came to rest after the flood. It is located in Armenia near Lake Van, on the northern border of modern Turkey.

**Araunah** (uh-**raw**-nuh)
The Jebusite man who sold his threshing floor, and the land around it, to David. This small piece of land became the site of Solomon's temple. — *2 Samuel 24:24; 1 Chronicles 21:25*

A

**archangel** (**ark-ayn**-juhl)
A word used only of the angel *Michael*, also called prince of Israel. Michael is the chief or most powerful angel. — *Daniel 10:13, 21; 1 Thessalonians 4:16; Jude 9*

**Areopagus** (**air**-ee-**ah**-puh-guhss)
- A hill northwest of the *Acropolis* in Athens. — *Acts 17:19*
- The council of officials that met on the Areopagus hill. This council had power to allow or deny permission to teach certain religious ideas. — *Acts 17:22*

**Ariel** (**air**-ee-uhl)
- One of the men who helped *Ezra* lead the reform in Israel. — *Ezra 8:16*
- A name for Jerusalem used by the prophet Isaiah. — *Isaiah 29:1*

**Arimathea** (air-i-muh-**thee**-uh)
"A city of the Jews" in New Testament times, hometown to *Joseph*. — *Matthew 27:57*

*Genesis 14:1, 9*

*Daniel 2:14-15*

**Arioch** (**air**-ee-ok)

• One of the kings whose army attacked and plundered *Sodom* when Lot lived there.

• The man who was commander of the king's guard when *Nebuchadnezzar* was ruler in Babylon. Arioch had been ordered to execute all the wise men of Babylon for not being able to interpret the king's dream, until Daniel told him that he could do it.

*Acts 19:29*
*Acts 20:4*

**Aristarchus** (air-i-**star**-kuhss)

One of the men who traveled with the apostle Paul and helped him in his ministry.

*Genesis 7:7-8*
*2 Peter 2:5*

**ark** (**ark**)

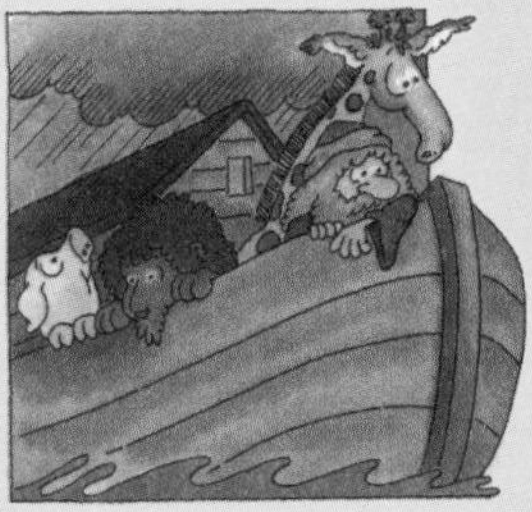

A box or chest used as a place of safety. In the Bible, this word is used to describe the boat that God told Noah to build. It kept *Noah*, his family, and the animals safe during the flood. Noah built it exactly as long, high, and wide as God told him. It was made of gopher wood and waterproofed with tar.

See also *Ark of the Covenant*

*Deuteronomy 31:26*
*Hebrews 9:2-4*

**Ark of the Covenant**
(**ark** uhv the **kuh**-vuh-nuhnt)

The most sacred object in Israel's worship. It was a box or chest made of acacia wood and overlaid with gold. On top was a "mercy seat" of gold, so called because the blood of the sacrificial lamb was sprinkled there once a year on the *Day of Atonement*. Two cherubim sat at either end of the lid. Inside were the two tablets of the Ten Commandments, a gold pot of manna, and Aaron's rod.

The ark was kept in the *Most Holy Place* of the *tabernacle* during the Exodus, and in the Most Holy Place of the *temple* after Solomon built it. The ark was never to be touched; it could only be carried by slipping two poles through rings at each of the four corners.

Other names for the Ark of the Covenant include Ark of the Testimony, Ark of the Lord, and Ark of God.

**Armageddon** (ar-muh-**ged**-uhn)

The place where all the armies of the world will meet in the very last rebellion against God. It is probably the valley between Mt. Carmel and Jezreel, though no one knows for sure.

*Revelation 16:16*

**armor bearer** (**ar**-mur **bair**-ur)

A person who carried a warrior's shield and sometimes spare weapons. Kings and officers always had an armor-bearer. Goliath had one.

*Judges 9:54*
*1 Samuel 14:6*

A

1 Chronicles 3:21

**Arnan** (**ar**-nuhn)

One of David's descendants.

Number 21:13
Joshua 1315-16

**Arnon** (**ar**-non)

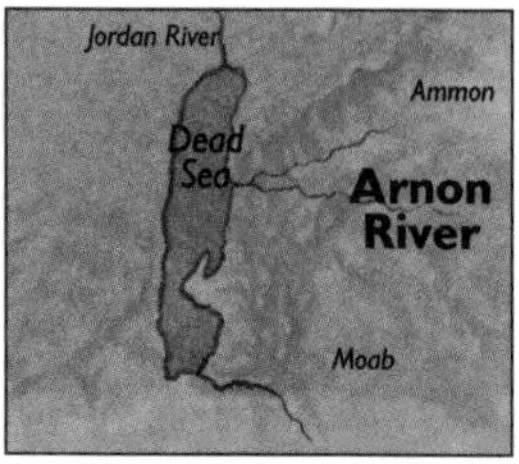


A river that flowed into the Dead Sea from the east. It served as the border between Moab on the south and *Ammon* on the north. The tribe of Reuben occupied the land north of this river after the conquest of Canaan.

**Aroer** (uh-**roh**-ur)

Deuteronomy 2:36
1 Chronicles 5:6-9

• An *Amorite* city on the north bank of the Arnon River, taken over by the tribes of Reuben and Gad after the conquest of Canaan.

1 Samuel 30:26-28
1 Chronicles 11:44

• A town in Judah southeast of *Beer Sheba*. David gave gifts to some men from this town.

**Arpad** (**ar**-puhd)

One of the Aramean cities conquered by the Assyrians. The Assyrian army that laid siege to Jerusalem during Hezekiah's reign bragged about their victory over this city in an effort to scare Hezekiah and his men.

Genesis 11:10-13
Luke 3:36

**Arphaxad** (ar-**fahk**-suhd)

One of *Shem's* sons and Noah's grandsons, born just two years after the *Flood*.

**Artaxerxes** (ar-tuh-**zurk**-seez)

*Nehemiah 2:1-5*

King of *Persia* during the time of *Ezra* and *Nehemiah*, the one who allowed these Jewish men to return to Jerusalem. His full name was Artaxerxes I Longimanus. He was the son of *Xerxes* I and ruled 40 years (464-424 B.C.).

A

**Artemis** (**ar**-tuh-mis)

*Acts 19:23, 24*

"Artemis of the Ephesians" was a Greek goddess of the moon and of hunting, known to the Romans as Diana. Paul ran into trouble with followers of Artemis while in *Ephesus*.

**Asa** (**ay**-suh)

*1 Kings 15:13*
*2 Chronicles 15:8*

Son of *Abijah* and third king of Judah. Asa was one of the few kings of Judah that obeyed God and led the people in doing the same. He reigned 41 years in Jerusalem.

**Asahel** (**ay**-suh-hel)

*2 Samuel 2:18-23*
*1 Chronicles 27:7*

Four people bore the name Asahel, the most famous of which was David's nephew and commander of David's fourth division. He was known for his amazing speed, but was also murdered for it by Abner. Asahel's death was avenged by his brother Joab.

**Asaiah** (uh-**say**-uh)

Four different men in the Old Testament, two of which were significant:

2 Chronicles 34: 19-21

• An officer in *Josiah's* court when the Book of the Law was discovered. Asaiah was one of those sent to ask the prophetess *Huldah* what they should do.

1 Chronicles 15: 6, 11

• A *Levite* family leader during the reign of David, one of the men ordered to help move the Ark of the Covenant to Jerusalem as soon as a place for it had been prepared.

1 Chronicles 16:5
Nehemiah 12:46

**Asaph** (**ay**-suhf)

One of David's three chief musicians. Asaph wrote Psalms 50 and 73–82. His descendants were the leaders of temple worship from David's time till the time of Ezra and Nehemiah.

John 20:17
Ephesians 4:9

**ascension, the** (uh-**sen**-shuhn, the)

The return of Jesus to heaven. After Jesus rose from the dead, he met and talked with his *disciples* over a period of 40 days. Then he went back to take his place at the Father's right hand, where he reigns as our King and serves as our High Priest.

**ascents, song of** (uh-**sentz**, **song** uhv)
See *song of ascents*

**Asenath** (**as**-uh-nath)
Egyptian mother of Manasseh and Ephraim; daughter of *Potiphera*; wife of Jacob's son Joseph.

Genesis 41:45, 50-52
Genesis 46:20

**Ashdod** (**ash**-dod)

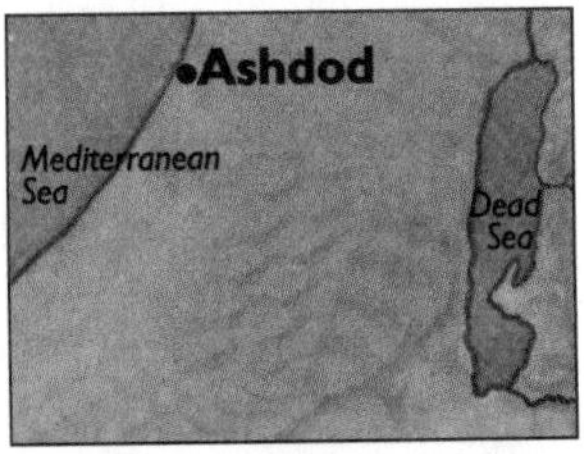


One of the five main cities of Philistia. When the Philistines captured the *ark of the covenant*, they carried it to the temple of *Dagon* in Ashdod.
See also *Ashkelon; Ekron; Gath; Gaza*

1 Samuel 5:1-2
Isaiah 20:1

**Asher** (**ash**-ur)

- Son of Jacob and the tribe of Israel named after him. *Zilpah* was his mother.
- The land allotted to the tribe of Asher.

See also *tribes of Israel*

Genesis 30:13
Luke 2:36-38

Numbers 26:44-47

**Asherah** (**ash**-ur-uh)
A goddess of the Canaanites and the *Aramean* peoples of Syria and Assyria. Worship of Asherah was so popular among Israel's neighbors that the Israelites themselves were often tempted to make and keep Asherah *idols*. God commanded them not to do this and to burn any idols they found.
See also *Asherah pole*

Exodus 34:13
1 Kings 16:29-33

1 Kings 16:33

**Asherah pole** (**ash**-ur-uh pohl)
An image or small statue of *Asherah* that the Canaanites worshiped. "Asherah pole" refers to the fact that they were usually made of wood.
See also *high place; shrine*

2 Kings 17:29-33

**Ashima** (uh-**shy**-muh)
The *idol* worshiped by the people of *Hamath* who settled in Samaria after the destruction of Israel.

Judges 14:19
Zephaniah 2:4

**Ashkelon** (**ash**-kuh-lon)
One of the five main *Philistine* cities. Israel occupied it for a brief time during the period of the judges, but the Philistines soon took it back.
See also *Ashdod; Ekron; Gath; Gaza*

Genesis 14:5
Deuteronomy 1:4

**Ashteroth-Karnaim** (**ash**-tur-oth-kar-**nay**-im)
One of the cities attacked and defeated by *Kedorlaomer* shortly before his attack on Sodom in the days of Abram and Lot. Its location is not known.

Judges 2:11-23
1 Samuel 7:3-4

**Ashtoreth** (**ash**-tur-eth)
A goddess of the *Sidonians*, also called Astarte. The kingdom of Israel was split in two partly because Solomon stopped worshiping God and worshiped Ashtoreth, against the first commandment (Exodus 20:3-4).

Acts 19:10
1 Corinthians 16:19

**Asia** (**ayzh**-yuh)
In New Testament times, a province of the Roman Empire

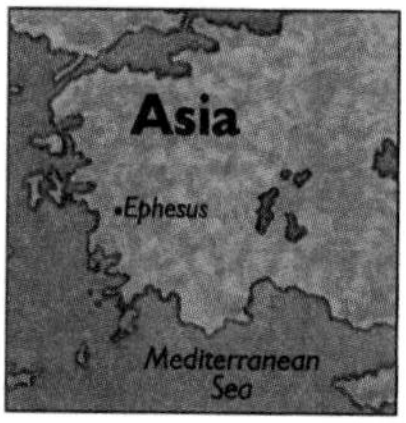

in the region later known as Asia Minor (modern Turkey). Major cities in the province of Asia included Ephesus, Smyrna, and Pergamum. The New Testament letter of Colossians was written to the Asian town of *Colosse*.

**assembly** (uh-**sem**-blee) *Exodus 12:6, James 2:2*
A meeting of believers; a *congregation*; a group of God's people gathered for worship.

**Asshur** (**ash**-ur) *Hosea 14:3*
The chief god of *Assyria*, the Assyrians, and the city that once served as their capital; Assyria.

**Asshurites** (**ash**-ur-ites) *Genesis 25:3*
Another name for the *Assyrians*.

**Assos** (**as**-os) *Acts 20:13-14*
A seaport on the northwest coast of the Roman province of *Asia*. Paul rendezvoused with some of his traveling companions there during his third missionary journey. Assos was in the region of Asia Minor known as *Mysia*.

**Assyria** (uh-**sihr**-ee-uh) *Genesis 10:11*
The *Aramean* people that lived in upper Mesopotamia; the land occupied by the Assyrians. The land of Assyria lay to the north of Babylonia. The Assyrians were among Israel's

A

bitterest enemies. During the time of the divided kingdom, God used the mighty Assyrian army to judge the northern kingdom of Israel.

**Astarte** (as-**tahr**-tee)
See *Ashtoreth*

*Isaiah 47:13*
*Daniel 2:2*

**astrologers** (uh-**strahl**-uh-jurz)
People who studied the stars. Some astrologers worshiped the stars or believed that the stars

affected people and life on earth. God forbade the worship of any false god, including stars and planets. The wise men of Babylon were astrologers. The magi who gave gifts to the baby Jesus were probably astrologers.

*2 Kings 11:1-3*
*2 Chronicles 22:12*

**Athaliah** (ath-uh-**lye**-uh)
Queen over Judah after Jehoahaz, the only queen ever to rule the Israelites and one of their most evil rulers. She murdered all but one of her grandsons,

*Joash*, who was rescued by his aunt. Athaliah reigned for six years.
See also *kings of Israel*

*Acts 17:15-16*
*1 Thessalonians 3:1*

**Athens** (**ath**-enz)
Greece's most famous city and a city in the Roman province of *Achaia* in New Testament

times. Paul preached at Athens on his second missionary journey, but got little response.

**atonement** (uh-**tohn**-ment) — *Romans 3:25*
Removal of God's anger against *sin* by means of a gift. *Jesus Christ* offered his life as the ultimate atonement.
See *born again; make atonement; salvation*

**Attalia** (at-uh-**lye**-uh) — *Acts 14:25*

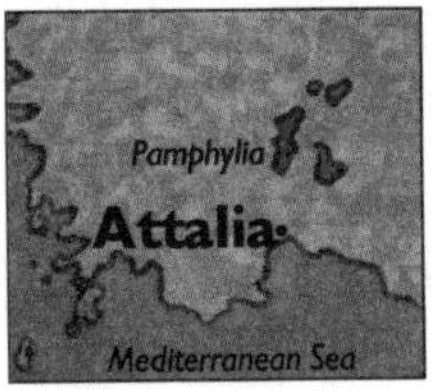


A port city in the Roman province of *Pamphylia* visited by the apostle Paul during his first missionary journey.
See also *Perga*

**Augustus** (uh-**guhs**-tuhss)
See *Caesar Augustus*

**Avva** (**ah**-vuh) — *2 Kings 17:24-25*
A province of *Assyria* whose inhabitants were sent to live in Samaria after the Assyrians took the Israelites of Samaria away.

**Azariah** (az-uh-**rye**-uh)
A very common name among the Israelites:
- Another name for King *Uzziah*. — *2 Kings 14:21*
- Israelite prophet in Judah who sparked *Asa's* reform. — *2 Chronicles 15:1-18*
- *Abednego's* Hebrew name. — *Daniel 1:6-7*, *Daniel 2:17*
- Two Levites who helped *Jehoiada* overthrow Athaliah; son of Jeroham and son of Obed. — *2 Chronicles 23:1*
- One of four leaders in the northern kingdom of Israel, together with *Jehizkiah*, *Berekiah*, and *Amasa*, — *2 Chronicles 28:12*

who spoke out against making slaves of 200,000 prisoners of war; son of Jehohanan. The prisoners were all fellow Israelites from the southern kingdom of Judah, captured after the defeat of Ahaz's forces.

*2 Chronicles 21:2*

• At least one of *Jehoshaphat's* sons.

*Jeremiah 43:2*

• Israelite army officer in league with *Johanan* son of Kareah; son of Hoshaiah.

• Several others mentioned only once.

**Baal** (**bay**-uhl)

The main god of many *Canaanite* peoples. Worship of Baal was a constant temptation for the Israelites. Many of Israel's kings promoted or allowed Baal worship in place of worship of the true God.

See also *idol; idolatry*

*Judges 6:25*
*1 Kings 18:25-26*

**Baal Peor** (**bay**-uhl **pay**-or)

A time when the Israelites of the *Exodus* joined with the people of Moab in worshiping the Baal of Peor. Their rebellion involved so much sin that 24,000 Israelites died in a plague.

*Numbers 25:1-9*
*Psalm 106:28*

**Baal-zebub** (**bay**-uhl-**zee**-bub)

The god of *Ekron*. King *Ahaziah* once tried to get this god to heal him.

*2 Kings 1:1-17*

**Baalath-Beer** (**bay**-uh-lath-**bee**-ur)

"*Ramah* of the Negev," a village in the land allotted to Judah.

*Joshua 19:8*

**Baanah** (**bay**-uh-nuh)

- A captain of Ish-Bosheth's raiding parties together with his brother *Recab*; son of Rimmon. Baanah and Recab tried to win favor with David by killing *Ishbosheth*.
  *2 Samuel 4:1-12*
- Two others mentioned only by name.
  *2 Samuel 23:29*
  *Ezra 2:2*

**Baasha** (**bay**-uh-shuh)

Third king of the northern kingdom of Israel. Baasha rose to power by assassinating his predecessor, King Nadab, and the entire royal family of Jeroboam.

*1 Kings 15:27-28*
*1 Kings 16:10-13*

B

B

*Genesis 11:4-9*

**Babel** (**bay**-buhl)

The great city of Genesis 11, where the tower of Babel was built, and once the capital of Babylonia. It was at the tower of Babel that God caused new languages to form as a punishment for human pride. Babel later became known as Babylon.

*Genesis 10:10*
*Daniel 1:1*

**Babylon** (**bab**-uh-lawn)

The capital of Babylonia. Babylon was founded by Nimrod and located on the Euphrates River.

*Isaiah 11:11*

**Babylonia** (bab-uh-**loh**-nee-uh)

The empire of southern Mesopotamia (modern Iraq). The Israelites spent 70 years as prisoners in Babylonia during the time of Daniel. It was ruled at different times by the Assyrians, the Babylonians, the Persians, the Greeks, and the Romans.

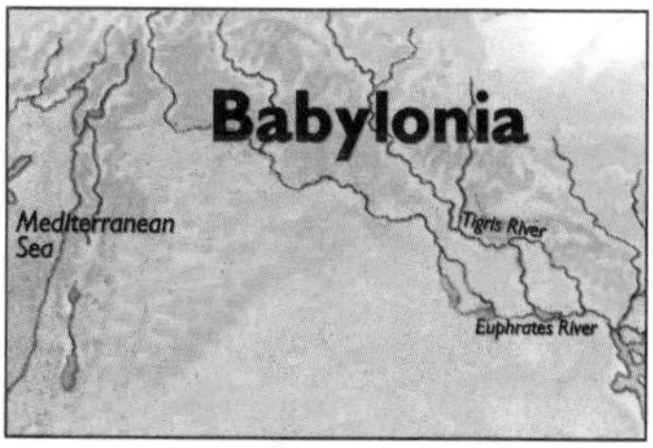


*Jeremiah 24:4-5*

**Babylonians** (bab-uh-**loh**-nee-uhnz)

The people of Babylonia.

**Balaam** (**bay**-luhm) — *Numbers 22:25-27*

An Israelite who did magic and claimed to be able to bless and curse people. The king of Moab hired Balaam to curse the people of Israel during the *Exodus*, but God stopped him with his donkey. He later advised the Israelites to worship *Baal*, and for this he was put to death.

**Balak** (**bay**-luhk) — *Numbers 22:1-6*

The king of Moab who hired Balaam to curse the Israelites during the *Exodus*.

**balm of Gilead** (**bawlm** uhv **gil**-ee-uhd) — *Jeremiah 8:22*

A cosmetic and a medicine that the Israelites made from either a spice or tree sap. No one knows for sure what this spice or sap was or how it got its name.

See also *stacte; incense*

**baptism** (**bap**-tiz-uhm) — *Matthew 21:25; Romans 6:4; Ephesians 4:5*

A special ceremony in which a pastor or other spiritual leader uses water to show that a person belongs to God. John the Baptist baptized Jesus in the Jordan River. Churches today often

B

sprinkle or dunk a person in water at the church. In some churches only babies are baptized, and in other churches only people who are old enough to ask to be baptized are baptized.
See also *baptist*

*Matthew 3:1, 5-6*

**baptist** (**bap**-tist)
A person who baptizes. John the Baptist was called this because he *baptized* people in the Jordan River to show that they loved God.

*Luke 3:16*

**baptize** (**bap**-tize)
To use water in a special ceremony to show that a person belongs to God. John the Baptist baptized people in the Jordan River.
See also *baptism*

**Bar-Jesus** (bar-**jee**-zuhss)
See *Elymas*

*Matthew 27:16-17*

**Barabbas** (buh-**rab**-uhss)
A Jewish man found guilty of murder and rebellion against Rome during the time of Jesus. Barabbas and Jesus were both prisoners at the same time. When Pontius Pilate found Jesus innocent, the crowd asked Pilate to release Barabbas instead.

**Barak** (**bair**-uhk)

Commander of the Israelite forces that defeated the Canaanites under Sisera. He was pressed into service by Deborah, who had received a prophecy ordering Barak to act.

*Judges 4:6*
*Judges 5:1*
*Hebrews 11:32*

**barley** (**bar**-lee)

A grain fed to horses, cows, and donkeys, and also used to make bread. People did not like barley bread as much as bread made from wheat, so it was considered a poor person's food.

*Ruth 1:22*
*Hosea 3:2*

**Barnabas** (**bar**-nuh-buhss)

A Jewish leader in the early church and one of those who helped the apostle Paul in his ministry. His real name was Joseph; people called him Barnabas because of his helpful way with words. *Barnabas* means "son of encouragement."

*Acts 4:36*
*Acts 15:36-39*
*Galatians 2:13*

**Barsabbas** (bar-**sab**-buhss)
See *Judas Barsabbas*

**Bartholomew** (bar-**thol**-uh-myoo)

One of Jesus' *Twelve* disciples, possibly the same man as *Nathanael*. Except for the fact that Bartholomew's name always appears next to

*Matthew 10:3*
*Mark 3:18*
*Luke 6:14*

B

*Philip's* in the lists of disciples, we know nothing about him.

Mark 10:46

**Bartimaeus** (bar-ti-**may**-uhss)
A blind beggar whom Jesus cured.

B

**Baruch** (bah-**rook**)

Jeremiah 32:12

• Jeremiah's assistant. Baruch wrote down Jeremiah's prophecies and read them to the people.

Nehemiah 3:20

• One of those who rebuilt a section of the walls of Jerusalem; a priest; son of Zabbai.

Nehemiah 11:5

• One of the Jewish leaders who settled in Jerusalem after the walls were rebuilt; son of Col-Hozeh.

2 Samuel 17:27-29

**Barzillai** (bar-**zil**-eye)
An Israelite from Gilead who helped David during Absalom's rebellion.

Deuteronomy 3:13-14

**Bashan** (**bay**-shuhn)
Territory to the east of the Sea of Galilee and north of *Gilead*. Bashan got plenty of rain and was well known for its rich soil. It was allotted to the tribe of Manasseh.
See also *Og*

Isaiah 5:10
Ezekiel 45:10-11

**bath** (**bath**)
A liquid measure equal to about 22 liters, or six gallons; equivalent to one *ephah*.

**Bathsheba** (bath-**shee**-buh)
The wife of Uriah with whom David committed adultery. Bathsheba became the mother of Shammua, Shobab, Nathan, and *Solomon*.

*2 Samuel 11:3*
*1 Kings 2:13*

**beast** (**beest**)
The being that comes from the *Abyss* in the prophesies of Revelation 11–20. This beast tries to take the place of God on earth by demanding to be worshiped. He is the ultimate *antichrist*, but will be thrown into the *lake of fire* with the *false prophet* in the end.

*Revelation 19: 19-20*

B

**Beatitudes** (bee-**at**-i-toodz)
"Blessings," the name given to the teachings of Jesus recorded in Matthew 5:3-12. The Beatitudes are part of the *Sermon on the Mount*.

*Matthew 5:3-12*

**Beelzebub** (bee-**el**-zuh-buhb)
Another name for Satan. Several of the people who opposed Jesus accused him of casting out demons by using power from Beelzebub.

*Matthew 10:25*
*Luke 11:15-19*

**Beelzebul** (bee-**el**-zuh-buhl)
See *Beelzebub*

B

*Genesis 21:31*
*1 Samuel 8:1-3*
*Nehemiah 11: 25-30*

**Beersheba** (bihr-**shee**-buh)

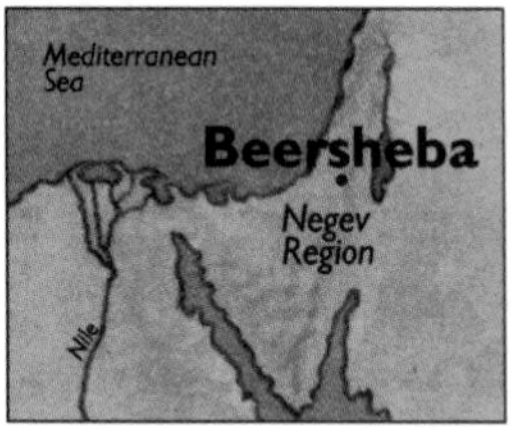


A town in the northern *Negev* that played a big part in Israel's history. Abraham lived in this area for a long time, as did his son Isaac. After the Israelites settled in Canaan, Beersheba was often spoken of as the southern border of Israel. There were several wells in Beersheba. The name means "well of the oath."

**begotten** (bee-**got**-uhn)
See *only begotten*

*Exodus 38:25-26*

**beka** (**bee**-kuh)
A unit of weight equal to about five and a half grams, or one-fifth of an ounce; 10 *gerahs*; one-half a *shekel*.

*Isaiah 46:1-2*
*Jeremiah 50:1-2*

**Bel** (**bel**)

Another name for Marduk, the main god of Babylonia. Jeremiah prophesied against Babylonia for its worship of Bel.

**Bela** (**bee**-luh)

*Genesis 36:31-33*
- King of Edom before the time of the Israelites.

*Genesis 46:21*
- Benjamin's firstborn son and father of the Belaite clan.

*1 Chronicles 5:8*
- A very wealthy member of the tribe of *Reuben*.

See also *Benjamin; Edom; Reuben*

**Belaites** (**bee**-luh-ites) *Numbers 26:38*

One of the clans of Benjamin; descendants of Bela.

**Belial** (**bee**-lee-uhl) *2 Corinthians 6:15*

Another name for Satan.

**Belshazzar** (**bel**-shuh-zar) *Daniel 5:1-6*

One of the kings of Babylonia during the time of Daniel. Belshazzar was the king who saw a hand write a message on the wall, which Daniel interpreted as a message from God. His name means "may Bel protect the king."

**Belteshazzar** (bel-tuh-**shaz**-ur) *Daniel 1:7*

The name that the Babylonians gave to Daniel. It means "protect his life." The spelling looks similar to that of one of the kings Daniel served, *Belshazzar*.

**Ben Hinnom** (ben-**hin**-uhm)

See *Valley of Hinnom*

**Ben-Hadad** (ben-**hay**-dad)

• Ben-Hadad I, king of Aram in Damascus during the reigns of Baasha, Asa, and Omri in Israel. *1 Kings 15:20-22*

*1 Kings 20:26* • Ben-Hadad II, king of Aram in Damascus during the reigns of Ahab and Joram.

*2 Kings 13:3* • Ben-Hadad III, son of Hazael and king of Aram in Damascus during the reigns of Jehoahaz and Jehoash in Israel.

**Ben-Hur (ben-hur)**

*1 Kings 4:8* "Son of Hur"; governor of the hill country of Ephraim under Solomon.

**Benaiah** (ben-**eye**-uh)

*1 Chronicles 27:5-6* • Commander of David's mighty men and of David's third militia of 24,000; son of Jehoiada of Kabzeel. He supported David when Adonijah laid claim to the throne. He replaced Joab as commander of the army under Solomon.

*1 Chronicles 27:14* • Commander of David's eleventh militia of 24,000; of the tribe of Ephraim.

*1 Chronicles 15:18* • A temple gatekeeper appointed to sing and play music during the return of the ark to Jerusalem from Kiriath Jearim.

**Benjamin** (**ben**-juh-min)

*Genesis 35:18*
*Genesis 43:14-16* • Jacob's youngest son and the tribe of Israel named after him. *Rachel* was his mother.

*Joshua 21:17* • The land allotted to the tribe of Benjamin.

See also *tribes of Israel*

**Benjamites** (**ben**-juh-mites) *Judges 3:15; 1 Samuel 9:1*
People of the tribe of Benjamin; people descended from Benjamin.

**Berea** (buh-**ree**-uh) *Acts 17:10-13*

A city in southern Macedonia during the time of Paul and his missionary journeys. Paul and Silas started a church there. Luke praised the Christians of Berea because they studied carefully everything Paul taught them.

**Bereans** (buh-**ree**-uhnz)
People who lived in *Berea*.

**Berekiah** (bair-uh-**kye**-uh)
- A descendant of Jehoiachin (who was a descendant of David and Solomon) who survived the exile in Babylonia. *1 Chronicles 3:17-20*
- Father of Asaph. *1 Chronicles 6:39*
- One of those who guarded the *Ark of the Covenant* when it was moved to Jerusalem in David's time. *1 Chronicles 15:23*

- Son of Meshillemoth; one of four leaders in the northern kingdom of Israel, together with *Azariah*, *Jehizkiah*, and *Amasa*, who spoke out against making slaves of 200,000 prisoners of war. The prisoners were *2 Chronicles 28:12*

all fellow Israelites from the southern kingdom of Judah, captured after the defeat of Ahaz's forces.

*Zechariah 1:1, 7*

• Father of the prophet Zechariah.

*Acts 25:13, 23*
*Acts 26:30*

**Bernice** (bur-**neess**)

Oldest daughter of Herod Agrippa I and sister of Herod Agrippa II. Bernice was present when Paul defended himself before Herod and Festus.

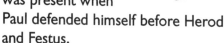

**Beroea** (buh-**ree**-uh)
See *Berea*

*Joshua 7:2*
*1 Samuel 13:5*

**Beth Aven** (**beth ay**-ven)

"House of nothing," a town on the northern boundary of Benjamin. Its exact location is unknown.

*Amos 1:3-5*

**Beth Eden** (**beth ee**-den)

"House of delight," a place in *Aram* that was a target of Amos's prophecies.

*Joshua 16:3, 5*
*1 Chronicles 7:24*

**Beth Horon** (**beth hor**-uhn)

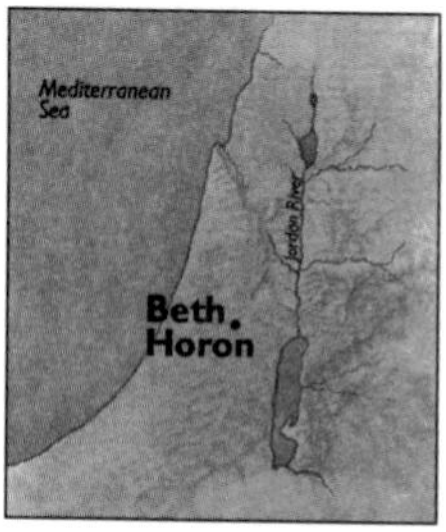


"House of the hollow," two towns in the valley of Aijalon, a very important trade route between the Mediterranean coast and the hill country of Ephraim. Joshua chased the Amorite forces down this valley after defeating them at Gibeon. It was in this battle the Joshua made the sun stand still. The Israelite towns of Upper Beth Horon and Lower Beth Horon were founded by Sheerah, Ephraim's daughter.

**Beth-shan (beth-shawn)**

*Joshua 17:12-16*
*1 Kings 4:12*

"House of rest," an important city in the territory of Manasseh between the Valley of Jezreel and the Jordan Valley. The city was valued for its place along a major trade route, rich soil, and an abundant supply of fresh water.

**Beth-shemesh (beth-shem-**uhsh)

"House of the sun":

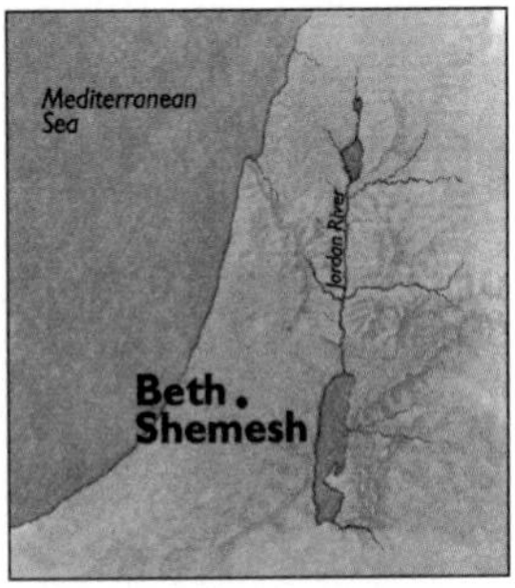


- One of the Canaanite cities given to the tribe of Judah; it lay along Judah's border with Dan. *Joshua 15:10*
- One of the Canaanite cities given to the tribe of Issachar. *Joshua 19:22*
- One of the Canaanite cities given to the tribe of Naphtali. *Judges 1:33*
- An Egyptian city during the time of Jeremiah. *Jeremiah 43:13*

**Beth-zur (beth-zoo-**ur)

*2 Chronicles 11:7*
*Nehemiah 3:16*

"House of rock," a city in the land of Judah. Rehoboam fortified it, and it was still around in the time of Nehemiah.

**Bethany** (**beth**-uh-nee)

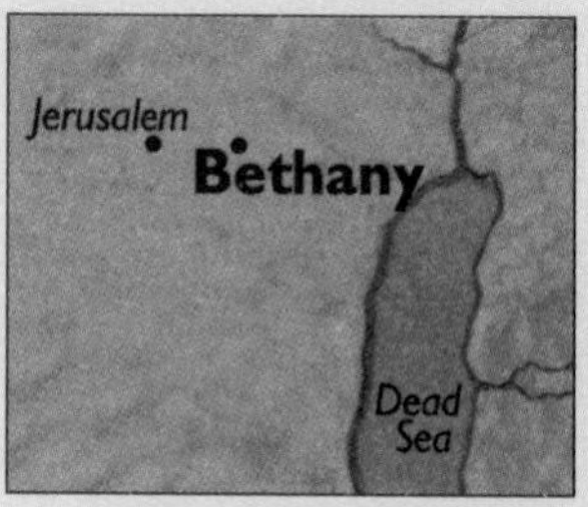


*Matthew 21:17*
*John 11:1*

• A village in Israel during the time of Jesus, just east of Jerusalem on the other side of the Mount of Olives. Bethany was Mary and Lazarus's home town. Jesus visited Bethany several times.

*John 1:28*

• The area or town east of the Jordan River where John baptized.

*Genesis 12:8*
*Genesis 28:10-22*
*Judges 20:26-28*

**Bethel** (**beth**-uhl)

A city in the land of Israel northwest of Ai. Abraham camped near Bethel when he first arrived in Canaan. Jacob had his dream there while fleeing from Esau. After Joshua's conquest, it was given to the tribe of Ephraim.

**Bethlehem** (**beth**-luh-hem)

*1 Samuel 16:1*
*Matthew 2:1*

• A small city in Judah nine kilometers south of *Jerusalem*. This is Bethlehem in *Judah*, where Jesus was born as predicted in Micah 5:2. It is called Bethlehem Ephrathah because it was originally known as Ephrath.

*Joshua 19:14-15*

• A town northwest of Nazareth in the land of Zebulun.

**Bethphage** (beth-**fayj**)
A small town on the Mount of Olives that Jesus visited on his way to Jerusalem from Bethany.
*Matthew 21:1*
*Luke 19:29*

**Bethsaida** (beth-**say**-duh)
A town on the north shore of the Sea of Galilee mentioned in the Gospels. Jesus singled it out for ignoring his miracles.
*Luke 10:13*

**Bethshean** (beth-**shawn**)
See *Beth Shan*

**Bethuel** (beth-**oo**-uhl)

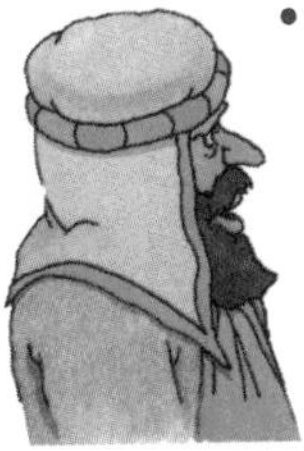

- Rebekah's father, one of those who had to give consent for Rebekah to marry Isaac. *Genesis 22:22*
- A town occupied by the tribe of Simeon. *Joshua 19:4*

**Bezalel** (**bez**-uh-lel)

- Foreman in charge of building the tabernacle when the Israelites were traveling in the wilderness (during the Exodus). God told Moses to give him the job. *Exodus 31:2-11*
- One of those who had to make some changes under Ezra's reform. *Ezra 10:30*

**Bigthana** (big-**thah**-nuh)
One of the eunuchs who plotted to assassinate *Ahasuerus* but was caught by *Mordecai*.
See also *Esther; Teresh*
*Esther 2:21-23*

*Job 2:11*
*Job 8:1-7*
*Job 18:1, 21*

**Bildad** (**bil**-dad)

One of *Job's* friends. Bildad believed that Job suffered because he and his children had sinned and were trying to hide it.

See also *Elihu; Eliphaz; Zophar*

*Genesis 29:29*

**Bilhah** (**bil**-huh)

• A *maidservant* given to Rachel by Laban. Rachel gave Bilhah to Jacob as a concubine. She became the mother of Dan and Naphtali.

*1 Chronicles 4:29*

• A city in the territory of Simeon.

*Genesis 25:29-34*

**birthright** (**burth**-rite)

The right of the firstborn son to become head of the family and to get a double share of the inheritance when the father died. Jacob became famous for getting Esau to trade his birthright for a single meal.

*Acts 16:7*
*1 Peter 1:1*

**Bithynia** (bi-**thi**-nee-uh)

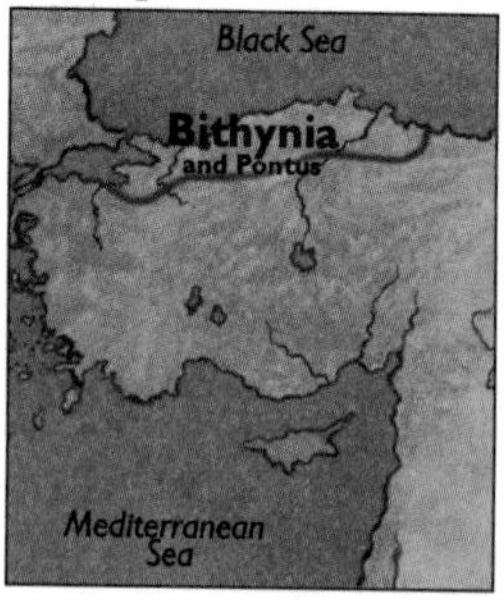


A region in Asia Minor along the southern side of the Black Sea that the Romans administered together with *Pontus* as a single province. Paul made plans to preach there, but God sent him instead to Troas. The apostle Peter addressed his first letter to believers in Bithynia.

See also *Peter, First*

**blameless (blaym**-less)
Innocent; not at fault; not guilty. A blameless person cannot be blamed for any wrongdoing.
See also *godly; holy*

*Genesis 6:9*
*Psalm 18:25*
*Philippians 2:14-15*

**bless (bless)**
• To wish well of someone else; to say words of belief in another person's promise for the future; to state a wish for someone's well being.
*Genesis 49:28*
*Hebrews 11:1*

• To ask God's favor on someone; to ask God to take care of someone.
*Matthew 5:44*

• To praise or extol.
*Psalm 103:1, 2*

B

**blessed (blest)**
Given special favor from God; happy.
*Matthew 5:3-11*

**blessing (bless**-ing)
A word or statement of hope for God's favor.
*Genesis 28:4*
*Hebrews 6:7*

**bloodguilt (bluhd**-gilt)
Probably a reference to murder.
*Psalm 51:14*

**Boaz (boh**-az)
Husband of Ruth; father of Obed; grandfather of Jesse; great-grandfather of David.
See also *Jakin and Boaz*
*Ruth 2:1-5*

**book of life (buk** uhv **life)**

The names of all those who will live with God forever in heaven; the list of all true believers in Christ.
*Revelation 3:5*
*Revelation 20:12*

*1 Kings 11:41*

**book of the acts of Solomon**
(**buk** uhv the **ann**-uhls uhv **sol**-uh-muhn)
A set of writings that that existed in Old Testament times but not today.

*2 Kings 14:15*

**book of the history of the kings of Israel**
(**buk** uhv the **ann**-uhls uhv the **kings** uhv **iz**-ree-uhl)
A set of writings that that existed in Old Testament times but not today.

*2 Kings 14:18*

**book of the history of the kings of Judah**
(**buk** uhv the **ann**-uhls uhv the **kings** uhv **joo**-duh)
A set of writings that that existed in Old Testament times but not today.

*Joshua 8:31*
*Joshua 23:6*

**Book of the Law**
(**buk** uhv the **law**)

The first five books of the Bible; Genesis, Exodus, Leviticus, Numbers, Deuteronomy; often called the *Pentateuch*, the Law of Moses, the Book of the Law of God, and the *books of history*.

B

**books of history** (**buks** uhv **hiss**-tuh-ree)
The Old Testament books of Joshua, Judges, Ruth, 1 Samuel, 2 Samuel, 1 Kings, 2 Kings, 1 Chronicles, 2 Chronicles, Ezra, Nehemiah, and Esther.

**books of law** (**buks** uhv **law**)
The Old Testament books of Genesis, Exodus, Leviticus, Numbers, and Deuteronomy; also called the *Pentateuch*.

**books of poetry** (**buks** uhv **poh**-i-tree)
The Old Testament books of Job, Psalms, Proverbs, Ecclesiastes, and Song of Songs.

**Booths, Feast of** (**boothz, feest** uhv)
See *Feast of Booths*

**born again** (**born** uh-**gen**)
Born of God's Spirit; reborn; *saved*. Jesus told Nicodemus, "I assure you, unless you are born again, you can never see the Kingdom of God" (John 3:3). Nicodemus did not understand this, so Jesus explained it in John 3:5-17.
See also *Jesus Christ; sin*

*John 3:1-21*

**bread of the Presence**
(**bred** uhv the **prez**-uhnss)
Twelve loaves of bread prepared and eaten weekly by the priests as part of their ritual duties. They were to bake one loaf for

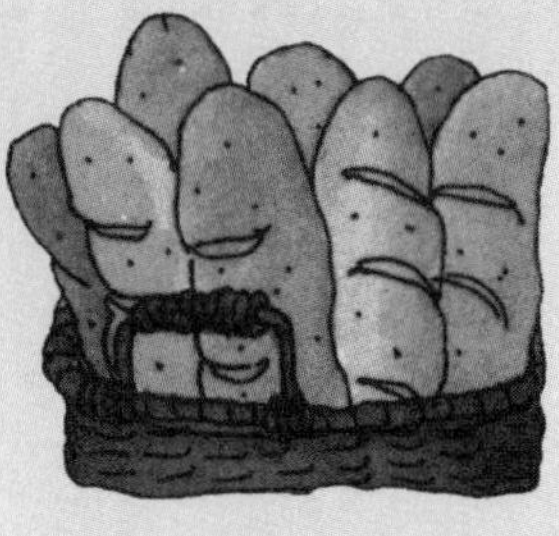

*Leviticus 24:8*

each tribe of Israel and place them all on a gold table in the holy place of the tabernacle (and later the temple). Leviticus 24:5-9 contains the instructions that God gave to Moses.

**brethren** (**brehth**-ren)
See *brothers in Christ*

B

*Isaiah 66:20*
*Acts 9:30*

**brothers in Christ**
(**bruh**-thurz in **kriste**)
An expression that refers to all believers; all Christians.

*Numbers 34:22*

**Bukki** (**buk**-eye)
The family leader of Dan chosen by God to help divide up the land after the conquest of Canaan.

*1 Kings 6:38*

**Bul** (**buhl**)
The eighth *month* of the Israelite year, overlapping October and November.

*Numbers 23:29*
*Ezra 6:9*

**bull** (**buhl**)
A male of cattle, one of the kinds of animals the Israelites were allowed to sacrifice for sin. People who could not afford a bull were allowed to sacrifice a *dove* or *pigeon* instead.

Some of the Canaanites made bull *idols*. The first of the Ten Commandments forbids this.

See *also offering*

**burnt offering** (**burnt awf**-ur-ing)

One of three kinds of sacrifices that the Israelites made to pay for sin. A person who wanted to make a burnt offering would bring a perfect young bull, sheep, goat, pigeon, or dove to the temple, place his hands on the animal's head, kill it, and give it to the priests. The priests would then burn the animal on the altar. This is the only kind of offering that was completely burned up; all other kinds of offerings were eaten by the priests. The rules for burnt offerings can be found in Leviticus 1:1-17 and 6:8-13.

See also *offering*

*Genesis 8:20*
*Hebrews 10:6-8*

B

C

2 Kings 6:25

**cab (kab)**
A liquid measure equal to about one liter, or one quart; one-eighteenth of an *ephah*.

Matthew 22:17, 21
John 19:12-15

**Caesar** (**see**-zur)
The emperor of Rome. "Caesar" was a title much like king or president. It started out as a family name. Over time, people started using Caesar as a title for their leader.

Luke 2:1

**Caesar Augustus** (**see**-zur uh-**guhs**-tuhss)
A title for the office of emperor adopted by Caesar Octavianus, the Roman emperor in power when Jesus was born. It was Caesar Augustus who ordered the census that required Mary and Joseph to travel to Bethlehem.

Acts 8;40
Acts 21:8-9

**Caesarea** (sess-uh-**ree**-uh)
A major seaport city in New Testament times

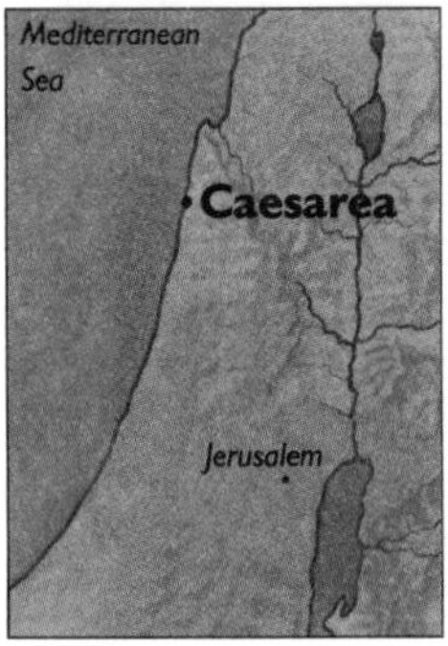


on the eastern Mediterranean coast in Palestine. The emperor Caesar Augustus gave it to *Herod the Great*, who thanked the emperor by naming the city after him. Paul set sail from this city's seaport in the course of his travels. Some of the city's ruins survive to this day.

Another city named after a Roman emperor was *Caesarea Philippi*.

**Caesarea Philippi** (sess-uh-**ree**-uh fil-i-pye)

A city in the Roman province of Judea at the southwest base of Mount Hermon, the source of the Jordan River. The emperor Caesar Augustus gave the city to *Herod the Great,* who built a temple to the emperor there. It passed to Herod's distant relative Philip the tetrarch after Herod's death. Philip added his own name to the city so people could tell it apart from Caesarea on the coast. This is the place where Jesus asked his disciples, "Who do people say that the Son of Man is?" (Matthew 16:13).

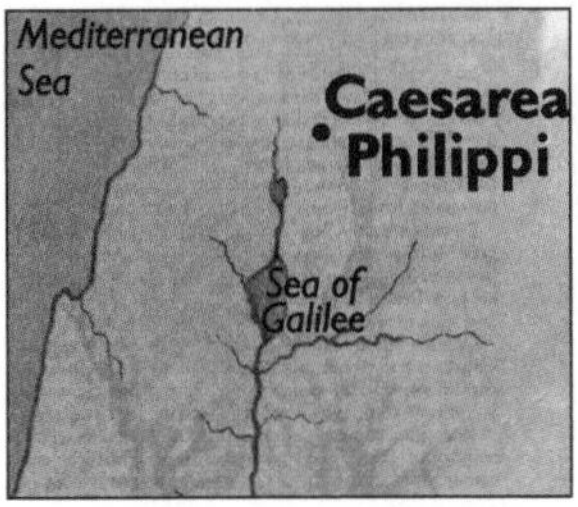


*Matthew 16:13-16*
*Mark 8:27-30*

**Caiaphas** (**kye**-uh-fuhss)

High priest of Israel from A.D. 18 to 36, when Jesus was an adult. Caiaphas was in charge of the trial that condemned Jesus to die.

*John 18:13-14*
*Acts 4:6*

**Cain** (**kane**)

Adam and Eve's firstborn son, who murdered his brother Abel. Cain is famous for the line, "Am I my brother's keeper?" (Genesis 4:9).

*Genesis 4:1-8*
*Hebrews 11:4*
*1 John 3:12*

C

**Caleb** (**kay**-leb)

*Numbers 13:6*
*Joshua 14:7*
*Judges 1:12-15*

• An Israelite of the tribe of Judah; son of Jephunneh. Moses chose him to represent Judah on the team of spies sent into the land of Canaan when the Israelites had reached *Kadesh-Barnea* during the Exodus. Besides *Joshua*, he was the only spy who believed God could give them victory over the Canaanites. He settled in *Hebron*.

*1 Chronicles 2:9, 18-19*

• One of Judah's great-great-grandsons; his father was Hezron.

*1 Chronicles 2:42*

• A "brother of Jerahmeel," otherwise unknown.

**calendar** (**kal**-uhn-dur)
See *month*

**calf** (**kaf**)

*Exodus 32:4-5*
*1 Kings 12:28-29*

A young *bull* or cow. Some of the offerings that God required of the Israelites involved sacrifice of a calf. Some of the meat from these offerings was given to the priests and their families for food.

Many false religions of Canaan involved worship of calf

*idols*. Aaron once tried to do this when Moses was receiving the Ten Commandments from God at Mt. Sinai.

**camel** (**kam**-uhl)

*Genesis 12:16*
*Genesis 30:43*
*Matthew 19:24*

An animal native to the middle east sometimes

used for transportation and hauling. Most people did not own camels because they cost too much. But wealthy people and rulers, such as Abraham, Solomon, and the queen of Sheba, owned them. Most people who could afford an animal for transportation owned a donkey.

**Cana** (**kay**-nuh)

*John 2:1, 11*
*John 21:2*

A village in Galilee where Jesus attended a wedding and did his first miracle. Its exact location is unknown.

**Canaan** (**kay**-nuhn)

- Son of *Ham* and therefore Noah's grandson. *Genesis 9:18*
- The land occupied by the descendants of Canaan, Noah's grandson; Palestine; the land directly south of Phoenicia or Lebanon, west of Syria, and northwest of Arabia. *Joshua 3:10*

**Canaanites** (**kay**-nuhn-ites)

*Exodus 33:2*

The descendants of Canaan, Noah's grandson. They lived in the land of Canaan.

C

Matthew 4:13
John 4:46-54

**Capernaum** (kuh-**pur**-nuhm)

A major city on the north shore of the Sea of Galilee during the time of Christ. Jesus settled there when he began his ministry (he had grown up in *Nazareth*), to fulfill the prophecy of Isaiah 9:1-2. Jesus called Simon, Andrew, James, John, and Matthew from their jobs in Capernaum.

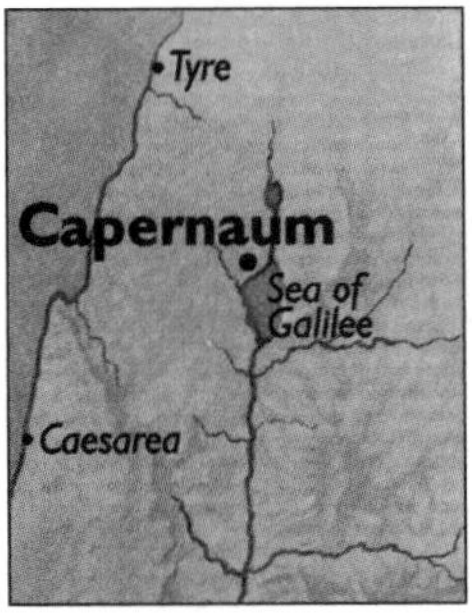


Acts 2:9
1 Peter 1:1

**Cappadocia** (kap-uh-**doh**-shuh)

A Roman province in Asia Minor (modern Turkey), east of Galatia and north of Cilicia. Some of the people who witnessed the coming of the Holy Spirit in Jerusalem at *Pentecost* were from Cappadocia. And Peter wrote his first letter to Christians in Cappadocia (among others).

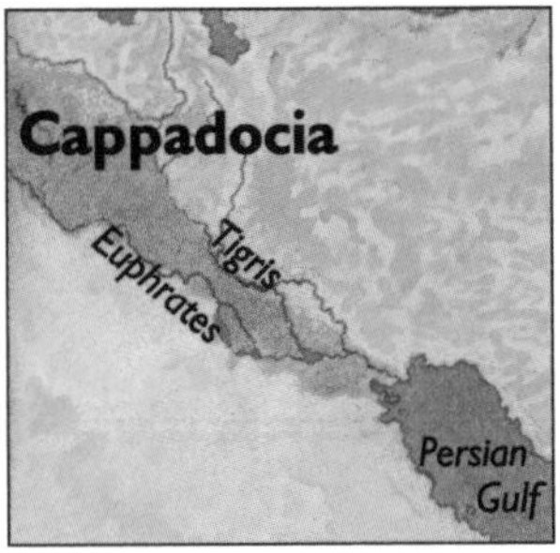


See also *First Peter*

Psalm 118:22
Romans 9:33
Ephesians 2:20

**capstone** (**kap**-stone)

A word that means "the head of the corner," sometimes translated as *cornerstone*.

**Carchemish** (**kar**-kuh-mish)

A city on the upper Euphrates River that thrived throughout Old Testament times. The Assyrians controlled it during Isaiah's time; the Egyptians and the Babylonians during Jeremiah's. Both Jeremiah and Isaiah mention the city in their prophecies.

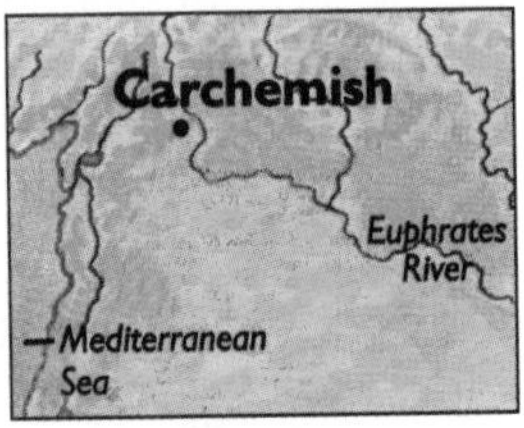


*2 Chronicles 35:20*
*Isaiah 10:9*

**Carmel** (**kar**-muhl)

• A range of mountains running northwest-southeast in the western region of northern Palestine, in the territory allotted to the tribe of Asher. Mount Carmel is the main peak in this range; it lies about 37 kilometers north of Caesarea. Elijah confronted Ahab's prophets of Baal on Mount Carmel.

*2 Kings 2:25; 4:25*
*Isaiah 35:2*

• A town in the hills of Judah about 12 kilometers south-southeast of Hebron; Nabal's hometown.

*1 Samuel 25:1-2*

**carnal** (**kar**-nul)

An older word for *worldly* or *unspiritual.*

*1 Corinthians 3:1-3*

*Esther 3:7*
*Jonah 1:7*
*Matthew 27:35*

**cast lots** (**kast lots**)
A method of decision-making used by believers both in the Old Testament and the New Testament. When Joshua and the leaders of Israel divided up the land of Canaan, they cast lots. When the apostles chose a replacement for Judas, they cast lots.
See also *Urim and Thummim*

C

*Acts 28:11*

**Castor and Pollux** (**kast**-ur and **pol**-uhks)
Two gods of Greek mythology, supposedly the sons of Zeus and Leda. Paul sailed on a ship decorated with figureheads of these two.

*Acts 18:18*

**Cenchrea** (**sen**-kruh-ee)

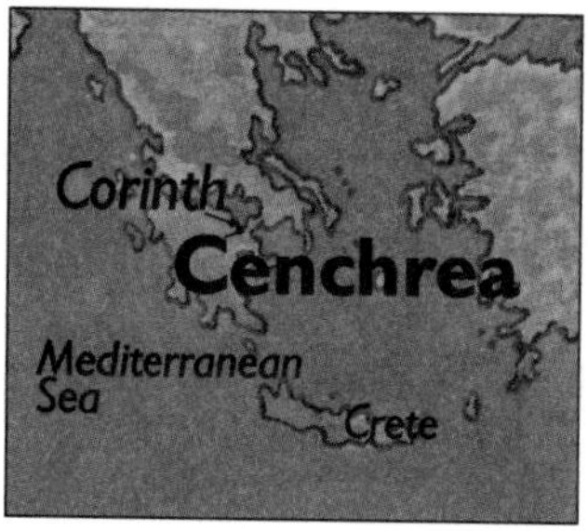


A port city 11 kilometers southeast of *Corinth* in New Testament times. The apostle Paul set sail from Cenchrea while on his second missionary journey.

*Numbers 16:6-7*
*1 Kings 7:50*

**censer** (**sen**-sur)
A place where incense was burned. Some censers were portable; others, such as an altar, were fixed. God gave specific instructions for how incense was to be used in worship. During the time of the Exodus Nadab and Abihu died for breaking those rules.

**census** (**sen**-suhss)
A count of a population. The book of Numbers is so named because it records a census of Israel. Mary and Joseph traveled to Bethlehem because the emperor Augustus ordered a census of the Roman Empire.

*2 Samuel 24:1*
*Luke 2:1*

**centurion** (sen-**tyur**-ee-uhn)
A Roman officer in command of 100 men, one-sixtieth of a Roman legion. Jesus once praised a centurion for showing great faith.

*Matthew 8:5-13*
*Acts 22:25*

**Cephas** (**see**-fuhss)
The Aramaic word for rock, equivalent to the Greek *Peter*. Jesus gave this nickname to his disciple Simon.

*John 1:42*

**cereal offering** (**seer**-ee-uhl **awf**-ur-ing)
Another term for *grain offering*

*Leviticus 2:1-3*
*Numbers 15:1-4*

**ceremonially clean** (**sair**-ee-uh-**mohn**-ee-uh-lee **kleen**)
See *clean*

**ceremonially unclean** (**sair**-ee-uh-**mohn**-ee-uh-lee uhn-**kleen**)
See *unclean*

**Chaldea** (kal-**dee**-uh)
A major region in southern *Babylonia*, where the Tigris and Euphrates empty into the Persian

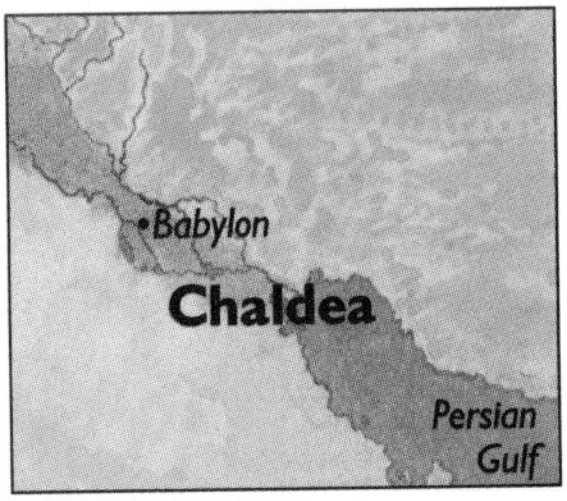


*Acts 7:4*

Gulf. The word was often used as another name for all of Babylonia.

Genesis 11:28

**Chaldeans** (kal-**dee**-uhnz)
The people of *Chaldea*. The word was sometimes used as another term for all the people of Babylonia (the Babylonians).



Genesis 41:43
Psalm 68:17

**chariot** (**chair**-ee-uht)
A carriage of two wheels pulled by one or more horses. The Egyptians, several Canaanite peoples, and David and Solomon used chariots in their armies. Chariots gave attackers a deadly advantage against infantry.

1 Kings 22:34

**charioteer** (chair-ee-uh-**teer**)
A chariot driver.

1 Corinthians 8:1
1 Corinthians 13:1-3
Colossians 3:14

**charity** (**chair**-uh-tee)
An older word for love that appears in some translations of the Bible.

**Chebar** (**kee**-bar)
See *Kebar*

**Chedorlaomer** (ked-or-**lay**-oh-mur)
See *Kedorlaomer*

Numbers 21:29
1 Kings 11:7, 33
2 Kings 23:13

**Chemosh** (**kee**-mosh)
The national god of the *Moabites*. Solomon built a *high place* to Chemosh in Jerusalem for his Moabite wives. Ahaz and Manasseh actually

practiced the Moabite rituals of worship, which involved sacrifice of children. Josiah destroyed these high places in his famous reform.

See also *idolatry; Molech*

**cherub** (**chair**-uhb)

*Exodus 25:19*
*Genesis 3:24*
*Psalm 18:10*

A spiritual being much like an *angel* but with a different function. The main job of a cherub is to guard and uphold God's holiness. God sent *cherubim* to guard the way to the tree of life in the garden of Eden after Adam and Eve's sin. The top of the Ark of the Covenant was adorned with a pair of golden cherubim statues. Descriptions of God's throne often mention cherubim. Cherubim, in other words, are God's attendants.

**Cherub** (**keh**-ruhb)

*Ezra 2:59*

A place in Babylonia during the time of Ezra and Nehemiah. Its location is unknown.

**cherubim** (**chair**-uh-bim)

*Exodus 25:19-20*

Plural of *cherub*

**chief priest** (cheef **preest**)

*2 Chronicles 26:20*
*John 11:47*

A leader among the priests of Israel and a member of the *Sanhedrin* in New Testament times. The chief priests were subordinate to the *high priest*.

C

C

**children of God** (**chil**-dren uhv **god**)
See *sons of God*

**Chinnereth, Chinneroth**
(**kin**-uh-reth, **kin**-uh-roth)
See *Kinnereth*

**Chislev** (**kiss**-lev)
See *Kislev*

**Chorazin** (**kor**-uh-zin)
See *Korazin*

*1 Chronicles 16:13*
*James 2:5*

**chosen** (**choh**-zuhn)
A word often used in the Bible to describe God's people. God chose the people of Israel to be his, and he chooses people today to be his children. The idea is that God does not leave us to our sins but reaches out to us in love of his own free will.

*Matthew 1:16*
*John 11:27*
*Romans 3:24*

**Christ** (**kriste**)
The Greek form of the Hebrew word *Messiah*. Jesus is called the Christ because he fulfilled the Old Testament prophecies about the coming of the Messiah.

See also *Jesus Christ*

**Christian** (**kris**-chuhn)

A follower of Christ; a "Christ-one." The word was first used in the New Testament city of *Antioch*.

*Acts 11:26*
*Acts 26:28*

C

**Chronicles** (**kron**-uh-kuhlz)

Two books of the Old Testament, *First Chronicles* and *Second Chronicles*. These two books tell about the life of Israel under David and Solomon, and about the southern kingdom of Judah after them.

*Nehemiah 12:23*
*Esther 2:23*

**Chronicles, First** (**kron**-uh-kuhlz, **furst** )

Thirteenth book of the Old Testament and eighth of the books of history. First Chronicles tells about David's deeds as king, especially his efforts to organize the worship of God in Jerusalem. No one knows who wrote it.

See also *Second Chronicles*

*1 Chronicles 29: 26-30*

**Chronicles, Second** (**kron**-uh-kuhlz, **sek**-uhnd)

Fourteenth book of the Old Testament and tenth of the books of history. Second Chronicles tells about Solomon's deeds as king, and about the southern kingdom of Judah under Rehoboam, Asa, Jehoshaphat, Jehoram, Joash, Uzziah, Ahaz, Hezekiah, Manasseh, and Josiah. Like 1 Chronicles, it deals mainly with how well each of these leaders obeyed God. No one

*2 Chronicles 7:14*

knows who wrote it. Where Second Chronicles leaves off, the book of Ezra picks up.
See also *First Chronicles*

*Exodus 28:15, 17-20*
*Daniel 10:6*
*Revelation 21:20*

**chrysolite** (**kris**-oh-lite)
A word used for yellow topaz and yellow quartz, two gemstones.

*1 Corinthians 1:2*
*1 Thessalonians 1:1*

*Matthew 16:18*
*1 Timothy 3:15*

**church** (**church**)
• A group of Christians that meets in a particular area. Many of the New Testament letters were written to such churches.
• All Christians everywhere.

*Acts 6:9*
*Galatians 1:21-22*

**Cilicia** (si-**lish**-uh)

A region of southern Asia Minor on the northern side of the Mediterranean Sea directly north of *Cyprus*; also a Roman province. Paul was from the capital city of Cilicia, *Tarsus*.

**circumcise** (**sur**-kuhm-size)
See *circumcision*

*Genesis 17:12*
*Acts 16:3*

**circumcision** (**sur**-kuhm-**si**-zhuhn)
Removal of the foreskin of the penis. Israelite males were circumcised on the eighth day after birth. God required this as a part of his covenant with Israel. It was a sign of their belonging to him.

**cistern** (**sis**-turn)

A hole or structure built to hold rain water. People of Old Testament and New Testament times used water collected in cisterns for drinking, cleaning, and bathing.

See also *well*

*Genesis 37:22-23*
*Isaiah 36:16-17*

**citadel** (**sit**-uh-duhl)

A fortified city, tower, or walled palace; any place of defense against attack.

*1 Kings 16:18*
*Nehemiah 2:8*

**cities of refuge** (**si**-teez uhv **ref**-yooj)

Six *Levite* cities in Israel set aside for the protection of people guilty of accidentally killing another person (manslaughter): *Kedesh*, *Golan*, *Ramoth Gilead*, *Shechem*, *Bezer*, and *Hebron*. Without the protection of these cities, vengeful relatives were allowed to kill the offender. The cities were spaced evenly throughout Israel, three to the west of the Jordan River and three to the east.

*Deuteronomy 4:41-43*
*Joshua 20:1-3*

**cities of the plain** (**si**-teez uhv the **plane**)

Five cities around the Dead Sea: Sodom, Gomorrah, Admah, Zeboiim, and Zoar. Abram's nephew Lot settled in Sodom.

*Genesis 13:10-12*
*Genesis 19:29*

**city** (**si**-tee)

A town and its villages. A city was not just one town, but a large area of homes, businesses, and farms. It included the main town or place where

*Joshua 18:21-24*

lots of people had homes and businesses, the farms around it, and all the smaller villages nearby. Some cities were *fortified cities*.

*2 Samuel 5:9*

**City of David** (**si**-tee uhv **day**-vid)

An Israelite nickname for Jerusalem, so named because David captured the city from the Jebusites and declared it his capital.

See also *Zion*

*Genesis 36:15-16*

**clan** (**klan**)

A group of people who all trace their roots to the same person; a family unit larger than a single family but smaller than a *tribe*. All members of a clan belong to the same tribe. Many lists of people in the Bible organize the names by clan.

*Acts 11:28*
*Acts 18:2*

**Claudius** (**klaw**-dee-uhss)

Roman emperor during the time of *Agabus* and during Paul's first two missionary journeys. Claudius Caesar reigned from A.D. 41 to 54.

*Acts 21:31*
*Acts 24:22*

**Claudius Lysias**
(**klaw**-dee-uhss **lis**-ee-uhss)

Commander of the Roman regiment at Jerusalem who saved Paul from a violent mob just after Paul's third missionary journey.

**clean (kleen)**
Holy; pure. The word was often used to describe a person who had obeyed rules about what to eat or touch. A clean person was allowed to worship with others.
See also *unclean*

*Leviticus 14:1, 7*
*Ephesians 5:25-26*

**cleansing (klen-**zing)
See *clean*

**Cleopas (klee-**oh-puhss)
One of the two disciples who walked with Jesus on the road to Emmaus after he rose from the dead. We know nothing else about him.

*Luke 24:18*

**Colosse** (kuh-**lah**-see)
A city in the Roman province of Asia about 15 kilometers east of Laodicea. Paul wrote the letter of *Colossians* to the Christians of Colosse. As far as we know Paul never visited the city, though his third missionary journey did take him through Laodicea.

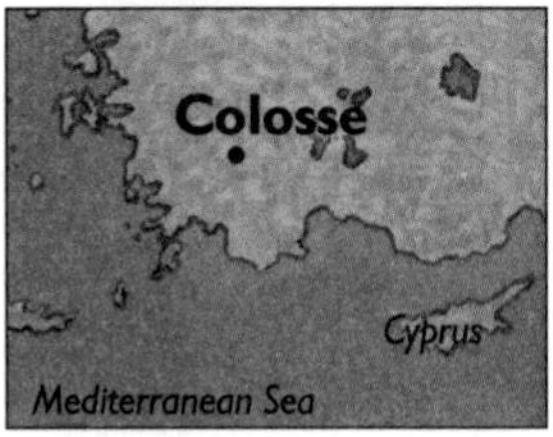


*Colossians 1:2*

**Colossians** (kuh-**lah**-shuhnz)
- People who lived in the city of *Colosse.*
- Christians of the church in Colosse.

See also *Colossians, book of*

*Colossians 1:2*

**Colossians, book of** (kuh-**lah**-shuhnz, **buk** uhv)
Twelfth book of the New Testament, a letter written by Paul to the churches of *Colosse*. Paul

*Colossians 3:17*

wrote this letter to teach the Colossians about life in Christ. They had some mistaken ideas about who Christ is, and Paul wanted to set them on the right track.

*Exodus 34:32*
*Psalm 147:15*
*John 14:15*

**commandment**
(kuh-**mand**-ment)
A rule or command given by God that applies to all people everywhere.

**Commiphora myrrha** (kom-i-**for**-uh **mur**-uh)
Name of the shrub from which *myrrh* is made.

**Communion** (kuh-**myoo**-nyuhn)
Another word for the *Lord's Supper.*

**Conaniah** (kon-uh-**nye**-uh)

*2 Chronicles 31:12*
- Levite chosen by Hezekiah to be in charge of the temple storerooms.

*2 Chronicles 35:9*
- A Levite leader who gave generously to the Levites during Josiah's reforms.

*Genesis 25:5-6*
*1 Kings 11:3*

**concubine** (**kon**-kyoo-bine)
A female slave who was allowed to have sex with a man. Kings and wealthy families of Old Testament times often had concubines. Most concubines took care of the household and were treated much like wives. Their children were part of the family and shared in the estate. A concubine was not the same as a *maidservant*.

**confess** (kuhn-**fess**)

• To admit *sin*. The Bible tells us to confess our sin to God and to each other. A person who wants to be forgiven of sin must confess it to God. *1 John 1:9*

• To say publicly what you believe. Peter confessed his belief in Christ. *Philippians 2:10-11*

See also *confession*

**confession** (kuhn-**fe**-shuhn)

• An admission of *sin*. *Ezra 10:11*

• A statement of belief. *Romans 10:10*

See also *confess*

**congregation** (**kon**-gruh-**gay**-shuhn) *Psalm 107:32*

A group of believers; a gathering of God's people, usually for the purpose of worship; an *assembly*.

**conscience** (**kon**-shunss) *Acts 23:1* *1 Timothy 1:18-19*

A sense of goodness or badness about something you did or might do; the feeling that you have done right or wrong. A bad or evil conscience tells you that you have done wrong. A good or clear conscience tells you that you have done right or have been forgiven.

C

C

Exodus 30:30
2 Chronicles 26:18

**consecrate** (**kon**-si-krate)
To set aside for God's service. God required the Israelite *priests* and *Levites* to consecrate themselves before serving in the temple.

Acts 15:3
Acts 3:19

**convert** (kuhn-**vurt** or **kon**-vurt)
• Verb: To change your own or someone else's belief about God and how to be saved from sin.
• Noun: A person who has changed his belief about God and how to be saved from sin.

John 16:7-11

**convict** (**kuhn**-vikt)
To find guilty.

**cor** (**kor**)
See *homer*

Acts 18:1-2
2 Corinthians 1:1

**Corinth** (**kor**-inth)
A major city on the narrow strip of land between the mainland of Greece and the

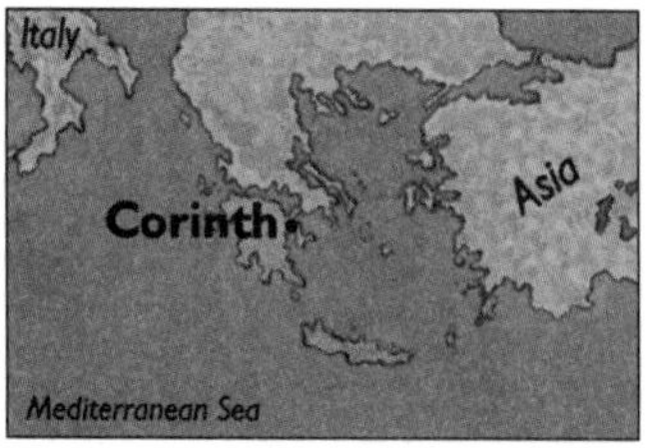


*Peloponnesus*. During New Testament times, this city lay in the Roman province of Achaia. Paul visited it for 18 months during his second missionary journey. He later wrote the letters of *First Corinthians* and *Second Corinthians* to the Christians of that city.

**Corinthians** (kuh-**rin**-thee-uhnz)

- People who lived in *Corinth*.
- Christians of the church in Corinth. 2 Corinthians 6:11
- Two books of the New Testament: *First Corinthians* and *Second Corinthians*.

**Corinthians, First** (kuh-**rin**-thee-uhnz, **furst**) 1 Corinthians 1:1-3

Seventh book of the New Testament, a letter written by the apostle Paul to the Christians at the church in Corinth. Paul wrote the letter to help the believers fix some of the problems they were having. Some of its main topics are church unity, marriage, spiritual gifts, worship, and the return of Christ.

See also *Second Corinthians*

**Corinthians, Second** 2 Corinthians 1:1-2

(kuh-**rin**-thee-uhnz, **sek**-uhnd)

Eighth book of the New Testament, a letter written by the apostle Paul to the Christians at the church in Corinth. Paul wrote Second Corinthians to defend his ministry against false teachers who were questioning his authority and the gospel message he preached.

See also *First Corinthians; false prophet*

**cormorant** (**kor**-mor-uhnt) *Leviticus 11:17* *Deuteronomy 14:17*

A bird that lives near the sea and eats fish. The Israelites were not allowed to eat cormorants.

C

*Acts 10:1-2*

**Cornelius** (kor-**neel**-yuhss)

A Roman centurion from Caesarea who was the first Gentile to become a Christian. His dramatic story is told in Acts 10:1-48.

*Psalm 118:22*
*Romans 9:33*

**cornerstone** (**kor**-nur-stone)

The stone placed at the top or bottom corner of a building. The cornerstone had a special place in the construction of stone buildings because of its size and prominence. Some passages in the Bible use it as a symbol of Christ because of his importance to our salvation.

See also *capstone*

**corrupt** (kuh-**ruhpt**)

*Deuteronomy 4:15-16*
*Daniel 11:32*
*2 Corinthians 7:2*

- Verb: To cause to sin; to cause to do evil.

*Genesis 6:11*
*1 Timothy 6:3-5*
*2 Peter 1:4*

- Adjective: Sinful; bad; wicked; evil.

**corruption** (kuh-**ruhp**-shuhn)

Evil; wickedness; badness; the effect of sin in our lives.

*Acts 21:1*

**Cos** (**kos**)

An island off the southwest coast of Asia Minor and a part of the Roman province of Asia. Paul's ship stopped briefly at Cos during his third missionary journey.

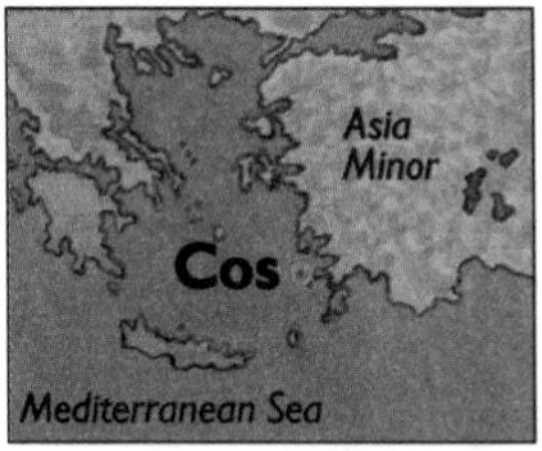

**Council** (**koun**-suhl)
Another word for the *Sanhedrin*.
*Matthew 10:17*
*Mark 15:43*

**council of the elders** (**koun**-suhl uhv **el**-durz)
- Any official gathering of local leaders. *Psalm 107:32; Luke 22:66; Acts 25:12*
- The *Sanhedrin*. *Matthew 26:59*

**covenant** (**kuh**-vuh-nuhnt)
A pact or agreement of loyalty between two people. The most famous covenant in the Bible is God's covenant with Israel at Mount Sinai during the Exodus. God promised to protect and provide for the people of Israel if the people of Israel kept the Law.
*See also Ten Commandments*
*Genesis 17:7*
*1 Samuel 18:3-4*
*Hebrews 8:8-13*

**covet** (**kuh**-vit)
To crave something that belongs to someone else; to envy someone else's possessions. The tenth of the *Ten Commandments* tells us not to covet.
*Exodus 20:17*
*Romans 13:9*

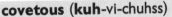

**covetous** (**kuh**-vi-chuhss)
Filled with envy; envious; craving what belongs to someone else; coveting.
*See also covet*
*Luke 12:15*
*Romans 7:7-8*

Job 39:28

**crag (krag)**

An outcropping of rock. Crags in the wilderness of Israel provide shade and shelter from the rain.

Titus 1:12-14

**Cretans (kree-tuhnz)**

People of *Crete.*

C

Acts 27:12-13
Titus 1:5

**Crete (kreet)**

A large island (about 250 kilometers long) in the

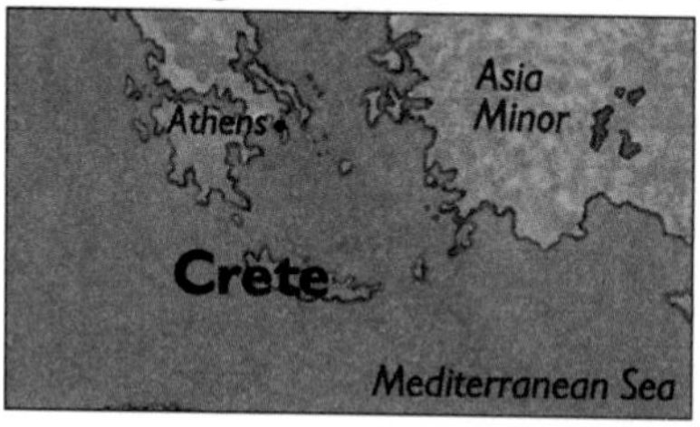


Mediterranean Sea, south of the Aegean Sea and southeast of the Greek *Peloponnesus.* It was part of the Roman province of Cyrenaica during New Testament times. Paul and several others got shipwrecked there while on his way to trial in Rome. The Christian leader Titus had a ministry on Crete.

2 Chronicles 2:7
Isaiah 1:18
Jeremiah 4:30

**crimson (krim-zuhn)**

Deep or dark red; scarlet. Isaiah made use of this word to describe how dramatic God's forgiveness is.

Acts 18:7-8
1 Corinthians 1:14

**Crispus (kriss-puhss)**

A Corinthian Jew who believed in Jesus when he heard the gospel from Paul. Crispus was one of the few converts Paul himself baptized.

**cross** (**kross**)

The two pieces of wood used in *crucifixion*. Jesus was crucified on a cross. This simple, ghastly sign became one of the most important symbols in Christianity.

*Mark 8:34*
*John 19:25*
*Ephesians 2:16*

**crucible** (**kroo**-si-buhl)

A pot used for melting silver so other metals and debris could be removed.

*Proverbs 17:3*

**crucifixion** (kroo-si-**fick**-shun)

A method of execution used by the Romans in New Testament times. The person to be crucified was nailed to two beams of wood in the shape of a cross. One nail was driven through both feet, and one through each wrist. The victim died of hunger, exhaustion, or exposure rather than the wounds themselves.

Only criminals convicted of serious crimes were crucified. The false charge used to justify the crucifixion of Jesus was treason against Rome.

*See also Jesus Christ*

*John 19:16, 18*
*Galatians 2:20*

**crucify** (**kroo**-si-fye)

To kill by means of *crucifixion*.

*John 19:6*

**cubit** (**kyoo**-bit)

The distance from the elbow to the tip of the middle finger. In Old Testament times, the Israelites and many nations around them consid-

*Exodus 27:1*
*Revelation 21:17*

C

ered the cubit their most basic unit of length. It was equal to about one-half a meter, or 18 inches; two *spans*; six *handbreadths*.

*Leviticus 11:3-4*
*Deuteronomy 4:6-8*

**cud (kuhd)**

Food that an animal brings up from the stomach. Some animals chew the cud and some do not. The Old Testament laws against eating certain kinds of meat used this as a test. The Israelites were not allowed to eat animals that did not chew the cud.

*Isaiah 28:25*
*Matthew 23:23*

**cummin (kyoo-min)**

A spice used to season food.

*2 Chronicles 9:4*
*Nehemiah 1:11*

**cupbearer (kuhp-bair-ur)**

An attendant of the king, sometimes called a butler. Cupbearers served the king's wine and often gave advice as well. This was an official position that required the king's highest trust. *Nehemiah* was a cupbearer to King Artaxerxes.

*Genesis 18:8*
*2 Samuel 17:27-29*

**curds (kurdz)**

A treat made from churning milk, similar to yogurt.

**curse** (**kurss**)

• Verb: To utter a wish of harm on someone else; to condemn; to damn; the opposite of *bless*. *Genesis 3:14* *Genesis 9:25* *Romans 9:3*

• Noun: The state of being condemned, judged, hurt, damned, or broken; the opposite of *blessing*. Adam and Eve's sin brought a curse on the earth that will last until God creates a new earth after Christ's return. *Matthew 26:73-74* *Galatians 3:10*

C

**Cush** (**kush**)

• Son of Ham and therefore Noah's grandson; father of *Nimrod*. *Genesis 10:6*

• An Israelite from the tribe of Benjamin who opposed David and prompted the writing of Psalm 7. *Psalm 7:1*

• *Ethiopia*. *Genesis 2:13*

• An area of Mesopotamia somewhere down-river from Eden; its exact location is unknown. *Genesis 2:10-14*

**Cushites** (**kush**-ites) *Numbers 12:1*

People of the land of Cush.

**Cuth** (**kooth**)

See *Cuthath*

**Cuthah** (**koo**-thuh) *2 Kings 17:24*

A city in Babylonia whose inhabitants were sent to live in Samaria after the Assyrians took the Israelites of Samaria away.

**cypress, cypress wood** (**sye**-pruhss **wud**) *Genesis 6:14* *Isaiah 60:13*

An evergreen tree native to the middle east. Idol worshipers used cypress wood to make idols.

Acts 4:36
Acts 15:39

**Cyprus** (**sye**-pruhss)

A large island in the eastern Mediterranean Sea, about 100 kilometers off the coast of Syria and 90 kilometers south of modern Turkey. It was part of the Roman province of Cilicia in New Testament times. Paul and Barnabas preached the gospel all over the island during their first missionary journey. Barnabas returned later with *John Mark*.

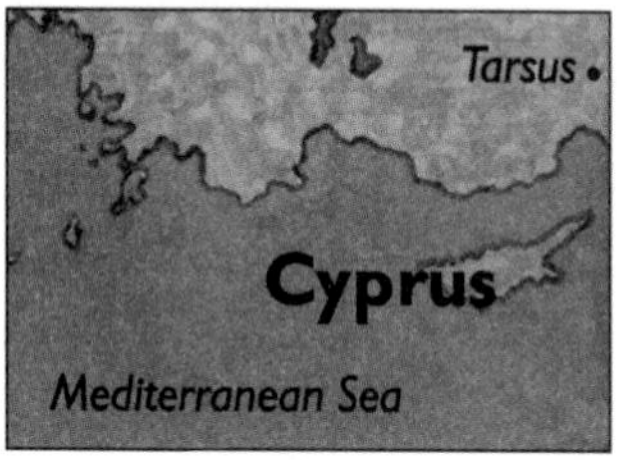


Matthew 27:32
Acts 6:9

**Cyrene** (sye-**reen**)

A port city in the Roman province of Cyrenaica on the Mediterranean coast of western Africa (in modern Lybia) in New Testament times. The man who carried Jesus' cross was from this city.

Ezra 1:1
Daniel 1:21

**Cyrus** (**sye**-ruhss)

King of *Persia* during the time of *Esther* and the last of the kings served by Daniel. This is the Cyrus who allowed the Jews to return to their homeland under Zerubbabel and Nehemiah after 70 years of captivity in Babylonia.

Cyrus the Persian is also known as Cyrus II or Cyrus the Great.

**Dagon** (**day**-gon)

One of the gods worshiped by the Philistines during the time of Samson, Saul, and David. The Philistine city of *Ashdod* had a temple of Dagon. God caused the idol in that temple to fall over when the Philistines tried to keep the Ark of the Covenant there.

*Judge 16:23*
*1 Samuel 5:2-5*

**Damascus** (duh-**mas**-kuhss)

A major city in *Aram* throughout all of biblical history. Abram's servant *Eliezer* was from Damascus. *Hazael* of Syria was a bitter enemy of *Jehu*. Saul of Tarsus (the apostle Paul) was converted while on his way to Damascus. Today the city is capital of Syria. It lies about 100 kilometers east of the Mediterranean coast, opposite *Sidon*.

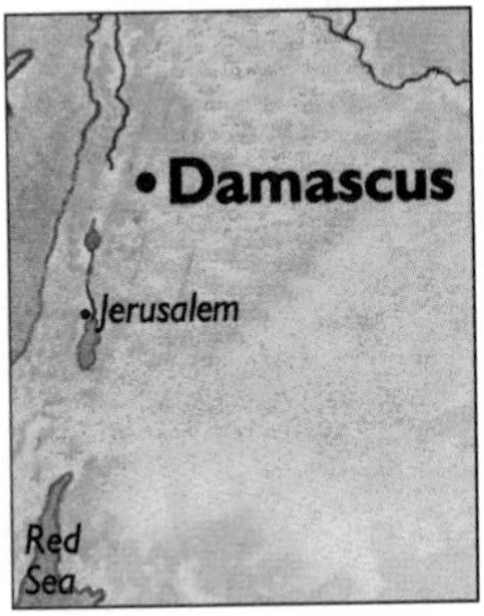


*Genesis 14:15*
*2 Chronicles 28:23*
*Acts 9:2-8*

**Dan** (**dan**)

• Jacob's son and the tribe of Israel named after him. *Bilhah* was his mother.

*Genesis 35:25*

• The land allotted to the tribe of Dan.

*Joshua 19:47-48*

• One of the northernmost cities in the tribal territory of Dan. During the time of the judges this was also the north-

*Genesis 14:14*

ern boundary of Israel ("all the Israelites, from Dan to Beersheba," Judges 20:1).

See also *tribes of Israel*

**Daniel** (**dan**-yuhl)

*1 Chronicles 3:1*

• David's second son, born to Abigail. We know nothing about him, in contrast to his brothers *Absalom* and *Adonijah*.

D

*Ezra 8:2*

• One of the family leaders who returned to Israel with Ezra and backed *Ezra's reform*.

*Daniel 1:6-11*

• A member of the royal family of Judah taken

captive to Babylon by the army of King Nebuchadnezzar during the reign of *Jehoiakim*. This is the Daniel who served four kings of Babylonia and wrote the *book of Daniel*. He is famous for surviving a night in a den of lions.

*Daniel 1:19-21*
*Ezekiel 28:3*

**Daniel, book of** (**dan**-yuhl, **buk** uhv)

Twenty-seventh book of the Old Testament. It was written by a Jewish nobleman taken captive during the reign of Jehoiakim.

See also *Daniel*

*Joshua 19:47*
*Judges 18:22-23*

**Danites** (**dan**-ites)

People who trace their roots to Dan, fifth son of Jacob; people of the tribe of Dan.

**Darius** (**dair**-ee-uhss)

• "Darius the Mede," king in Babylonia who took power after the death of Belshazzar; possibly another name for Cyrus II.

*Daniel 5:31*
*Daniel 11:1*

• Darius I, king in Babylonia during the time of Ezra and Nehemiah. He was the king who allowed Ezra to lead a large group of Jews back to Israel. The prophets *Haggai* and *Zechariah* mention him in their books. He ruled from 521 to 486 B.C.

*Haggai 1:1, 15*
*Zechariah 1:1, 7*

• Darius II, or Nothus, king in Babylonia from 423 to 404 B.C. He is called "Darius the Persian" by Nehemiah. He reigned shortly after the time of Malachi.

*Ezra 6:12-13*
*Nehemiah 12:22*

**Dathan** (**day**-thuhn)

One of the rebels against Moses in league with *Korah*. He and his brother *Abiram* were Reubenites.

*Numbers 16:12*
*Deuteronomy 11:5-7*

**Daughter of** (**daw**-tur uhv)

An emotional term for "people of." Many of the *major prophets* and *minor prophets* use this term in their prophecies to Judah and their enemies. "Daughter of Zion" means something like, "beloved people of Judah"; "Daughter of Edom" means something like, "poor people of Edom."

*Isaiah 62:11*
*Lamentations 4:22*
*John 12:15*

D

**David's mighty men** (**day**-vidz **mye**-tee **men**)
See *mighty men, David's*

*1 Samuel 16:13, 19-23*
*1 Samuel 17:22-50*
*Matthew 21:9, 15*

D

**David** (**day**-vid)

Son of Jesse and second king of Israel after Saul. He was from the tribe of Judah and the youngest of seven brothers.

David is the most famous king of Israel and one of the most important people in the Bible. His defeat of Goliath is a model of faith. He followed God's will at every step of his rise to power. He wrote psalms, ruled with justice, and fought bravely. His life was such a big part of God's plan that his name appears over 1,000 times in the Bible.

God chose David to be king over Israel, but he also promised that David's kingdom would never end. One of David's descendants would one day be born in Bethlehem, grow up to be king, and reign forever. This would be the "anointed one," the Messiah. This is why the New Testament often calls Jesus "son of David."

The story of David is told in *First Samuel* and *Second Samuel*.

See also *City of David; mighty men, David's; Samuel; Saul*

**day's journey** (**dayz jur**-nee)
See *day's walk*
See also *Sabbath day's journey*

**day's wages** (**dayz way**-juhz)
The amount of money paid to a person for one day of work. In New Testament times, this was one *denarius*.

*Matthew 20:2*
*Revelation 6:6*

**day's walk** (**dayz wok**)
The amount of distance a normal person could walk in one day, probably about 40 kilometers.
See also *Sabbath day's journey*

*Acts 1:12*

**Day of Atonement** (**day** uhv uh-**tohn**-ment)
The tenth day of the seventh month of every year. The Hebrew name is *Yom Kippur*. On this day, all the people would hold a fast. The high priest would enter the Holy of Holies and offer a sacrifice to make atonement for the nation's sin. This most holy day and its rituals were a reminder that no single sacrifice was enough to pay for their sin. The rules for the Day of Atonement are in Leviticus 16:1-34.

*Leviticus 23:27*
*Leviticus 25:9*

**day of his coming** (**day** uhv hiz **kuhm**-ing)
A reference to the *return of Christ*, a time still in the future when Jesus Christ will come back, defeat all his enemies, judge the earth, and set up his kingdom. No one knows when this day will come.
See also *day of judgment; day of the* L*ORD; judgment; last day*

*Malachi 3:1-4*
*1 Thessalonians 4:16*

D

*Matthew 12:36*
*2 Peter 3:7*
*1 John 4:17*

**day of judgment** (**day** uhv **juhj**-ment)
Another term for the *last day*; the final *day of the Lord*.

**day of Pentecost**
See *Pentecost*

*Isaiah 13:6-9*
*Joel 3:14*

**day of the Lord** (**day** uhv the **lord**)
• A generic term for any judgment that God brings on the wicked. Some of the disasters that befell enemy nations of Israel came under this description.

*1 Thessalonians 5:2*
*2 Peter 3:10*

• A reference to the *last day.*

*Philippians 1:1*
*1 Timothy 3:8, 12*

**deacon** (**dee**-kuhn)
A Greek word that generally means servant, aid, or helper. The word is used in the New Testament to refer to Christians who did important jobs of service or ministry.

*Genesis 14:3*
*Joshua 18:19*

**Dead Sea** (**ded see**)
The salty body of water in the great rift valley of Palestine. Its main source is the Jordan River. David camped in the nearby caves of En-gedi while hiding from Saul. The Dead Sea lies at the lowest point on earth.

**death** (**deth**)

• Physical death: The end of life; permanent stopping of all vital functions. — *2 Corinthians 4:11*

• The "second death": Eternal punishment for sin; eternal separation from God; going to hell; the *lake of fire*. — *Revelation 20:6*

• The name of the rider of the fourth (pale) horse of *four horsemen of the Apocalypse*. — *Revelation 6:8*

See also *life; eternal life*

**debauchery** (de-**baw**-chuh-ree)

A lack of self-control; doing whatever you want to whether it is right or wrong. — *2 Corinthians 12:21*, *Ephesians 5:18*

**Debir** (de-**beer**)

• King of Eglon during the time of Joshua. Debir and four other Amorite kings allied themselves against Gibeon in an effort to stop the Israelite march through Canaan. — *Joshua 10:1-4*

• A city in the Judean hills southwest of Hebron that was conquered by Joshua and given to the Levites. — *Joshua 11:21*

• A place in the northern territory of Judah. — *Joshua 15:5-7*

• A place in the northern territory of Gad. — *Joshua 13:24-26*

**Deborah** (**deb**-uh-ruh)

Wife of Lappidoth and fourth judge of Israel after Shamgar. She is famous for enlisting *Barak* to command the armies of Israel against *Sisera*. She judged Israel 40 years. — *Judges 4:4, 14*

Matthew 6:11-12
Matthew 18:25-32
Romans 13:8

**debtor (det-ur)**
A person who owes something to someone else; someone who has a debt. In some translations of the Lord's Prayer, the word debtor is used to describe anyone who has sinned against another person.

Matthew 4:25
Mark 5:20
Mark 7:31

**Decapolis** (de-**kap**-uh-liss)
A large area south and east of the Sea of Galilee. It is called the Decapolis because deca is Greek for ten, and there were ten towns in the region. Jesus visited this area and drew crowds.

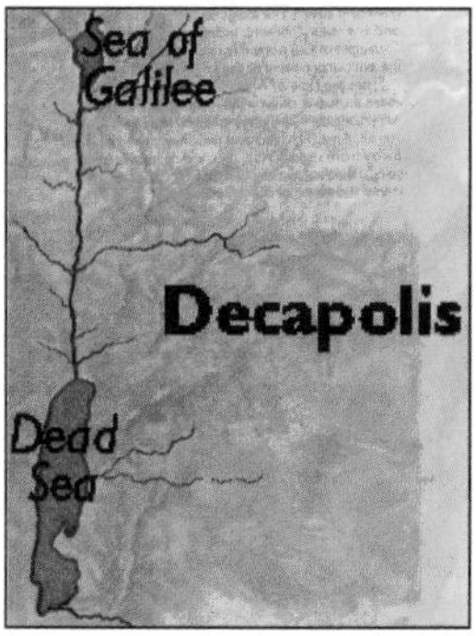


See also *Gadarenes, region of the*

Psalm 2:7
Daniel 2:13
Luke 2:1

**decree** (di-**kree**)
An edict or *law* that is declared publicly.

**Dedan** (**dee**-duhn)

Genesis 10:6-7

- A son of Raamah and great-great-grandson of Noah through Ham.

Jeremiah 49:8

- A city in northwest Arabia where the descendants of Dedan lived.

Jeremiah 49:8

- The people who lived in the city of Dedan.

Isaiah 21:13

**Dedanites** (**dee**-duhn-ites)
People of *Dedan*.

**dedicate** (**ded**-uh-kate)
To set aside an object for God's service. The priests dedicated the altar and many of the gold and silver furnishings of the temple before using them in worship.
See also *consecrate; Feast of Dedication*

*Leviticus 27:26*
*Proverbs 20:25*
*Ezekiel 43:26*

**defile** (di-**file**)
To make unfit for God's use; to make *unclean*.

*Leviticus 18:30*
*Daniel 1:8*
*Hebrews 12:14-15*

**Deity, the** (**dee**-i-tee, the)
All of God's nature; all that God is.

*Colossians 2:9*

**Delilah** (duh-**lye**-luh)
The woman who betrayed *Samson* to the Philistines. The Philistines paid her 1,100 pieces of silver to find his weakness. Samson fell in love with her and told her what she wanted to know.

*Judges 16:6, 18*

**Demas** (**dee**-muhss)
A Christian who worked with Paul in Rome, but then later deserted him.

*Colossians 4:14*
*2 Timothy 4:10*
*Philemon 1:24*

**Demetrius** (duh-**mee**-tree-uhss)
• A Christian man praised in 3 John for his excellent reputation.

*3 John 1:12*

• A silversmith who made and sold shrines of Artemis during the time of Paul. He started a riot in Ephesus when Paul told people not to worship idols.

*Acts 19:24*
*Acts 19:38*

*Matthew 9:32-33*
*1 Timothy 4:1*
*James 2:19*

**demon** (**dee**-muhn)
An evil spirit. Demons live in Hades, hate God, and serve the devil. They will be thrown into the lake of fire on the day of judgment.
See also *Abyss*

*Matthew 8:28-33*

**demon-possessed** (**dee**-muhn puh-**zest**)
Controlled by a demon. Jesus freed several people from demon-possession in the course of his healings. This led his enemies to accuse him of being the prince of demons. But as Paul explained in Romans 8:38-39, God has infinite power over all forces. God wants us to be possessed and controlled by the *Holy Spirit*. Demon-possession is not the same as illness.

D

*Matthew 18:28*
*Luke 7:41*

**denarii** (duh-**nair**-ee-eye)
Plural form of *denarius*.

*Matthew 20:2*
*Matthew 22:19*

**denarius** (duh-**nair**-ee-uhss)
A silver coin minted by the Roman empire in New Testament times and often used to pay one *day's wages*. It was equal to one twenty-fifth of the gold aureus.

*Ezekiel 23:11*
*Romans 1:28*
*Philippians 2:15*

**depraved** (de-**praved**)
Corrupt; sinful; prone to do wrong. Because of sin, every person is depraved.

*Romans 1:29*
*2 Peter 2:19*

**depravity** (de-**prav**-i-tee)
The state of being *depraved*.

**Derbe** (**dur**-bee)

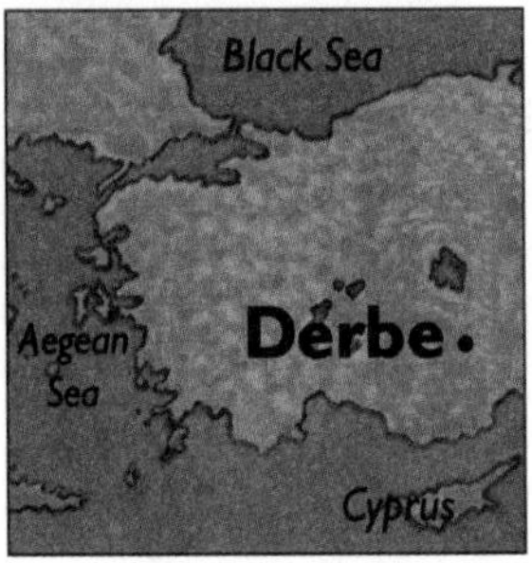


A city in the region of Asia Minor known as Lycaonia, part of the Roman province of Galatia. It is in the southeast portion of Asia Minor. Paul visited this city on his first and second missionary journeys.

*Acts 14:6*
*Acts 16:1*
*Acts 20:4*

D

**desecrate** (**des**-uh-krate)

To violate or misuse something that is holy.

*Leviticus 21:11-12*
*Ezekiel 7:22*
*Acts 24:5-8*

**desert** (**dez**-urt)

A dry and barren area, also called wilderness.

The Bible mentions many places in the desert and many desert regions. Mount Sinai, the Dead Sea, and Beersheba are all in wilderness areas. The Negev is one of Israel's most famous desert areas.

See also *Desert of Sin; Sinai*

*Exodus 3:1*
*Numbers 14:2*
*Luke 3:4; 4:1*

**Desert of Paran** (**dez**-urt uhv **pair**-uhn)

An area of wilderness between Mount Sinai and the *Desert of Zin* in the Sinai peninsula. Abraham and Hagar's son Ishmael lived in the Desert of Paran for a while. The Israelites passed through this desert on their way to the promised land during the Exodus.

*Genesis 21:20*
*Numbers 13:26*

D

*Exodus 15:22-24*

**Desert of Shur** (**dez**-urt uhv **shoor**)
An area of wilderness on the northwest edge of the Sinai peninsula and right outside of Egypt. The Israelites wandered around in this desert region right after leaving Egypt during the Exodus. This is where they first complained of having no water.

*Exodus 16:1*
*Exodus 17:1*
*Numbers 33:11-12*

**Desert of Sin** (**dez**-urt uhv **sin**)
An area of wilderness between the Red Sea of Egypt (the Sea of Reeds) and the *Desert of Sinai* in the Sinai peninsula. The Israelites passed through this desert on their way to Sinai during the Exodus. It is not the same as Zin or the *Desert of Zin*.

*Exodus 19:1*

**Desert of Sinai** (**dez**-urt uhv **sye**-nye)
The area of wilderness around Mount *Sinai* in the south of the Sinai peninsula.

*Joshua 15:1-3*

**Desert of Zin** (**dez**-urt uhv **zin**)
The area of wilderness between *Beersheba* and *Kadesh Barnea*; the desert north of *Paran*; the southern half of the *Negev*.

*Deuteronomy 1:1*

**Deuteronomy, book of**
(**dyoo**-tuh-**ron**-uh-mee, **buk** uhv)
Fifth book of the Old Testament and fifth of the *books of law*. The word deuteronomy means "second law"; the book got this name because it is a copy of the Law given to Moses (see 17:18).

It tells about what God did for Israel and reviewed the terms of the covenant between the people and God. The book was written by Moses.

See also *Pentateuch*

**devil, the** (**de**-vuhl, the)
Another word for *Satan*.

*Matthew 4:1-3*
*1 John 3:8*
*Revelation 12:9*

**devoted to destruction**
(di-**voh**-tid too di-**struhk**-shuhn)
A phrase applied to anything that was so sinful or corrupt that it had to be completely destroyed. It was applied to many of the cities of Canaan during Joshua's campaign. These cities were not to be spared in any way.

*Leviticus 27:29*
*Joshua 7:12*

**devout** (di-**vout**)
Careful to obey all of God's commands and sincere in wanting to; true to God; respectful of God and his ways.

*1 Kings 18:3*
*Luke 2:25*
*Acts 22:12*

**diadem** (**dye**-uh-dem)
A crown; chief symbol of royalty.

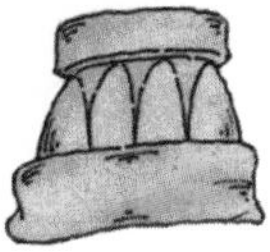

*Leviticus 8:9*
*Isaiah 62:3*

**Dibon** (**dye**-buhn)
• A town in the territory of Judah. It is mentioned only in Nehemiah, and its location is unknown.

*Nehemiah 11:25*

• Also called Dibon Gad, a city in Moab north of the Arnon River and east of the Dead Sea. It

*Numbers 32:34*

was given to the tribes of Reuben and Gad after the conquest of Canaan. The Gadites built it up, hence the name.

*John 11:16*
*John 20:24*
*John 21:2*

**Didymus** (**did**-i-muhss)
The Greek version of the name *Thomas*.

*Genesis 30:21*
*Genesis 46:15*

**Dinah** (**dye**-nuh)
Jacob and Leah's only daughter.

*Genesis 36:32*
*1 Chronicles 1:43*

**Dinhabah** (din-**huh**-buh)
The city where Bela, son of Beor, ruled as king over Edom. The city was destroyed long ago and its location is unknown.

*Acts 17:34*

**Dionysius** (**dye**-uh-**nish**-uhss)

A member of the *Areopagus* and one of the few people of Athens who converted to Christianity under Paul's preaching there.

*3 John 1:9*

**Diotrephes** (dye-**ah**-truh-feez)
A leader among some in the early church who opposed the authority of the apostle John. He is mentioned only in the letter of Third John.

**disciple** (duh-**sye**-puhl)
A person who follows another; a student of a teacher; a learner. Jesus had many disciples. The most famous were *The Twelve* whom he called to be with him. Joseph of Arimathea and Nicodemus were secret disciples.

*Matthew 10:42*
*Luke 9:18*
*Acts 14:20*

**district** (**dis**-trikt)
An area of land or group of cities marked off for one reason or another.

*1 Samuel 9:4*
*Nehemiah 3:14*
*Acts 16:12*

**divination** (**di**-vuh-**nay**-shuhn)
Use of magic, sorcery, witchcraft, astrology, or any other occult practice to learn what will happen in the future or far away. Sometimes a *diviner* would also try to influence events; this is what Balaam tried to do. Deuteronomy 18:10-11 lists the kinds of divination God forbids.

*Joshua 13:22*
*Ezekiel 13:9*
*Micah 3:6*

**diviner** (duh-**vye**-nur)
A person who tries to determine the future or influence events through use of *magic*, soothsaying, or other occult means.

*1 Samuel 6:2*
*Zechariah 10:2*

**doctrine** (**dok**-truhn)
A set of beliefs or teachings.

*1 Timothy 4:16*
*Titus 2:1*

**Dorcas** (**dor**-kuhss)
A Christian in the early church known for her acts of good will toward others.

*Acts 9:36-39*

D

*Genesis 37:17*
*2 Kings 6:13*

**Dothan** (**doh**-thuhn)

A city and fertile plain near Shechem in the hills of Samaria midway between the Jordan River and the Mediterranean coast. This is where Joseph's brothers threw him into a pit. It was easy for merchants to find him because Dothan lay on a major trade route to Egypt.

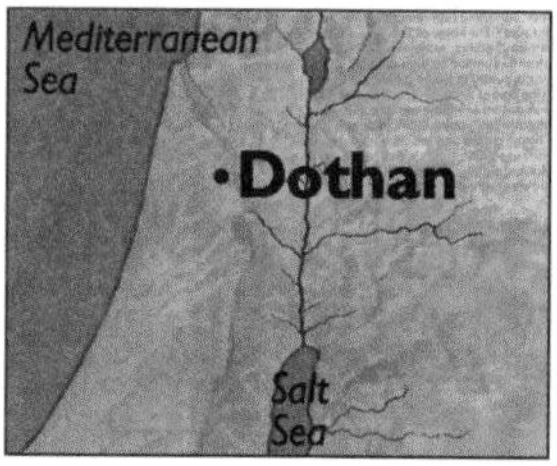


*Genesis 8:8-12; 15:9*
*Psalm 55:6*
*Mark 1:9-11*

**dove** (**duhv**)

A medium-sized, plump bird closely related to the *pigeon*, one of the kinds of animals the Israelites were allowed to sacrifice for sin. Doves were lighter in color than pigeons. Doves and pigeons were chosen by those who could not afford bulls, sheep, or goats. People who could not afford a dove or pigeon were allowed to sacrifice a tenth of an *ephah* of fine flour instead.

See also *offering*

**drachma** (**drok**-muh)

*Ezra 2:69*

• A coin of gold minted by the Persians during the time of Ezra and Nehemiah.

*Matthew 17:24, 27*

• A silver coin equal to about one denarius. Though it was a Greek coin, it still circulated in Roman provinces during New Testament times.

**dragon** (**drag**-uhn)
Another term for Satan.

*Revelation 12:9*
*Revelation 20:2*

**dream** (**dreem**)

A means by which God has sometimes communicated with people. Jacob learned of God's care for him in a dream. Daniel interpreted dreams for Nebuchadnezzar and Belteshazzar. An angel used a dream to warn Joseph about Herod.

*Genesis 20:3-7*
*Matthew 2:19*
*Acts 2:17*

**drink offering** (**dringk awf**-ur-ing)
An *offering* of liquid such as wine or oil.

*Genesis 35:14*
*Philippians 2:17*

**dropsy** (**drop**-see)
A buildup of fluid inside the body. Jesus once healed a victim of dropsy, even though the Pharisees thought that it was unlawful to heal on the Sabbath.

*Luke 14:2*

**Drusilla** (droo-**sil**-uh)

Jewish wife of Felix who went with her husband to cross-examine Paul in Jerusalem.

*Acts 24:24*

**Dura** (**doo**-ruh)
A plain or valley in Babylonia where Nebuchadnezzar set up a gold statue during the time of Daniel.

*Daniel 3:1*

*Leviticus 15:31*
*Psalm 33:14*
*Revelation 13:6*

D

**dwelling place, the LORD's**
(the **lordz dwel**-ing **playss**)
Another name for God's home; heaven; God's presence.

**East Gate (eest gate)**
One of the gates in the walls of Jerusalem. The east wall of the city doubled as the east wall of the temple, so the East Gate was also part of the *temple*. Nehemiah's repair of the city walls involved the restoration of this gate.
See also *North Gate; South Gate; West Gate*

*1 Chronicles 26:14*
*Nehemiah 3:29*
*Ezekiel 40:10*

**east wind (eest wind)**
A very strong wind of hot and dry air that stirs up dust and debris from the desert. It is very destructive.

*Genesis 41:6*
*Psalm 48:7*
*Jonah 4:8*

**East, the (eest,** the)
A term generally referring to the land east of the land of Canaan, especially Mesopotamia and the lands beyond.

*Genesis 2:8*
*Joshua 11:3*
*Matthew 24:27*

**Ebal (ee**-bawl)
• The larger of two mountains that overshadow the city of Shechem. Mount Gerizim is the other. Moses told the Israelites to place a copy of the Ten Commandments on Mount Ebal.

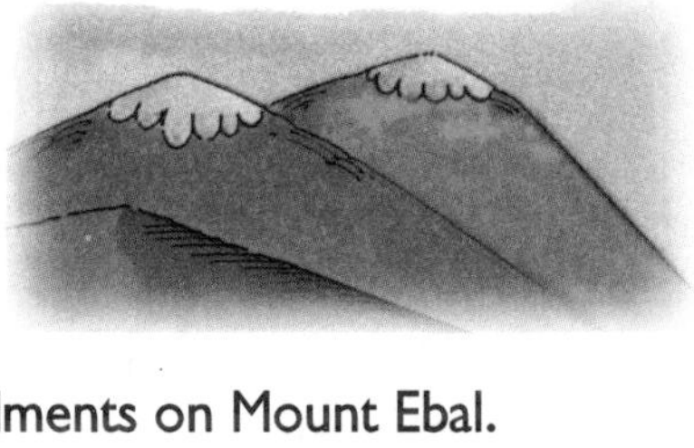

*Deuteronomy 11:29*
*Joshua 8:30*

• Alternate spelling for Obal, a son of Joktan whose descendants settled in Arabia.

*Genesis 36:10-29*

• One of Esau's descendants.

*Genesis 36:19, 23*

E

**Ebed-Melech** (e-bed-**mel**-ek)

*Jeremiah 38:7-11*

An Ethiopian eunuch in the service of King Zedekiah who rescued the prophet Jeremiah from a *cistern*.

**Ebenezer** (eb-uh-**nee**-zur)

*1 Samuel 4:1*
*1 Samuel 5:1*

• A place near and east of *Aphek* in the territory of Ephraim; the site where the Philistines defeated the Israelites and captured the Ark of the Covenant during the time of Eli.

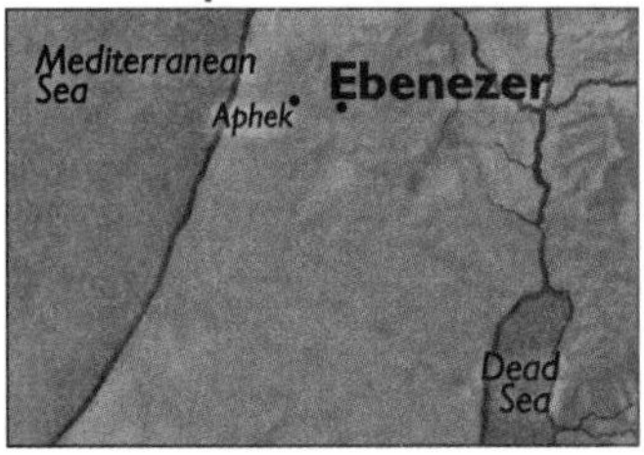


*1 Samuel 7:12*

• A stone that Samuel set up at Ebenezer (the place; see above) to commemorate the victory of the Israelites over the Philistines at the same site as their earlier defeat.

**Eber** (**ee**-bur)

*Genesis 10:21*

• A great-grandson of Shem; son of Salah; father of Peleg and Joktan. He lived 464 years.

*1 Chronicles 5: 11-13*

• One of the members of the tribe of Gad.

*1 Chronicles 8:12*

• One of the sons of Elpaal, from the tribe of Benjamin.

*Nehemiah 12: 12, 20*

• The head of a priestly family that returned to Jerusalem with Nehemiah.

**Ecclesiastes, book of** (e-**klee**-zee-**as**-teez, **buk** uhv)

Twenty-first book of the Old Testament and fourth of the books of poetry. Ecclesiastes is a collection of wise sayings and proverbs written by Solomon. "Ecclesiastes" means "a member of the assembly." The author calls himself "the Teacher."

*Ecclesiastes 1:1*

**Eden** (**ee**-den)

• The land where God placed Adam and Eve. It was "in the east," and a river flowed through it that was connected in some way to four other rivers: Pishon, Gihon, Tigris, Euphrates. Its exact location is unknown. Adam and Eve were forced to leave Eden after their sin.

*Genesis 2:15*
*Genesis 3:23-24*

• One of the Levites who purified the temple for Hezekiah's reform.

*2 Chronicles 31:14-15*

• *Beth Eden.*

**edification** (**e**-di-fuh-**kay**-shuhn)

Help given to another person that keeps adding more and more to that person's ability; the building up of another person.

*Romans 14:19*

**edify** (**e**-duh-fye)

To build up; to help another person improve or get better at something.

*1 Corinthians 14:4, 16-17*

E

Genesis 25:30
Genesis 36:8

**Edom** (**ee**-dom)
• A nickname for Esau.

Genesis 32:3

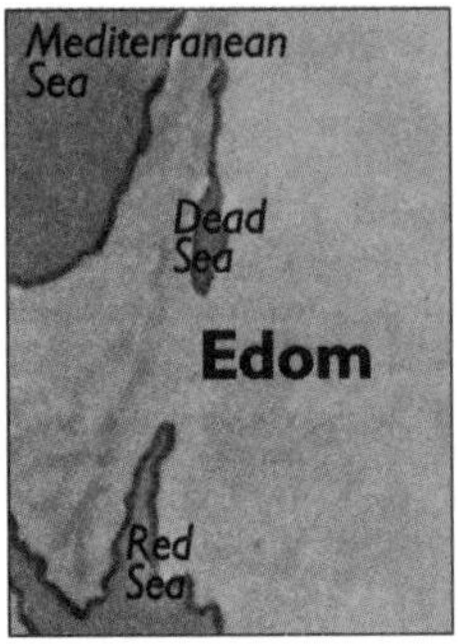


• The area south of the Dead Sea where the descendants of Esau (Edomites) lived, bounded on the west side by the western Arabah and on north by the wadi Zered. Moab lay to the north, Midian to the south. The *king's highway* passed through the eastern side of Edom.

Genesis 36:9, 43

**Edomites** (**ee**-duhm-ites)
People of *Edom*; descendants of Esau.

2 Samuel 3:5

**Eglah** (**eg**-luh)
One of David's wives and mother of *Ithream*. We know nothing else about her.

Judges 3:17-23

**Eglon** (**eg**-lon)
• King of Moab during the time of the judges. The book of Judges gives a detailed account of his assassination at the hands of *Ehud*.

Joshua 10:3, 23
Joshua 10:36

• A city conquered by Joshua's forces in the territory allotted to Judah.

Genesis 12:10-11
Matthew 2:13-14
Acts 7:9-17

**Egypt** (**ee**-jipt)
The nation and kingdom at the northeastern corner of Africa. Israel's entire history involves Egypt. Abram visited Egypt before settling in

Canaan. Jacob's whole family settled there and grew to become the Hebrew nation. God called Moses to lead the Hebrews out of slavery in Egypt. Several Israelite kings tried to ally themselves with Egypt before the Exile. An angel directed Mary and Joseph to hide there when Herod was trying to kill the baby Jesus. And people from Egypt were present at *Pentecost*. Even some of the messianic prophesies mention Egypt.

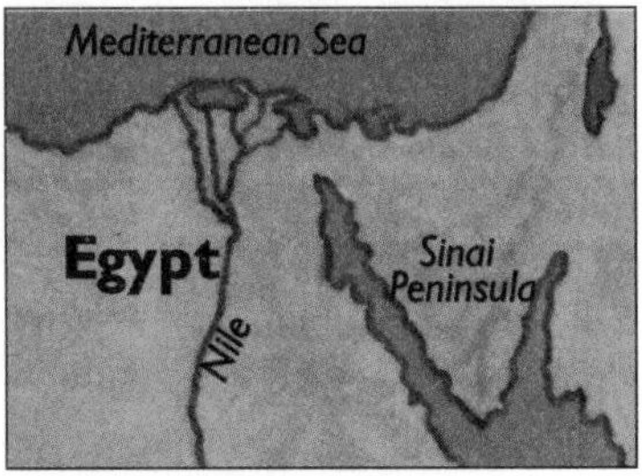


**Egypt, plagues of**
See *plagues of Egypt*

**Egyptians** (ee-**jip**-shuhnz)
People of *Egypt*.

*Genesis 12:11-14*

**Ehud** (**ee**-huhd)

Son of Gera and second judge of Israel after Othniel. He earned fame for the left-handers of Benjamin by assassinating the king of Moab when the Moabites were oppressing the Israelites. He judged Israel 80 years.

*Judges 3:15-23*
*Judges 4:1*

Joshua 13:3
1 Samuel 5:10

**Ekron** (**ek**-ron)

One of the five main Philistine cities. It lay on the border of Judah and Dan, but the Israelites never got control of the city for very long. The Philistines tried to keep the Ark of the Covenant there after taking it from Israel. The people of Ekron worshiped *Baal-Zebub*.

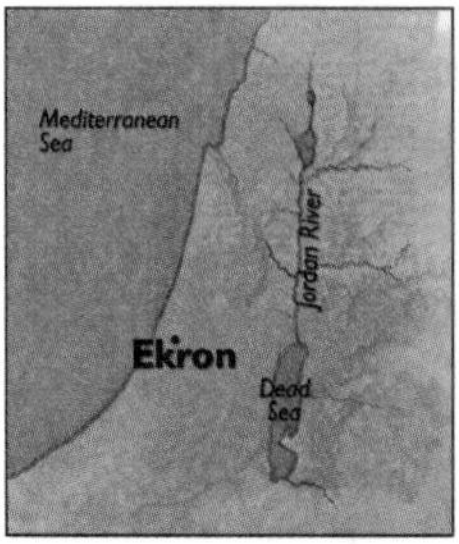


Genesis 28:3
Psalm 91:9

**El Shaddai** (**el** shuh-**dye**)

"God Almighty," a name for God.

1 Samuel 17:19
1 Samuel 21:9

**Elah** (**ee**-luh)

Site of the Israelite camp during the battle of David and Goliath. Elah is a valley near Jerusalem in the territory of Judah.

Isaiah 11:11
Daniel 8:2

**Elam** (**ee**-luhm)

A large plain in southern Mesopotamia and east of the Tigris River, known today as the plain of Khuzistan in Iran, and the people who lived there. This is where *Susa* was located during the time of Esther. Isaiah predicted that this nation would conquer Babylon and then later be conquered itself.

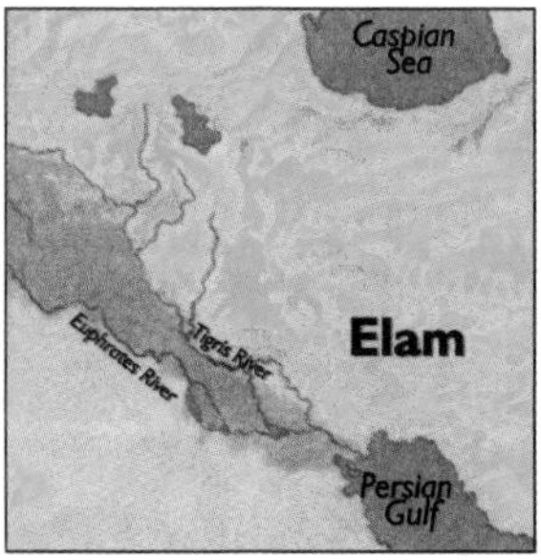


Ezra 4:9
Acts 2:9

**Elamites** (**ee**-luhm-ites)

People of *Elam*.

**Eldad** (**el**-dad)

One of the 70 elders of Israel chosen by Moses to help lead the nation. Eldad and *Medad* were the only two elders not present at the tent of meeting when God gave them his Spirit.

*Numbers 11:26-30*

**elders** (**el**-durz)

A word for leaders:

• Elders of Israel: In Old Testament times, every city, town, and village had elders who held authority over all civil affairs. Another group of elders held authority over all Israel; these are the ones who asked Samuel for a king. They continued to have influence even when Israel had kings. In New Testament times, they shared power with the priests of the Sanhedrin.

*Exodus 3:16*
*Acts 4:23*

• Elders of the church: The New Testament mentions elders who held authority over local congregations. These elders were the church's leaders.

*James 5:14*

**Eleazar** (el-ee-**ay**-zur)

A very common name among the Israelites, especially among the descendants of Aaron:

• Third son of Aaron, father of Phinehas, and one of the leaders of Israel in its earliest days. He was in charge of the tabernacle during the Exodus.

*Exodus 28:1*

E

*1 Samuel 7:1* • One of those who guarded the Ark of the Covenant when it was being held at *Kiriath Jearim*.

*2 Samuel 23:9* • One of the elite of David's mighty men; son of Dodai. He became a hero for refusing to join the retreat at *Pas Dammim*.

*1 Chronicles 23:21-22* • A Levite family leader during the time of David; son of Merari.

*Ezra 8:33* • One of those who returned to Israel with Ezra; son of Phinehas.

*Ezra 10:25* • One of the family leaders who complied with Ezra's reforms; son of Parosh.

*Matthew 1:15-16* • Great-grandfather of Joseph, Mary's husband.

*Matthew 24:22*
*2 Timothy 2:10*

**elect** (e-**lekt**)
Another word for *chosen*.

*2 John 1:1-2*

**elect lady** (e-**lekt lay**-dee)
The person to whom John addressed the letter of Second John, either a woman whose name is unknown, a woman named Electa, or a church; also called the "chosen lady."

*Matthew 20:6, 9*

**eleventh hour** (e-**lev**-uhnth **our**)
The last twelfth of the day before sundown.
See *also hour*

**Elhanan** (el-**hay**-nuhn)

*1 Chronicles 11:26* • One of David's *mighty men*.

*1 Chronicles 20:5* • The Israelite who killed *Lahmi*.

**Eli** (**ee**-lye)

High priest of Israel who reared Samuel in the tabernacle at Shiloh when the Lord called Samuel to prophesy. Eli's sons Hophni and Phinehas became famous for their disrespect toward their priestly duties. Eli's story is told in 1 Samuel 1:1–4:22.

*1 Samuel 1:3, 9*
*1 Kings 2:27*

**Eliab** (ee-**lye**-ib)

A common name among the Israelites:

- Jesse's oldest son and David's brother. As a soldier in Saul's army, he scoffed at David for trying to challenge Goliath. He was also called Elihu. *1 Samuel 17:13, 28*
- One of the family leaders from the tribe of Zebulun, chosen by God to help Moses take a census of Israel while camped at Sinai. *Numbers 2:7, 24*
- An Israelite of the tribe of Reuben; son of Pallu. Two of his sons, Dathan and Abiram, died in *Korah's rebellion*. *Numbers 16:1* *Numbers 26:8*
- Third in command among the warriors of Gad who defected to David when David was on the run from Saul. Their great bravery and skill is described in 1 Chronicles 12:8-15.
- A Levite musician who played when the Ark of the Covenant was returned to Jerusalem from Kiriath Jearim. *1 Chronicles 15: 19-22*

*1 Chronicles 6:25-27*
• Son of Nahath; a Levite and ancestor of Samuel.

**Eliakim** (ee-**lye**-uh-kim)

*2 Kings 18:18*
• Israelite chosen by God to replace Shebna as assistant to king Hezekiah; son of Hilkiah. His position was a place of great honor and responsibility. He negotiated with the Assyrian Rabshakeh during the siege of Jerusalem.

*2 Chronicles 36:4*
• King *Jehoiakim's* original name.

*Nehemiah 12:40-41*
• A priest during the time of Nehemiah.

*Matthew 1:13*
• One of Zerubabbel's grandsons.

*Luke 3:30*
• One of those listed in Luke's genealogy of Jesus.

**Eliasaph** (ee-**lye**-uh-saf)

*Numbers 1:14; 7:42*
• Leader of the tribe of Gad during the Exodus; son of Deuel.

*Numbers 3:24*
• Leader of the clan of Gershon during the Exodus; son of Lael.

**Eliashib** (ee-**lye**-uh-shib)

*Nehemiah 3:1*
• High priest of Israel during the time of Nehemiah. He helped rebuild the *Sheep Gate*.

*1 Chronicles 3:24*
• A member of the royal family of David who lived sometime after the Exile.

*1 Chronicles 24:6, 12*
• One of the family leaders among the priests during the time of David.

**Elidad** (ee-lye-dad) *Numbers 34:21*
The family leader of Benjamin chosen by God to help divide up the land after the conquest of Canaan.

**Eliezer** (el-i-**ee**-zur)
A common name among the Israelites:
- Abraham's chief servant, a man from Damascus. Abraham complained to God that Eliezer would inherit his estate before Ishmael or Isaac were born. *Genesis 15:2*

- Moses' second son. *Exodus 18:2-4*
- One of Benjamin's grandsons. *1 Chronicles 7:6-8*
- One of the priests who played a trumpet when the Ark of the Covenant was brought into Jerusalem from Kiriath Jearim. *1 Chronicles 15:24*
- Family leader of the tribe of Reuben during the time of David; son of Zichri. *1 Chronicles 27:16*
- A prophet who prophesied against Jehoshaphat, king of Judah; son of Dodavahu. *2 Chronicles 20:37*
- One of the men sent by Ezra to find Levites for the return to Jerusalem after the Exile. *Ezra 8:16*
- Three different men who complied with Ezra's reform. *Ezra 10:18, 23, 31*
- One of those listed in Luke's genealogy of Jesus. *Luke 3:29*

E

**Elihu** (ee-**lye**-hoo)

Job 32:2

• One of the friends of Job who tried to make sense of Job's suffering.

Elihu believed that God was trying to teach Job a lesson. Neither Job nor God responded to his speeches.

1 Samuel 1:1

• Samuel's great-grandfather; also called Eliab and Eliel.

1 Chronicles 12:20

• A commander in Saul's army who defected to David along with several others from the tribe of Manasseh. Elihu became a commander in David's army.

1 Chronicles 27:18

• David's oldest brother, usually called Eliab, who became commander of the forces of Judah in David's army.

**Elijah** (ee-**lye**-juh)

1 Kings 17:1
2 Chronicles 21:12
James 5:17

A prophet to the northern kingdom of Israel during the reigns of Ahab, Ahaziah, and Joram. He became famous for his defeat of 400 prophets of Baal at Mount Carmel. Elijah was from Tishbe. His story is told in 1 Kings17:1–2 Kings 2:11.

**Elim** (**ee**-lim)
An oasis in Sinai between the Red Sea and Mount Sinai; the second place the Israelites stopped after crossing the Red Sea. Its exact location is unknown.

*Exodus 15:27*
*Numbers 33:9*

**Elimelech** (uh-**lim**-uh-lek)
Naomi's husband, a wealthy man from the tribe of Judah. He moved his family from Bethlehem to Moab to escape a famine.

*Ruth 1:1-3*

**Eliphaz** (**el**-i-faz)
One of the three men who tried to explain Job's suffering. Eliphaz believed that God was punishing Job for his sins. God said that Eliphaz was wrong.

*Job 2:11*
*Job 42:7-9*

**Elisha** (ee-**lye**-shuh)
A friend of Elijah and a prophet to the southern kingdom of Judah, the northern kingdom of Israel, Moab, and Aram. He prophesied during the reigns of Jehu and Jehoahaz in Israel; and Jehoram, Ahaziah, Athaliah, and Joash in Judah. Elisha is well-known for his many miracles, including the healing of Namaan and raising a woman's son to life. He ministered for over 50 years. Elisha's story is told in 1 Kings 19:16–2 Kings 13:20.

*1 Kings 19:16*
*2 Kings 8:1-5*
*Luke 4:27*

E

Luke 1:5-7, 13, 39-42

**Elizabeth** (e-**liz**-uh-beth)
Wife of Zechariah the priest, mother of John the Baptist, and a relative of Jesus' mother Mary.

Numbers 34:25

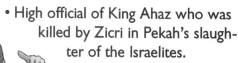

**Elizaphan** (e-li-**zay**-fuhn)
The family leader of Zebulun chosen by God to help divide up the land after the conquest of Canaan.

**Elkanah** (el-**kay**-nuh)

1 Samuel 1:1 — • Hannah's husband and father of Samuel.

Exodus 6:24 — • One of Korah's sons.

2 Chronicles 28:5-8 — • High official of King Ahaz who was killed by Zicri in Pekah's slaughter of the Israelites.

1 Chronicles 12:1-6 — • One of David's mighty men.

1 Chronicles 15:23 — • Several Levites mentioned in the genealogies of 1 Chronicles.

**Elon** (**ee**-lon)

Judges 12:11-12 — • Tenth judge of Israel after Ibzan. He was from the tribe of Zebulun and judged Israel 10 years.

Numbers 26:26 — • One of Zebulun's sons.

Genesis 36:2 — • A Hittite father-in-law of Esau's.

1 Kings 4:7-9 — • A town in the south territory of Dan.

**Elul** (**ee**-luhl)

The sixth *month* of the Israelite year, overlapping August and September.

*Nehemiah 6:15*

**Elymas** (**el**-i-muhss)

"Sorcerer," the nickname given to a Jewish false prophet who served as counsel to *Sergius Paulus* at Paphos during Paul's first missionary journey. His real name was Bar-Jesus. The man was struck blind when he tried to stop Paul from persuading the people to believe in Christ.

*Acts 13:8-9*

**Emim** (**ee**-mim)

See *Emites*

**Emites** (**ee**-mites)

"Terrifying beings" who lived in the land of Moab during the time of Abraham; also called Rephaites. They were legendary for their size and strength, but defeated by *Kedorlaomer*.

*Genesis 14:5*
*Deuteronomy 2:10-11*

**Emmaus** (e-**may**-uhss)

The village where the resurrected Jesus revealed his identity to two disciples after talking with them on the road. It lay about 11 kilometers from Jerusalem, but no one knows exactly where it was.

*Luke 24:13*

E

Acts 25:25

**emperor** (**em**-pur-ur)
Title of the supreme Roman ruler. *Caesar Augustus* was emperor during the time of Jesus' birth.

1 Samuel 24:1
2 Chronicles 20:2
Ezekiel 47:10

**En-gedi** (en-**ged**-ee)

An oasis in the desert of Negev on the western shore of the Dead Sea, in the territory allotted to Judah. David hid in the caves of En-gedi while on the run from Saul.

1 Samuel 28:7
Psalm 83:10

**Endor** (**en**-dor)
A Canaanite town on the north slope of the hill Moreh (Shunem was on the south slope). Saul made Endor famous by hiring a witch from there. It lay in the territory allotted to Manasseh, but the Israelites never got control of it.

**Enoch** (**ee**-nok)

Genesis 5:18-20
Hebrews 11:5

• Son of Jared and father of Methuselah who had a close relationship with God; one of the only people in the Bible who was taken from this earth directly by God. He is mentioned in Hebrews 11 as an example of faith.

Genesis 4:17-18

• Son of Cain.

Colossians 1:7
Colossians 4:12
Philemon 1:23

**Epaphras** (**ep**-uh-frass)
A close associate of the apostle Paul who planted the church at Colosse and several other

churches. Paul praised him for his prayer for the Colossians, concern for others, and hard work in preaching the gospel. He served some time in prison with Paul. "Epaphras" can be a nickname for "Epaphroditus," but this is not the same man as the *Epaphroditus* named in the New Testament.

**Epaphroditus** (ee-**paf**-roh-**dye**-tuhss)
A Christian from the church at Philippi who delivered a gift of money to Paul when Paul was in prison. Epaphroditus got very ill during his visit and almost died. Paul praised him as a brother and fellow worker. "Epaphroditus" was a very common Greek name in New Testament times.

*Philippians 2:25-30*
*Philippians 4:18*

**ephah** (**ee**-fuh)
A dry measure equal to about 22 liters, or three-fifths of a bushel; 10 *omers*.

*Exodus 16:36*
*Ezekiel 46:14*

**Ephes-dammim** (**ee**-fess dahm-**im**)

Site of the Philistine camp during the battle of David and Goliath. It is also called *Pas Dammim* and was the site of another great Israelite victory later.

*1 Samuel 17:1*
*2 Samuel 23:9*
*1 Chronicles 11:13*

E

Acts 19:28, 34
Acts 21:27-29
Ephesians 1:1

**Ephesians** (e-**fee**-zhuhnz)

- People who lived in the city of *Ephesus*.
- Christians of the church in Ephesus.

See also *Ephesians, book of*

Ephesians 1:1

**Ephesians,** book of (e-**fee**-zhuhnz, **buk** uhv)

Tenth book of the New Testament, a letter to the church at Ephesus. The apostle Paul wrote the letter to encourage and teach the Christians there.

Acts 19:35
1 Corinthians 16:8
1 Timothy 1:3

**Ephesus** (**ef**-uh-suhss)

A major city in the Roman province of Asia on the southwestern coast of the Aegean Sea (in

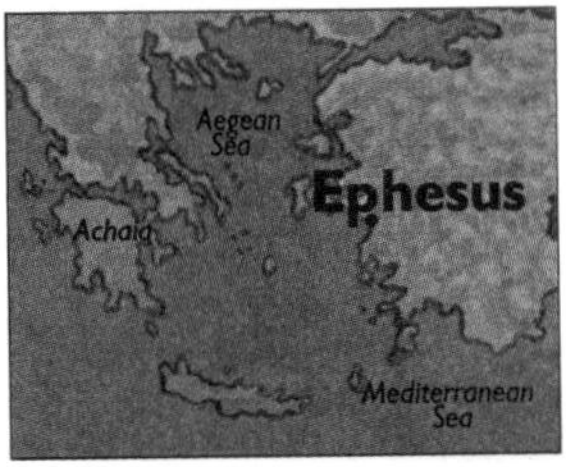


modern Turkey). Paul visited Ephesus on his second and third missionary journeys, once staying for three years. He was nearly killed in a riot started by *Demetrius* for upsetting the local business of Artemis statue making. The church that Paul started there became strong and lasted a long time.

1 Chronicles 2: 36-37

**Ephlal** (**ef**-lol)

A descendant of Judah; son of Zabad.

Numbers 34:18-19, 23

**Ephod** (**ee**-fod)

Father of *Hanniel*.

**ephod** (**ee**-fod)
An item of clothing much like a tunic worn by the high priest when performing his duties. It was an elaborate piece decorated with gold and other expensive materials. Exodus 28:4-40 and 39:2-30 describe it in detail. Priests wore more ordinary ephods during the time of the judges and the kings.

*Exodus 39:4-7*
*Judges 8:27*
*Hosea 3:4*

**Ephraim** (**ee**-free-uhm)
• Joseph's second son and the tribe of Israel named after him. *Asenath* was his mother. *Genesis 46:20*
• Another word for the nation of Israel. *Hosea 7:11*
• The land allotted to the tribe of Ephraim. *Joshua 20:7*
See also *tribes of Israel*

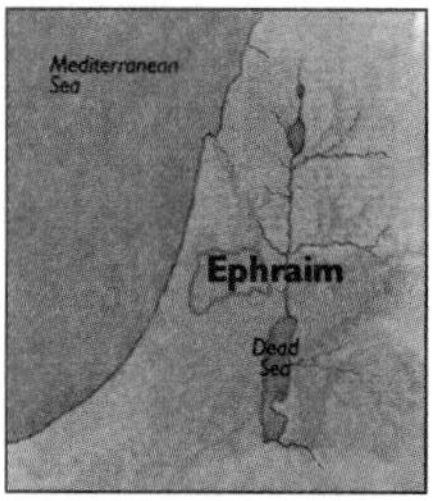


**Ephraimites** (**ee**-free-uhm-ites)
People of the tribe of Ephraim.

*Joshua 16:8-9*
*Zechariah 10:7*

**Ephrath** (**ef**-roth)
An old name for Bethlehem; also called Ephrathah.

*Genesis 35:19*
*Genesis 48:7*

**Ephrathah** (**ef**-rah-thah)
See *Ephrath*

**Ephrathite** (**ef**-rah-thyte)
Any person from *Bethlehem* (*Ephrath*).

*1 Samuel 17:12*

E

E

*Genesis 23:10-15*

**Ephron** (**ee**-fron)
The Hittite man who sold Abraham a field and cave at *Mamre* for burial of Sarah's body.

*Acts 17:18*

**Epicurean** (ep-uh-**kyur**-ee-uhn)
A person who subscribes to the philosophy of Epicurus, a Greek philosopher of the fourth century B.C. Epicureans believed that happiness came from a "don't worry, be happy" outlook and had no concern for life after death. They debated with Paul when he went to evangelize in *Athens* during his second missionary journey. They laughed at Paul's teaching about the resurrection.

See also *Stoic*

*Colossians 4:16*
*2 Thessalonians 3:14*

**epistle** (ee-**pis**-uhl)
Another word for *letter*.

*Genesis 38:6-7*

**Er** (**ur**)
One of two sons of *Judah* who died for their wickedness (the other was *Onan*).

*Romans 16:23*

**Erastus** (uh-**ras**-tus)
One of those who sent greetings to the Roman Christians at the conclusion of Paul's letter to the Romans. He was "city treasurer."

**Esau** (**ee**-saw)

Son of Isaac and fraternal twin brother of *Jacob*. Esau is famous for trading his birthright for a meal of stew, then being tricked out of his father's blessing by Jacob. Esau became the ancestor of the Edomite tribe and all its clans.

*Genesis 25:25-30*
*Malachi 1:2*
*Hebrews 12:16*

**Esh-Baal** (**esh**-bay-uhl)

Another name for *Ishbosheth*.

*1 Chronicles 8:33*

**Eshtaol** (**esh**-tuh-ahl)

A city in the lowlands of Judea shared by the tribes of Judah and Dan. Eshtaol is always mentioned together with *Zorah*, and between the two lay *Mahaneh Dan*, a location that became very important to Samson.

*Judges 13:24-25*
*Judges 16:30-31*

**Esther** (**es**-tur)

A Jewish woman born in captivity in Babylonia among the exiles of Judah. This was more than 50 years after *Zerubabbel* led the first group of exiles back to Israel. By Esther's time, Babylonia was ruled by the Persians, and it was the Persian king Xerxes who chose her to replace *Vashti* as queen. She became famous for her heroic effort to save the Jewish people from extinction at the hands of

*Esther 2:7-8*
*Esther 5:3-6*
*Esther 9:29*

E

Haman. *Mordecai* was her cousin. Esther was also known as Hadassah. Her story is told in the *book of Esther*.

*Esther 2:16-17*

**Esther, book of** (**es**-tur, **buk** uhv)
Seventeenth book of the Old Testament. It tells the story of the Jewish woman who became queen in Persia, only to find her and all her people in danger of slaughter. It is one of the only books of the Bible that never mentions God's name. No one knows who wrote it.

*1 Kings 10:9*
*John 5:24*
*1 Timothy 1:16-17*

**eternal** (ee-**tur**-nuhl)
Neverending; timeless; something that goes on forever; something that never ends.

*John 3:16-17*

**eternal life** (ee-**tur**-nuhl **life**)
Life forever in heaven with God. *Jesus Christ* came into the world so that people could have eternal life.
See also *born again; salvation*

*Psalm 93:2*
*Proverbs 8:23*
*Ecclesiastes 3:11*

**eternity** (ee-**tur**-ni-tee)
All of space and time and everything before and after it.

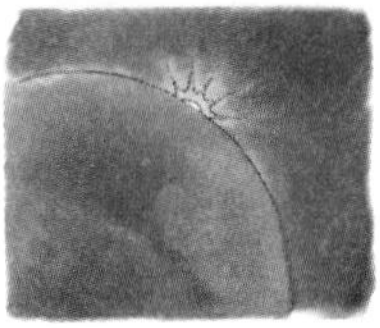

*1 Kings 4:31*
*Psalm 89:1*

**Ethan the Ezrahite**
(**ee**-thuhn thee **ez**-ruh-hite)
Author of Psalm 89, a man so wise he was compared to Solomon.

*1 Kings 8:2*

**Ethanim** (**eth**-uh-nim)
The seventh *month* of the Israelite year, overlapping September and October.

**Ethiopia** (ee-thee-**oh**-pee-uh)
The land settled by the descendants of *Cush*, the son of Ham; Nubia, south of Egypt.

*Genesis 2:13*

**Ethiopian** (ee-thee-**oh**-pee-uhn)
A person from *Ethiopia*.

*Jeremiah 13:23*
*Acts 8:27*

**Eunice** (**yoo**-niss)
Jewish mother of Paul's protégé *Timothy*. Eunice was praised for her faith and diligent instruction of Timothy from a young age. Her husband was a Gentile.

*2 Timothy 1:5*

**eunuch** (**yoo**-nik)
A man who has been castrated. Most eunuchs were trusted court officials in the service to the king or the royal family.

*Esther 2:14*
*Acts 8:27*

**Euodia** (yoo-**oh**-dee-uh)
A Christian woman who had a dispute with another Christian at Philippi, Syntyche. In the *book of Philippians*, Paul pleaded with the two to settle their differences.

*Philippians 4:2*

**Euphrates** (yoo-**fray**-teez)
A major river that flows through Mesopotamia and empties into the Persian Gulf. It is the largest river in southwestern Asia, with its sources in the mountains of Armenia. Major biblical cities along the Euphrates include Carchemish, Babylon, and Ur.

*Genesis 2:14*
*Jeremiah 46:6*
*Revelation 16:12*

*Acts 20:9*

**Eutychus** (**yoo**-tik-uhss)

Young man who fell out the window and died while listening to Paul teach late into the night. Paul raised Eutychus back to life.

*Acts 21:8*
*2 Timothy 4:5*

**evangelist** (ee-**van**-juh-list)

A person who tries to persuade others to

believe in Christ. Paul, Epaphras, Barnabas, and many others mentioned in the book of Acts were evangelists.

*Genesis 3:20; 4:1*
*2 Corinthians 11:3*
*1 Timothy 2:13*

**Eve** (**eev**)

The woman created by God from one of Adam's ribs.

*Genesis 9:16*
*Psalm 119:142*
*John 6:47*

**everlasting** (**ev**-ur-**last**-ing)

See *Eternal*

*Matthew 12:43*
*Acts 19:15-16*

**evil spirit** (**ee**-vuhl **spihr**-it)

A *demon*.

**exile** (**ek**-sile)

*2 Samuel 15:19*
*Matthew 1:17*

• Noun: A person forced to live in a foreign land; the state of being forced to live in a foreign land. The Israelites were exiles in Babylonia for over 70 years.

*Isaiah 27:13*
*Isaiah 49:21*

• Verb: To send away from home permanently.

See also *Exile, the*

**Exile, the** (**ek**-sile, the)

A period of 70 years that the people of the southern kingdom (Judah) spent as captives in Babylonia. The first wave of captives were taken when Nebuchadnezzar's armies captured Jerusalem. Others were taken in two waves afterward. The prophet Jeremiah warned of this, but the people did not listen. Ezekiel preached to the exiles while in Babylonia. Daniel, Esther, Mordecai, and other Jews served the Babylonian kings during and after this time.

*1 Chronicles 5:22*
*Matthew 1:17*

**exiles** (**eg**-zilz)
See *exile*
See also *Exile, the*

**Exodus** (**ek**-suh-duhss)

The event described in the books of *Exodus*, *Numbers*, and *Deuteronomy*; the journey of the Israelites from slavery in Egypt to the east side of the Jordan River under Moses' leadership. Because the Israelites refused to enter Canaan at Kadesh-Barnea, the journey took forty years instead of two.

*Hebrews 11:22*

E

Exodus 1:7-10

**Exodus, book of** (**ek**-suh-duhss, **buk** uhv)
Second book of the Old Testament. Moses wrote it to describe the journey of the people of Israel out of slavery in Egypt.

Genesis 1:6, 20

**expanse** (ek-**spanss**)
Another word for sky.

E

Ezekiel 24:24

**Ezekiel** (ee-**zee**-kee-uhl)
Prophet to the people of Israel in Babylonia during the Exile. Ezekiel was taken captive at the same time as Jehoiachin. He lived by the Kebar River and was called to prophesy five years later. Ezekiel's work and prophecies are recorded in the *book of Ezekiel*.

Ezekiel 1:3

**Ezekiel, book of** (ee-**zee**-kee-uhl, **buk** uhv)
Twenty-sixth book of the Old Testament and third of the *major prophets*. The prophet Ezekiel wrote this book during his exile in Babylonia. It tells about how God gave him the job of prophesying, the visions God gave him, and the messages God told him to give to Israel and other nations. The book is famous for Ezekiel's visions of heaven.

**Ezel** (**ee**-zuhl)

*1 Samuel 20:19*

The name of a stone where David was to hide while waiting for a signal from Jonathan. David was on the run from Saul, and Jonathan was going to indicate whether Saul's attitude toward David had changed. Ezel's exact location is unknown.

E

**Ezer** (**ee**-zer)

- Commander of the warriors of Gad who defected to David when David was on the run from Saul. "The weakest among them could take on a hundred regular troops, and the strongest could take on a thousand!" (1 Chronicles 12:14) — *1 Chronicles 12:8-9*

- Ruler of Mizpah who helped repair the walls of Jerusalem under Nehemiah's direction. — *Nehemiah 3:15-19*
- A musician in Nehemiah's service. — *Nehemiah 12:42*
- Several others named only in genealogies. — *Genesis 36:20-21*, *1 Chronicles 4:4*

**Ezion Geber** (**ez**-ee-uhn **gee**-bur)

*Deuteronomy 2:8*
*1 Kings 9:26*
*1 Kings 22:48*

A port city on the north shore of the Gulf of Aqaba, in the south of Edom. The Israelites stopped there twice on their way to the land of Canaan during the Exodus, once before their arrival at Kadesh Barnea and once afterward. Solomon built a fleet of ships there when he was king.

E

Nehemiah 8:5-9, 18

**Ezra's reform** (**ez**-ruhz ree-**form**)

A time when *Ezra* led the Jews in a change of ways. The people had just returned to the land of Israel from Babylonia, but they were disobeying many of God's commands. Together with Nehemiah, Ezra gathered the people in Jerusalem for a public reading of the Law of Moses. The people vowed to obey all of God's commands and to make any changes that they needed to make. The story of Ezra's reform is told in Nehemiah 8:1–10:39.

Ezra 7:10
Nehemiah 12:36

**Ezra** (**ez**-ruh)

A Jewish *scribe* who lived during the time of the Exile. Ezra led a group of Jewish exiles back to Judah about ten years after the return led by *Zerubabbel*. Ezra lived in Jerusalem at the same time as Nehemiah; they worked together to bring about *Ezra's reform*.

Ezra 7:1-6

**Ezra, book of** (**ez**-ruh, **buk** uhv)

Fifteenth book of the Old Testament. It records the history of Israel as the Exile came to an end. The book is famous for describing the reforms that Ezra the scribe started among the people who returned to the land of Israel. The books of Ezra, Nehemiah, and Esther all deal with this period of time.

F

**Fair Havens** (**fair hay**-venz)

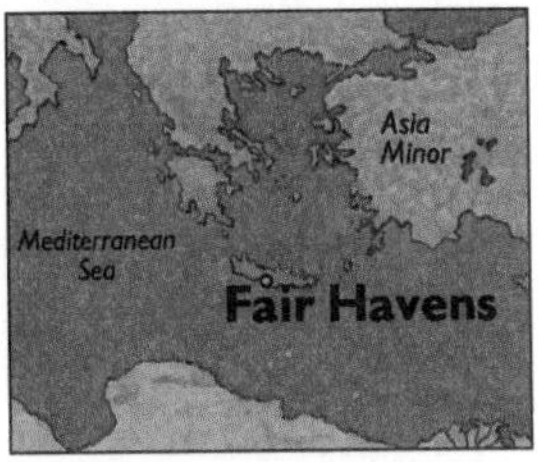


A harbor on the south side of Crete. A ship carrying Paul and many others stopped there on its way to Rome. See also *Phoenix*

*Acts 27:8*

**faith** (**fayth**)

Trust in God; belief that God can and will do what he has promised; doing something because God said to, without any other reason to do it. Faith is one of the most important topics in the Bible because God is invisible. Pleasing him requires that we act only on what he has said. All of the Bible's heroes became heroes because of their faith; *Hebrews* 11 lists many of them by name.

*2 Chronicles 20:20*
*Matthew 9:2*
*James 2:24*

**faithful** (**fayth**-fuhl)

Dependable; reliable; trustworthy. A person who is faithful does what he or she says. The Bible often describes God as faithful and asks his people to be faithful too. Faithful is the opposite of *unfaithful*.

*1 Samuel 2:35*
*Psalm 25:10*

F

*Joshua 24:14*
*Proverbs 16:6*
*3 John 1:3*

**faithfulness** (**fayth**-fuhl-ness)
Dependability; reliability; trustworthiness.
See also *faithful*

*Deuteronomy 8:14-20*
*Acts 13:6*
*Revelation 20:10*

**false prophet** (**fawlss prof**-uht)
• A person who claims to speak for God when he or she really does not; a person who pretends to be a prophet; a phony prophet. God told the Israelites to execute false prophets.
• A being described in the prophecies of Revelation 16–20. The false prophet does fake miracles and persuades people all over the world to worship the *beast*. He will be thrown into the *lake of fire*.
See also *false teacher*

*2 Corinthians 11:13*
*Galatians 4:17*
*2 Peter 2:12-15*

**false teacher** (**fawlss tee**-chur)
A person who teaches what is false about God. False teachers were a big problem in the churches at *Corinth* and *Galatia* during the early days of Christianity.
See *also Second Corinthians; Second Peter; Galatians, book of*

*Zechariah 7:3*
*Matthew 6:16-17*
*1 Kings 21:12*

**fast** (**fast**)
• Verb: To go without food for an unusual length of time; to skip one or more meals.

• Noun: A period of time when a person willingly eats nothing.
Sometimes people fast during prayer or a time of repentance. Fasting was part of the

annual *Day of Atonement*. Jesus fasted several times. Satan once tempted Jesus after Jesus had fasted 40 days.

**fasting** (**fast**-ing)
To *fast*.

Psalm 109:24
Matthew 4:2
Acts 13:2

**father** (**fah**-thur)
This word has at least three meanings in the Bible:

- A person's father.
- A person's ancestor, such as a grandfather, great-grandfather, or even someone related from hundreds of years ago.
- First person of the *Trinity*; a title for God. Jesus taught his disciples to address God as Father in their prayers.

Genesis 2:24
Genesis 4:20-21
Luke 11:2
Luke 23:34

**fear of the LORD** (**feer** uhv the **lord**)
Respect for God; respect for God's power and authority.

2 Chronicles 17:10
Job 28:28
Acts 9:31

**feast** (**feest**)
An official day of celebrating, resting, or marking an important event. God instructed the Israelites to hold several feasts, including the *Feast of Unleavened Bread*, the *Feast of Booths*, the *Feast of Weeks*, the *Feast of Trumpets*, *Passover*, *Sabbath*, and the *Day of Atonement*. Five of these happened once a year; three were known as "annual festivals." They are all described in Leviticus 23:1-44.

Exodus 23:15, 16
Mark 15:6
Acts 12:3

F

*Nehemiah 8:14*

**Feast of Booths** (**feest** uhv **boothz**)
One of the three annual *festivals*; a celebration of God's care for his people in the desert during the Exodus. The people harvested the fruit and lived in handmade booths for seven days. It was also called the Feast of Tabernacles and the Feast of Ingathering.

*John 10:22*

**Feast of Dedication**
(**feest** uhv **ded**-uh-**kay**-shun)
The term used in the New Testament for *Hanukkah*.

*Numbers 28:16*

**Feast of Firstfruits** (**feest** uhv **furst**-froots)

A day of celebrating God's provision. The people gave the first part of the barley harvest to the Lord.
See also *Feast of Booths; Feast of Weeks*

*Exodus 23:16*

**Feast of Harvest** (**feest** uhv **har**-vist)
Another name for the *Feast of Weeks*.

*Exodus 23:16*
*Exodus 34:22*

**Feast of Ingathering**
(**feest** uhv **in**-ga-thur-ing)
Another name for the *Feast of Booths*.

*Ezekiel 45:21*
*Mark 14:1*
*John 13:1*

**Feast of Passover** (**feest** uhv **pass**-oh-vur)
The longer name for *Passover*.

*Leviticus 23:24*
*Zechariah 14:18-19*
*John 7:2*

**Feast of Tabernacles**
(**feest** uhv **tab**-ur-nak-uhlz)
Another name for the *Feast of Booths*.

**Feast of Trumpets**
(**feest** uhv **truhm**-pits)

A day of rest and praise to God. This feast took place on the first day of the month of *Ethanim*.

*1 Kings 8:2*

**Feast of Unleavened Bread**
(**feest** uhv **uhn-lev**-uhnd **bred**)

One of the three annual *festivals*; a time of remembering when the Israelite slaves left Egypt. The unleavened bread is a reminder that the Israelite slaves had to leave quickly, with no time to add leaven (yeast) to their bread dough. The feast lasts for seven days and begins on the fourteenth day of *Nisan*.

*Exodus 23:15*
*Ezra 6:22*
*Mark 14:12*

**Feast of Weeks (feest** uhv **weeks)**

One of the three annual *festivals*; a time of thanking God for the harvest. This feast became known as Pentecost because it took place 50 days after the beginning of the Passover. It is also called the Feast of Harvest.

*Exodus 34:22*
*Deuteronomy 16:10, 16*

**Felix (fee**-liks)

Roman *procurator* (governor) of Judea from A.D. 52 to 59, during Paul's imprisonment in Jerusalem. Paul was being held on false charges and Felix was supposed to judge Paul's case. Instead he kept Paul in prison for two years as a

*Acts 24:22-26*

F

favor to Paul's enemies, hoping that Paul would bribe him.

*Leviticus 7:11-15*
*Numbers 7:88*

**fellowship offering** (**fel**-oh-ship **awf**-ur-ing)

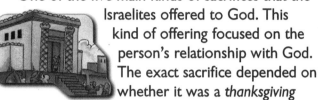

One of the five main kinds of sacrifices that the Israelites offered to God. This kind of offering focused on the person's relationship with God. The exact sacrifice depended on whether it was a *thanksgiving offering*, a *vow offering*, or a *freewill offering*.

See also *offering*

*Exodus 12:14*
*1 Kings 12:32*
*1 Corinthians 5:8*

**festival** (**fest**-uh-vuhl)

A once-a-year celebration that God commanded the Israelites to observe. There were three such festivals: the *Feast of Unleavened Bread*, the *Feast of Weeks*, and the *Feast of Booths*.

See also *feast*

*Acts 25:1-5*
*Acts 26:24-25*

**Festus** (**fest**-uhss)

Roman *procurator* (governor) of Judea after Felix, during the time of Paul's arrest and trial for leading an uprising against Rome. Festus is the one who heard Paul's defense and appeal to Caesar. His full name was Porcius Festus.

**final judgment** (**fye**-nuhl **juhj**-ment)

See *last day*

**firmament** (**fur**-muh-ment)
Another word for sky.

*Genesis 1:8-9*
*Jeremiah 4:25*
*Matthew 24:29-30*

**firstborn** (**furst**-born)

The child born first in a family. In Old Testament times, the firstborn son got the *birthright*. The New Testament describes Jesus as the firstborn among all Christians because he is their redeemer.

*Genesis 27:19*
*Luke 2:7*
*Colossians 1:15-18*

**firstfruits** (**furst**-froots)
The first crops to be harvested, first wool to be shorn from the sheep, or first result of any other labor. The *Feast of Weeks* and the *Feast of Firstfruits* are celebrations of the harvest's first-fruits. The people of Israel supported the priests and Levites (in part) by giving them the first-fruits of grain, wine, and wool.

*Leviticus 2:14*
*Nehemiah 10:35*
*James 1:18*

**firstling** (**furst**-ling)
Another word for *firstborn*.

*Genesis 48:14*
*2 Chronicles 21:3*

**Fish Gate** (**fish gate**)
One of the gates in the walls of Jerusalem. Nehemiah's repair of the city walls involved the repair of this gate. It was on the north side. It got its name from the nearby fish markets. This gate was not a part of the city that David captured from the *Jebusites*.

*2 Chronicles 33:14*
*Nehemiah 3:3; 12:39*
*Zephaniah 1:10*

F

F

**flax (flaks)**

*Exodus 9:31*
*Joshua 2:6*
*Judges 15:14*

A thin straight plant with needle-like leaves and blue flowers. The fiber of the stalk was used to make thread, and the seeds were used to make linseed oil. *Rahab* hid the Israelite spies under sheaves of flax that were drying on her roof.

**flesh (flesh)**

*Galatians 5:13*

• The corrupt part of human nature; evil desires. The apostle Paul wrote a famous passage (Romans 7:14-25) about doing battle with this part of himself.

*1 Corinthians 15:39*

• Meat; the body of an animal or person.

*1 John 4:2*

• People; human beings.

**flint (flint)**

*Isaiah 5:28*
*Ezekiel 3:9*

A type of quartz very common to the lands of Canaan and Egypt. God told Joshua to use it to make knives for the circumcision of all Israelite men just before entering Canaan.

**flocks and herds (floks and hurdz)**

*Genesis 47:1*
*Psalm 8:6-8*
*John 4:12*

Cattle, sheep, and goats kept by farmers, herdsmen, or shepherds; domesticated animals. Many people of Bible times kept flocks and herds or worked for those who did. David was a shepherd before he was king.

**flogged (flogd)**
Whipped by a *scourge*.

*Deuteronomy 25:2-3*
*Matthew 27:26*
*Acts 16:23*

**flood (fluhd)**
• The time when God covered the earth with

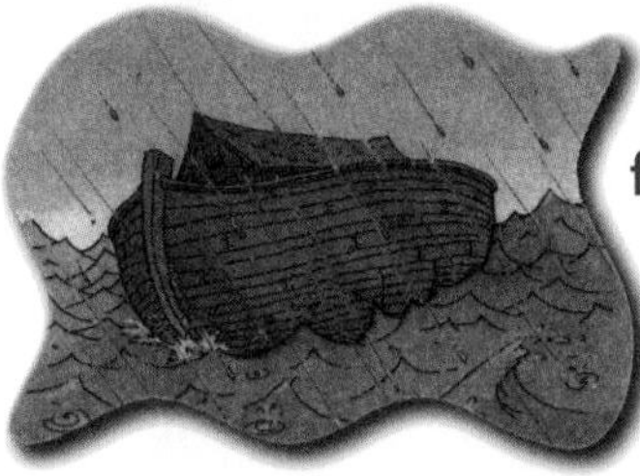

water to destroy everyone but Noah and his family. God did this because all people everywhere were constantly doing evil. Only the people and animals in Noah's *ark* survived.

*Genesis 7:7*
*Genesis 9:11*
*Luke 17:27*

• A deluge; an excess of water. This term was sometimes used as a symbol of terror, disaster, or chaos.

*Joshua 3:15*
*Job 20:28*

**food (food)**
See *barley; grain; oil; wheat*

**foolish (fool-ish)**
Weak of character; prone to evil; senseless; wicked.
See also *wise*

*1 Chronicles 21:8*
*Proverbs 8:5*
*Matthew 25:2-3*

**forbearance** (for-**bair**-inss)
Acting patient and calm; being self-controlled; showing restraint; holding back.

*Romans 3:25*

**forefather** (**for**-fah-thur)
An ancestor; a person related to you from long ago.

*Joshua 21:10-11*
*Jeremiah 35:6*
*Romans 4:1*

*Deuteronomy 15:3*
*2 Samuel 15:19*
*Acts 7:29*

**foreigner** (**for**-uh-nur)

A person from another country, land, or nation. God gave the Israelites two rules about foreigners: (1) Be kind to them. (2) Do not become like them. The Israelites were to be kind to foreigners because the Israelites were once foreigners in Egypt. But they were not to adopt the worship or immoral ways of other peoples.

**foreordained** (**for**-or-**daned**)
See *chosen*

*Psalm 105:18-19*
*Acts 3:18*
*Jude 1:17*

**foretold** (for-**tohld**)

Predicted; told before the happening. The prophets foretold many details about the Messiah.

*Genesis 50:17*
*Jeremiah 36:3*
*Matthew 6:14-15*

**forgive** (for-**giv**)

To pardon, release, or free from obligation; cancel a debt; let go. This word is one of the most important in the Bible because all people everywhere need God's forgiveness, and most of the Bible's stories and messages tell of God's desire to forgive people. Jesus came and died to make it possible. This is also one reason God wants his people always to forgive each other.

**fornication** (**for**-ni-**kay**-shuhn)
Sex with anyone who is not the person's husband or wife; sex before marriage or outside of marriage; any wrong act of sex.

*Matthew 15:19*
*Romans 1:24*
*1 Corinthians 5:1*

**forsake, forsaken** (for-**sake,** for-**sake**-uhn)
To give up on; abandon; leave alone. The Bible promises that God will never forsake his people.

*Deuteronomy 31:6*
*Judges 10:13*
*Mark 15:34*

F

**forsook** (for-**suk**)
Past tense of *forsake*.

*Judges 2:12*
*2 Kings 21:22*

**fortified city** (**fort**-i-fide **sit**-ee)
A city protected by stone walls. Most towns and villages of ancient times had no walls. Farms surrounded a cluster of houses, with no defense against attack. Larger and more important cities would often have a perimeter or circle of stone walls around them to keep out invading armies, raiders, and wild animals. *Jericho* was the first Canaanite fortified city to fall to Joshua's army.

*2 Kings 3:19*
*Proverbs 10:15*
*Daniel 11:15*

**fortress** (**for**-tress)
Another word for *fortified city*.

*Psalm 18:2*
*Daniel 11:7*
*Zechariah 9:12*

**Fountain Gate** (**foun**-ten **gate**)
One of the gates in the walls of Jerusalem. Nehemiah's repair of the city walls involved the repair of this gate. It was on the south side right

*Nehemiah 2:14*
*Nehemiah 3:15*
*Nehemiah 12:37*

beside the *Pool of Siloam*, a source of water for the city. This gate was not a part of the city that David captured from the Jebusites.

*Revelation 6:2-8*

**four horsemen of the Apocalypse (for horss-**mihn uhv the uh-**pah**-kuh-lipss)

Four riders described in the prophesies of Revelation 6:2-8. Each rides a horse of a different color: white, red, black, or pale.

See also *death*

**four living creatures (for liv**-ing **kree**-churz)

See *living creatures*

*Proverbs 6:5*

**fowler (foul**-ur)

A bird-catcher.

*Exodus 30:34*
*Matthew 2:11*
*Revelation 18:13*

**frankincense (frang**-kin-senss)

A dry perfume or incense made from the sap of the Boswellia tree. Frankincense has a strong, pleasant smell when burned. The *magi* who visited the child Jesus brought him a gift of frankincense.

See also *myrrh*

*1 Corinthians 7:22*

**freedman (freed**-man)

A slave who has been freed.

F

**freewill offering** (**free**-wil **awf**-ur-ing)

One of three kinds of *fellowship offerings*; a sacrifice that a person offers to God as a gift. The rules about freewill offerings are the same as for *vow offerings* and appear in Leviticus 7:16-18.

See also *offering*

*Psalm 54:6*
*Ezekiel 46:12*

F

**fruit of the Spirit** (**froot** uhv the **spihr**-it)

The result of devotion to God; ways a person acts and lives when he or she surrenders control to the *Holy Spirit.*

*Galatians 5:22-23*

**fruitful** (**froot**-fuhl)

Productive; fertile.

*Genesis 1:22*
*Psalm 107:37*
*John 15:2*

G

*Judges 9:26-33*

**Gaal** (**gay**-uhl)

A man who organized a rebellion against *Abimelech* at Shechem; son of Ebed.

*Daniel 9:21*
*Luke 1:19*
*Luke 1:26*

**Gabriel** (**gay**-bree-uhl)

An angel who appeared to Daniel and to Elizabeth's husband *Zechariah*. He and Michael are the only two angels mentioned by name in the Bible.

**Gad** (**gad**)

*Genesis 30:11*

• Jacob's son and the tribe of Israel named after him. *Zilpah* was his mother.

*Joshua 22:13*

• The land allotted to the tribe of Gad.

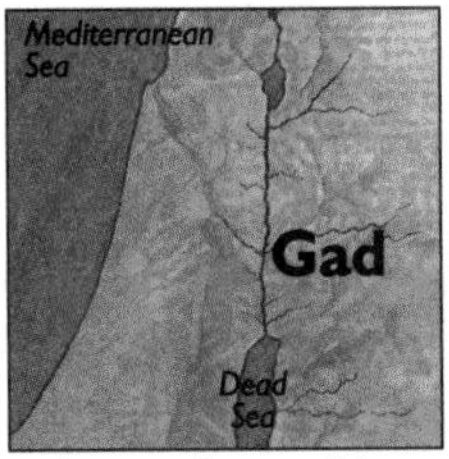


*2 Samuel 24:11-14*

• A prophet during the reigns of Saul and David. Gad gave David advice, criticism, and instructions several times, and David always acted on Gad's words.

See also *tribes of Israel*

*Matthew 8:28*

**Gadarenes, region of the**
(**gad**-uh-reenz, **ree**-juhn uhv the)

An area on the southeast shore of the Sea of Galilee, a part of the larger Gerasene region of the *Decapolis*. Jesus once cast demons out of a man from this area.

See also *Gerasenes*

**Gaddi** (**gad**-eye) — *Numbers 13:3, 11*

One of the 12 men chosen by Moses at Kadesh Barnea to spy out the land of *Canaan*; a leader of the tribe of Manasseh; son of Susi.

**Gaddiel** (**gad**-i-uhl) — *Numbers 13:3, 10*

One of the 12 men chosen by Moses at *Kadesh Barnea* to spy out the land of Canaan; a leader of the tribe of Zebulun; son of Sodi.

G

**Gadites** (**gad**-ites) — *Numbers 32:1, 31*

People of the tribe of Gad.

**Gaius** (**gay**-uhss)

A common name in New Testament times and the name of four Christians known to the apostles Paul and John:

- One of the men seized by the mob during the riot in Ephesus (the other was *Aristarchus*). Gaius was from Macedonia and had been traveling with Paul during Paul's third missionary journey. — *Acts 19:29*
- Another of Paul's traveling companions, this one from Derbe, who met Paul at Troas. — *Acts 20:4*

- One of the few converts Paul baptized (the other was *Crispus*). — *1 Corinthians 1:14*
- The person to whom John addressed *Third John*. — *3 John 1:1*

G

Galatians 1:2

**Galatia** (guh-**lay**-shuh)

• A country in the north of Asia Minor that was settled by the Gauls and later absorbed into the Roman Empire.

Acts 16:6
Acts 18:23
1 Peter 1:1

• A Roman province in Asia Minor that included the country of Galatia plus several other regions, including Isauria, *Lycaonia*, Paphlagonia, *Pisidia*, *Phrygia*, and Pontus.

See also *Galatians*

**Galatians** (guh-**lay**-shuhnz)

• People who lived in *Galatia* in New Testament times, either the northern country of Galatia or the entire Roman province.

Galatians 3:1

• Christians of the church in Galatia. Paul visited this region during his first missionary journey and started several churches there. No one knows for sure whether this included only the northern country of Galatia or the entire Roman province.

See also *book of Galatians*

Galatians 1:1

**Galatians, book of** (guh-**lay**-shuhnz, **buk** uhv)

Ninth book of the New Testament, a letter written by the apostle Paul to the churches of *Galatia*. Paul wrote it to explain freedom in Christ. Some people in the church were saying that Gentiles had to become Jews before they could be forgiven of their sins. Paul wrote that Christians were free of Jewish regulations.

**galbanum** (gal-**ba**-nuhm)
One of four ingredients that the Israelites used to make holy *incense*. It was probably the sap of the *Ferula galbaniflua* plant of Persia (related to carrots).

*Exodus 30:34*

**Galileans** (gal-i-**lee**-uhnz)
People who lived in *Galilee*.

*John 4:45*
*Acts 2:7*

**Galilee** (**gal**-i-lee)
The general area of north Palestine in New Testament times. Jesus grew up in Galilee, preached there, and healed many people there.

*1 Kings 9:11*
*Matthew 11:1*
*Acts 10:37*

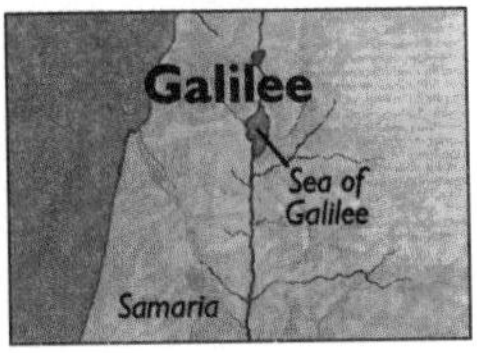


**Galilee, Sea of**
See *Sea of Galilee*

**Gallio** (**gal**-ee-oh)
*Proconsul* (governor) of Achaia who freed Paul from the charges brought against him by his Jewish enemies in Corinth during Paul's second missionary journey.

*Acts 18:12-17*

**Gamaliel** (guh-**may**-lee-uhl)
Member of the Sanhedrin who persuaded the Council to let the apostles preach about Christ; an early teacher of Paul's.

*Acts 5:34*
*Acts 22:3*

**Garden of Eden** (**gar**-den uhv **ee**-den)
See *Eden*

G

2 Samuel 18:26

**gatekeeper** (**gate**-keep-ur)

• city gatekeeper: A person who guarded a city gate. Also called a watchman.

1 Chronicles 9:21
1 Chronicles 26: 1-19

• temple gatekeeper: A priest or *Levite* who guarded the entrance to the *temple*, collected offerings from worshipers, and generally cared for the temple grounds.

1 Samuel 17:23
Amos 6:2

**Gath** (**gath**)

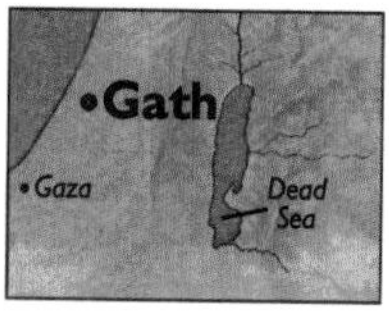


One of the five main Philistine cities. At the time of Joshua, Gath was occupied by the Anakites, the giants that scared the Israelite spies out of entering Canaan during the Exodus. The city was allotted to the tribe of Judah. *Goliath* was from Gath.

See also *Ashdod; Ashkelon; Ekron; Gaza; Gittites*

Joshua 10:41
Judges 16:1-3
Acts 8:26

**Gaza** (**gah**-zuh)

One of the five main Philistine cities, the southernmost of the five and the southern border of Canaan. Gaza was allotted to the tribe of Judah during the time of Joshua, but the Israelites never permanently took the city. Samson once visited Gaza and ripped the gates off.

See also *Gath; Ekron; Ashdod; Ashkelon*

**Gedaliah** (ge-duh-**lye**-uh)

• Governor of Judah appointed by Nebuchadnezzar after the sack of Jerusalem; son of *Ahikam*; grandson of *Shaphan*. The Babylonian army had taken most of the Jews captive to Babylonia, leaving only farmers behind. Gedaliah was in charge. The prophet Jeremiah came to live with him soon after the Babylonians left. Gedaliah was assassinated by *Ishmael* son of Nethaniah. *Jeremiah 40:5*

• One of the musicians appointed by David to serve in the choir; son of Jeduthun. *1 Chronicles 25:3*

• One of the four royal officials who put Jeremiah in a cistern; son of *Pashhur*. *Jeremiah 38:1-6*

• *Zephaniah's* grandfather. *Zephaniah 1:1*

• A priest who responded to Ezra's reform. *Ezra 10:18*

**Gehazi** (guh-**hay**-zee)

Elisha's servant and helper, mentioned by name in 2 Kings 4, 5, and 8. Gehazi is featured in the story of the woman from Shunem and the story of Naaman. He got leprosy for trying to steal from Elisha. *2 Kings 4:11-14* *2 Kings 5:27* *2 Kings 8:4-5*

**gehenna** (geh-**hen**-uh)

Hell. The term is Greek for "valley of *Hinnom*." *Matthew 10:28* *2 Peter 2:4*

G

**general letters** (**jen**-ur-uhl **let**-urz)
New Testament books of Hebrews, James, First Peter, Second Peter, First John, Second John, Third John, and Jude.

*Genesis 1:1*

**Genesis, book of**
(**jen**-uh-sis, **buk** uhv)

First book of the Old Testament and first of the *books of law*. Moses wrote this book of beginnings. It tells of God's plan for humankind from Adam to the settling of Jacob's family in Egypt. Genesis is followed by the book of Exodus.

*Matthew 14:34*
*Luke 5:1*

**Gennesaret** (guh-**ness**-uh-ret)
The very fertile plain on the northwest of the Sea of Galilee. Many people lived in Gennesaret in New Testament times. Jesus did a lot of his preaching and healing in this area.

*Nehemiah 5:9*
*Acts 10:28*
*Romans 10:12*

**gentile** (**jen**-tile)
A non-Jew; a person who is not a Jew. Jesus and all his disciples were Jews, and all of their first converts were Jews. Acts 15, Romans 11, and the book of Galatians talk about how God let gentiles become Christians.
See also *foreigner; Greeks*

*Exodus 30:13*
*Ezekiel 45:12*

**gerah** (**gee**-rah)
A unit of weight equal to about six-tenths of a gram, or one-fiftieth of an ounce; one-tenth of a *beka*.

**Gerar** (**gihr**-ar)

A town southeast of *Gaza* in the *Negev*. Both Abraham and Isaac lived in Gerar for a while before settling elsewhere.

See also *Valley of Gerar*

Genesis 20:1
2 Chronicles 14:13-14

**Gerasenes** (**gair**-uh-seenz)

People who lived in the region of Gerasa, a major city of the *Decapolis* in New Testament times. This area was quite large and probably included the smaller area of the Gadarenes, where a herd of pigs drowned in the sea.

Luke 8:26, 37

**Gergesenes** (**gur**-guh-zeenz)

See *Gadarenes, region of the*

**Gerizim** (**gair**-uh-zim)

An important mountain in the hill country of Manasseh, four kilometers northwest of Shechem. On this mountain, Joshua and the Israelites reenacted the giving of the Law to Moses.

In New Testament times, the Samaritans worshiped on this mountain. Its twin is Mount Ebal to the north; the two mountains overlook the Nablus Valley.

Joshua 8:33
Judges 9:7

**Gershom** (**gur**-shuhm)

- Moses' firstborn son, born in Midian.

Exodus 2:22

- One of the family leaders who returned to Israel with Ezra; a descendant of Phinehas.

Ezra 8:2

*Genesis 46:11*

• One of Levi's sons, also known as Gershon, whose descendants became the *Gershonites*.

*Numbers 3:24-25*
*2 Chronicles 29:12*

**Gershonites (gur**-shuh-nites)

Descendants of Levi's son Gershom, *Levites* who served Israel from David's time to after the Exile. The Gershonites were given charge of two cities of refuge: *Kedesh* and *Golan*.

See also *Kohathites; Merarites*

G

*Nehemiah 6:1-2*

**Geshem (ge**-shum)

An Arab who tried to stop *Nehemiah* from rebuilding the walls of Jerusalem.

See also *Sanballat; Tobiah*

*2 Samuel 14:23*
*1 Chronicles 3:2*

**Geshur (gesh**-ur)

A city in Syria during the time of David. Absalom fled there after murdering his brother Amnon because Geshur was ruled by Absalom's grandfather, *Talmai*.

*Deuteronomy 3:14*
*Joshua 13:2*
*1 Samuel 27:8*

**Geshurites (gesh**-ur-ites)

A small group that occupied the Negev during the conquest of Canaan (not people of Geshur in Syria). David raided them while Saul was king.

**Gethsemane** (geth-**sem**-uh-nee)

A garden on the Mount of Olives, across from the Kidron Valley, just east of Jerusalem. Judas betrayed Jesus there.

*Mark 14:32*

**Geuel** (**goo**-el)

One of the 12 men chosen by Moses at Kadesh Barnea to spy out the land of Canaan; a leader of the tribe of *Gad*; son of Maki.

*Numbers 13:3, 15*



**Gezer** (**gee**-zur)

A strong and important Canaanite city in the territory of Ephraim. Gezer was one of the cities given to the Levites. Solomon built it up.

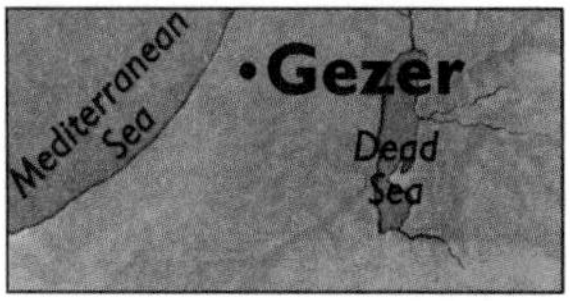


*1 Kings 9:15*
*1 Chronicles 6:67*

**Gibbethon** (**gib**-uh-thon)

A Canaanite city in the territory of Dan. It was one of the cities given to the *Kohathites*, but the Philistines controlled it for a long time. Several kings of Israel tried to take it. Baasha assassinated Nadab during the siege of Gibbethon.

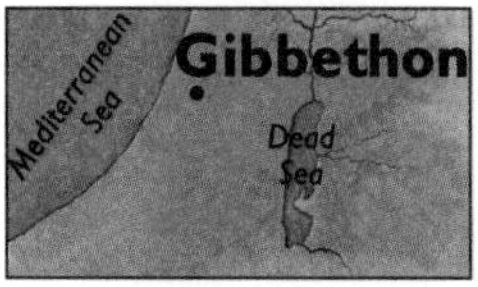


*1 Kings 15:27*
*1 Kings 16:17*

**Gibeah** (**gib**-ee-uh)

A Hebrew word for hill and the name of three places:

• A city in Benjamin. It was Saul's hometown, and he lived there while he was king.

*Judges 19:16*

G

*Joshua 15:20, 57*

• A Canaanite town allotted to the tribe of Judah. Its location is unknown.

*Joshua 24:33*

• A town in the hill country of Ephraim where Aaron's son Eleazar was buried.

*Joshua 10:1-2, 12*
*Isaiah 28:21*

**Gibeon** (**gib**-ee-uhn)

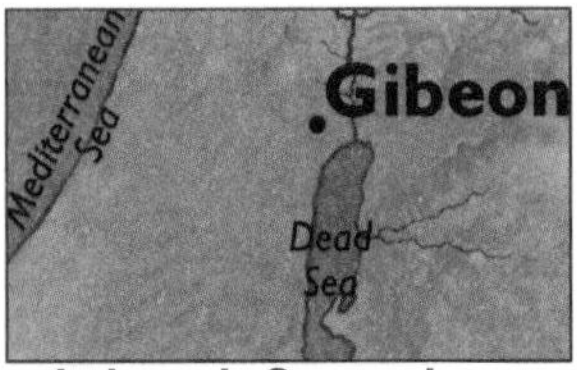


A large Canaanite city during the time of Joshua. After Joshua's defeat of Ai, the *Gibeonites* made a treaty with Israel. Several Canaanite kings south of Gibeon then attacked the city, and Joshua came to Gibeon's aid. It was at this battle that the sun stood still for a day.

*Joshua 9:16*

**Gibeonites** (**gib**-ee-uhn-ites)

People who lived in the city of Gibeon.

*Judges 6:11-22*

**Gideon** (**gid**-ee-uhn)

Son of Joash the Abiezrite and fifth judge of Israel after Deborah. Gideon became famous for putting out a fleece to test God's message that he would defeat the Midianites. Gideon judged Israel 40 years.

**Gihon** (**gye**-hon)

*Genesis 2:13*

• One of the four rivers that flowed out of the garden of Eden.

*2 Chronicles 33:14*

• A spring in the Kidron Valley, just east of Jerusalem's walls. Solomon was anointed king at

Gihon. Hezekiah built a tunnel to bring the water to the pool of *Siloam*.

**Gilboa** (gil-**boh**-uh)

1 Samuel 28:4
1 Chronicles 10:8

A range of mountains in the territory of Issachar. King Saul died atop the main peak of this range after a battle against the Philistines.

G

**Gilead** (**gil**-ee-uhd)

• First ancestor of the Gileadite *clan*, a clan in the tribe of Manasseh; son of Makir; grandson of Manasseh. *Numbers 26:29*

• Father of *Jephthah* the judge. *Judges 11:1*

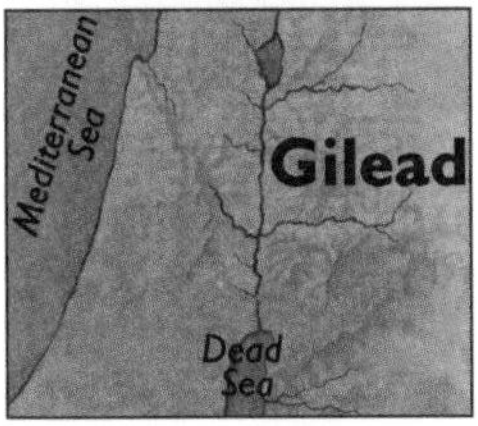


• The Old Testament name of the region directly east of the Jordan River. This land was allotted to the tribes of Gad, Reuben, and half of Manasseh. It included the land of Ammon. *Numbers 32:1*

• A member of the tribe of Gad named only in the genealogies of 1 Chronicles. *1 Chronicles 5:14*

**Gileadites** (**gil**-ee-uhd-ites)

*Joshua 17:1*
*Judges 12:4-5*

The Gileadite *clan*; people who traced their roots to *Gilead*, grandson of Manasseh.

**Gilgal** (**gil**-gal)

• "Gilgal on the plains of Jericho," the site where Joshua launched the conquest of Canaan. *2 Samuel 19:15*

It lay just east of the city of *Jericho*. The name is explained in Joshua 5:9.

Hosea 9:15

• Several other places in Palestine that no one has been able to identify with certainty.

Deuteronomy 7:1
Nehemiah 9:8

G

**Girgashites (gur**-guh-shites)

A tribe of people who traced their roots to Canaan (son of Ham) and settled in the land of Canaan. The Israelites destroyed them in the conquest of Canaan.

2 Samuel 15:18

**Gittites (git**-ites)

The people of the Philistine city of Gath. Goliath was a Gittite. Because some of David's loyal men were Gittites, David fled to Gath twice while on the run from Saul.

1 Corinthians 13:12
James 1:23-24

**glass (glass)**

An older word for *mirror* found in some translations of the Bible.

Ruth 2:3-8
Job 24:6

**glean (gleen)**

To harvest grain or other crops left in the field. God required the Israelites to leave some of their crops in the field unharvested so that the poor could glean and get food. The most famous Bible story about gleaning is the story of *Ruth*.

**glorification** (**glor**-i-fi-**kay**-shun)
The Christian doctrine that in heaven every believer will be like Christ. Glorification is explained in the *book of Romans*.
See also *glory*

*Romans 8: 18-19, 30*

**glorify** (**glor**-i-fye)
To praise, honor, or extol. The *book of Psalms* is devoted to glorifying God with music.

*Psalm 34:3*
*John 8:54*
*1 Peter 2:12*

G

**glory** (**glor**-ee)
Honor; greatness; majesty. The word is usually used to describe God.

*Exodus 16:7*
*Psalm 115:1*
*John 1:14*

**goad** (**gode**)
An *ox goad*.

*Judges 3:31*

**goat** (**gote**)
An animal that chews the cud and has divided hooves and a beard in the male, one of the kinds of animals the Israelites were allowed to sacrifice for sin. Goats are closely related to *sheep* but have no woolly coat. People who could not afford goats or sheep were allowed to sacrifice a *dove* or *pigeon* instead.

In some parts of the Bible, goats are used as a symbol of those who do not love God. Matthew 25:31-46 is one famous example.
See also *offering*

*Genesis 15:9*
*1 Samuel 16:20*
*Luke 15:29*

*Matthew 25:32*

G

Genesis 1:1
2 Kings 21:22
Romans 15:13

**God (god)**

Creator of all and Lord over all; the only one that has always existed and always will; the one true God; the *Trinity*. The Bible is the story of God's deeds and efforts to restore a broken friendship with people. The first of the Ten Commandments forbids the making or worshiping of false *gods*.

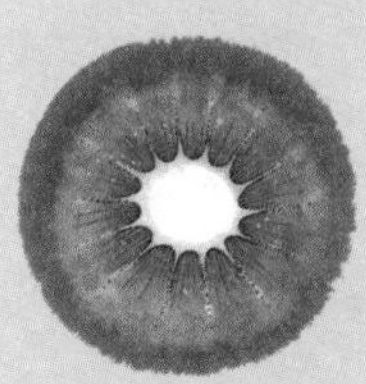

Genesis 31:19
Exodus 23:24
1 Corinthians 8:5-6

**god, gods (god, godz)**

Deities of the Canaanites, Egyptians, Assyrians, and other ancient peoples; false, man-made substitutes for *God*; *idols*. The Israelites were supposed to destroy the Canaanites partly because of Canaanite *idolatry*. Instead, many Israelites themselves became worshipers of *Asherah*, *Baal*, *Molech*, and other such gods. The first of the Ten Commandments forbids the making or worshiping of false gods.

2 Timothy 3:16

**God-breathed** (god-**breethd**)

A term used to describe *Scripture*. It means that God directed or guided the writers of Scripture to write what he wanted to say.

G

**God-fearing** (god-**fihr**-ing)
Another term for *devout*.
See also *fear of the* LORD.

*Ecclesiastes 8:12*
*Acts 13:26*
*Acts 17:17*

**godhead, the** (**god**-hed)
An older word for *Deity*.

*Colossians 2:9*

**godless** (**god**-less)
• Adjective: Wicked; against or opposed to God; hostile to God.

*Job 8:13*
*1 Timothy 4:7*
*2 Timothy 2:16*

• Noun: People who are wicked, against God, or hostile to God.

*Isaiah 33:14*
*Proverbs 11:9*

**godliness** (**god**-lee-ness)
Respect for God; *fear of the Lord*; holiness; piety; sincere devotion to God.

*1 Timothy 4:8*
*1 Timothy 6:3-6*
*2 Timothy 1:6-7*

**godly** (**god**-lee)
• Adjective: Devoted to God; holy; pious; *devout*.

*2 Corinthians 7:10-11*
*2 Timothy 3:12*

• Noun: People who are devoted to God, *holy*, pious, devout.

*Psalm 4:3*
*Micah 7:2*

**Gog** (**gog**)
King of *Magog*, an enemy of Israel mentioned in the prophecies of Ezekiel. The prophesies say that Gog and his kingdom will be utterly destroyed. They may be related to the prophesies against *Gog and Magog* in the book of Revelation.

*Ezekiel 38:2*
*Ezekiel 38:14*

*Revelation 20:8*

**Gog and Magog** (**gog** and **may**-gog)
The armies that Satan will muster against God, and which God will defeat once and for all, at the end of time. These events are described in the book of Revelation.
See also *Gog; last day; Magog*

G

*Genesis 14:1, 9*

**Goiim** (**goi**-im)
A city and group of people that allied with the kings of Shinar, Ellasar, and Elam to attack the *cities of the plain*. Abram's nephew Lot was captured in the raid. Goiim was ruled by *Tidal*.

*Deuteronomy 4:41-43*
*Joshua 21:27*
*1 Chronicles 6:71*

**Golan** (**goh**-luhn)
A city in the country of Bashan east of the Sea of Galilee, in the territory allotted to Manasseh. It was one of the six *cities of refuge*, administered by the *Gershonites*.

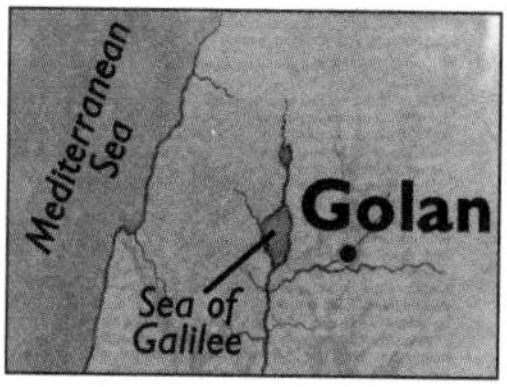


*Mark 15:22*
*John 19:17*

**Golgotha** (**gohl**-guh-thuh or gohl-**gah**-thuh)

"Place of the skull," the place where Jesus and two criminals were crucified. It was in Jerusalem, probably just outside the city walls.

**Goliath** (guh-**lye**-uhth)
Philistine warrior of *Gath* who challenged the armies of Israel to a one-man duel. The famous story of Goliath's defeat by David is told in 1 Samuel 17.

1 Samuel 17:4
2 Samuel 21:19



**Gomer** (**goh**-mur)
• One of the sons of *Japheth*, and therefore Noah's grandson; father of Ashkenaz, Riphath, and Togarmah.

Genesis 10:2

• Wife of the prophet *Hosea*; daughter of Diblaim; a prostitute. Gomer was unfaithful to Hosea, and this became an illustration of Israel's unfaithfulness to God.

Hosea 1:3, 6

**Gomorrah** (guh-**mor**-uh)
One of the five *cities of the plain*, often mentioned with *Sodom*. It was destroyed in the same rain of fire that destroyed Sodom, and for the same reason.

Genesis 14:8
2 Peter 2:6
Jude 1:7

**gopher wood** (**goh**-fur **wud**)
An older word for *cypress wood*.

Genesis 6:14
Isaiah 44:14
Ezekiel 27:6

G

**Goshen** (**goh**-shin)

*Genesis 46:28-29*
*Genesis 50:8*

• A region in the delta of the Nile River in Egypt that Pharaoh gave to Joseph and his family. Joseph's family settled there and grew to become the Hebrew nation. They were living in Goshen when they became slaves of the Egyptians, and they were living there when Moses led them out of Egypt.

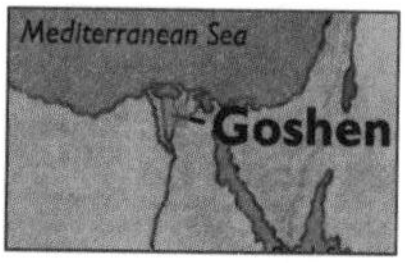


*Joshua 15:20, 51*

• A Canaanite town in the hill country of Judah allotted to that tribe.

**gospel** (**gos**-puhl)

*Mark 1:1*
*Acts 20:24*
*Galatians 2:5*

"Good news," the news that Jesus Christ paid the penalty for our sins and invites us to receive his offer of forgiveness. The *Gospels* tell of Jesus' life, death, and resurrection.

See also *justification*

**Gospel of John** (**gos**-puhl uhv **jon**)
See *John, Gospel of*

**Gospel of Luke** (**gos**-puhl uhv **luke**)
See *Luke, Gospel of*

**Gospel of Mark** (**gos**-puhl uhv **mark**)
See *Mark, Gospel of*

**Gospel of Matthew** (**gos**-puhl uhv **math**-yoo)
See *Matthew, Gospel of*

**Gospels (gos-**puhlz)

The first four books of the New Testament: Matthew, Mark, Luke, John. They are called Gospels because they tell the good news about Christ.

See also *gospel*

*Mark 1:1*

**grace (grayss)**

• Favor; kindness. The Bible often uses this word to describe God's love for people.

• The special favor of God by which people are saved from their sins; God's free gift of salvation; God's forgiveness, mercy. "God saved you by his special favor" (Ephesians 2:8).

See also *justification*

*Proverbs 3:34*
*Isaiah 26:10*
*John 1:14*
*Romans 3:24*
*2 Corinthians 6:1*

**grain (grane)**

*Wheat* or *barley*. Grain played a big part in the story of Jacob's son *Joseph*.

See also *food; grain offering; millstone*

*Genesis 41:1-40*
*Mark 2:23-28*

**grain offering (grane awf-**ur-ing)

One of the five main kinds of sacrifices that the Israelites offered to God. The *offering* of grain always went with the *burnt offering*. Part of it was burned and part was eaten by the priests. The rules for grain offerings are in Leviticus 2:1-16.

See also *offering*

*Leviticus 2:1*
*2 Kings 16:15*
*Ezekiel 46:11*

*Matthew 28:19-20*
*Luke 10:1-4*

**Great Commission, the**
(**grate** kuh-**mish**-uhn, the)

A term used to describe Jesus' command to tell others about him and teach them to follow him. The most famous example is in Matthew 28:19-20.

G

*Acts 6:1*
*Acts 9:29*

**Grecian** (**gree**-shuhn)

Greek-speaking. Some of the first Christians were described as Grecian Jews because they spoke Greek even though they were Jews.

*Isaiah 66:19*
*Daniel 11:2*
*Acts 20:2*

**Greece** (**greess**)

The land of the Greeks, from Mount Olympus on the north to the Mediterranean Sea on the south and all the land in between. The Romans ruled Greece in New Testament times as the province of Achaia, neighbor to Macedonia. Famous Greek cities include Athens and Corinth.

**Greeks** (**greeks**)

*Ezekiel 27:19*
*Joel 3:6*
*Romans 1:14*

• People of the land of Greece.

*Acts 21:28*
*1 Corinthians 1:23*
*1 Corinthians 12:13*

• *Gentiles*. The New Testament sometimes refers to all gentiles as Greeks.

**guilt offering (gilt awf**-ur-ing)

One of three kinds of sacrifices that the Israelites made to pay for sin. Like the *sin offering*, the guilt offering was required of anyone who broke God's commands accidentally or without meaning to. But the guilt offering also required the person to make *restitution* for his or her sin, and only a ram could be offered. The rules for guilt offerings can be found in Leviticus 5:14–6:7 and 7:1-10.

*Leviticus 5:18*
*Ezra 10:19*
*Ezekiel 46:20*

H

**Habakkuk** (huh-**bak**-uhk)

*Habakkuk 1:1*
*Habakkuk 3:1*

Israelite prophet and author of the book of Habakkuk. We know nothing else about him.

**Habakkuk, book of** (huh-**bak**-uhk, **buk** uhv)

*Habakkuk 1:1-4*

Thirty-fifth book of the Old Testament and eighth of the *minor prophets*. The book records *Habakkuk's* frustration with the wicked people of Judah, and what God said to him in response.

**Hadad** (**hay**-dad)

*1 Kings 11:14, 25*

• A prince of Edom during the time of David and Solomon. He escaped a raid on Edom by Joab, lived for a while in Egypt, and returned to Edom to make trouble for Israel. His story is told in 1 Kings 11:14-22.

*Genesis 36:35*

• A king of Edom during the time of the *patriarchs*; son of Bedad. He ruled from the city of Avith.

*Genesis 36:39*

• Another king of Edom during the time of the patriarchs; husband of Mehetabel. He ruled from the city of Pau.

*1 Chronicles 1:29-30*

• One of *Ishmael's* twelve sons; grandson of Abraham.

**Hadadezer** (**hay**-dad-**ee**-zur)

*2 Samuel 8:3-6*
*1 Chronicles 19:19*

King of Zobah in Syria during the time of David. David defeated Hadadezer's forces twice.

**Hadassah** (huh-**das**-uh)

*Esther 2:7*

*Esther's* Hebrew name.

**Hades** (**hay**-deez)

The New Testament word for *Sheol*, the place where the wicked go after they die. It is a place of darkness and separation from God.

See also *Abyss; lake of fire; gehenna; hell*

Matthew 16:18
Revelation 1:18
Revelation 20:13-14

**Hagar** (**hay**-gar)

An Egyptian maidservant of *Sarai*. Sarai gave Hagar to Abraham as a *concubine* after growing impatient for a child. Hagar became the mother of Ishmael.

Genesis 16:1-4
Genesis 16:15-16

**Haggai** (**hag**-eye)

A prophet of Israel after the Exile. Haggai helped rebuild the temple during the time of Ezra. He wrote the *book of Haggai* and prophesied at the same time as *Zechariah*.

Ezra 5:1
Ezra 6:14
Haggai 1:1

**Haggai, book of** (**hag**-eye, **buk** uhv)

Thirty-seventh book of the Old Testament and tenth of the *minor prophets*. The prophet Haggai wrote the book during the time of Ezra to encourage the Jews to rebuild the temple in Jerusalem. It contains the prophecies he delivered to *Zerubbabel* the governor and *Joshua* the high priest.

Haggai 1:1

2 Kings 17:6
2 Kings 18:11
1 Chronicles 5:26

**Halah** (**hay**-luh)
A place in Assyria where *Shalmaneser* exiled some of the Israelites who were captured during the reign of Hoshea. Its location is unknown.

Joshua 11:17
Joshua 12:7

**Halak** (**hay**-luhk)
A mountain in the *Negev* at the southern border of the land allotted to Judah. Its exact location is uncertain.

H

Psalm 106:1
Revelation 19:1, 3-4, 6

**hallelujah** (**hah**-le-**loo**-yuh)
"Praise the LORD," a call to praise. The term comes from "Hallelu" (praise) and "Yah," a short form of *Yahweh*. The term often appears in the Psalms and in Revelation 19.

Matthew 6:9

**hallowed** (**hal**-ohd)
Set apart as *holy*; held in respect; honored; revered.

Genesis 5:32
Genesis 9:22
1 Chronicles 1:8

**Ham** (**ham**)
One of Noah's three sons. Ham was with Noah on the ark. He became the father of *Canaan* and therefore the ancestor of the Canaanites.

**Haman** (**hay**-min)
The official of Xerxes' court who hated *Mordecai* and plotted to massacre the Jews while Esther was queen; son of Hammedatha.

Esther 3:1-2, 5-6
Esther 8:5

**Hamath** (**hay**-muhth)
A large and important city of *Aram* on the west bank of the Orontes River at the farthest northern boundary of Solomon's kingdom. Hamath was settled at one time by the descendants of Canaan. It was not included in the list of cities conquered by Joshua, but Solomon and Jeroboam both controlled it. Hamath is mentioned in the prophecies of Isaiah, Jeremiah, Ezekiel, Amos, and Zechariah.

2 Samuel 8:9
1 Kings 8:65
Amos 6:2

H

**Hamathites** (**hay**-muhth-ites)
People of *Hamath*.

Genesis 10:15-16
1 Chronicles 1:13-14

**Hammedatha** (ham-uh-**day**-thuh)
Father of *Haman*.

Esther 3:1
Esther 9:24

**Hamor** (**hay**-mor)
Father of *Shechem* and ruler of the city that he named Shechem after his son. Hamor and all the men of Shechem were killed for his son's rape of *Dinah*.

Genesis 34:8
Joshua 24:32
Acts 7:16

**Hananel, Tower of** (**han**-uh-nel, **tou**-ur uhv)
See *Tower of Hananel*

**Hananiah** (**han**-uh-**nye**-uh)

A very common name among the Israelites:

*Jeremiah 28:1-9* • A false prophet who opposed *Jeremiah*; son of Azur, from Gibeon. Hananiah said that the Exile would last not 70 years, as Jeremiah said, but two years. The people believed him.

*Daniel 1:6, 19*
*Daniel 2:17* • *Shadrach's* Hebrew name.

*1 Chronicles 8:1, 24* • A descendant of Benjamin listed in the genealogy of *First Chronicles*.

*2 Chronicles 26:11* • A royal official in *Uzziah's* service. He had command of Uzziah's well-trained army.

*Nehemiah 3:8* • One of the men who helped *Nehemiah* rebuild the walls of Jerusalem; a perfume-maker.

*Nehemiah 7:2* • Commander of the *fortress* in Jerusalem during the time of Nehemiah.

*Ezra 10:28*
*Jeremiah 37:13* • Several others mentioned only by name.

*1 Kings 7:26*
*Ezekiel 40:43*

**handbreadth** (**hand**-bredth)

The width of four fingers. In Old Testament times, the Israelites considered the handbreadth a standard unit of length. It was equal to about eight centimeters, or three inches; one-third of a *span*; one-sixth of a *cubit*.

**handmaid, handmaiden**
(**hand**-mayd, **hand mayd**-uhn)

See *maidservant*

**Hannah** (**han**-uh)

One of *Elkanah's* two wives; mother of *Samuel*. — *1 Samuel 1:1-20*

**Hanniel** (han-**ee**-el)

• The family leader of Manasseh chosen by God to help divide up the land after the conquest of Canaan. — *Numbers 34:23*

• One of the "skilled warriors and prominent leaders" in the tribe of Asher. — *1 Chronicles 7:40*

**Hanukkah** (**hah**-nuh-kuh)

A Jewish *festival* that celebrates the restoration of the *temple*; also called the Feast of Dedication and the Feast of Lights. — *John 10:22*

**Hanun** (**hay**-nuhn)

• Ammonite son of *Nahash* and king of the Ammonites after his father. Hanun warred against David and lost. His brother *Shobi* took a wiser path. — *2 Samuel 10:1-19*

• Israelite who helped repair the *Valley Gate* during the time of Nehemiah. — *Nehemiah 3:13, 30*

See also *Rabbah*

**Haran** (**hay**-run)

• Son of Terah; Lot's father; Abram and Nahor's younger brother. — *Genesis 11:27*

• City in *Paddan Aram* that was home to Abram and Laban. — *Genesis 27:43*

H

H

Esther 2:8-9

**harem** (**hair**-uhm)

"House of the women" where wives of the king stayed, in the care of a *eunuch*. Esther was part of Ahasuerus's harem.

Isaiah 1:21
Nahum 3:4

**harlot** (**har**-luht)

A prostitute; a person who gives sexual favors for money or religious ritual. Many Canaanite religions used harlots in their rituals, and this was just one reason God told Israel not to worship the Canaanite gods. *Rahab* was a harlot.

1 Samuel 16:16, 23
Psalm 33:2
Revelation 5:8

**harp** (**harp**)

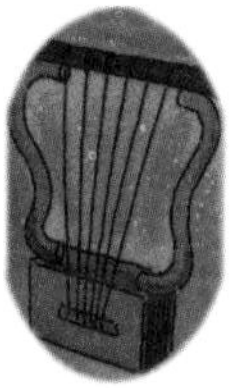

A small stringed instrument often used by Levite musicians in Old Testament times. David was famous for his harp-playing.

**Hashabiah** (hash-uh-**bye**-uh)

A very common name among the Israelites:

1 Chronicles 26:30

• Chief of the clan from *Hebron* that was in charge of all territory west of the Jordan River during the time of David.

1 Chronicles 27:17

• Commander of the forces of *Levi* in David's army; son of Kemuel.

• A Levite leader who gave generously to the Levites during Josiah's reforms. *2 Chronicles 35:9*
• Ruler of *Keilah* who repaired the city walls in Jerusalem under Nehemiah's direction. *Nehemiah 3:17*
• Several others mentioned only briefly.

**Havilah** (**hav**-il-uh)
• An area inhabited by the *Amalekites*, probably in the northeastern portion of Sinai. *Genesis 25:18*
• An area near *Eden* rich in gold and gemstones; its location is unknown. *Genesis 2:10-11*
• A descendant of Shem; son of Joktan. *1 Chronicles 1:23*
• A descendant of Ham; son of Cush. *Genesis 10:7*

**Hazael** (**hay**-zye-el) *1 Kings 19:15; 2 Kings 9:14*
King of *Damascus* during the time of Elijah, Elisha, and *Jehu*. Elijah prophesied that God would use Hazael to purge Israel of idol worship. These prophecies came true. Hazael defeated Israel's kings time after time, especially Jehu, and took a lot of territory from them. Only God's mercy stopped him from completely destroying the northern kingdom.

**Hazeroth** (**haz**-ur-oth) *Numbers 11:35—12:10; Deuteronomy 1:1*
A place in Sinai where the Israelites stopped during the *Exodus*. Hazeroth is where *Miriam* got leprosy for complaining about Moses' wife.

**Hazor** (**hay**-zor)
Several places mentioned in the Old Testament:
• A fortified Canaanite city in the territory allotted to Issachar, on the west side of the Jordan *Joshua 11:1*

River just south of *Lake Huleh*. Kings named Jabin ruled Hazor during Joshua's time and during Deborah's, but both kings were defeated by Israel. Solomon rebuilt the walls.

*Joshua 15:21-23*
• A town in the Negev allotted to Judah.

*Joshua 15:12, 25*
• "Hazor Hadattah," or New Hazor, also in the Negev and allotted to Judah.

*Nehemiah 11: 31-35*
• A village in the territory of Benjamin during the time of Nehemiah.

*Jeremiah 49:28*
• A tribe of Arabs destroyed by *Nebuchadnezzar*.

**heart (hart)**

*Genesis 6:5*
*Proverbs 27:19*
*2 Timothy 2:22*
• A person's true feelings, attitudes, and beliefs; character.

*Hebrews 12:3*
• Determination.

*Jonah 2:3*
• The center or middle.

**heaven, heavens (hev-en, hev-enz)**

*Genesis 24:7*
*Matthew 28:18*
*Galatians 1:8*
• God's home and the home of all who love him. The angels live in heaven with God. Jesus promised to prepare a place for his people in heaven. Sometimes the word *heavens* refers to the same place.

*Genesis 1:1*
*Haggai 1:10*
*Matthew 26:64*
• The sky and everything beyond it; the stars.

**Heber** (**hee**-bur)

- One of the Israelites who went with Jacob and his family to settle in *Goshen* in Egypt; grandson of Asher; son of Beriah. *Genesis 46:17*
- *Jael's* husband. *Judges 4:17*
- Two others named only in the genealogies of *First Chronicles*. *1 Chronicles 4:18; 1 Chronicles 7:31-32*

H

**Hebrew** (**hee**-broo)

- Any descendant of Abraham, Isaac, and Jacob; an Israelite. *Genesis 14:13; Jonah 1:9; Philippians 3:5*
- Language of the Hebrew people. *2 Kings 18:26; Revelation 9:11*

**Hebrews, book of** (**hee**-brooz, **buk** uhv)

Nineteenth book of the New Testament and first of the *general letters*. The book of Hebrews is a letter to the Hebrew Christians of the first century. Some Jewish Christians were thinking about returning to *Judaism*. Hebrews was written to remind them that Jesus Christ fulfilled the *messianic prophesies* and had made the final, perfect sacrifice for all sins. *Hebrews 13:24-25*

**Hebron** (**hee**-bruhn)

- A Canaanite city in the *Negev* about 30 kilometers south-southwest of Jerusalem; also called Kiriath Arba. Abraham lived in Hebron several different times throughout his life, and he buried Sarah in this area. It was allotted to the tribe of Judah after the conquest of Canaan. *Genesis 23:2; Joshua 10:23; 1 Chronicles 6:1-2*
- One of Caleb's grandsons. *1 Chronicles 2:42*

*Numbers 3:27*
*1 Chronicles 26:23*
*1 Chronicles 26:30-31*

**Hebronites (hee-bruhn-ites)**
People of *Hebron*.

*Genesis 15:9*
*1 Samuel 16:2*
*Hebrews 9:13*

**heifer (hef-ur)**
A young cow; a cow that has not yet given birth to a calf.

H

**Helez (hee-lez)**

*2 Samuel 23:24, 26*

• Commander of David's seventh militia of 24,000; of the tribe of Ephraim.

*1 Chronicles 2:39*

• Son of *Azariah* and father of Eleasah.

*Matthew 5:22*
*James 3:6*
*2 Peter 2:4*

**hell (hel)**
The final place where the devil, all demons, and all the wicked will suffer for their sins; *Gehenna*; the *lake of fire*. Hell is a place of darkness, fire, pain, suffering, and separation from God.

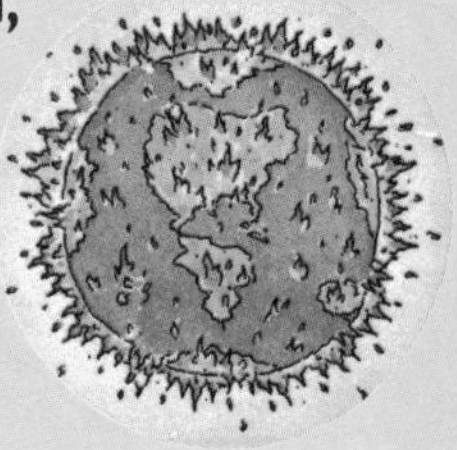

**Heman (hee-muhn)**

*1 Chronicles 15:19*
*1 Chronicles 25:1*
*Psalm 88:1*

• A Levite musician appointed by David to lead the temple chorus; a Kohathite. He was also a *seer* to King David and possibly the author of Psalm 88.

*1 Kings 4:31*

• A man so wise he was compared to Solomon; a son of *Mahol*.

**Hepher** (**hee**-fur)
• Head of the Hepherites, a clan of *Manasseh*. Joshua 17:2
• One of David's *mighty men*; a Mekerathite. 1 Chronicles 11: 26-36
• A man of Judah named only in the genealogy of *First Chronicles*. 1 Chronicles 4:5-6

H

**herbs, bitter** (**urbz, bit**-ur) Exodus 12:8
A salad of greens eaten as part of the *Passover* meal, after the lamb. The Passover today includes lettuce, chicory, eryngo, horseradish, and sow-thistle.

**heresies** (**hair**-uh-seez) 2 Peter 2:1
Plural of heresy:
• Strong opinions; views that a person holds stubbornly.
• Divisions in the church caused by strong opinion or stubborn will.

Most people think of heresy as wrong beliefs. But in the New Testament the term "heresies" refers to strong beliefs that a person uses to cause needless conflict and division. The apostle Paul urged believers not to pick fights over their views.

H

*Joshua 12:1, 5*
*1 Chronicles 5:23*

**Hermon** (**hur**-muhn)

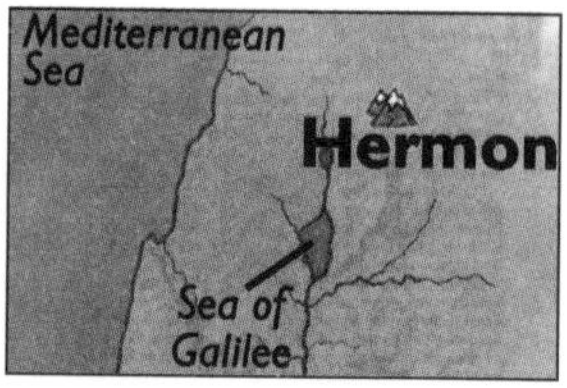


Highest peak in the mountains of south Lebanon. Mount Hermon is covered with snow most of the year. Its western slope hosts the headwaters of the Jordan River. Joshua's conquest of Canaan went no further than this mountain.

*Acts 4:27*
*Acts 12:23*

**Herod Agrippa I**
(**hair**-uhd uh-**grip**-uh the **furst**)

Roman king of Judea and Samaria during the early events of Acts (A.D. 37-44); also known as "Herod the king." Herod Agrippa I had the apostle James executed and the apostle Peter imprisoned. He was the son of Aristobulus and grandson of Herod the Great. Herod Agrippa I received his title and power from the Roman emperor Caligula. His gruesome death is recorded in Acts 12.

*Acts 25:22-26*
*Acts 26:27*

**Herod Agrippa II**
(**hair**-uhd uh-**grip**-uh the **sek**-uhnt)

Son of Herod Agrippa I and Roman king of north territories in Palestine and Syria during the later events of Acts (A.D. 50-100). Herod Agrippa II received his title and power from the Roman emperor Claudius; Nero gave him even more territories. His capital was Caesarea Philippi, which he renamed Neronias to honor Nero. Herod Agrippa II is famous for hearing

Paul's defense and saying, "Do you think you can make me a Christian so quickly?"

**Herod Antipas** (**hair**-uhd an-**tip**-uhss)
"Herod the Tetrarch," king of the regions of Galilee and Perea during the time of Jesus (4 B.C.-A.D. 34). His brother was Philip. Herod Antipas was a son of Herod the Great. He is famous for beheading John the Baptist and for taking part in Jesus' trial. Jesus called him a fox.

*Mark 6:16*
*Luke 3:1*
*Luke 23:8*

**Herod the Great** (**hair**-uhd the **grate**)
*Procurator* (governor) of Judea in the time just before the time of Christ (47-4 B.C.); son of Antipater. Julius Caesar first gave Herod his position and power over Judea. Caesar Augustus gave him the title "king of the Jews" in 40 B.C. The Jews protested this, so Herod killed the whole Jewish Hasmonean ruling family. Over time Augustus granted Herod rule over most of Palestine. Herod is famous for rebuilding the temple in Jerusalem, a project he began in 19 B.C.; this is the magnificent temple that Jesus said he could rebuild in three days if it were torn down.

*Matthew 2:1*
*Mark 15:29*

*Matthew 22:16*
*Mark 3:6*
*Mark 12:13*

**Herodians** (huh-**roh**-dee-uhnz)
Jewish supporters of Herod's rule who also opposed Jesus.

*Mark 6:17-22*

**Herodias** (huh-**roh**-dee-uhss)
Wife of Herod Antipas who had John the Baptist beheaded.

H

*Deuteronomy 3:2-6*
*Joshua 13:8-10*
*Nehemiah 9:22*

**Heshbon** (**hesh**-bon)
A city of Moab about 24 kilometers east of the Jordan River at the north end of the Dead Sea. The Israelites took Heshbon from King *Sihon* during the Exodus. It was allotted to the tribe of Reuben and eventually settled by the tribe of Gad.

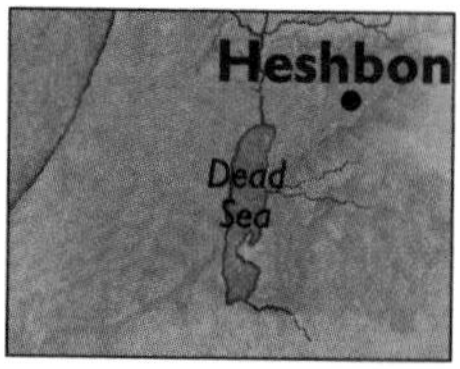


*Genesis 23:3*
*Judges 1:26*
*Nehemiah 9:8*

**Heth** (**heth**)
Canaan's second son and father of the *Hittites*.

*2 Chronicles 32:27*
*Jeremiah 26:19*
*Matthew 1:9-10*

**Hezekiah** (**hez**-uh-**kye**-uh)
Son of *Ahaz* and thirteenth king of Judah after his father. Hezekiah is famous for his great faithfulness to God and courage in resisting the Assyrian siege of Jerusalem. He also built the tunnel from the spring Gihon to the pool of Siloam. Hezekiah is mentioned in the prophesies of Isaiah and in the lineage of Joseph, Jesus' earthly father. His story is told in 2 Kings 16:20–20:21; 2 Chronicles 28:27–32:33; and Isaiah 36:1–39:8.

See also *kings of Judah*

**Hezron** (**hez**-ruhn)

- Son of Reuben and head of the Hezronite clan. *Exodus 6:14*
- One of Judah's great-grandsons; son of Perez. *Ruth 4:18-19*
- A town in the south of Judah between Kadesh Barnea and Addar. *Joshua 15:3*

**Hierapolis** (**hye**-ur-**op**-uh-liss)

A city in the Roman province of *Asia*, about 10 kilometers north of Laodicea. It is mentioned in the book of *Colossians*.

*Colossians 4:13*

**high place** (**hye playss**)

A Canaanite *shrine*, usually set on a hill or pole. The Canaanites worshiped their gods at high places, and this is why God told the Israelites to destroy these shrines. Most kings of Israel built more of them instead of destroying them.

See also *Asherah pole; idolatry*

*1 Samuel 9:12-13*
*Isaiah 16:12*

**high priest** (**hye preest**)

The highest office of the priesthood in Israel. It was the high priest's duty to represent Israel on the Day of Atonement and to interpret the *Urim and Thummim*. Only one high priest held office at a time. In New Testament times, the Roman governor appointed the high priest who served as head of the *Sanhedrin*. Today, *Jesus* is our high priest.

See also *Levite; priest*

*Leviticus 16:32*
*Matthew 26:57*
*Hebrews 7:23-28*

**Hilkiah** (hil-**kye**-uh)

A common name among the Israelites:

*2 Kings 22:8*
- *High priest* of Israel who found the lost Book of the Law during the time of *Josiah*.

*Isaiah 22:20*
- Father of Hezekiah's official *Eliakim*.

*Jeremiah 1:1*
- Jeremiah's father, a priest of the tribe of Benjamin.

*Nehemiah 8:4*
*Jeremiah 29:3*
- Several others mentioned only by name.

*Genesis 10:30*
*2 Chronicles 19:4*
*Luke 1:65*

**hill country** (**hil kuhn**-tree)

Hilly areas. The land of Palestine has many such places. The territory of Ephraim was especially noted for its hills.

**hill of Ophel** (**hil** uhv **oh**-fel)
See *Ophel, hill of*

*Leviticus 19:36*

**hin** (**hin**)

A liquid measure equal to about four liters, or one gallon; one-sixth of a *bath*.

*2 Kings 23:10*
*Jeremiah 32:35*

**Hinnom** (**hin**-uhm)

A deep valley just outside the south walls of Jerusalem. Hinnom was the scene of Israel's worst examples of idol worship: child sacrifice. *Ahaz* sacrificed children to Baal; *Manasseh* sacrificed them to Molech. Later the valley was used for burning garbage. Because of its history and its fires, Hinnom became a symbol of hell. "Hinnom" is a Hebrew word; the Greek is *gehenna*.

**Hiram** (**hye**-ruhm)

King of *Tyre* during the time of David and Solomon. Hiram greatly admired David and proved to be a strong ally of both Israelite kings. He helped David build his palace, and helped Solomon build the temple.

*2 Samuel 5:11*
*2 Chronicles 8:18*

H

**Hittites** (**hit**-ites)

People who traced their roots to *Heth*. The Hittites lived in the central areas of Canaan during the time of the patriarchs. Abram lived among them at Hebron. Bathsheba's first husband, *Uriah*, was a Hittite.

*Genesis 10:15*
*2 Samuel 11:3*
*Nehemiah 9:8*

**Hivites** (**hiv**-ites)

Descendants of Canaan and one group of Canaanites conquered by the Israelites. They lived mostly in the north of Palestine and south Lebanon. *Hamor* was a Hivite.

*Genesis 34:2*
*Joshua 24:11*

**holiness** (**hoh**-lee-ness)

Perfection; purity; complete separation from everything else.

See also *holy*

*Genesis 2:3*
*Psalm 103:1*
*Ephesians 1:4*

**holy** (**hoh**-lee)

Perfect; pure; separate; given to God's service. Above all else, God is holy. Everything associated with God is holy.

See also *holiness*

*Psalm 29:2*
*Isaiah 29:23*
*2 Corinthians 1:12*

H

*Psalm 2:6*

**Holy City** (**hoh**-lee **si**-tee)

Another name for *Jerusalem*.

See also *Zion*

**holy kiss** (**hoh**-lee **kiss**)

See *kiss*

**Holy of Holies** (**hoh**-lee uhv **hoh**-leez)

See *Most Holy Place*

*Psalm 51:11*
*John 14:26*
*Romans 15:16*

**Holy Spirit** (**hoh**-lee **spihr**-it)

Third person of the *Trinity*. The Bible speaks of God's Holy Spirit as the one who saves us, lives inside God's people, and convicts the world of *sin*. Jesus told his disciples he would send the Holy Spirit to guide and teach all Christians.

See also *God*

*Leviticus 27:16*
*Ezekiel 45:11, 14*
*Hosea 3:2*

**homer** (**hoh**-mur)

A dry measure equal to about 220 liters, or six bushels; also called a cor; 10 *ephahs*.

*1 Samuel 1:3*
*1 Samuel 4:4-11*

**Hophni and Phinehas** (**hof**-nee and **fin**-ee-uhss)

Two sons of *Eli* and priests of Israel during the time of the Judges. Hophni and Phinehas had no respect for God or their duties as priests. The boy Samuel prophesied against them. They died in the battle of Aphek

and Ebenezer when the Philistines captured the ark of the covenant.

**Hophra** (**hof**-ruh)

*Jeremiah 44:30*

King of *Egypt* during the reign of *Zedekiah* in Jerusalem. Zedekiah made the mistake of asking Hophra for help in resisting Nebuchadnezzar. Jeremiah had warned Zedekiah not to do this, and Jeremiah's prophesies came true.

**Hor** (**hor**)

*Numbers 21:4*
*Deuteronomy 32:50*

A mountain ridge in *Edom* where *Aaron* died and was buried during the Exodus. Its exact location is unknown.

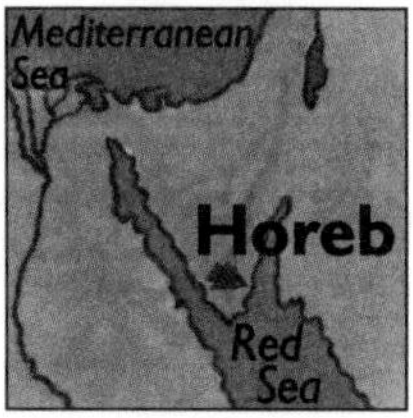


**Horeb** (**hor**-eb)

*Exodus 3:1; 17:6*
*2 Chronicles 5:10*
*Malachi 4:4*

Another name for Mount *Sinai*.

**Horites** (**hor**-ites)

*Genesis 14:5-6*
*Deuteronomy 2: 12, 22*

People who lived in the land of *Edom* before it was settled by the *Edomites*. The Horites were among those defeated by *Kedorlaomer's* alliance against the *cities of the plain*.

**Hormah** (**hor**-muh)

*Numbers 14:45*
*Judges 1:17*

"Destruction," name given to a *Canaanite* city in the Negev taken by Joshua's forces and first assigned to Judah, then later to Simeon. The original Canaanite name was Zephath. Its exact location is unknown.

H

*Exodus 27:2* *Exodus 19:13* *Psalm 81:3* *1 Samuel 16:1, 13* *2 Samuel 22:3*

**horn** (**horn**)

- Point at the corners of an altar. The blood of the *offering* was smeared on these horns.

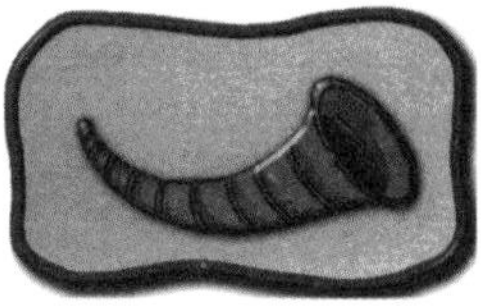

- The horn of a ram.
- A wind instrument made from a ram's horn.
- A flask or cup made from a ram's horn.
- A symbol of power.

*Matthew 21:9*

**hosanna** (hoh-**zan**-uh)

The Greek form of a Hebrew term in Psalm 118:25, "Save us, Lord!" The crowd that welcomed Jesus at Jerusalem on Palm Sunday was quoting the Psalm 118:25-26.

See also *Triumphal Entry*

*Hosea 1:1*

**Hosea** (hoh-**zay**-uh)

Israelite prophet to the northern kingdom of Israel in its final 30 years; son of Beeri. Hosea's marriage to *Gomer* was part of his message. His prophesies are recorded in the *book of Hosea*. *Amos* was one of his peers.

*Romans 9:25*

**Hosea, book of** (hoh-**zay**-uh, **buk** uhv)

Twenty-eighth book of the Old Testament and first of the *minor prophets*. It records the prophesies of Hosea to the northern kingdom of Israel during the reigns of Zechariah, Shallum,

Menahem, Pekahiah, *Pekah*, and Hoshea of Jeroboam II. The message was this: God loves you, Israel, and wants you to come back to him. The Israelites had abandoned God for idolatry.

**Hoshea** (hoh-**shee**-uh)

• Son of Elah and last king of Israel after *Pekah*. Hoshea came to power by assassinating Pekah. He reigned for nine years. *2 Kings 17:1*

• *Joshua's* original name. *Numbers 13:16*

• Officer over the tribe of Ephraim in David's army; son of Azaziah. *1 Chronicles 27:16, 20*

• One of the leaders of Israel who agreed to Ezra's reform. *Nehemiah 10:14, 23*

**host, hosts** (**host**)

• Army or armies. *Daniel 8:13*

• Star or stars; heavenly bodies. *2 Kings 21:5*

• Angel or angels. *Luke 2:13*

• A person who gives a party. *Luke 14:9-12*

**hour** (**our**)

One-twelfth of daylight. The counting of hours starts at sunrise. The most common hours mentioned in the Bible are the third, sixth, and ninth hours. *Matthew 8:13*

See also *third hour; sixth hour; ninth hour; tenth hour; eleventh hour*

**house** (**houss**)

*Genesis 19:2* • A home or residence. The patriarchs lived in tents; the Israelites of David's time and later lived in flat-roofed structures. The "house of God" referred to the tabernacle and the temple.

*Judges 1:22* • Family; household; a home and the people who lived there. Joseph had charge of Potiphar's household.

*2 Samuel 2:7* • Family line; dynasty. "The house of David" was the family line of his descendants.

**household** (**houss**-hold)

*Genesis 12:17* • The people living in a home.

*Acts 18:8* • All the members of an extended family.

**Huldah** (**huhl**-duh)

*2 Kings 22:14*
*2 Chronicles 34:22*

*Prophetess* of Israel during the time of *Josiah*; resident of Jerusalem. When the high priest *Hilkiah* found the Book of the Law and read it to Josiah, the king sent Hilkiah to Huldah to find out what they should do. Jeremiah and Zechariah were two of Huldah's peers.

**humble** (**huhm**-buhl)

*Ephesians 4:2* • Adjective: Meek; lowly; small; modest; plain; simple. Its opposite is arrogant; conceited; smug.

*Psalm 18:27* • Noun: A person who is meek, lowly, small, modest, plain, or simple.

• Verb: To make small, plain, or low; to force down; to reduce; to shame. — *2 Chronicles 33:23*

**humility** (hyoo-**mil**-ih-tee)
The quality of being *humble*. Its opposite is arrogance; conceit; smugness. — *Proverbs 18:12; Philippians 2:3*

**Hundred, Tower of the**
(**huhn**-druhd, **tou**-ur uhv the)
See *Tower of the Hundred*

H

**Hur** (**hur**)
• Assistant to *Moses* during the *Exodus*. Hur worked together with *Aaron*. — *Exodus 17:10*
• One of five *Midianite* kings killed trying to stop the Israelite Exodus, the same battle at which *Balaam* was killed. — *Joshua 13:21*
• Two fathers of notable sons: *Ben-Hur* and *Rephaiah*. — *1 Kings 4:8; Nehemiah 3:9*
• Several Israelites mentioned only by name in the genealogies of *First Chronicles*. — *1 Chronicles 2:50; 4:1*

**Huram** (**hur**-uhm)
An expert metalworker sent by *Hiram* to help Solomon build the temple. Huram made many special-purpose pieces of bronze for the temple. — *1 Kings 7:13-14; 2 Chronicles 4:16*

H

Zechariah 13:5
James 5:7

**husbandman** (**huhz**-buhnd-muhn)

An older word for "farmer" that is found in some translations of the Bible.

2 Samuel 16:16
1 Chronicles 27:33

**Hushai** (**hoo**-shye)

Close friend and wise counselor to David. Hushai is the one who joined Absalom's staff of advisors so he could give *Absalom* bad advice.

Hushai was an "Archite," from the town of Archi in the land of Benjamin.

1 Timothy 1:20
2 Timothy 2:17

**Hymenaeus** (hye-**men**-ee-uhss)

A *false teacher* in the church at *Ephesus* who opposed Paul. Hymenaeus taught that there would be no resurrection.

See also *Philetus*

Psalm 40:3
Matthew 26:30
1 Corinthians 14:26

**hymn** (**him**)

A sacred song; a song of praise to God.

**hypocrisy** (hi-**pah**-kri-see)
Acting; pretending; falseness.

*Matthew 23:28*
*Galatians 2:13*
*1 Peter 2:1*

**hyssop** (**hiss**-uhp)
A plant, or several different plants, used in some Israelite ceremonies of Old Testament times. No one knows for sure what this plant was.

*Leviticus 14:51*
*Psalm 51:7*
*John 19:29*

I

2 Samuel 5:14-15
1 Chronicles 14:3-6

**Ibhar** (**ib**-har)
One of David's sons. We know nothing about him except that he is always listed after Solomon.

Judges 12:8-10

**Ibzan** (**ib**-zan)
An Israelite from Bethlehem who served as ninth judge of Israel after *Jephthah*. He judged Israel seven years.

Acts 14:19-21
2 Timothy 3:10-11

**Iconium** (eye-**koh**-nee-uhm)
A large and important city in the Roman province of Galatia during the time of Paul's travels. Paul visited Iconium at least three times and suffered a lot of trouble there.

**Iddo** (**id**-oh)
A common name among the Israelites:

1 Chronicles 27:16, 21

• A commander in David's army, officer over half the tribe of Manasseh in Gilead; son of Zechariah.

2 Chronicles 9:29; 12:15

• A *seer* who wrote down what happened during the reigns of Solomon, Rehoboam, and Abijah.

Nehemiah 12:1, 4

• One of the priests or Levites who returned to Jerusalem with Zerubbabel.

1 Kings 4:14
Ezra 6:14

• Several others mentioned only by name.

**idol** (**eye**-duhl)

A false god; an image of a god made of stone, wood, or metal; a statue that people worshiped. Most Canaanites worshiped idols of *Ashtoreth*, *Baal*, *Chemosh*, *Dagon*, or *Molech*. The second of the Ten Commandments says, "Do not make idols of any kind" (Exodus 20:4).

*Exodus 32:4*
*Psalm 24:4*
*1 Corinthians 10:19*

**idolater** (eye-**dol**-uh-tur)

A person who worships an *idol*; a person who tries to get guidance and help from a false god.
See also *idolatry*

*1 Corinthians 5:11*
*Ephesians 5:5*

**idolatry** (eye-**dol**-uh-tree)

Worship of idols. Idolatry was a constant temptation for the Israelites. It is one of the main reasons for the *Exile*.
See also *Amos; Ezekiel; idol; Isaiah; Jeremiah; Micah; Nahum.*

*1 Samuel 15:23*
*Colossians 3:5*

**Idumea** (id-yoo-**mee**-uh)

The Greek word for *Edom*. By the time of the New Testament, Idumea included all of southern Palestine and not just the area around the *Arabah*.

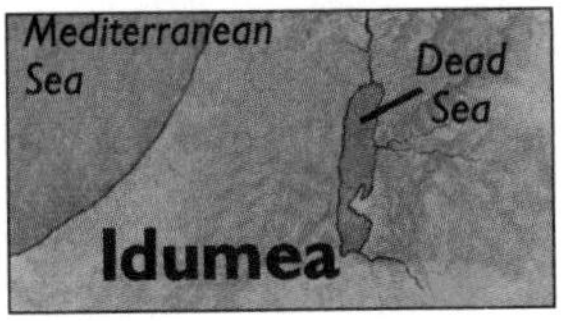

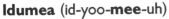

*Numbers 20:14*
*Mark 3:8*

**Igal** (**eye**-gal)

*Numbers 13:3, 7*
• One of the 12 men chosen by Moses at Kadesh Barnea to spy out the land of Canaan; a leader of the tribe of Issachar; son of Joseph.

*2 Samuel 23:24, 36*
• One of David's *mighty men*, a member of the *Thirty*; son of Nathan.

*1 Chronicles 3:10, 22*
• A descendant of David who returned to Israel after the *Exile*.

**Ijon** (**eye**-jon)

*2 Kings 15:29*
*2 Chronicles 16:4*

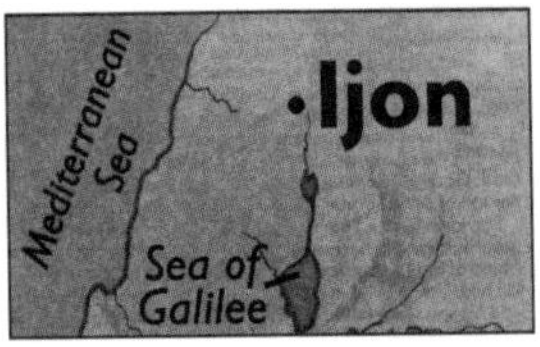


A town in the far north of Naphtali that was captured from *Baasha* by the Syrian forces of Ben-Hadad. Ben-Hadad attacked Ijon at *Asa's* request because Asa and Baasha were at war.

**Illyricum** (il-**ihr**-i-kuhm)

*Romans 15:19*

A Roman province across the Adriatic Sea from Italy during the time of Paul's travels. Paul wrote in Romans that he went as far as Illyricum in his missionary journeys.

**image** (**im**-ij)

*Genesis 1:27*
*Acts 17:29*
• A likeness, portrayal, representation, copy, replica, or picture. God created people in his image.

See also *image of God*

*Leviticus 26:1*
*Revelation 13:14*
• An *idol*.

**image of God** (**im**-ij uhv **god**)

This term has two meanings in the Bible:

• A copy or likeness of God. The Bible describes people in this way. It means that we are like God in some ways. *Genesis 1:27*

• God himself in a body. The Bible describes Jesus Christ in this way. It means he is "visible God." This is often called the *Incarnation*. *2 Corinthians 4:4*

**Immanuel** (i-**man**-yoo-el)

A Hebrew word that means "God with us." Isaiah's prophesies use it to describe the *Messiah*. *Isaiah 7:14; Isaiah 8:8; Matthew 1:23*

**Immer** (**im**-uhr)

• One of the family leaders among the priests during the time of David. *1 Chronicles 24:6, 14*

• Father of *Pashhur*. *Jeremiah 20:1*

• A town in Babylonia where some of the Jews lived during the time of the Exile. *Nehemiah 7:61*

**immoral** (im-**or**-uhl)

• Adjective: Corrupt, bad, evil, wicked, unlawful, depraved; hostile to God's will. *Proverbs 6:23-24; Ephesians 5:5*

• Noun: A person who is corrupt, bad, or evil; a person who purposely breaks God's law; a *wicked* person. *Hebrews 13:4; Revelation 22:15*

1 Timothy 3:16

**Incarnation** (**in**-car-**nay**-shuhn)

The appearance of God in the flesh; God taking on a human body; God becoming a human being. The term describes the coming of *Jesus Christ*. The word itself does not appear in the Bible, but the idea does: "So the Word became human and lived here on earth among us" (John 1:14).

See also *image of God*

Exodus 30:35
Luke 1:11

**incense** (**in**-senss)

A dried sap or spice burned for its strong, pleasant scent. God told the Israelites to make a special blend of incense for use only in the temple, a blend that included *frankincense*. Only priests were allowed to burn this holy incense as an offering to God.

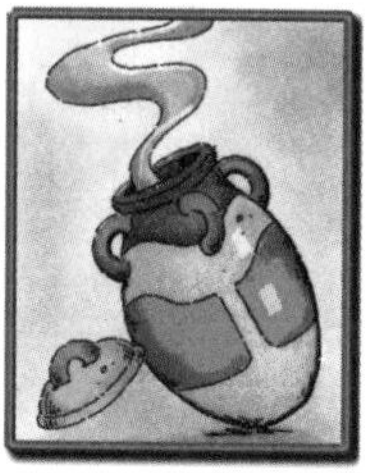

Genesis 31:14
Ephesians 5:5

**inheritance** (in-**hair**-i-tenss)

Money, property, or anything else that passes from a parent to a child because of the family relationship. The Bible often uses the word "inheritance" to describe Canaan because of God's *covenant* with Israel. It also

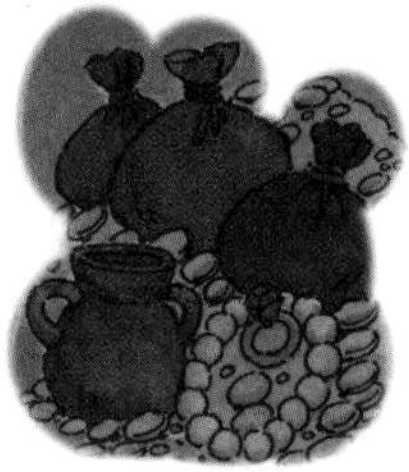

describes salvation, heaven, glory, immortality, the earth, the kingdom of God, and eternal life as blessings that every Christian inherits.

**iniquity** (in-**ik**-wi-tee)

An older word for *sin* that is found in some translations of the Bible.

*Psalm 25:11*
*Micah 2:1*

**inspiration** (in-spur-**ay**-shuhn)
See *God-breathed*

**inspired** (in-**spy**-yurd)
See *God-breathed*

**intermarry** (**in**-tur-**mair**-ee)

To change religious practices in order to marry someone who serves a different god; to stop worshiping God, stop obeying God, or turn away from what is right in order to marry someone who worships a false god. God told the Israelites not to intermarry because it would lead them to *idolatry*. Ezra's reform came about because the Jews who returned from Babylonia had begun to intermarry.

*Joshua 23:12*
*Ezra 9:14*

**Isaac** (**eye**-zik)

Only son of Abraham and Sarah; the "son of promise"; half-brother of Ishmael; father of *Jacob* and *Esau*. Isaac became the ancestor of the *Israelites* and is famous for his part in many of the stories of Genesis.
See also *Rebekah*

*Genesis 21:3-5*
*Hebrews 11:9*

I

2 Kings 19:2
2 Chronicles 32:20
Romans 10:20

**Isaiah** (eye-**zay**-uh)

An Israelite prophet who preached to the southern kingdom of Judah during the reigns of Jotham, Ahaz, Hezekiah, and Manasseh. Isaiah is famous for the statement, "I am a sinful man and a member of a sinful race. Yet I have seen the King, the LORD Almighty!" (Isaiah 6:5). He was the son of Amoz and lived in Jerusalem. During Hezekiah's reign, he served as a key part of the king's faith and resistance to the Assyrian siege of Jerusalem. *Micah* lived and prophesied at about the same time. Isaiah's prophesies are recorded in the *book of Isaiah*.

Isaiah 2:1
Romans 15:12

**Isaiah, book of** (eye-**zay**-uh, **buk** uhv)

Twenty-third book of the Old Testament and first of the major prophets. The book of Isaiah records God's call of the prophet Isaiah, his messages to Judah, and the dramatic defeat of Sennacherib's army. The book is famous for its many prophesies about the Messiah, especially those in chapters 9 and 53.

See also *Micah*

**Iscariot** (is-**kair**-ee-uht)

See *Judas Iscariot*

**Ishbak** (**ish**-bak)

One of Abraham and Keturah's sons. We know nothing else about him.

*Genesis 25:1-2*
*1 Chronicles 1:32*

**Ishbosheth, Ish-Bosheth** (**ish**-boh-sheth)

Son of Saul who laid claim to the throne after Saul's death at Gilboa; brother of *Jonathan*, *Malki-Shua*, and *Abinadab*. *Abner* supported Ishbosheth's claim at first, then later deserted him. He was murdered by his own captains after losing a two-year war against David's armies. Ishbosheth was also called Esh-Baal.

*2 Samuel 2:10*
*2 Samuel 4:12*

**Ishmael** (ish-may-el)

- Son of Abraham and *Hagar*, and half-brother of Isaac; ancestor of the Ishmaelites (Arabs). Ishmael was born 13 years before Isaac and lived with the family until Isaac was two years old. Sarah grew jealous and sent Ishmael and his mother away. But God promised to protect Ishmael and make him into a great nation. *Genesis 16:15-16*

- Israelite army officer who betrayed and assassinated *Gedaliah*; son of Nethaniah. *2 Kings 25:25*
- Israelite commander who helped *Jehoiada* restore Joash to the throne; son of Jehohanan. *2 Chronicles 23:1*
- Several others who are mentioned only by name. *Ezra 10:22*

**Ishmaelites** (**ish**-may-el-ites)

*Genesis 37:27*
*Judges 8:24*

People who trace their roots to Ishmael; the Arabs.

**Ishmaiah** (ish-**may**-uh)

*1 Chronicles 12:1-4* • An Israelite warrior from the tribe of Benjamin who defected to David at Ziklag and became a leader of the *Thirty*; a Gibeonite.

*1 Chronicles 27:16, 19* • An officer in David's army in command of the tribe of Zebulun; son of Obadiah.

**Ishtar** (**ish**-tar)

*Jeremiah 44:25*

A goddess of Mesopotamia that some Jews worshiped during the time of Jeremiah. Jeremiah's prophesies rebuked God's people for worshiping this false god, also known as the *Queen of Heaven*. He told them that they would be taken captive to Babylonia if they did not stop worshiping her.

**Ishvi** (**ish**-vye)

*Numbers 26:44* • Third son of *Asher*.

*1 Samuel 14:49* • One of Saul's sons.

**Israel** (**iz**-ree-uhl)

*Genesis 32:28* • The name that God gave to Jacob after they wrestled in Peniel. The name means "strive."

*Exodus 12:19* • The nation that descended from Isaac's son Jacob; the Israelites; the Hebrews; God's chosen people.

*2 Chronicles 27:7* • The northern kingdom of ten tribes that split from Rehoboam and chose Jeroboam as their king after Solomon's death (the southern kingdom became *Judah*). This kingdom had 21 kings.

See also *kings of Israel; prophets to Israel*

**Israelites** (**iz**-ree-uhl-ites)

The nation of Israel; people who trace their roots to Isaac's son Jacob. — *Genesis 32:32; Genesis 47:27; 2 Corinthians 11:22*

**Issachar** (**iss**-uh-kar)

- Jacob's son and the tribe of Israel named after him. *Leah* was his mother. — *Genesis 30:18*
- The land allotted to the tribe of Issachar. — *Ezekiel 48:25-26*
- A temple gatekeeper during the time of David; son of Obed-Edom. — *1 Chronicles 27:18*

See also *tribes of Israel*

**Isshiah** (ish-**eye**-uh)

- A chief among the clans of Issachar during the time of David; son of Izrahiah. — *1 Chronicles 7:3*
- An Israelite warrior from the tribe of Benjamin who defected to David at Ziklag. — *1 Chronicles 12:2, 6*
- A Levite appointed by David to serve in the temple; firstborn son of Rehabiah. — *1 Chronicles 24:21*
- A Kohathite musician in David's service; son of Uzziel. — *1 Chronicles 23:20*

I

Exodus 6:23
Numbers 7:7-8

**Ithamar** (**ith**-uh-mar)
Youngest son of Aaron and brother of Eleazar, Nadab, and Abihu. Ithamar helped with construction of the tabernacle and was given charge of the *Gershonites* and the *Merarites*.

2 Samuel 3:2, 5

**Ithream** (**ith**-ree-uhm)
Sixth son born to David during his reign over Judah in Hebron. His mother was David's wife *Eglah*.

**Ittai** (**it**-eye)

2 Samuel 15:19

• One of three generals in David's army during Absalom's rebellion. Ittai was a *Gittite*.

2 Samuel 18:12

• One of the *Thirty* among David's mighty men, from the tribe of Benjamin.

Luke 3:1-2

**Iturea** (i-**toor**-ee-uh)
A tribe of Arabs and the land they inhabited in the hills of south Lebanon. This area was part of the kingdom of Philip the tetrarch during the time of John the Baptist.

**Iye-abarim** (**eye**-uh **ah**-buh-rim)

"Ruins of the Abarim," a place along the southeastern edge of Moab where the Israelites stopped during the Exodus after leaving *Oboth*. No one knows where this place was.

*Numbers 21:10-11*
*Numbers 33:44*

I

J

**Jaazaniah** (jay-**az**-uh-**nye**-uh)

A common name among the Israelites:

2 Kings 25:23 • Israelite army officer who served during the time of *Gedaliah*.

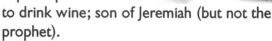

Jeremiah 35:3 • A leader in the family of Recab during the time of Jeremiah who kept his promise not to drink wine; son of Jeremiah (but not the prophet).

Ezekiel 8:11 • An Israelite elder who burned incense to idols during the time of Ezekiel; son of Shaphan.

Ezekiel 11:1 • A corrupt Israelite leader named in Ezekiel's prophesies; son of Azzur.

**Jaaziel** (**jay**-uh-**zye**-uhl)

1 Chronicles 15:18

A temple *gatekeeper* appointed to sing and play music during the return of the Ark to Jerusalem.

**Jabbok** (**jab**-ok)

Genesis 32:22
Judges 11:13

A river in the territory of the *Ammonites* that flows into the Jordan River from the east. Jacob forded this river after wrestling with God the night before (he had already sent his family across). Today the Jabbok River is known as Wadi Zerqa.

**Jabesh** (**jay**-besh)

1 Samuel 11:3

A short form of *Jabesh-gilead*.

**Jabesh-gilead (jay-besh gil-ee-ad)**

A city of Israel in the territory of Manasseh east of the Jordan River. Saul secured Israel's loyalty by routing the Ammonites at Jabesh Gilead right after he became king.

*Judges 21:8*
*1 Chronicles 10:11-12*

**Jabez (jay-bez)**

• A "distinguished" Israelite of the tribe of Judah mentioned in the genealogies of First Chronicles. *1 Chronicles 4:9-10*

• A place in Judah whose location is unknown. *1 Chronicles 2:55*

**Jabin (jay-bin)**

• King of *Hazor* during the conquest of Canaan. Jabin and his Canaanite allies were defeated by Joshua. *Joshua 11:1, 6*

• King of Hazor during the time of Deborah. It was Jabin's forces under Sisera's command that were defeated by Barak and Deborah. *Judges 4:1-4*

**Jabneel (jab-nee-el)**

• A Canaanite city on the border of the land allotted to Judah, possibly another name for the Philistine city of Jabneh that Uzziah captured. *Joshua 15:1, 11*

• A Canaanite town in the land allotted to Naphtali. *Joshua 19:31-33*

J

Genesis 25:27-34
Genesis 29:18
Genesis 32:28

**Jacob** (**jay**-kuhb)

Son of *Isaac* and *Rebekah* and ancestor of the Israelites; grandson of *Abraham*; fraternal twin brother of *Esau*. Jacob is famous for tricking his brother into selling his birthright, for stealing Esau's blessing, and for moving his family to Egypt. God named him Israel after they wrestled at Peniel.

Jacob's story is told in Genesis 26-50.

See also *tribes of Israel*

Judges 4:17-22

**Jael** (**jay**-el)

Wife of Heber who murdered *Sisera* in her tent after the rout of Sisera's forces by Barak and Deborah. The gruesome details appear in Judges 4:17-24.

**Jahaziel** (juh-**hah**-zee-el)

2 Chronicles 20:14

• An Israelite from the clan of Asaph who urged *Jehoshaphat* king of Judah to resist the Moabite and Ammonite invaders. Jahaziel's words were a prophesy and promise of victory.

1 Chronicles 12:1-7

• An Israelite warrior from the tribe of Benjamin who defected to David at Ziklag.

1 Chronicles 23:19
1 Chronicles 24:23
Ezra 8:5

• Several other Israelites mentioned only by name.

**Jair** (**jay**-ur)

Judges 10:3-5

• Israelite from Gilead who served as seventh judge of Israel after *Tola*. He judged Israel 22 years.

• Israelite from the tribe of Manasseh who captured 60 towns of Bashan during the conquest of Canaan.
*Numbers 32:41*
*1 Kings 4:13*

• *Mordecai's* father.
*Esther 2:5*

• *Elhanan's* father or clan.
*1 Chronicles 20:5*

**Jairus** (**jye**-ruhss)
A Jewish *synagogue* ruler who brought his daughter to Jesus for healing.
*Luke 8:40-42*

**Jakin and Boaz** (**jay**-kin and **boh**-az)
*2 Chronicles 3:17*

The two bronze pillars at the entrance to Solomon's temple. Jakin and Boaz were each about nine meters high and one meter in diameter. Nebuchadnezzar's army broke them down and hauled them away when they destroyed Jerusalem.

**Jambres** (**jam**-breez)
See *Jannes and Jambres*

**James** (**jaymz**)

• Jewish fisherman from Galilee who followed Jesus as one of the *Twelve*; son of Zebedee; brother of John.
*Matthew 4:21*

• Another of Jesus' Twelve disciples; son of *Alphaeus*.
*Matthew 10:2-3*

• Jesus' half-brother and author of the *book of James*. This James did not
*Galatians 1:19*
*Mark 6:3*

believe in his brother's message until after Jesus died and rose again. He gave an important speech in Jerusalem shortly after the church got started; it is recorded in Acts 15:13-21.

*Luke 6:16*

• Father of *Thaddaeus*.

*James 1:1*

**James, book of (jaymz, buk** uhv)

Twentieth book of the New Testament and second of the *general letters*; a letter from Jesus' half-brother James to Jewish Christians all over the world. The book of James tells how to live as a Christian. It was written around A.D. 49.

*2 Timothy 3:8*

**Jannes and Jambres** (**jan**-uhz and **jam**-breez)

Two of the Egyptian magicians who faked miracles for *Pharaoh* when Moses was asking him to let the Hebrew slaves go free. Jannes and Jambres' names do not appear in the Old Testament, only in Jewish tradition. But Paul mentioned them in his second letter to Timothy as examples of false teachers who would, in the end, be exposed.

**Janoah** (juh-**noh**-uh)

*Joshua 16:5-7*

• A Canaanite town in the territory allotted to Ephraim, southeast of Shechem on Ephraim's border with Manasseh.

• A town in the territory of Naphtali captured by *Tiglath-Pileser* during the reign of *Pekah*. All of Janoah's people were taken away to Assyria. *2 Kings 15:29*

**Japheth** (**jay**-feth)

Son of Noah and one of only eight people who survived the *flood*. Noah blessed Japheth for showing more respect than Ham.

*Genesis 7:13*
*Genesis 9:27*

**Japhia** (juh-**fye**-uh)

A town on the southern boundary of Zebulun two and a half kilometers southwest of Nazareth; modern Yafa.

*Joshua 19:12*

**Jashobeam** (juh-**shoh**-bee-uhm)

• Chief among the *Three*; highest-ranking of David's most elite *mighty men*. *1 Chronicles 11:11*

• An Israelite warrior from the tribe of Benjamin who defected to David at Ziklag; a *Korahite*. *1 Chronicles 12:1, 6*

**Jason** (**jay**-suhn)

Jewish Christian in *Thessalonica* who opened his home to Paul and Silas during Paul's second missionary journey. Jealous opponents of Paul kidnapped Jason and had him arrested on false charges of causing a riot. The Jason named in Romans 16:21 may be the same man.

*Acts 17:6-7, 9*
*Romans 16:21*

Genesis 10:4

**Javan** (**jay**-vuhn)
One of *Japheth's* sons; a grandson of Noah.

Joshua 8:18
1 Samuel 17:45

**javelin** (**jav**-uh-lin)

A throwing spear. Goliath approached David with a javelin slung on his back.

J

Judges 19:10-11
1 Chronicles 11:4

**Jebus** (**jee**-buhss)
Another name for Jerusalem. The *Jebusites* got their name from this city.

Numbers 13:29
2 Samuel 5:6-7

**Jebusites** (**jeb**-yoo-sites)
A small clan that lived in and around *Jebus* during the time of the judges; descendants of Canaan. The Jebusites were a smaller group than the Amorites, Canaanites, and Girgashites that lived around them. They disappeared as a distinct clan some time after David captured Jebus for Israel.

1 Chronicles 12:20

**Jediael** (juh-**dye**-uhl)
A commander in Saul's army who defected to David along with several others from the tribe of Manasseh. Jediael became an officer in David's army.

1 Chronicles 25:1, 6
2 Chronicles 5:12

**Jeduthun** (juh-**dyoo**-thuhn)
A Levite musician appointed by David to lead the temple chorus. Jeduthun played the harp and supervised six of his sons in their duties as

temple musicians. His family still had this job during the time of Nehemiah. David wrote two Psalms for him (39 and 62), and *Asaph* wrote one (Psalm 77). Jeduthun worked together with *Heman* and Asaph.

**Jehiel** (juh-**hye**-el)

A common name among the Israelites:

- Tutor of David's sons; son of Hacmoni. *1 Chronicles 27:32*
- Temple treasurer during the time of David; a Gershonite. *1 Chronicles 29:8*
- A temple *gatekeeper* appointed to sing and play music during the return of the Ark to Jerusalem from *Kiriath Jearim*. *1 Chronicles 16:4-5*

- A temple supervisor appointed by Hezekiah. *2 Chronicles 31:11-13*
- A temple supervisor and official in Josiah's service who gave generously to the priests and Levites during Josiah's reforms. *2 Chronicles 35:7-8*
- King *Jehoshaphat's* son. *2 Chronicles 21:2*
- Several others mentioned only once. *Ezra 10:21, 26*

**Jehizkiah** (juh-hiz-**kye**-uh) *2 Chronicles 28:12*

One of four leaders in the northern kingdom of Israel, together with *Azariah*, *Berekiah*, and *Amasa*, who spoke out against making slaves of 200,000 prisoners of war. The prisoners were all fellow Israelites from the southern kingdom of Judah, captured after the defeat of Ahaz's forces.

J

**Jehoahaz** (juh-**hoh**-uh-haz)

2 Chronicles 25: 17, 23

• Another name for *Ahaziah*, sixth king of Judah.

2 Kings 10:35

• Son of Jehu and eleventh king of Israel after his father. Jehoahaz reigned 17 years.

2 Kings 23:30

• Son of *Josiah* and seventeenth king of Judah after his father; also called Shallum. Jehoahaz reigned only three months because Judah was under Egypt's control, and Pharaoh Neco did not approve of him. Neco placed his brother *Jehoiakim* on the throne in his place. Jehoahaz died in Egypt as the prophet Jeremiah predicted.

**Jehoash** (juh-**ho**-ash)
See *Joash*

**Jehoiachin** (juh-**hoi**-uh-kin)

2 Kings 24:6
Esther 2:5-6
Jeremiah 52:33-34

Son of *Jehoiakim* and nineteenth king of Judah after his father. Jehoiachin came to power when Nebuchadnezzar put down Jehoiakim's revolt against Babylonia and made Jehoiachin king in his place. Nebuchadnezzar changed his mind after only three months and 10 days, and replaced Jehoiachin with his brother *Zedekiah*. Jehoiachin was carried off to Babylon with his wife and family.

**Jehoiada** (juh-**hoi**-uh-duh)

A common name among the Israelites:

- Priest of Israel during the reigns of Ahaziah, Athaliah, and Joash; husband of *Jehosheba*. Jehoiada became famous for hiding young Joash in the temple after his wife rescued the baby prince from Athaliah's slaughter of princes. He served as Joash's counselor for many years. — 2 Chronicles 24:2-3

- Father of David's officer *Benaiah*. — 1 Chronicles 11:22
- Leader of 3,700 men of the clan of Aaron who defected to David at Hebron. — 1 Chronicles 12:27
- Counselor to David who took *Ahithophel's* place. — 1 Chronicles 27:34
- A priest who lived during the time of Jeremiah. — Jeremiah 29:26

**Jehoiakim** (juh-**hoi**-uh-kim) — 1 Chronicles 3:15, Jeremiah 22:18, Daniel 1:1

Son of *Josiah* and eighteenth king of Judah after his younger brother *Jehoahaz*. *Neco* made Jehoiakim king in place of his brother at a time when Egypt controlled Judah. Jehoiakim's given name was Eliakim, but Neco made him change it. Jehoiakim reigned 11 years.

J

**Jehoram** (juh-**hor**-uhm)

A common name among the Israelites, sometimes shortened to Joram:

2 Kings 8:16
• Son of Ahab and Jezebel, and ninth king of Israel after Ahaziah. Jehoram was assassinated by *Jehu*. He reigned 12 years.

1 Kings 22:50
• Son of *Jehoshaphat* and fifth king of Judah after his father. Jehoram murdered his six brothers, married the wicked Athaliah, and lost territory to the Philistines. He reigned eight years.

1 Chronicles 18:10
• A prince from Hamath who visited David; also known as Hadoram.

2 Chronicles 17:8
• Two others mentioned only once.

**Jehoshabeath** (juh-hoh-**shab**-ee-uth)

See *Jehosheba*

2 Chronicles 20:1
2 Chronicles 22:9

**Jehoshaphat** (juh-**hoh**-shuh-fat)

Son of *Asa* and fourth king of Judah after his father. Jehoshaphat arranged for the marriage of his son Jehoram to Ahab's daughter Athaliah in order to improve relations with Israel. Jehoshaphat was known as a good king who followed God's ways. He reigned 25 years.

2 Chronicles 22:11

**Jehosheba** (juh-**hoh**-shi-buh)

Daughter of Jehoram king of Judah; sister of Ahaziah king of Judah; wife of *Jehoiada*; *Joash's* aunt. Jehosheba is the one who rescued her one-year-old nephew Joash from being killed by Athaliah. Athaliah was trying to kill off the royal line of David. Jehosheba and Jehoiada kept Joash hidden in the temple for six years.

**Jehovah** (juh-**hoh**-vuh)
God's name. This form of the name comes from a combination of YHWH, the Hebrew name for God, with the vowels in *adonai*, the Hebrew word for Lord.
See also *Yahweh*

*Exodus 6:3*
*Psalm 83:18*
*Isaiah 12:2*

J

**Jehovah-jireh** (juh-**hoh**-vuh **jye**-ruh)
"The LORD will Provide," a name for God.

*Genesis 22:14*

**Jehovah-nissi** (juh-**hoh**-vuh **niss**-eye)
"The LORD is my Banner," a name for God.

*Exodus 17:15*

**Jehovah-shalom** (juh-**hoh**-vuh-shah-**lohm**)
"The LORD is Peace," a name for God.

*Judges 6:24*

**Jehovah-shammah** (juh-**hoh**-vuh **shah**-muh)
"The LORD is There," a name for God.

*Ezekiel 48:35*

**Jehovah-tsidkenu** (juh-**hoh**-vuh tsid-**ken**-oo)
"The LORD is our Righteousness," a name for God.

**Jehu** (**jay**-hoo)

2 Kings 9:14, 20
2 Kings 10:30-31

- Son of *Jehoshaphat* and tenth king of Israel after *Jehoram*. Jehu came to power by assassinating Jehoram and taking his place. Jehu reigned for 28 years, but lost a lot of territory to *Hazael*, king of Syria.

1 Chronicles 12:1-3

- An Israelite warrior from the tribe of Benjamin who defected to David at Ziklag; a man from Anathoth.

1 Kings 16:1-2
2 Chronicles 19:2

- A seer and scribe who prophesied to Baasha and Jehoshaphat; son of Hanani.

**Jehudi** (juh-**hoo**-dye)

Jeremiah 36:14, 21, 23

An official in the service of King Jehoiakim during the time of Jeremiah; son of Nethaniah. Jehudi is the official who got a scroll of Jeremiah's prophesies from *Baruch* and read them to the king. He was also among the officials who told Baruch and Jeremiah to hide from the king. Jehoiakim burned the scroll.

See also *Jerahmeel*

**Jeiel** (juh-**eye**-uhl)

A common name among the Israelites:

1 Chronicles 16:5

- A temple gatekeeper appointed to sing and play music during the return of the Ark to Jerusalem from Kiriath Jearim.

2 Chronicles 35:9

- A Levite leader who gave generously to the Levites during Josiah's reforms.

• One of David's *mighty men*; brother of *Shama*; son of Hotham. *1 Chronicles 11:26, 44*

• Several others mentioned only once. *Ezra 10:43; 2 Chronicles 26:11*

**Jephthah** (**jef**-thuh) *Judges 11:1; Hebrews 11:32*

Son of Gilead and eighth judge of Israel after *Jair*. Jephthah defeated the Ammonites and judged Israel six years.



**Jerahmeel** (juh-**rah**-mee-el)

• A descendant of Judah and father of the clan named after him. *1 Chronicles 2:3-9*

• Son of King *Jehoiakim* who was ordered to arrest Baruch and Jeremiah. *Jeremiah 36:26*

• Levite son of Kish (not Saul's father). *1 Chronicles 24:29*

See also *Jerahmeelites*

**Jerahmeelites** (juh-**rah**-meel-ites) *1 Samuel 27:10*

People who traced their roots to *Jerahmeel* of Judah; the clan of Jerahmeel. The Jerahmeelites lived in the Negev during the time of David, then eventually mixed in completely with other clans in the tribe of Judah.

**Jeremiah** (**jer**-uh-**mye**-uh)

A common name among the Israelites:

• Son of *Hilkiah* and Israelite prophet to Judah for 40 years. Jeremiah prophesied during the reigns of Judah's last five kings: Josiah, Jehoahaz, Jehoiakim, Jehoiachin, and Zedekiah. He is famous for being *2 Chronicles 36:21-22; Jeremiah 19:14*

ignored by almost everyone in Judah despite everything he did to get their attention. King Jehoiakim burned a scroll of Jeremiah's prophesies; Zedekiah ordered him put him in prison; several court officials tried to kill him. Jeremiah's story and prophesies are recorded in the *book of Jeremiah*. The prophets Zephaniah and Habakkuk also lived during this time.

J

1 Chronicles 12:1, 4

• An Israelite warrior from the tribe of Benjamin who defected to David at Ziklag.

1 Chronicles 12: 8-13

• Two skilled Israelite soldiers from the tribe of Gad who defected to David at Ziklag; fifth and tenth in command under *Ezer*.

2 Kings 23:31

• Several others known only by name.

Jeremiah 1:1

**Jeremiah, book of** (**jer**-uh-**mye**-uh, **buk** uhv)

Twenty-fourth book of the Old Testament and second of the *major prophets*. This book tells how God gave Jeremiah words to say, what he said to the people of Judah, and what happened when the people got sick of hearing all the bad news. The book of Jeremiah is famous for ending exactly as God predicted it would.

The book of Habakkuk was written during the same time period.

See also *Baruch*

Joshua 6:1-5
2 Kings 2:4
Mark 10:46

**Jericho** (**jer**-uh-koh)

First Canaanite city taken by the Israelites during the conquest of Canaan and a famous city in the Bible.

Rahab hid the Israelite spies in Jericho. Joshua's army destroyed Jericho's walls with seven days of marching and playing music. And the parable of the Good Samaritan is set on the road to Jericho. Jericho was about seven kilometers west of the Jordan River and 16 kilometers north-northwest of the Dead Sea. It lay in the territory allotted to Benjamin.



**Jerimoth** (**jer**-i-moth)

- An Israelite warrior from the tribe of Benjamin who defected to David at Ziklag. *1 Chronicles 12:5*
- A temple supervisor appointed by Hezekiah. *2 Chronicles 31:11-13*
- Several others mentioned only once. *1 Chronicles 25:4; 2 Chronicles 11:18*

**Jeroboam** (**jer**-uh-**boh**-uhm)

Two kings of Israel:

- Jeroboam I: Son of Nebat and first king of the northern kingdom of Israel. *1 Kings 12:15; 2 Chronicles 13:6* Solomon put Jeroboam in charge of the labor forces in the northern tribes while Solomon was still king. After Solomon's death, Jeroboam pressed *Rehoboam* to ease the working conditions, but Rehoboam refused and Jeroboam led a revolt. All Israelite tribes but Benjamin and Judah joined Jeroboam, and the northern kingdom was formed. It all happened as the prophet *Ahijah* predicted.

Because the temple was in Jerusalem, Jeroboam started a new religion. He built two large shrines and created a new priesthood. Jeroboam's new religion replaced the true worship of God and led all of Israel into idolatry. Not one king of the northern kingdom ever led them back to the Lord.

Jeroboam I reigned 22 years and was succeeded by *Nadab*.

*2 Kings 14:27*
*Amos 1:1*

• Jeroboam II: Son of *Joash* and thirteenth king of Israel after his father. The prophet Jonah lived during Jeroboam II's reign; the prophet Amos spoke out against his sins. He reigned 41 years.

*Joshua 10:3*
*Isaiah 31:5*
*Acts 1:8*

**Jerusalem** (juh-**roo**-suh-lem)
Most important city of the Bible and home to the Jewish people. Jerusalem was the city of Salem when Abraham came to Canaan, and Jebus when Joshua's forces reached it during the conquest of Canaan. This is the *fortified city* that David captured from the Jebusites and made his capital. David, Solomon, and all the kings of Judah ruled from the palace in Jerusalem. It was the site of Solomon's *temple* and of the temple that Zerubbabel rebuilt. Nehemiah rebuilt the city walls after the Exile. Jesus preached, healed, and was crucified in Jerusalem.

Jerusalem is also called the Holy City, the City of David, *Zion*, and Mount Zion. It is located about 50 kilometers east of the Mediterranean Sea in the hills of Judea.

See also *new Jerusalem*

**Jeshua** (je-**shoo**-uh)

A common name among the Israelites and another form of Joshua:

• One of those who helped Zerubbabel rebuild the temple in Jerusalem after the Exile; son of Jozadak. *Ezra 3:2; Nehemiah 12:1*

• Several other people known only by name. *2 Chronicles 31:15; Nehemiah 12:24*

• An area of Judah settled by the Jews who returned from Exile. *Nehemiah 11:26*

**Jesse** (**jess**-ee)

*Ruth 4:17; Luke 3:23, 32, 38*

Father of David and of eight other children: Eliab, Abinadab, Shimea, Nethanel, Raddai, Ozem, Elihu, Zeruiah, and Abigail. Jesse belonged to the tribe of Judah and was from Bethlehem. He was the son of Obed and the grandson of Boaz.

J

J

*Matthew 1:18*
*Acts 16:18*
*Romans 3:22*

**Jesus Christ (jee**-zuhss **kriste)**

The most important man in the Bible; *Son of God*; *Messiah*; our Savior and Lord. The Old Testament tells of Jesus' coming. The *Gospels* tell of his birth, life, death, and resurrection.

The New Testament explains that Jesus Christ is both God and man. He is one person in the *Trinity*, one with the Father and Holy Spirit. He existed before the creation of the world and brought it into existence.

Jesus came to earth to take away our sins. He was born without sin, lived a perfect life, and gave his life as a perfect sacrifice for our sins. All people who come to him in faith and ask him to take away their sins will be *saved*.

Jesus went back to his Father in heaven to act on behalf of his people. He sent his Spirit to be with us in his absence, pleads our case before the Father, and is preparing a place for us in heaven. He will return at the *last day* and reign forever as King of kings and Lord of lords.

Jesus Christ is the one who fulfilled the *messianic prophesies* of the Old Testament. Some of the most famous are Isaiah 7:14; Isaiah 53:1-12; Micah 5:2; Zechariah 9:9; and Psalm 22:7-18. These prophesies predicted who the Messiah would be and what would happen to him.

The name "Jesus" is the Greek form of the Hebrew *Joshua*; it means "the LORD saves." "Christ" is the Greek form of the Hebrew *Messiah*; it means "anointed one." Jesus Christ is the one God chose and *anointed* to save us from our sins.

There are many other names for Jesus in the Bible, including *Alpha and Omega*, Christ Jesus, *Immanuel*, Judge, Lamb, Shepherd, Son of David, Son of God, and Son of Man.

*See also God; image of God; Incarnation; sacrifice; Trinity*

J

**Jether** (**jee**-thur)

- Gideon's oldest son. *Judges 8:19-20*
- Four other Israelites known only by name. *2 Samuel 17:25; 1 Chronicles 2:32; 1 Chronicles 4:17; 1 Chronicles 7:38*

**Jethro** (**jeth**-roh)

Moses' father-in-law, a Midianite; also called Reuel; father of Moses' wife Zipporah. *Exodus 18:1, 27*

Jethro is famous for advising Moses to get help with the leadership of Israel during the Exodus.

**Jew** (**joo**)

A person from the southern kingdom of Judah or any Israelite who lived during or after the Exile. *Esther 2:5; John 4:9; Romans 10:12*

1 Kings 19:1-2
2 Kings 9:30

**Jezebel** (**jez**-uh-bel)

• Wife of King *Ahab* and enemy of *Elijah*.

Jezebel was the daughter of the king of Sidon and a devoted worshiper of idols, especially Asherah and Baal. She had 450 prophets of Baal and 400 prophets of Asherah until her losing battle with Elijah on Mount Carmel.

Revelation 2:20

• A wicked woman and false teacher named in Jesus' letter to the church in Thyatira in the *book of Revelation*.

1 Chronicles 12:3

**Jeziel** (**jee**-zi-uhl)

An Israelite warrior from the tribe of Benjamin who defected to David at Ziklag; brother of Pelet and son of Azmaveth.

**Jezreel** (**jez**-ree-uhl)

Joshua 19:17-18
1 Kings 21:23

• A city in the territory allotted to Issachar. This area was the scene of many events related to the northern kingdom of Israel, especially those of *Jezebel*.

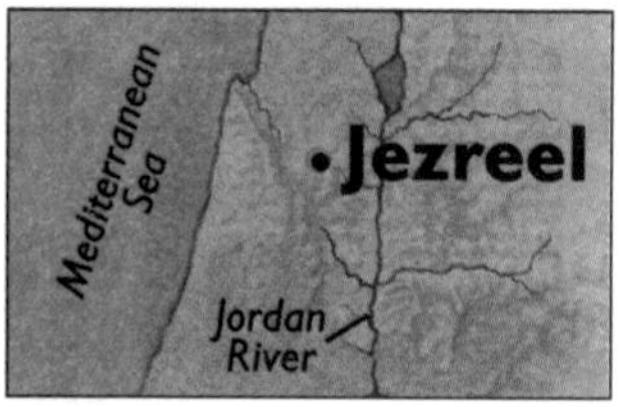


Joshua 15:21, 56

• A town in the territory allotted to Judah.

Hosea 1:4-5

• *Hosea's* first son.

1 Chronicles 4:1, 3

• A descendant of Judah.

See also *Valley of Jezreel*

1 Kings 21:4

**Jezreelite** (**jez**-ree-uhl-**ite**)

A person from the city of *Jezreel*.

**Joab** (**joh**-ab)

• Commander-in-chief of David's army through most of David's reign. Joab was a brave but reckless warrior. He defeated many of David's enemies but also killed some of David's friends and allies. In the end Joab joined *Adonijah's* revolt and was killed for it by Benaiah. Joab was the son of David's half-sister *Zeruiah*, and brother of *Asahel* and *Abishai.*

*2 Samuel 2:13*
*1 Kings 2:28*

• A family that returned to Jerusalem with Zerubbabel. *Ezra 2:1-6*

• A descendant of Judah. *1 Chronicles 4:14*

**Joah** (**joh**-uh)

• King Hezekiah's "royal historian," one of the three officials who spoke with the Assyrian officers during the siege of Jerusalem; son of Asaph. *2 Kings 18:18*

• King Josiah's royal historian, one of the three officials appointed by Josiah to repair the temple; son of Joahaz. *2 Chronicles 34:8*

• Two others mentioned only by name. *1 Chronicles 6:21*, *1 Chronicles 26:4*

**Joanna** (joh-**an**-uh)

One of the women who followed Jesus and who gave of her own money so he could travel and preach. Jesus had healed her of some kind of illness, so she traveled with Jesus and the

*Luke 8:3*
*Luke 24:10*

Twelve. Joanna went to the tomb on Easter morning, saw the empty tomb, and reported Jesus' resurrection to the Twelve. Joanna's husband Cuza worked for Herod Antipas.

**Joash** (**joh**-ash)

*2 Kings 11:2, 21*
*2 Kings 14:1*

J

• Son of Ahaziah and eighth king of Judah after *Athaliah*. Joash is famous for becoming king at the age of seven. He came to power when his uncle Jehoiada conspired with the Levites and the elders of Israel to overthrow Athaliah and restore the kingdom to David's line. Joash was assassinated by his own officials. He reigned 40 years.

*2 Kings 14:1, 13*

• Son of *Jehoahaz* and twelfth king of Israel after his father; also called Jehoash. Joash is noted for visiting Elisha on his death bed. He reigned 16 years.

*Judges 6:11*

• Gideon's father, an Israelite of the clan of *Abiezer* and an idol worshiper.

*1 Chronicles 12:1, 3*

• An Israelite warrior from the tribe of Benjamin who defected to David at Ziklag; a man from Gibeah.

*2 Chronicles 18:25*

• Ahab's son.

**Job** (**johb**)

Wealthy man of God whose story is told in the *book of Job.* Job lost his children, possessions, and health when God allowed Satan to take them all away. Job became famous for saying, "The LORD gave me everything I had, and the LORD has taken it away. Praise the name of the LORD!" (Job 1:21).

*Job 1:1*

**Job, book of** (**johb, buk** uhv)

Eighteenth book of the Old Testament and the first of the *books of poetry*. The book of Job is a record of *Job's* suffering and how four of his friends tried to explain it. *Eliphaz*, *Bildad*, *Zophar*, and *Elihu* each tell Job their ideas, but God rejects all of them and reminds them of his vast power and wisdom. In the end, Job's family and wealth are restored.

*Job 1:8*

**Jochebed** (**jok**-uh-bed)

Mother of Moses and Aaron; a Levite and wife of Amram.

*Exodus 6:20*
*Numbers 26:59*

**Joel** (**joh**-uhl)

A very common name among the Israelites:

• The prophet who wrote the *book of Joel*; son of Pethuel. We know nothing else about him.

*Acts 2:16*

J

1 Chronicles 11:38

1 Chronicles 27: 16, 20

• One of David's *mighty men*.
• Officer over half the tribe of Manasseh in David's army; son of Pedaiah.
• At least eight others mentioned only by name.

J

Joel 1:1

**Joel, book of** (**joh**-uhl, **buk** uhv)

Twenty-ninth book of the Old Testament and second of the *minor prophets*. The book of Joel is a set of prophecies to the southern kingdom of Judah. They were written by the prophet *Joel*. It is famous for its mention of locust plagues.

1 Chronicles 12:7

**Joelah** (joe-**ee**-luh)

An Israelite warrior from the tribe of Benjamin who defected to David at Ziklag; son of Jeroham and brother of *Zebadiah*.

1 Chronicles 12:1, 6

**Joezer** (joe-**ee**-zer)

An Israelite warrior from the tribe of Benjamin who defected to David at Ziklag; a Korahite.

**Johanan** (joh-**han**-uhn)

A common name among the Israelites:

2 Kings 25:23
Jeremiah 40:7-8; 41:15

• Important Israelite army officer and leader after the fall of Jerusalem; son of Kareah. Johanan was a hero to his people but a major villain to the prophet Jeremiah. He warned *Gedaliah* of Ishmael's plot, and tried to catch

Ishmael after Gedaliah's murder. He was leader of the officers who were loyal to Gedaliah. Together they rescued many hostages taken by Ishmael.

Johanan was also bitterly opposed to the prophet *Jeremiah* and misled many people of Judah. Johanan and his friend *Azariah* son of Kareah led the disastrous retreat to Egypt after Gedaliah's death, even though Jeremiah warned them that this was not God's plan and would cost them their lives. The sad story is told in Jeremiah 41:16–45:5.



• A skilled Israelite soldier from the tribe of Gad who defected to David at Ziklag; eighth in command under *Ezer*. *1 Chronicles 12:1, 8, 12*

• An Israelite warrior from the tribe of Benjamin who defected to David at Ziklag. *1 Chronicles 12: 1, 4*

• At least six others mentioned only by name.

**John (jon)**

• Son of Zebedee and brother of James; Jesus' disciple; an *apostle*. This is the John who wrote the Gospel of John. He was one of Jesus' three closest disciples (along with *Peter* and *James*) and an eyewitness to the *Transfiguration*. *Mark 1:19*

• *Simon Peter's* father. *John 21:15*

• *John Mark* *Acts 15:37*

• *John the Baptist* *Matthew 3:1-3*

• A relative of the high priest Annas present at the trial of the apostles Peter and John. *Acts 4:6-7*

Acts 12:25
Acts 15:37

**John Mark (jon mark)**

Assistant to Paul and Barnabas during Paul's first missionary journey and author of the Gospel of *Mark*. Mark's mother's name was Mary, and their home was one of the first meeting places of the early church. After his journey with Paul and Barnabas, John Mark returned to Cyprus to encourage the churches there.

Matthew 3:1
Matthew 11:11-12
Mark 8:27-28

**John the Baptist (jon** the **bap**-tist)

Prophet who prepared the people of Israel for the coming of the Messiah in fulfillment of Isaiah 40:3-5. John's birth to Elizabeth and Zechariah was foretold by the angel Gabriel shortly before the angel appeared to Mary to announce the coming of Jesus. John preached in the wilderness of Judea. He identified Jesus as the Messiah. John was put in prison and beheaded by *Herod Antipas*.

1 John 1:9

**John, First (jon, furst)**

Twenty-third book of the New Testament, a letter written by the apostle John to *Gentile* Christians. John wrote this letter to help God's people know they have *eternal life*. It is famous for an important verse about *forgiveness*, 1:9.

See also *Second John; Third John*

**John, Second (jon, sek-**uhnd)

Twenty-fourth book of the New Testament, a letter written by the apostle John to the chosen lady. Its theme is truth.

See also *First John; Third John*

*2 John 1:1-2*

**John, Third (jon, thurd)**

Twenty-fifth book of the New Testament, a letter written by the apostle John to *Gaius*. John wrote the letter to commend Gaius for his hospitality toward traveling *evangelists*.

See also *First John; Second John*

*3 John 1:1-4*



**John, Gospel of (jon, gos-**puhl uhv)

Fourth book of the New Testament and fourth of the *Gospels*. It was written by the apostle John to prove that Jesus is the Messiah, the Son of God. For this reason is it often called the Gospel of belief. Most of the details in this Gospel do not appear in the other three. John has some of the most famous verses in Scripture, especially 3:16; 13:14; 14:6; 15:12; and 16:33.

See also *First John; Second John; Third John; Luke; Mark; Matthew*

*John 1:19*

**Jokneam (jok-**nee-uhm)

A Canaanite city in the land allotted to Zebulun. It was given to the Levites.

*Joshua 19:10-11*
*Joshua 21:34*

J

*Genesis 10:25-29*

**Joktan** (**jok**-tuhn)

A son of *Eber* and ancestor of 13 tribes that settled in south Arabia.

*Jeremiah 35:6-10*

**Jonadab** (**joh**-nuh-dab)

Ancestor of the *Recabites* who set up the Recabite way of life.

*Jonah 1:17*
*Luke 11:29-32*

**Jonah** (**joh**-nuh)

Israelite prophet to the northern kingdom of Israel during the reign of Jeroboam II; son of Amittai. Jonah is famous for refusing to preach in Nineveh, trying to escape to Tarshish, and being brought back to Israel by a fish. His story is told in the *book of Jonah*.

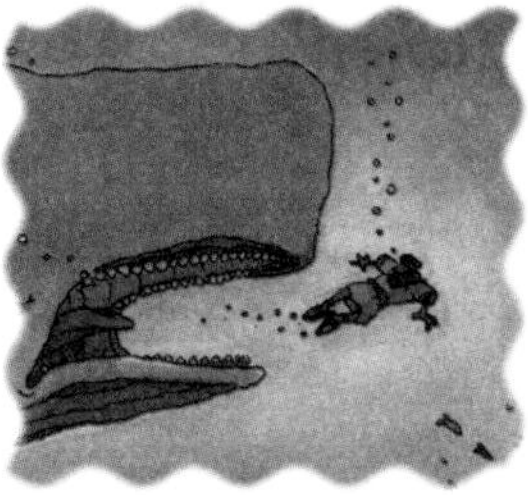

*Jonah 1:1-3*

**Jonah, book of** (**joh**-nuh, **buk** uhv)

Thirty-second book of the Old Testament and fifth of the *minor prophets*. Unlike all other books of prophecy, the book of Jonah tells only about what happened to the prophet and very little of the prophet's message. It tells the famous story of Jonah's attempt to escape from God's assignment to preach in Nineveh. It was written during the time of Jeroboam II.

**Jonathan** (**jon**-uh-thuhn)

A very common name among the Israelites:

*1 Samuel 13:16*
*1 Samuel 19:1*
*2 Samuel 1:12, 17*

• Firstborn son of Saul, prince of Israel, and David's loyal friend. Jonathan was a brave and

skilled warrior who gained fame for helping his father repel the Philistines. Later, after David's fame in Israel made Saul jealous, Jonathan helped David escape Saul's plots of murder. He was killed at Gilboa with his father.

• Son of Gershom and descendant of Moses who served as private priest for "a man named Micah" during the time of the judges. Though Jonathan was a Levite, Micah's place of worship was an idol *shrine*, not the valid place of worship in Shiloh. This led to more and more idolatry in Israel. — *Judges 18:30*

• Courier to David during Absalom's revolt; son of Abiathar the priest. — *2 Samuel 15:36*

• David's nephew; son of David's brother *Shimei* (also called Shimea). Jonathan became a hero for killing the six-fingered Philistine from Gath. — *2 Samuel 21:21; 1 Chronicles 20:7*

• One of David's *mighty men*. — *1 Chronicles 27:23-25*

• David's uncle and royal advisor. — *1 Chronicles 27:32*

• Brother of *Johanan* and Israelite army officer loyal to *Gedaliah*; son of Kareah. — *Jeremiah 40:8*

• Many others mentioned only by name.

**Joppa** (**jop**-uh) — *2 Chronicles 2:16; Acts 9:36; Acts 11:13*

Port city on the Mediterranean coast in the territory allotted to *Dan*; modern Jaffa. The Philistines controlled Joppa during

most of Israel's history. The apostle Peter was in Joppa when Cornelius's two servants went there to fetch him.

2 Kings 8:28

**Joram** (**jor**-uhm)

A short form of *Jehoram*.

Genesis 13:10-11
Joshua 13:23
John 3:26

**Jordan** (**jor**-duhn)

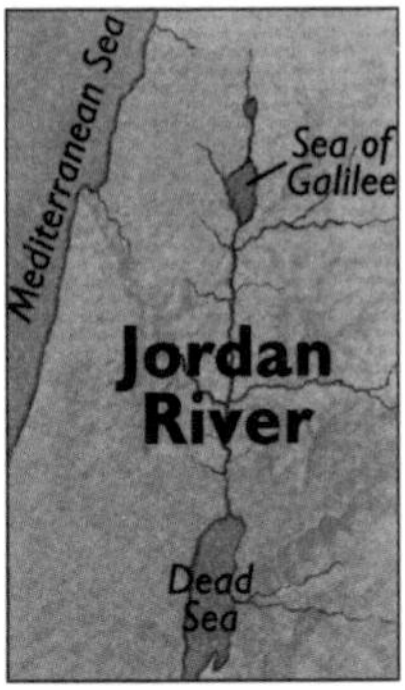


A major river in Palestine and key to many events of the Bible. The Israelites began their conquest of Canaan after crossing the Jordan. *Naaman* washed in the Jordan. John the Baptist baptized in the Jordan. The river flows north-south from the mountains of south Lebanon to the Dead Sea. The headwaters flow into Lake Huleh from mountain springs and pass through the Sea of Galilee on their way to the salty waters of the Dead Sea.

See also *Valley of Salt*

**Joseph** (**joh**-seph)

A very common name among the Israelites:

Genesis 35:24

• Son of Jacob and *Rachel*, and father of *Ephraim* and *Manasseh*. Joseph is famous for his dreams of being ruler, being sold to merchants by his jealous brothers, and then becoming ruler of Egypt under Pharaoh. Joseph's story is told in Genesis 37:1–50:26.

• Mary's husband and earthly father to Jesus, a descendant of David. We know little about Joseph except that he was a righteous and devout man. An angel appeared to him four times, and he followed the angel's instructions each time. The Gospels mention him only in connection with Jesus' birth and boyhood. *Luke 1:26-27* *Luke 3:23*

• "Joseph called Barsabbas," or Justus, one of the two men, along with Matthias, nominated to replace Judas Iscariot. *Acts 1:23*

• "Joseph of Arimathea," member of the Sanhedrin and secret disciple of Jesus. This is the Joseph who donated his tomb for the burial of Jesus' body and helped Nicodemus carry out the gruesome task. *John 19:38*

• *Barnabas'* real name. *Acts 4:36*

• One of Jesus' half-brothers. *Mark 6:3*

• Many others mentioned only by name.

**Josheb-Basshebeth** (**joh**-sheb-bass-**shee**-beth)
See *Jashobeam*

**Joshua** (**josh**-oo-uh)

• Israelite who commanded the armies of Israel during the conquest of Canaan; son of Nun. Joshua was one of the Hebrews who left Egypt in the Exodus, and one of the twelve spies who explored Canaan from Kadesh Barnea. He was named Hoshea until Moses changed it. He and *Numbers 14:6-8* *Numbers 27:18-23* *Acts 7:45*

J

*Caleb* were the only ones to enter Canaan from the original group that left Egypt. Joshua wrote most of the *book of Joshua*.

*Zechariah 3:1*

• High priest of Israel during the time of *Ezra*; son of Jehozadak. He is mentioned in the prophesies of *Zechariah*.

J

*1 Samuel 6:14, 18*

• "Joshua of Beth Shemesh": When the Philistines sent the *Ark of the Covenant* back to Israel, the cart stopped at his field.

*Joshua 1:1-2*

**Joshua, book of** (**josh**-oo-uh, **buk** uhv)

Sixth book of the Old Testament and first of the *books of history*. The book of Joshua records the Israelite conquest of Canaan. It tells the famous stories of Rahab, the attack on Jericho, and the day the sun stood still.

**Josiah** (joh-**zye**-uh)

*2 Kings 21:24; 22:1*
*2 Chronicles 35: 1-10*

• Son of *Amon* and sixteenth king of Judah after his father; grandson of Manasseh. His mother's name was Jedidah. Josiah was one of the best kings Judah ever had. He repaired the broken-down temple, held a national reform when *Hilkiah* found the lost *Book of the Law*, and cleared the land of idols and *high places*. He is also famous for becoming king at the age of

eight, only one year older than Joash was when he became king. Josiah's story is told in 2 Kings 21:24–23:30 and 2 Chronicles 33:25–35:26. He reigned 31 years.
• Unidentified Israelite who lived during the time of *Zechariah*. *Zechariah 6:10*

**jot and tittle** (**jot** and **tit**-uhl) *Matthew 5:18*
An expression that means every little stroke or letter; every little bit; even the smallest part. A jot is the smallest letter of the alphabet. A tittle is a minor stroke of a letter.

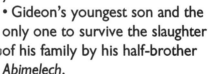

**Jotham** (**joth**-uhm)
• Son of *Uzziah* and eleventh king of Judah after his father. His mother's name was Jerusha. Jotham's story is told in 2 Chronicles 27:1-9. He reigned 16 years. *2 Kings 15:32* *2 Chronicles 26:21*

• Gideon's youngest son and the only one to survive the slaughter of his family by his half-brother *Abimelech*. *Judges 9:21*
• A descendant of Caleb mentioned in the genealogies of First Chronicles. *1 Chronicles 2:46-47*

**Jozabad** (**joz**-uh-bad)
• An Israelite warrior from the tribe of Benjamin who defected to David at *Ziklag*; from the town of Gederah. *1 Chronicles 12:4*

*1 Chronicles 12:20*

• Two commanders in Saul's army who defected to David along with several others from the tribe of *Manasseh*. Both became officers in David's army.

*2 Chronicles 31:11-13*

• A temple supervisor appointed by Hezekiah.

*2 Chronicles 35:9*

• A Levite leader who gave generously to the Levites during Josiah's reforms.

*Leviticus 25:13, 33*
*Numbers 36:4*

**Jubilee (joo-buh-lee)**

A special custom that the Israelites were supposed to observe every 50 years. The Year of Jubilee was to be a time of *Sabbath*, or rest, from debt, bondage, and work. The people were to forgive all debts, release all slaves, return property to its original owners, and stop planting or harvesting any crops that year. The Year of Jubilee is explained in Leviticus 25:8-55, but the Bible records no examples of it ever being observed.

**Judah (joo-duh)**

*Genesis 29:31-35*
*Genesis 37:26*
*Hebrews 7:14*

• Jacob's fourth son and the tribe of Israel named after him. *Leah* was his mother.

*Joel 3:18*
*Matthew 2:6*

• The land allotted to the tribe of Judah.

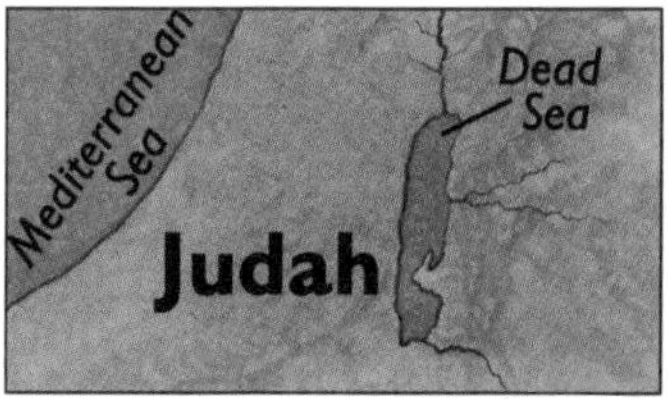

• The southern kingdom of Israel that was formed after the split between *Rehoboam* and Jeroboam I. The southern kingdom became known as Judah because only Judah and Benjamin stayed loyal to Rehoboam, and Judah was the larger of the two tribes. This kingdom had 19 kings and one queen.
See also *kings of Judah; prophets to Judah*

*1 Kings 15:9*
*Hebrews 8:8*

J

**Judaism** (**joo**-dee-iz-uhm)
The religion of the Jews. Judaism is belief in the God of the Old Testament and in the Law of Moses as the only rule of life.

Judaism does not recognize Jesus as the Messiah.

*Acts 13:43*
*Galatians 1:13-14*

**judaizer** (**joo**-dee-ize-ur)
A person who insists that only Jews can become Christians. Paul wrote the book of Galatians to explain that the judaizers were wrong.

See also *Cornelius; Judas Barsabbas*

*Galatians 1:13-17*

**Judas Barsabbas** (**joo**-duhss bar-**sab**-buhss)
A Christian prophet and leader in the early church. Judas Barsabbas went with Silas, Paul, and Barnabas to Antioch to deliver the news that Gentile Christians would not be required to become Jews.

*Acts 15:22*

J

*Mark 14:10*
*Luke 22:47*
*John 6:71*

**Judas Iscariot** (**joo**-duhss is-**kair**-ee-uht)

The disciple who betrayed Jesus. Judas was one of the *Twelve* and keeper of their money box. But his love of money made him steal from Jesus, criticize Mary for her gift of perfume, and take 30 pieces of silver for Jesus' arrest. Judas committed suicide after Jesus' trial. He was replaced by *Matthias*.

*Jude 1:1*

**Jude** (**jood**)

Half-brother of Jesus and author of the *book of Jude*. Jude is short for Judas, but he is not the same as Judas Iscariot. We know nothing about Jude except that he, like his brother *James*, did not believe that Jesus was the Christ until after his ascension.

*Jude 1:1*

**Jude, book of** (**jood, buk** uhv)

Twenty-sixth book of the New Testament and eighth of the *general letters*. This letter was written by Jude to all Christians everywhere. It urges God's people to watch out for false teachers.

**Judea** (joo-**dee**-uh)
The Greek word for Judah used by people of the Roman Empire in New Testament times.

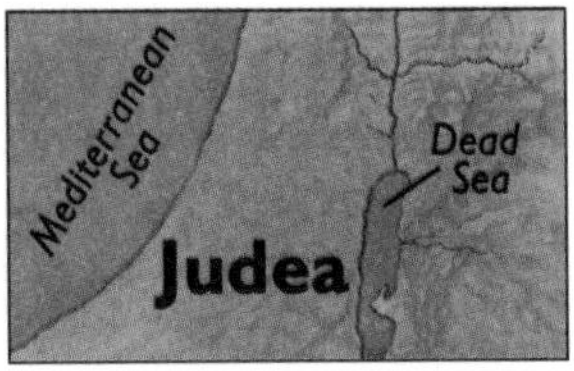


*Matthew 2:5, 6*
*2 Corinthians 1:16*

**Judean** (joo-**dee**-uhn)
Adjective: In Judea; from Judea; of Judea.

*1 Chronicles 4:18*
*John 3:22*

**judge, judges (juhj, juhj**-ez)
• A leader of Israel after the time of Joshua and before the time of the kings. Judges were servants of God who led the people and fought against Israel's enemies. Their deeds are recorded in the *book of Judges*.

*Judges 2:18*

• A person who hears disputes and rules on them. Moses acted as judge during the Exodus. The Bible describes God as the only perfect judge.

*Exodus 18:13-14*

• To pass judgment; to rule on whether something is right or wrong; to find a person guilty or not guilty.

*1 Kings 8:32*

• To condemn; to find fault; to find guilty.

*1 Corinthians 5:12*

**Judges, book of**
(**juhj**-iz, **buk** uhv)
Seventh book of the Old Testament and second of the *books of history*. The book of Judges tells about the nation of Israel during the

*Judges 2:16*

time when the judges ruled, including Gideon and Samson. This was a dark and violent time because "the people did whatever seemed right in their own eyes" (21:25).

**judgment** (**juhj**-ment)

Ezekiel 38:22
Revelation 14:7

• Punishment for sin. Many books of prophecy use the word judgment in this sense. There will be a final judgment on the *last day*.

Deuteronomy 1:17
Proverbs 3:21

• Wisdom; sense; ability to see right from wrong. The Proverbs use the word judgment in this sense.

See also *foolish; last day; wise*

Romans 14:10
2 Corinthians 5:10

**judgment seat, judgment seat of Christ** (juhj-ment **seet** uhv **kriste**)

A reference to the last day, when all people will stand before Christ to be judged by him.

**judgment, last** (**juhj**-ment, **last**)

See *last day*

See also *judgment*

Acts 27:1, 3

**Julius** (**joo**-lee-uhss)

The *centurion* in charge of Paul and several others during the shipwreck on Malta.

Romans 4:25
Romans 5:16-18

**justification** (**juhst**-i-fi-**kay**-shuhn)

The Christian doctrine that God can treat a person as just; that God can find a person not guilty, and therefore accept the person as perfect and sinless, even though he or she is not. This is how a person can be *saved* or *born again*. The book of Romans explains that a person's justification comes by faith in Christ.

See also *justified*

**justified (juhst-i-fide)**
Declared or treated as just, perfect, and sinless. The books of Romans and Galatians explain that people are justified by faith in Christ. A person who places his or her *faith* in Christ is justified by God. As a result, that person becomes a Christian. God promises that all who are justified by Christ will escape *judgment* on the *last day*.
See also *justification*

*Romans 3:24-28*
*Galatians 2:17*

**Justus (juhst-uhss)**

- A Jewish Christian also known as Jesus who helped Paul in his ministry. *Colossians 4:11*
- *Titius Justus* *Acts 18:7*
- *Joseph* called Barsabbas. *Acts 1:23*

**Juttah (juh-tuh)**
A *fortified city* eight kilometers south of Hebron in the hill country of Judah. Juttah was assigned to the priests.

*Joshua 21:13-16*

Joshua 10:41
2 Samuel 24:6

**Kadesh** (**kay**-desh)
- *Kadesh Barnea*
- An ancient city of the *Hittites* in the far north of Lebanon on the Orontes River, probably just a ruin or landmark by David's day.

Joshua 14:6-7

**Kadesh Barnea** (**kay**-desh bar-**nee**-uh)
An important city and area on the south side of the *Desert of Zin* and the north side of Paran. The Israelites were camped at Kadesh Barnea when they sent 12 men to spy out the land of Canaan. Its exact location is unknown.

Ezra 3:9
Nehemiah 9:4

**Kadmiel** (**kad**-mee-uhl)
A leader among those who helped *Zerubbabel* rebuild the temple in Jerusalem after the Exile.

Genesis 15:18-20

**Kadmonites** (**kad**-muhn-ites)
Literally, "easterners," or "people of the east."

Ezekiel 1:1-3
Ezekiel 10:20-22

**Kebar** (**kee**-bar)
A river in Babylonia whose location is unknown. The prophet *Ezekiel* and some of the Jewish *exiles* lived by the Kebar River.

**Kedar** (**kee**-dar)
Ishmael's second son and the tribe of Arabians descended from him; Abraham's grandson. *Isaiah* prophesied against the people of Kedar.
Genesis 25:13
Isaiah 21:16

**Kedesh** (**kee**-desh)
• A Canaanite city in the land allotted to Naphtali and one of the *cities of refuge*; also called "Kedesh in Naphtali." Kedesh was northwest of Lake Huleh in Galilee. Judges 4:6
• A *levitical city* in the land allotted to Issachar. Its exact location is unknown. 1 Chronicles 6:72
• A town in the south of Judah near Edom; possibly *Kadesh Barnea*. Joshua 15:20-23

**Kedorlaomer** (ked-or-**lay**-oh-mur)
King of *Elam* who led a force of four allies against the *cities of the plain* when Lot was a resident of Sodom. Kedorlaomer plundered Sodom and carried off Lot, then was killed by Abram's rescue force.
Genesis 14:8-17

**Keilah** (kuh-**eye**-luh)
A *fortified city* in the lowlands of Judah about 14 kilometers northwest of Hebron.
1 Samuel 23:10

**Kemuel** (**kem**-yoo-el)
• The family leader of *Ephraim* chosen by God to help divide up the land after the conquest of Canaan. Numbers 34:24
• Son of Nahor and Milcah and therefore Abraham's nephew; father of *Aram*. Genesis 22:20-21

K

1 Chronicles 27:17

• Father of the Levite commander *Hashabiah* during the time of David.

Numbers 32:42

**Kenath** (**kee**-nath)

A city in the northern portion of Manasseh east of the Jordan River. Kenath was captured by *Nobah*.

K

**Kenaz** (**kee**-naz)

Genesis 36:15

• Grandson of Esau and father of the *Kenizzite* clan; son of Eliphaz.

Joshua 15:17

• Caleb's brother and father of *Othniel* and Seraiah.

1 Chronicles 4:15

• *Caleb's* grandson; son of Elah.

Genesis 15:18-19

**Kenites** (**ken**-ites)

A tribe of people that settled in the Negev across from Midian. God promised their land to *Abram*.

Genesis 15:18-19
Genesis 36:15

**Kenizzites** (**ken**-i-zites)

People who traced their roots to Esau's grandson *Kenaz;* the Kenizzite clan.

2 Samuel 20:23
Ezekiel 25:16

**Kerethites** (**kair**-i-thites)

A group of people that settled in the *Negev* across from the Philistines. The Kerethites were among those who served as David's bodyguards under *Benaiah's* command.

See also *Pelethites*

**Keturah** (kuh-**too**-ruh)

Abraham's second wife and the mother of *Zimran*, *Jokshan*, *Medan*, *Midian*, *Ishbak*, and *Shuah*.

*Genesis 25:1-4*
*1 Chronicles 1:32-33*

**Kibroth Hattaavah** (**kib**-roth hah-**tay**-uh-vuh)

A place one day's journey from the *Desert of Sinai*, northeast of it. The Israelites stopped at Kibroth Hattaavah on their way to the promised land after receiving the Ten Commandments. Kibroth Hattaavah got its name from the disasters that befell the Israelites at that location. The name means "graves of craving."

*Numbers 11:34-35*
*Numbers 33:16-17*
*Deuteronomy 9:22*

**Kidron Valley** (**kid**-ruhn **val**-ee)

The valley directly east of Jerusalem's east wall; also called the Valley of Jehoshaphat. The Kidron Valley is dry most of the year; during the rainy season it serves as a river bed.

*2 Kings 23:6*
*John 18:1*

**Kilion** (**kil**-ee-uhn)

One of *Naomi* and Elimelech's two sons; brother of Mahlon.

*Ruth 1:2*
*Ruth 4:9*

**king's highway** (**kingz hye**-way)

A trade route that cut through the territories of *Edom*, *Moab*, and *Ammon*. During the Exodus, the Israelites were denied permission to use the king's highway.

*Numbers 20:17*
*Numbers 21:22*

**King David** (**king day**-vid)

See *David*

K

**King Herod (king hair**-uhd)
See *Herod*

**King Saul (king sawl)**
See *Saul*

*Luke 7:28*
*1 Corinthians 4:20*

**Kingdom of God (king**-duhm uhv **god)**
Any place where God rules; the kingdom ruled by Jesus Christ. Both John the Baptist and Jesus preached that "the Kingdom of God is near" because Jesus came to rule in the hearts of his people. The Gospels of Mark, Luke, and John use this term, while Matthew uses *Kingdom of Heaven*.

*Matthew 5:3*
*Matthew 19:14*

**Kingdom of Heaven (king**-duhm uhv **hev**-en)
Another term for *Kingdom of God*. The Gospel of Matthew uses Kingdom of Heaven instead of Kingdom of God because it was written to Jews, and Jews revered God's name too highly to pronounce it. Matthew records that John the Baptist said, "Turn from your sins and turn to God, because the Kingdom of Heaven is near."

*Numbers 31:8*
*1 Kings 10:23*
*1 Timothy 6:13-15*

**kings (kingz)**
Rulers of specific territories or land, usually based in a *fortified city*. Most ancient cities and nations were ruled by kings. Power usually

passed from father to firstborn son, though there were many exceptions to this. The elders of Israel rejected the rule of the *judges* because they wanted a king.

See also *First Kings; Second Kings*

**kings of Israel** (**kingz** uhv **iz**-ree-uhl)

*1 Kings 1:43*

*2 Chronicles 21:6*

• Kings of the united kingdom in order of their rule: Saul, David, Solomon.

• Kings of the northern kingdom in order of their rule: Jeroboam I, Nadab, Baasha, Elah, Zimri, Omri, Ahab, Ahaziah, Jehoram (Joram), Jehu, Jehoahaz, Joash, Jeroboam II, Zechariah, Shallum, Menahem, Pekahiah, Pekah, Hoshea.

**kings of Judah** (**kingz** uhv **joo**-duh)

*1 Kings 22:45*
*1 Chronicles 3: 10-16*

Kings of the southern kingdom in order of their rule: Rehoboam, Abijah, Asa, Jehoshaphat, Joram, Jehoahaz (Ahaziah), Athaliah (queen), Joash, Amaziah, Uzziah, Jotham, Ahaz, Hezekiah, Manasseh, Amon, Josiah, Jehoahaz, Jehoiakim, Jehoiachin, Zedekiah.

**Kings, First** (**kingz**, **furst**)

*1 Kings 2:1-4*

Eleventh book of the Old Testament and sixth of the books of history. This book tells about Solomon's reign as king over Israel, the revolt of the northern tribes, and the first kings of Israel and kings of Judah. It tells how God's people turned away from God during this time, and how God used the prophet Elijah. No one knows who wrote the book.

See also *Second Kings*

*2 Kings 17:13-14*

**Kings, Second** (**kingz, sek**-uhnd)

Twelfth book of the Old Testament and seventh of the books of history. Second Kings tells about the nation of Israel through most of its history under the kings of Israel and the kings of Judah. It records the destruction of the northern kingdom of Israel and the Exile of Judah to Babylonia. No one knows who wrote it.

See also *First Kings*

**Kinnereth** (**kin**-uh-reth)

*Joshua 19:31-35*

• A fortified Canaanite city in the land allotted to *Naphtali*. Kinnereth was on the northwest shore of the Sea of Galilee.

*Joshua 12:3*

• An older name for the *Sea of Galilee*. This name was used because of the size and importance of the fortified city of Kinnereth.

*Ruth 3:2*
*Proverbs 7:4*

**kinsman** (**kinz**-muhn)

A relative or family member. The relation can be close, as in an immediate family member, or distant, as in a *clan* member.

*Ruth 2:20*
*Ruth 4:14*

**kinsman-redeemer** (**kinz**-muhn ree-**dee**-mur)

A person who steps forward to take care of a needy relative or family member. *Boaz* became

*Ruth's* kinsman-redeemer when he realized that she was a distant relative with no husband and no means to support herself.

**Kir-hareseth** (**kihr-har**-uh-seth)
A fortified city of *Moab* south of Ar; also known as Kir of Moab. Kir Hareseth is featured in the prophesies of Isaiah and Jeremiah. Its most likely location is Kerak, 18 kilometers east of the Dead Sea, site of a Crusader castle.

*2 Kings 3:25*
*Isaiah 16:11*

**Kiriath-arba** (**kihr**-ee-ath-**ar**-buh)
"City of four," an older name for *Hebron*. Abraham buried his wife Sarah there.

*Genesis 23:2*

**Kiriath-jearim** (**kihr**-ee-ath-**jee**-uh-rim)
A Canaanite town allotted to Judah on the border between Judah and Benjamin; also called Kiriath-baal. Kiriath-jearim became famous for housing the Ark of the Covenant after the Philistines returned it. The Ark stayed in *Eleazar's* keeping for 20 years before David finally brought it back to Jerusalem.

*Joshua 15:60*
*1 Samuel 6:21*
*1 Samuel 7:7*

**Kish** (**kish**)
- King *Saul's* father.
- *Mordecai's* great-grandfather.
- Several others mentioned only briefly.

*1 Samuel 9:3*
*1 Samuel 10:11*
*Esther 2:5*

K

**Kishon (kish-on)**

Judges 4:7 • A river that flows from the hills of northern Samaria to the Mediterranean Sea just north of *Mount Carmel*; also called "Megiddo's springs" and "the brook east of Jokneam."

1 Kings 18:40 • The "Kishon Valley" through which the Kishon River flows.

The Kishon Valley and River are featured in the stories of *Deborah* and *Elijah*.

**Kislev (kiss-lev)**

Nehemiah 1:1 The ninth *month* of the Israelite year, overlapping November and December.

**kiss (kiss)**

Romans 16:16 • A method of greeting that was and is very common among many peoples of the near east.

Song of Songs 1:2 • A show of affection or love between two family members.

**Kittim (kit-im)**

Genesis 10:4 • One of *Javan's* sons and the people descended from him.

Jeremiah 2:10 • The Hebrew name for the island of *Cyprus*, where the people of Kittim settled.

**Kohath (koh-hath)**

1 Chronicles 6:22 One of *Levi's* sons and the clan named after him; brother of *Gershon* and *Merari*; father of the *Kohathites*.

**Kohathites** (koh-hath-ites)
The *clan* of Kohath; people who traced their roots to *Kohath*. The Kohathites were one of three divisions of *Levites*. Their job was to look after the Ark of the Covenant and all the pieces of furniture related to it.
See also *Gershonites; Merarites*

*Numbers 4:18*

**kor** (**kor**)
See *homer*

**Korah's rebellion** (**kor**-uhz ri-**bel**-yuhn)
The uprising against Moses led by *Korah* during the *Exodus*. Korah, *Dathan*, *Abiram*, and 250

other Israelite leaders said that Moses was wrong to set aside priests for special duties. They said that it was not fair for Aaron and his clan to get "special treatment" and be the only ones allowed to approach God at the tabernacle, burn incense, and offer sacrifices. Korah and all his supporters died after ignoring God's warning.

*Numbers 26:10*
*Jude 1:11*

**Korah** (**kor**-uh)
• Levite who led a rebellion against the priesthood of Israel during the *Exodus*; son of Izhar; grandson of Kohath; great-grandson of Levi.

*Numbers 16:1; 26:10*

K

Genesis 36:5
- One of Esau and Oholibamah's sons.

Genesis 36:15-16
- A clan chief descended from Esau.

1 Chronicles 2: 42-43
- One of Caleb's great-grandsons.

See also *Korah's rebellion*

1 Chronicles 9:19
**Korahites** (**kor**-uh-hites)
People who traced their roots to *Korah*; the clan of Korah.

Luke 10:13
**Korazin** (**kor**-uh-zin)
A city singled out by Jesus for its unbelief. Korazin was four kilometers north of *Capernaum*.

See also *Bethsaida*

1 Kings 10:28
**Kue** (**koo**-uh)
One of the cities that supplied Solomon with horses, probably *Cilicia*.

**Laban** (**lay**-buhn)

• Son of Bethuel and descendant of Nahor who played a big part in Jacob's life during the time of the *patriarchs*. Laban was Jacob's uncle, but also Rebekah's father and therefore Jacob's father-in-law. Jacob fled to Laban's home in Haran after Esau vowed to kill him. *Genesis 28:2* *Genesis 46:25*

• A place in Moab near where Moses gave final instructions to the Israelites. Its exact location is unknown. *Deuteronomy 1:1*

**Lachish** (**lay**-kish) *Joshua 10:23, 34-35* *2 Chronicles 32:9* *Isaiah 36:2*

A large fortified city of Canaan defeated by Joshua and featured in the history of Judah's kings. Rehoboam rebuilt the fortress destroyed during the conquest of Canaan. Lachish was about 40 kilometers southwest of Jerusalem, a little more than halfway between Jerusalem and Gaza.

**Lahmi** (**lah**-mye) *1 Chronicles 20:5*

*Goliath's* brother, a Philistine. Lahmi was killed by Elhanan, one of David's mighty men.

**Laish** (**lay**-ish)

• A city at the base of Mount Hermon during the time of the judges; also called Dan and Leshem. Laish was the scene of the ruthless slaughter of innocent people described in Judges 18. *Judges 18:7, 14*

*1 Samuel 25:44*

• Father of *Palti*.

**Lake Huleh (lake hoo**-luh)

The lake north of the *Sea of Galilee*.

*Revelation 20:14*

**lake of fire (lake** uhv **fye**-ur)

The term for *hell* used in the book of Revelation; also called the "lake of burning sulfur" and the "second death"; *gehenna*. The *beast*, the *false prophet*, the devil, all demons, and all the wicked will be thrown into the lake of fire.

See *also last day*

*John 1:29*
*John 1:36*

**Lamb of God (lam** uhv **god)**

A name or title for Jesus. Just as the lambs were sacrificed as a substitute for people in Old Testament times, Jesus was our substitute.

See *also lamb*

**lamb, Lamb (lam)**

*Exodus 29:40-41*
*Ezra 6:20*
*1 Corinthians 5:7*

• A young *sheep*, one of the kinds of animals the Israelites were allowed to sacrifice for sin.

People who could not afford a lamb or goat were allowed to sacrifice a *dove* or *pigeon* instead.

*1 Peter 1:18-19*
*Revelation 5:12*

• A short form of *Lamb of God*.

See *also goat; offering*

**Lamech** (**lay**-mek)

• One of Cain's descendants and the first person ever to have two wives; son of Methushael.

Genesis 4:18-19
Genesis 5:25

• One of Seth's descendants and the father of *Noah*; son of Methuselah.

Genesis 5:28-31
1 Chronicles 1:1-3

L

**lament** (luh-**ment**)

• Noun: Sadness; a word, song, or expression of sadness.

2 Samuel 3:33
Ezekiel 27:2

• Verb: To wail, weep, or express sadness.

Isaiah 16:7
Ezekiel 24:16

See also *Lamentations, book of*

**Lamentations, book of**
(**lam**-en-**tay**-shuhnz, **buk** uhv)

Lamentations 2:8

Twenty-fifth book of the Old Testament and third of the *major prophets*. The prophet Jeremiah wrote Lamentations as a sequel to the *book of Jeremiah*. It records Jeremiah's great sadness over Judah's *Exile*, but also the promise of God's mercy. The book is famous for the verses, "The unfailing love of the LORD never ends! By his mercies we have been kept from complete destruction. Great is his faithfulness; his mercies begin afresh each day" (3:22-23).

**lamp** (lamp)

2 Kings 4:10
Psalm 119:105
Matthew 6:22

A bowl made of pottery or metal and shaped to hold a wick at the rim. Such a lamp held olive oil for the fuel; wicks would be made of *flax*. Some lamps had more than one wick holder.

Exodus 25:31
Numbers 8:2
Hebrews 9:2

**lampstand** (**lamp**-stand)
A post or pole that held a *lamp* up off the floor. God directed the people of Israel to make several golden lampstands for the tabernacle.



**land of Canaan** (**land** uhv **kay**-nuhn)
See *Canaan*

**land of promise** (**land** uhv **pro**-miss)
See *Promised Land*

Colossians 4:15
Revelation 3:14

**Laodicea** (**lay**-oh-di-**see**-uh)
A city in the Roman province of Asia and one of the stops on Paul's third missionary journey. Paul started a church in Laodicea. Jesus addressed one of the letters in the book of Revelation to this church. The city was only 18 kilometers west of *Colosse*.

Colossians 4:16

**Laodiceans** (**lay**-oh-di-**see**-uhnz)
People who lived in the city of *Laodicea*.

Galatians 5:19
Ephesians 4:19
1 Peter 4:3

**lasciviousness** (luh-**siv**-ee-uhss-ness)
Doing whatever your body feels like doing without trying to control the desire; sensual indulgence; sexual excess.

**last day** (**last day**)

A time still in the future when God will punish all sin once and for all. This day will come shortly after the return of Christ. God will judge all people who ever lived. Those who belong to Christ will be accepted into *heaven*. All others will be condemned to the *lake of fire*.

John 6:39-40, 44, 54
John 11:24
John 12:48

**last judgment** (**last juhj**-ment)

See *last day*
See also *judgment*

**Last Supper, the** (**last suhp**-ur, the)

The time when Jesus ate with his disciples for the last time. During the Last Supper, Jesus gave some final instructions, Judas left to betray Jesus, and Jesus served the first *Lord's Supper*. This important event is recorded in all four Gospels.

See also *Passover*

Matthew 26:18-23
Luke 22:17-20
Mark 14:14-16
John 13:1-5

**laver** (**lay**-vur)

A bronze basin on a stand made for the tabernacle so that priests could wash before performing their duties. Solomon ordered ten lavers made for the temple.

1 Kings 7:38
Jeremiah 52:19

**law of Moses, Law of Moses** (**law** uhv **moh**-zess)
All of the laws given to the Israelites through Moses, the most important of which were the *Ten Commandments*.

*Joshua 23:6*
*John 7:23*

**law, Law** (**law**)
• The *Law of Moses*; all of the laws given to the Israelites through Moses. *Joshua 8:30-32; Luke 24:44*
• The *Ten Commandments*. *Exodus 24:12*
• Every command of God. *Mark 12:28; John 7:19*
• Any command or rule that tells people what they should or should not do. *Leviticus 24:22; John 7:51*

See also *commandment; oracle; ordinance; precept; statute*

**lawbreaker** (**law**-bray-kur)
A person who breaks the law, usually God's *law*; a person who makes a habit of *lawlessness*.

*Romans 2:27*
*Galatians 2:18*
*James 2:11*

**lawlessness** (**law**-less-ness)
Disregard for the God's will; hostility toward any of God's rules for living.
See also *law; lawbreaker*

*2 Thessalonians 2:3, 7*
*1 John 3:4*

**laying on of hands** (**lay**-ing **on** uhv **handz**)
A special show of *blessing*, support, or approval.

*1 Timothy 5:22*
*Hebrews 6:2*

**Lazarus** (**laz**-ur-uhss)

- Mary and Martha's brother, the man Jesus raised back to life after a terrible illness. Lazarus was from Bethany. *John 11:1-5 John 12:9*
- The main person in Jesus' parable of The Rich Man and Lazarus. *Luke 16:20-24*

**Leah** (**lee**-uh)

Wife of Jacob and mother of Reuben, Simeon, Levi, Judah, Issachar, Zebulun, and Dinah; daughter of Laban. *Genesis 29:16-28 Genesis 35:23*

**leaven, leavened** (**lev**-en, **lev**-end)

- Noun: Fermented bran, barley, or bread flour. Leaven was added to bread dough to make it rise. *Exodus 13:6-7 Judges 6:20-21 Matthew 26:17*
- Verb: To add fermented bran, barley, or bread dough to make a piece of bread dough rise.

The Passover feast features *unleavened bread* because leaven takes time to make the bread rise, and the Israelites had to leave Egypt in great haste. Leaven also became a symbol for evil and for contamination.

**Lebanon** (**leb**-uh-non)

A range of mountains to the north of Palestine between the Mediterranean coast and the land of *Aram* east of those mountains. Lebanon is famous for its cedar forests, from which Solomon bought a lot of timber for construction of the temple. The name means "white" and takes its name from the snow that caps the *Deuteronomy 1:7 1 Kings 5:6 Isaiah 35:2* mountains six months of the year, and from the limestone hills. Famous cities of Lebanon include Sidon and Tyre.

*1 Kings 8:65*
*Ezekiel 48:1*

**Lebo-hamath** (**lee**-boh-**hay**-muhth)

"The entrance of *Hamath*." Lebo Hamath may have been a town or small city on the outskirts of Hamath.

L

*Numbers 11:5*

**leeks** (**leeks**)

An herb used for flavoring foods. Leeks have a flavor like onions, only stronger. They were grown and eaten in Egypt and Palestine.

*Mark 5:7-9*
*Luke 8:30*

**legion** (**lee**-juhn)

A regiment of six thousand men in the Roman army. Each legion had sixty centuries of one hundred men, each commanded by a *centurion*. In the Gospels, the term is sometimes used for very large numbers of angels or demons because of their power.

*Judges 15:9, 14, 19*

**Lehi** (**lee**-hye)
See *Ramath Lehi*

*Proverbs 31:1, 4*

**Lemuel** (**lem**-yoo-uhl)

Author of Proverbs 31:1-9. Lemuel was a king, but we know nothing else for sure about him. He wrote that he learned his proverbs from his mother.

**leper** (**lep**-ur)

A person who has *leprosy*. Some of the Bible's most famous stories feature lepers. Miriam, Naaman, and Uzziah all had it. Jesus healed many lepers. The law considered lepers *unclean* and required them to live in isolation.

*Mark 14:3*

**leprosy** (**lep**-ruh-see)

A term used for several different kinds of serious diseases that affected the skin and had no cure. The laws of Leviticus 13 include rules for dealing with leprosy. A person with leprosy had to stay away from others.

*Numbers 12:10*
*2 Chronicles 26:21*
*Luke 5:12-13*

**lethek** (**leh**-thek)

A dry measure found only in Hosea 3:2; its exact meaning is unknown.

*Hosea 3:2*

**letter** (**let**-ur)

A message from one person to another or to a group of other people. The Bible contains many letters. Several *books of history* contain important letters. But the most famous letters of all are the New Testament books of Romans, First Corinthians, Second Corinthians, Galatians, Ephesians, Philippians, Colossians, First Thessalonians,

*2 Samuel 11:14*
*Jeremiah 29:1*
*2 Peter 3:1*

Second Thessalonians, First Timothy, Second Timothy, Titus, Philemon, Hebrews, James, First Peter, Second Peter, First John, Second John, Third John, and Jude. Most New Testament letters were written to specific churches or people. But the letters also record the *apostles'* instructions to all Christians everywhere. Paul told the Colossian Christians to be sure to exchange letters with the Laodicean Christians. The word *epistle* is another word for letter.

**Levi** (**lee**-vye)

*Genesis 29:34*
*Deuternomony 21:5*
*Hebrews 7:5*

• Son of Jacob and Leah and the tribe of Israel named after him. We know little about Levi except for his and Simeon's attack on *Shechem*. The tribe of Levi was the only one not to receive an inheritance of land after the conquest of Canaan.

• Another name for *Matthew*.

See also *Levites; levitical city*

**leviathan** (le-**vye**-uh-thuhn)

*Job 41:1*
*Psalm 74:14; 104:26*
*Isaiah 27:1*

A large animal that lives in or near water named several times in the Bible. No one knows for sure what leviathan was, but a long description of it appears in Job 41.

**Levite, Levites** (**lee**-vite, **lee**-vytes)
A descendant of Levi and member of that tribe. God gave the Levites special duties in the tabernacle and temple worship instead of an inheritance of land. They worked together with the priests. The Levites also administered the six *cities of refuge*.
See also *levitical city*

*Exodus 4:14*
*2 Chronicles 20:14*
*Acts 4:36*

**levitical** (le-**vit**-i-kuhl)
Related to the *Levites*; having to do with the Levites.

*Leviticus 25:32*
*1 Chronicles 15:12*
*Hebrews 7:11*

**levitical city** (le-**vit**-i-kuhl **si**-tee)
Any one of the cities allotted to the tribe of Levi. Eleven of the tribes of Israel received large areas of land, each area having dozens or even hundreds of cities, towns, and villages. This land was the inheritance each tribe got as God's chosen people. The Levites, however, did not get any land. Their inheritance was to oversee the tabernacle and the temple, the worship of God, and many other priestly duties. Because they still needed a place to live, God directed Joshua to set aside cities for the Levites in each tribe's territory. These became the levitical cities.

*Leviticus 25:32*

**Leviticus, book of** (le-**vit**-i-kuhss, **buk** uhv)
Third book of the Old Testament and third of the *books of Law*. Moses wrote this book to

*Leviticus 17:5*

record God's instructions to the priests and Levites. Leviticus explains all the *offerings*.

**Libnah (lib**-nuh)

Joshua 10:29
2 Kings 8:22

• A Canaanite city in the lowlands of Judah that Joshua conquered. Libnah became a *levitical city*. Its exact location is unknown.

Numbers 33:20-21

• One of the places the Israelites stopped during the Exodus. Its exact location is unknown.

**Libya (lib**-ee-uh)

Ezekiel 30:5
Nahum 3:9
Acts 2:10

The land and people to the west of Egypt throughout Bible times. *Simon of Cyrene* was from Libya.

**licentiousness** (lye-**sen**-shuss-ness)

Another word for *lasciviousness*.

**Life, Book of (life, buk** uhv)

See *book of life*

**Life, Tree of (life, tree** uhv)

See *tree of life*

**lifeblood (life**-bluhd)

Genesis 9:4-5
Jeremiah 2:34

Blood.

**lintel (lin**-tuhl)

Exodus 12:21-23

A beam of wood across the top of a doorway

that holds up the wall above the doorway. The angel of death that swept through Egypt on the eve of the Exodus passed over every home that

had the blood of the *Passover lamb* on the lintel and doorposts.
See also *Passover*

**Linus (lye-**nuhss)

A Christian who sent greetings to Timothy in the conclusion of Paul's second letter to Timothy. We know nothing else about him.

*2 Timothy 4:21*

**living creature**
(**liv**-ing **kree**-chur)

An animal, insect, or any other kind of living thing that is neither a plant nor a human being. God gave Adam and Eve charge of all living creatures. Ezekiel used this term to describe "four living beings" he saw in a vision of heaven.

*Genesis 1:24-28*
*Ezekiel 10:15*
*Revelation 4:6*

**locust (loh**-kust)

A leaping species of grasshopper very common in the middle east. The *plagues of Egypt* and the prophecies of *Joel* feature locusts.

*Exodus 10:19*
*Joel 2:25*

**log (loge)**

A liquid measure equal to about three-tenths of a liter, or one-third of a quart; one-twelfth of a *hin*.

*Leviticus 14:15, 21, 24*

Job 12:18

**loincloth** (**loin**-kloth)
A short piece of clothing worn around the *loins*.

**loins** (**loinz**)
Leviticus 3:14-15
Job 40:16
• The midsection of the body; the part of the body between the ribs and the thighs.
2 Kings 4:29
• Clothing that hangs down below the waist. The old phrase "gird up your loins" means "pick up your skirt" or "get ready to run."

L

2 Timothy 1:5

**Lois** (**loh**-iss)
Timothy's grandmother, noted for her Christian faith.

Ecclesiastes 7:8
Galatians 5:22

**longsuffering** (long-**suhf**-ur-ing)
An older word for patience.

Revelation 1:10

**Lord's Day, the** (**lordz day**, the)
The first day of the week, Sunday. The term is found only once in Scripture.

Luke 11:2-4

**Lord's Prayer, the** (**lordz prair**, the)

The prayer of Jesus that serves as a pattern for our own prayer. Jesus taught this prayer to his disciples when they asked him to teach them how to pray.

**Lord's Supper, the (lordz suhp**-ur, the)
A ceremony in which Christians meet to remember the Lord's death and payment for their sins; also called Communion. Jesus set the pattern for this important ceremony at the *Last Supper*.

*Luke 22:13-23*

**LORD (lord)**
English word for *Yahweh*. Most Bibles use the small capital letters to distinguish this word from *Lord*.

*Genesis 2:4-5*
*Psalm 72:18*

**LORD of hosts (lord** uhv **hohsts)**
"God who is Lord of all," or LORD Almighty, a name for God.

*1 Samuel 1:11*
*Psalm 84:3*

**Lord Sabaoth (lord sab**-ay-oth)
An older term for *LORD of hosts*.

**lord, Lord (lord)**
English word for the Hebrew "adonai" and the Greek "kurios"; ruler, king, or master. The word often refers to *God*, but people also addressed kings as "lord" or "my lord," and those in authority as "sir" or "master."
See also *LORD*

*Psalm 73:20*
*Mark 12:29-30*

**Lot (lot)**
Son of Abram's brother Haran and therefore Abram's nephew. Lot went with his father and Abram when they left Ur to set out for Canaan.

*Genesis 11:27-31*
*Genesis 19:15*
*Luke 17:28*

Lot settled among the *cities of the plain*. He is famous for being rescued from Sodom by angels.

*Leviticus 16:8*
*John 19:23-24*

**lot, lots (lot, lots)**
Any object used to *cast lots*.

*Jude 1:12*

**love feast (luhv feest)**
A meal shared by Christians for the purpose of fellowship.

*Psalm 25:6*
*Isaiah 63:7*

**lovingkindness (luhv-ing-kined-ness)**
An older word for love or unfailing love.

*Isaiah 14:12*

**Lucifer (loo-si-fur)**
An older word for *morning star*.

**Lucius (loo-shuhss)**

*Acts 13:1*

• Jewish Christian and prophet at Antioch during Paul's first missionary journey. Lucius was from *Cyrene*.

*Romans 16:21*

• One of those who sent greetings to the Roman Christians at the conclusion of Paul's letter to the Romans. He also was a Jewish Christian.

*Genesis 10:22*

**Lud (luhd)**
One of Shem's sons.

*Genesis 10:13*

**Ludites (lood-ites)**
People who traced their roots to *Lud*.

**Luke** (**luke**)
Gentile Christian who wrote the *Gospel of Luke* and the *book of Acts*. Luke traveled with the apostle Paul on his first and third missionary journeys, and on his journey to Rome. Paul referred to him as "Dear Doctor Luke."

*Colossians 4:14*
*2 Timothy 4:11*
*Philemon 1:24*

**Luke, Gospel of** (**luke, gos**-puhl uhv)
Third book of the New Testament and third of the *Gospels*. The Gospel of Luke often refers to Jesus as the Son of Man and has more detail about the birth of Jesus than any other Gospel. It also has a large number of Jesus' parables. It was written by the Gentile Christian Luke to give a complete and accurate account of Jesus' life (1:1-4).

*Luke 1:1-4*

**lust of the eyes** (**luhst** uhv the **eyez**)
Craving for things that a person sees.

*1 John 2:16*

**lust of the flesh** (**luhst** uhv the **flesh**)
Craving for things that a person feels.

*1 John 2:16*

**Lycaonia** (**lik**-ay-**oh**-nee-uh)
A region in the Roman province of *Galatia* in New Testament times.

*Acts 14:5-6*

**Lycaonian** (**lik**-ay-**oh**-nee-uhn)
Any person who lived in *Lycaonia*.

*Acts 14:6*

Acts 27:5

**Lycia (lish-yuh)**

Roman province directly south of *Pisidia* on the Mediterranean coast of Asia Minor. The apostle Paul passed through Lycia on his way to Rome.

**Lydia (lid-ee-uh)**

Acts 16:14

- A Jewish woman from *Thyatira* who believed in Christ during Paul's first missionary journey.

Jeremiah 46:9

- A nation mentioned with Put and Cush in the Old Testament whose identity is unknown.
- A country in western Asia Minor ruled by the Romans and made part of the Roman province of Asia. *Sardis* was its capital.

Psalm 57:8
Pslam 144:9

**lyre (lye-ur)**

A stringed instrument much like the harp only smaller. Lyres were common among the Israelites and are often mentioned in the Psalms.

**Lysias (liss-ee-uhss)**

*Claudius Lysias*

Acts 16:1

**Lystra (lye-struh)**

A small town in *Lycaonia* and one of Paul's stops on all three missionary journeys. *Timothy* was from Lystra.

**Maacah** (**may**-uh-kuh)

A common name among the Israelites:

- Abraham's nephew; son of Nahor and *Reumah*. — *Genesis 22:23-24*
- David's wife and Absalom's mother; daughter of *Talmai*. — *2 Samuel 3:3*
- Absalom's daughter or granddaughter, who married King *Rehoboam*. She was queen mother to both *Abijah* and *Asa*, kings of Judah. — *2 Chronicles 11: 18-20*
- Father of *Achish*. — *1 Kings 2:39*
- Caleb's *concubine*. — *1 Chronicles 2:48*
- Several other people mentioned only by name. — *1 Chronicles 7:15*
- A region in the territory allotted to Manasseh directly east and north of Lake Huleh. David conquered this region after he became king. — *Joshua 13:11*

**Maaseiah** (**may**-uh-**see**-uh)

A very common name among the Israelites:

- A temple *gatekeeper* appointed to sing and play music during the return of the Ark to Jerusalem. — *1 Chronicles 15: 15-18*

- A Levite who helped *Jehoiada* overthrow *Athaliah*. — *2 Chronicles 23:1*
- A son of King *Ahaz* slain in battle. — *2 Chronicles 28:1-7*
- Governor of Jerusalem during the reign of *Josiah* who helped repair the temple. — *2 Chronicles 34:8*

• Many others, most of them priests or Levites, mentioned only once or only in passing.

1 Chronicles 12: 8, 13

**Macbannai** (**mak**-ba-nye)
A skilled Israelite soldier from the tribe of Gad who defected to David at Ziklag; eleventh in command under *Ezer*.

M

Acts 16:9
1 Thessalonians 1:7
1 Timothy 1:3

**Macedonia** (**may**-suh-**doh**-nee-uh)

Roman province directly north of *Achaia*. Macedonia saw a lot of Christians come and go during Paul's missionary journeys. Major churches took root in the Macedonian cities of Berea, *Philippi*, and *Thessalonica* early in the New Testament era.

2 Corinthians 9:2, 4

**Macedonians** (**may**-suh-**doh**-nee-uhnz)
People who lived in *Macedonia*.

**Machir** (**may**-kur)
See *Makir*

Genesis 23:9, 17, 19
Genesis 49:30
Genesis 50:13

**Machpelah** (mok-**pel**-uh)

The area near Hebron where Abraham buried his wife Sarah. Abraham bought the burial place from a local Hittite named Ephron for 400 pieces of silver. The story is told in Genesis 23.

**Madmannah** (**mad**-man-uh)

• A descendant of Caleb. *1 Chronicles 2:49*

• A Canaanite town in the south of the Negev near Edom; also called Beth-marcaboth. This town was allotted to Judah. *Joshua 15:21, 31*

**Madmen** (**mad**-men) *Jeremiah 48:2*

A town in the land of *Moab* mentioned in Jeremiah's prophesies against Moab. Madmen's exact location is unknown.



**Magdalene** (**mag**-duh-leen)

See *Mary Magdalene*

**Magdiel** (**mag**-dee-el) *Genesis 36:43*

Descendant of Esau and *Edomite* clan chief during the time of the *patriarchs*.

**magi, Magi** (**may**-jye) *Matthew 2:1, 7, 16*

The men "from eastern lands" who visited Jesus shortly after his birth and gave him gifts; also called wise men. We know little about these magi except that they came because of seeing a star that signaled to them the birth of the king of the Jews. The term magi usually referred to astrologers or magicians who interpreted dreams. It could also refer to magicians or sorcerers, like *Simon* the *sorcerer* and *Elymas*.

See also *magic; magician*

M

Ezekiel 13:18
Acts 8:11
Revelation 21:8

**magic** (**maj**-ik)
Use of supernatural forces or power to do miracles, affect events, or influence people; *sorcery*. Some of those who practiced magic got their power from demons. Others merely used trickery to give the appearance of power.

1 Samuel 28:7
Daniel 2:10, 27

**magician** (muh-**ji**-shun)
A person who practices *magic*. Kings often used magicians as advisors. Joseph and Daniel became famous for interpreting dreams that the royal magicians could not interpret. Moses' standoff with Pharaoh showed how God's power exceeded the magicians' power.

See also *sorcerer*

Luke 12:58

**magistrate** (**maj**-i-strate)
A ruler, administrator, judge, or other public official who has authority to judge disputes.

Ezekiel 38:2
Revelation 20:8

**Magog** (**may**-gog)
Land ruled by *Gog* and an enemy of Israel mentioned in the prophecies of Ezekiel. The prophesies say that Gog and his kingdom will be utterly destroyed. They may be related to the prophesies against *Gog and Magog* in the book of Revelation.

**Mahalalel** (muh-**hah**-luh-lel)

• One of those mentioned in the genealogy of Jesus; a descendant of David and ancestor of Jesus' earthly father Joseph; son of Kenan. — *Luke 3:23, 37*

• A resident of Jerusalem during the time of Nehemiah. — *Nehemiah 11:4*

**Mahalath** (muh-**hah**-luhth)

• A term that appears in the title of Psalms 53 and 88. Its meaning is unknown. — *Psalm 53 title*

• One of Esau's wives; daughter of Ishmael; sister of *Nebaioth*. — *Genesis 28:9*

• One of *Rehoboam's* wives; a granddaughter of David. — *2 Chronicles 11:18*

**Mahanaim** (**mah**-huh-**nay**-im)

*Genesis 32:2*
*1 Kings 2:8*

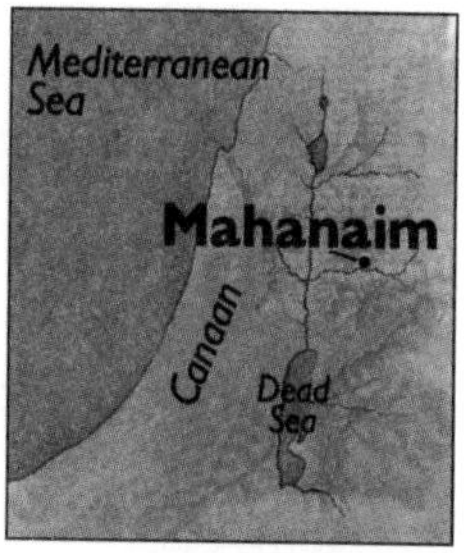


A fortified city in Gilead near Peniel. Jacob gave Mahanaim its name while on his way from Haran to meet Esau. After the conquest of Canaan, Mahanaim was made a levitical city in Gad. After Saul's death, *Ishbosheth* made it his capital. David hid in Mahanaim during Absalom's rebellion.

**Mahaneh-dan** (muh-**hah**-nuh-**dan**)

*Judges 13:25*
*Judges 18:12*

The place between the cities of *Eshtaol* and *Zorah* where the Spirit of the Lord first began to stir *Samson*. Mahaneh-dan was part of the territory of Dan.

**Mahli** (**mah**-lye)

Exodus 6:19

• Firstborn son of *Merari* and therefore one of Levi's grandsons. His family became one of the Levite clans.

1 Chronicles 23:23

• Son of *Mushi*, and therefore one of Levi's great-grandsons and nephew of the other Mahli.

**Mahlon** (**mah**-lon)

Ruth 1:2
Ruth 4:9

Ruth's first husband, an Israelite of Judah from Bethlehem. Mahlon was one of *Naomi* and *Elimelech's* two sons and brother of Kilion. He died while in Moab, leaving Ruth a widow.

See also *Boaz*

**Mahol** (**may**-hohl)

1 Kings 4:31

A person or a group known for being wise. Three Israelites (Heman, Calcol, and Darda) were called "sons of Mahol" and noted for their wisdom. But they were also called sons of Zerah. "Mahol" may have been something like a badge of honor.

**maiden** (**may**-den)

Proverbs 30:18-19
Isaiah 62:5

A young woman who is not married.

**maidservant** (**mayd**-sur-vuhnt)

A female slave. Kings and wealthy families of Old Testament times often had such servants. Most maidservants took care of the household and were treated much like family members. A maidservant was not the same as a *concubine*.

*Genesis 16:1-2*
*Judges 19:9*
*Proverbs 30:21-23*

M

**major prophets** (**may**-jur **prof**-uhtz)

Five books of prophecy in the Old Testament: Isaiah, Jeremiah, Lamentations, Ezekiel, and Daniel. They are called major prophets because they were written by prophets of great influence and importance.

See also *minor prophets*

*Isaiah 38:1*
*Jeremiah 1:5*

**make atonement** (**make** uh-**tohn**-ment)

To pay for sin. Sin is a violation of God's law.

The penalty for sin is death. Before Christ came, animal sacrifices paid for sins. That is why the Israelites sacrificed animals in the temple. God sent his perfect Son Jesus to die as a once-for-all sacrifice. His death paid for all sins once so that those who believe in him need not make atonement for their sins any longer.

*Exodus 29:36-37*
*Ezekiel 16:63*
*Hebrews 2:17*

**make restitution** (**make** ress-ti-**too**-shuhn)
See *restitution*

**Makir** (**may**-kur)

Genesis 50:23
Joshua 17:3

• Firstborn son of Manasseh and the clan named after him; father of *Gilead*. The Makir clan settled in Bashan and Gilead.

2 Samuel 9:2-5
2 Samuel 17:27-29

• Israelite who gave shelter to *Mephibosheth* after Saul's death; son of Ammiel. Makir also brought provisions to David at Mahanaim during Absalom's rebellion.

**Makirites** (**may**-kur-ites)

Numbers 32:40
Joshua 17:1

People who traced their roots to Manasseh's son *Makir*; the clan of Makir.

**Makkedah** (muh-**kee**-duh)

Joshua 10:16-21; 28-29
Joshua 12:16
Joshua 15:41

A town in the lowlands of central Palestine near *Lachish*. Makkedah was allotted to the tribe of Judah.

**Malachi** (**mal**-uh-kye)

Malachi 1:1

Last Israelite prophet to Judah and author of the *book of Malachi*. We know nothing else about Malachi except that he lived around 430 B.C., fifteen years after Nehemiah came to Jerusalem.

**Malachi, book of** (**mal**-uh-kye, **buk** uhv)

Malachi 1:1

Thirty-ninth book of the Old Testament and last of the *minor prophets*. The book of Malachi records prophecies to the people of Judah in Jerusalem after the Exile. It scolds God's people for their careless attitude toward worship and holy living.

**Malcam** (**mal**-kuhm)

- A *Benjamite* named in Saul's genealogy. *1 Chronicles 8:8-9*
- Another name for *Molech*. *Leviticus 18:21*

M

**Malchus** (**mawl**-kuhss) *John 18:10*

A servant of the high priest during the time of Jesus. Simon Peter cut off Malchus's ear in trying to defend Jesus from arrest.

**Malkishua** (**mal**-kye-**shoo**-uh) *1 Samuel 14:49* *1 Chronicles 10:2*

One of Saul's sons who died with Saul in the battle at Gilboa.

**Malkijah** (mal-**kye**-juh)

A very common name among the Israelites:

- Son of King *Zedekiah* and owner of the cistern that served as Jeremiah's prison for a while. *Jeremiah 38:1, 6*
- Many others mentioned only by name. *Nehemiah 3:31*

**Malluch** (**mal**-uhk)

A common name among the Israelites:

*Nehemiah 12:1-2* • One of the priests who returned to Judah with Zerubbabel.

*1 Chronicles 6:44* • Several others mentioned only by name.

*Acts 28:1*

**Malta** (**mawl**-tuh)

A small island in the Mediterranean Sea 93 kilometers south of Sicily. Paul was shipwrecked on Malta during his journey to Rome.

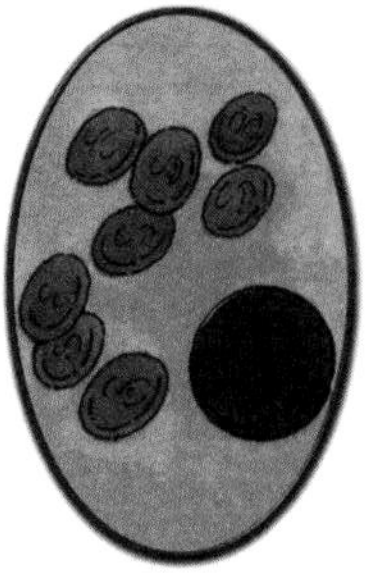

*Luke 16:13*

**mammon** (**mam**-uhn)

The Aramaic word for wealth or riches. Jesus used the word in his teaching about money.

**Mamre** (**mam**-ree)

*Genesis 18:1*
*Genesis 23:19* • An area just north of Hebron where Abraham and Isaac lived. Mamre was known for its oak trees.

*Genesis 14:13* • Amorite king who helped Abraham rescue Lot from Kedorlaomer.

*Acts 13:1*

**Manaen** (**man**-ay-en)

A Christian teacher and prophet in the church at Antioch before any of Paul's missionary journeys. Manaen taught alongside Barnabas, Simeon, Lucius, and Saul (Paul).

**Manahath** (**man**-uh-hath)

*1 Chronicles 8:6* • A place near Bethlehem during the time of the kings. Manahath is known mainly as the place to which some Benjamites were deported.

*Genesis 36:19, 23* • A descendant of Esau.

**Manahathites** (**man**-uh-hath-ites) — *1 Chronicles 2:52*

Descendants of Caleb who lived in *Manahath*.

**Manasseh** (muh-**nass**-uh)

• Joseph's firstborn son and the tribe of Israel named after him. *Asenath* was Manasseh's mother. — *Genesis 46:20*

• The land allotted to the tribe of Manasseh. — *Joshua 17:1-2*

• Son of *Hezekiah* and fourteenth king of Judah after his father. Manasseh was one of the most evil kings Judah ever had. He built many high places and shrines to *Ashtoreth* and *Molech*, and sacrificed children to Molech in the Valley of *Hinnom*. Manasseh repented in his later years and returned to God. — *2 Kings 20:21*

See also *kings of Judah; tribes of Israel*

**mandrake** (**man**-drake) — *Genesis 30:14-16*

An herb with egg-shaped leaves and forked roots common in *Palestine*. Some people of Old Testament times used the mandrake root as a mild drug.

**manger** (**mane**-jur) — *Proverbs 14:4*, *Luke 2:6-12*

A feeding trough for animals.

**manna** (**man**-uh) — *Exodus 16:31-32*, *Nehemiah 9:20*, *John 6:58*

One of the foods that God provided for the Israelites during the *Exodus*. Manna appeared with the dew every morning, six days of every week, for 40 years. It had a sweet taste and

M

could be used to make other foods. But the Israelites got tired of eating manna, and their complaints about it became a famous example of their ungrateful attitude. The word manna means "What is it?"

M

**Manoah** (muh-**noh**-ah)

Judges 13:2
Judges 16:31

*Samson's* father. Manoah is one of the few people ever to see and speak with an angel. He lived in Zorah and was a member of the tribe of Dan. His story is told in Judges 13–14.

**manservant** (**man**-sur-vuhnt)

Exodus 20:8-10
Deuteronomy 5:21

A male slave.

See also *maidservant*

**manslayer** (**man**-slay-ur)

Numbers 35:6-8, 10-11
Joshua 20:1-3

A person who has killed another person unintentionally or who is accused of murder. The term appears in passages that explain the *cities of refuge*.

**Maon** (**may**-on)

1 Samuel 23:24-25

• A hilltop town in south Judah about 11 kilometers south of Hebron. David and his men hid from Saul in Maon. It was also *Nabal's* hometown.

1 Chronicles 2:42-45

• A descendant of Caleb; son of Shammai.

**Maonites** (**may**-on-ites)
People who traced their roots to *Maon*; a group of people that oppressed the Israelites during the time of the judges.

*Judges 10:11-12*

**Mara** (**mar**-uh)
The nickname that *Naomi* gave herself after returning from Moab. Mara means "bitter."

*Ruth 1:20*

**maranatha** (**mair**-uh-**nath**-uh)
Aramaic for "Our Lord, come!"

*1 Corinthians 16:22*

**Marduk** (**mar**-dook)
See *Bel*

**Mareshah** (muh-**ree**-shuh)
A Canaanite town in the land allotted to Judah. Rehoboam built walls around Mareshah.

*2 Chronicles 14:10*
*Micah 1:15*

**Mark** (**mark**)
See *John Mark*

**mark of the beast** (**mark** uhv the **beest**)
A mark on the forehead or hand taken by people who worship the *beast*. Satan's beast will require this mark of anyone who wants to escape the *persecution* he inflicts on God's people. This mark is a sign of devotion to Satan and rejection of God. It appears in the prophecies of the *book of Revelation*.
See also *false prophet*

*Revelation 13:16-18*
*Revelation 16:2*
*Revelation 19:20*

M

*Mark 1:1-2*
*Acts 12:25*

**Mark, Gospel of (mark, gos-**puhl uhv)
Second book of the New Testament and second of the *Gospels*. The Gospel of Mark is the shortest of the four Gospels but records more miracles than any other. It tells all of the essential details of Jesus' life, death, burial, and resurrection. The book gets its name from its author, *John Mark*.

M

*Luke 10:38-42*
*John 12:2*

**Martha (mar-**thuh)

One of those who opened her home to Jesus during his ministry; sister of Mary and Lazarus. Martha is famous for complaining to Jesus when Mary stopped helping with housework to listen to Jesus.

*Acts 22:22*

**martyr (mar-**tur)

A person who is killed for his or her devotion to God. *Stephen* is called a martyr.

**Mary (mair-**ee)

*Matthew 1:18*
*Luke 1:26-30*

• Mother of Jesus. The Bible tells us little about Mary except that she was a devout Jewish woman chosen by God to give birth to the Son of God. She was engaged to the carpenter *Joseph* when the angel Gabriel first appeared to her. She wrote down a song of praise after

learning of her pregnancy. She and Joseph lived in Nazareth until Augustus's census forced them to go to Bethlehem. Her comments about Jesus at Cana and her presence at the cross show her devotion to Jesus and belief in him as Israel's Messiah.

• Mother of *James* and probably one of those who witnessed the crucifixion of Jesus. *Matthew 27:56*

• Sister of *Martha*. Jesus praised her for her attention to his teaching. *Luke 10:38-39*

• *Mary Magdalene.* *Matthew 27:56*

• Mother of *Mark.* *Acts 12:12*

• One of those greeted by Paul in the conclusion of the *book of Romans.* *Romans 16:6*

**Mary Magdalene** (**mair**-ee **mag**-duh-leen) *Luke 8:1-2 John 20:18*

One of those who followed Jesus, witnessed the crucifixion, and went to the tomb on the morning of Jesus' resurrection. "Magdalene" probably means that she was from Magdala, a town in Galilee. Before following Jesus, she was probably a *prostitute.*

**maskil** (**mas**-kil)

An older term that appears in the title of Psalms 32, 42, 44, 45, 52-55, 74, 78, 88, 89, and 142. "Maskil" may mean something like, "teaching song," but its exact meaning is unknown.

*Genesis 25:13-14*

**Massa** (**mass**-uh)

Seventh son of Ishmael and the tribe named after him.

*Exodus 17:7*
*Deuteronomy 6:16*
*Psalm 95:8*

**Massah** (**mass**-uh)

A place in the wilderness of Sinai where the Israelites tested God. "Massah" means "testing."

See also *Meribah*

*Matthew 9:9*
*Luke 6:13-16*
*Acts 1:13*

**Matthew** (**math**-yoo)

One of the Twelve among Jesus' disciples and an *apostle*; also known as Levi. Matthew was a tax collector; many Jews regarded tax collectors as outcasts because some worked for the Romans. Tradition says that Matthew wrote the *Gospel of Matthew*.

*Matthew 1:18*

**Matthew, Gospel of** (**math**-yoo, **gos**-puhl uhv)

First book of the New Testament and first of the *Gospels*. The Gospel of Matthew is most famous for the *Sermon on the Mount* and the *Great Commission*. It also has a lot of details that would appeal to a Jewish audience, such as Jesus' genealogy, the visit of the *magi*, Jesus' statements about the *Law*, the term *Kingdom of Heaven*, and Jesus' *Triumphal Entry*.

*Acts 1:23*
*Acts 1:26*

**Matthias** (muh-**thye**-uhss)

The man who took Judas's place among the *Twelve* after Jesus' ascension. The disciples *cast lots* to determine whether God had chosen Matthias or *Joseph* called Barsabbas to fill the slot.

**Mattithiah** (mat-uh-**thye**-uh) — 1 Chronicles 16:4-5

- A temple gatekeeper appointed to sing and play music during the return of the Ark to Jerusalem. He played the *lyre*.
- Levite in charge of baking the offering bread during the time of Ezra. — 1 Chronicles 9:31; Nehemiah 8:4

**mattock** (**mat**-ok) — 1 Samuel 13:20-21

A pole with a narrow blade at one end and a wider blade at the other. Farmers often used it for digging and scraping in Old Testament times.

**meal offering (meel awf**-ur-ing)

Another term for *grain offering*.

**meat offering (meet awf**-ur-ing)

Another term for *grain offering*.

**Meconah** (me-**koh**-nuh) — Nehemiah 11:25-28

A place near Ziklag in the lowlands of Judah where some Jews settled after returning from *Exile*.

**Medad** (**mee**-dad) — Numbers 11:26-27

One of the 70 elders of Israel chosen by Moses to help lead the nation. Medad and *Eldad* caused quite a stir when they began to prophesy in Moses' absence.

**Medan** (**mee**-dan) — Genesis 25:1-2

One of Abraham and Keturah's sons.

*Numbers 21:30*
*Joshua 13:16*

**Medeba** (**mee-**duh-buh)
A Moabite town allotted to the tribe of Reuben. Medeba was 10 kilometers south of Heshbon on the *king's highway*.

*2 Kings 17:6*
*Daniel 6:8*

**Medes** (**meedz**)
People of *Media*. The Medes ruled in Babylonia during the time of Daniel and Esther. Both Isaiah and Jeremiah prophesied against the Medes.

*Esther 1:3*
*Daniel 8:20*

**Media** (**mee**-dee-uh)
Land, nation, and kingdom southwest of the Caspian Sea. The people of Media were called *Medes*.

*Galatians 3:20*
*Hebrews 8:6*

**mediator** (**mee**-dee-**ate**-ur)
A go-between. Jesus is the mediator between God and people.

*Genesis 24:63*
*Joshua 1:8*
*Psalm 119:97*

**meditate** (med-i-tate)
To think over; ponder; reflect on.

*Leviticus 20:27*
*1 Samuel 28:7*
*1 Chronicles 10:13*

**medium** (**mee**-dee-uhm)
A person who talks to the dead in order to get advice. A medium's work is called necromancy. The penalty for consulting the dead was death, but the Bible records no examples of Israel enforcing this punishment. King *Saul* once hired a medium: the witch of *Endor*.
See also *divination; magic*

**meek (meek)**
Humble; gentle; tame.

*Psalm 37:11*
*Zephaniah 3:12*
*Matthew 5:5*

**meeting, tent of** (**meet**-ing, **tent** uhv)
See *tent of meeting*

**Megiddo** (me-**gid**-oh)
A large fortified Canaanite city in *Carmel*. Joshua captured Megiddo during the conquest of Canaan. It was given to the tribe of Manasseh. Solomon stationed some of his chariots and horses at Megiddo.

*Judges 1:27*
*2 Kings 23:29-30*

**Mekerathite** (muh-**ker**-uh-thite)
A person who traces his roots to *Mekerah*; a member of the Mekerathite clan.

*1 Chronicles 11:26, 36*

**Mekonah** (me-**koh**-nuh)
See *Meconah*

**Melchizedek** (mel-**kiz**-uh-dek)
"Priest of God Most High" and king of *Salem* during the time of Abraham. Melchizedek was unique because his priesthood did not come from the *Law* or from Aaron's family line. Abraham gave him a *tithe*. David mentioned Melchizedek in the *messianic prophesies* of Psalm 110. The *book of Hebrews* explains how Melchizedek helps us understand Christ.

*Genesis 14:18*
*Psalm 110:4*
*Hebrews 6:20*

M

Daniel 1:11, 16

**Melzar** (**mel**-zar)

The Babylonian official in charge of Daniel, Hananiah, Mishael, and Azariah. Melzar was a title, not a name.

Jeremiah 44:1
Ezekiel 30:13

**Memphis** (**mem**-fiss)

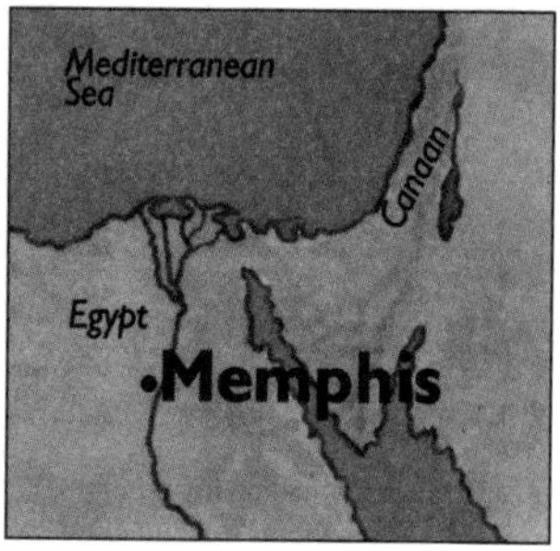


Capital city of Egypt during Old Testament times. Memphis was on the west bank of the Nile about 24 kilometers south of the Mediterranean shore. The prophets Isaiah, Jeremiah, Ezekiel, and Hosea used the term as a synonym for all Egypt.

Esther 1:16-22

**Memucan** (muh-**moo**-kuhn)

The advisor to King *Ahasuerus* who suggested that the king replace *Vashti*.

2 Kings 15:14-22

**Menahem** (**men**-uh-hem)

Seventeenth king of the northern kingdom of Israel; son of Gadi. Menahem came to power by assassinating *Shallum*. He was one of Israel's cruelest kings. He reigned 10 years and was succeeded by his son *Pekahiah*. Hosea and Amos prophesied during his reign.

**mene, mene, tekel, parsin** (**mee**-nee, **tek**-uhl, **par**-sin)
The four words written on the wall during *Belshazzar's* feast that Daniel interpreted as a prophesy against the Babylonian king. Daniel's words came true.

*Daniel 5:22-25*

**menservants** (**men**-sur-vuhntz)
See *manservant*

**Mephibosheth** (me-**fib**-oh-**sheth**)

- Grandson of Saul and Rizpah. Mephibosheth was executed by the people of Gibeon. *2 Samuel 21:7-8*
- Saul's grandson; son of David's friend Jonathan. The touching story of David's kindness to Mephibosheth, and Mephibosheth's gratitude, is told in the book of *Second Samuel*. *2 Samuel 4:4*

**Merari** (muh-**rar**-eye)
Third son of Levi and father of the clan named after him. *Gershon* and *Kohath* were his older brothers.

*Exodus 6:16*
*1 Chronicles 6:63*

**Merarites** (muh-**rar**-ites)
One of the three clans of Levites; the clan of Merari; people descended from Levi's son Merari. During the Exodus, the Merarites carried portions of the tabernacle and camped on its north side. During the time of David, they

*Numbers 3:36*
*2 Chronicles 29:12*

served as temple musicians, singers, and temple gatekeepers. They received 12 *levitical cities*.
See also *Gershonites; Kohathites*

Genesis 43:14
Nehemiah 13:22
James 3:17

**mercy** (**mur**-see)
Undue kindness; forgiveness. Mercy is a very important word in the Bible because it describes the way God treats all people. Mercy accounts for God's choosing of Abraham and promise to make him a great nation. Mercy is the reason that God sent Jesus Christ. One of the most famous verses about mercy says, "God blesses those who are merciful, for they will be shown mercy" (Matthew 5:7).

See *also mercy seat*

Hebrews 9:5

**mercy seat** (**mur**-see **seet**)
The top that covered the *Ark of the Covenant*; the "atonement cover" or "place of atonement." This is where the high priest sprinkled the blood on the *Day of Atonement*. The mercy seat was made of pure gold.

Exodus 17:7
Psalm 106:32

**Meribah** (**mair**-i-buh)
The nickname given to two places in the wilderness of Sinai, *Rephidim* and *Kadesh Barnea*, where the Israelites complained about the lack

of water. "Meribah" means "quarreling" or "strife."
See also *Massah*

**Meribah Kadesh** (**mair**-i-buh **kay**-desh)
"Strife at Kadesh," a nickname for Kadesh Barnea and the reason Moses was not allowed to enter Canaan.
*Numbers 27:14*
*Ezekiel 48:28*

**Merodach** (**mair**-oh-dok)
Another name for *Bel*.

**Merodach-baladan** (**mair**-oh-dok-**bal**-uh-dan)
King of Babylonia who congratulated Hezekiah on recovering from illness.
*Isaiah 39:1*

**Merom, Waters of** (**mee**-rom, **wah**-turz uhv)
See *Waters of Merom*

**Mesha** (**mee**-shuh)
- King of Moab during the reigns of Ahab and Ahaziah in Israel. Mesha paid tribute to Ahab, but rebelled against Israel after Ahab died. *2 Kings 3:4*
- Firstborn son of *Caleb*; father of Ziph. *1 Chronicles 2:42*
- A clan leader in the tribe of Benjamin; son of *Shaharaim*. *1 Chronicles 8:8-9*

**Meshach** (**mee**-shuhk)
Babylonian name given to Mishael, a Hebrew exile in the service of King *Nebuchadnezzar*. Meshach and his two friends *Shadrach* and
*Daniel 1:7*
*Daniel 3:19-20*

M

*Abednego* were thrown into a fiery furnace for refusing to bow down to an idol of gold.

1 Chronicles 1:5
Ezekiel 27:13

**Meshech** (**mee**-shek)

One of *Japheth's* sons and the tribe named after him. The people of Meshech traded in slaves and copper, and became known for their violent ways.

**Meshullam** (muh-**shoo**-luhm)

A very common name among the Israelites:

2 Chronicles 34:12

• One of the *Kohathite* priests who helped repair the temple during Josiah's reform.

Nehemiah 3:4

• One of those who helped repair the walls of Jerusalem during the time of *Nehemiah*; son of Berechiah.

Nehemiah 3:6

• Israelite who helped repair the *Old Gate* of Jerusalem during the time of Nehemiah; son of Besodeiah.

1 Chronicles 3:19

• One of *Zerubbabel's* sons.

1 Chronicles 9:11

• Several others who are hard to identify or who are mentioned only once.

Acts 2:8-9
Acts 7:2

**Mesopotamia** (**mess**-uh-poh-**tay**-mee-uh)

The land between the *Tigris* and *Euphrates* Rivers and the land watered by them. This land is in modern Syria and Iraq. Abraham and Sarah were from Haran in Mesopotamia. The Assyrian and Babylonian kingdoms also ruled this region.

The word "mesopotamia" means "between the rivers."

**Messiah** (muh-**sye**-uh)
A Hebrew word meaning "anointed one." It refers to the savior that the Old Testament prophets predicted would be born of a virgin in Bethlehem. The Greek form is *Christ*.

*John 1:41*
*John 4:25*

**messianic prophesies** (**meh**-see-**an**-ik **prof**-uh-seez)
Prophesies about the *Messiah*; predictions of who the Messiah would be, where he would be born, what he would do, and how people would respond to him. Some of the most famous messianic prophesies are in Psalm 110, Isaiah 53, Micah 5, and Zechariah 13. Acts and Hebrews quote several messianic prophesies.

*Acts 8:28-33*
*Romans 15:12*

**Methuselah** (muh-**thoo**-zuh-luh)

Son of *Enoch* and father of Lamech; one of those who lived before the *flood*. Methuselah lived 969 years—longer than any other person.

*Genesis 5:21*

M

M

**Micah** (**mye**-kuh)

A short form of *Micaiah* and a common name among the Israelites:

Micah 1:1
- "Micah of Moresheth," prophet of Israel who wrote the *book of Micah*. This Micah lived and preached during the reigns of Jotham, Ahaz, and Hezekiah, and during the time of *Isaiah*.

Judges 17:10-13
- Israelite of Ephraim who hired Jonathan (son of Gershom) as his own personal priest during the time of the judges.

1 Chronicles 8:34
- Son of *Mephibosheth*; grandson of David's friend Jonathan.

1 Chronicles 24:24
- A few other minor characters.

Micah 1:1

**Micah, book of** (**mye**-kuh, **buk** uhv)

Thirty-third book of the Old Testament and sixth of the *minor prophets*. The prophet *Micah* delivered his messages to both Israel and Judah during the reigns of Jotham, Ahaz, and Hezekiah. They warn the people that their sins will bring judgment unless they turn back to God. The book of Micah is famous for its *messianic prophesies*.

See also *Isaiah, book of*

**Micaiah** (mye-**kye**-uh)

A common name among the Israelites, often shortened to *Micah*:

• The royal official who first heard Baruch read from Jeremiah's scroll; son of Gemariah; grandson of Shaphan. Micaiah and his father both served in *Jehoiakim's* court. *Jeremiah 36:11-13*

• A prophet who lived during the time of *Elijah*; son of Imlah. *1 Kings 22:8-9*

• Several others mentioned briefly here and there. *Nehemiah 12:41*

See also *Delaiah; Elishama; Elnathan; Zedekiah*

**Michael** (**mye**-kuhl)

A very common name among the Israelites:

• One of only two angels named in the Bible (the other is *Gabriel*); "one of the archangels." The angel who appeared to Daniel called Michael the prince of Israel. *Daniel 10:13; Jude 1:9; Revelation 12:7*

• A commander in Saul's army who defected to David along with several others from the tribe of Manasseh. Michael became a commander in David's army. *1 Chronicles 12:20*

• Father of *Sethur*. *Numbers 13:3, 13*

• *Asaph's* great-grandfather. *1 Chronicles 6:39-40*

• Son of King *Jehoshaphat* who was murdered by his brother *Jehoram*. *2 Chronicles 21:2*

• Several others mentioned only by name. *1 Chronicles 8:16; 1 Chronicles 5:13-14*

M

1 Samuel 18:20
2 Samuel 3:13

**Michal** (**mye**-kuhl)
Daughter of *Saul* and David's first wife. Michal is the one who was ashamed to watch David dance before the Lord.

**Michmash** (**mik**-mash)
See *Micmash*

1 Samuel 13:5
Nehemiah 11:31

**Micmash** (**mik**-mash)
A city in the hill country of Benjamin 12 kilometers northeast of Jerusalem.

Genesis 25:1-4
Exodus 2:15
Acts 7:29

**Midian** (**mid**-ee-uhn)
One of Abraham and Keturah's sons. The people descended from Midian became a tribe that settled in the land south and east of Edom. Moses lived in this land for 40 years while tending sheep, until God appeared to him in a burning bush and made him go back to Egypt. The Israelites had to pass through this land before they could enter Canaan.

See also *Midianites*

Genesis 37:36
Judges 7:7

**Midianites** (**mid**-ee-uhn-ites)
The people of *Midian*. The Midianites gave the Israelites a lot of trouble during Exodus and the time of the judges. Gideon became famous for routing the Midianite forces with only 300 men.

**midwife** (**mid**-wife)

A woman who helps a mother give birth to a baby. The Hebrew midwives in Egypt became heroes for protecting newborn sons from being killed by Egyptian executioners.

*Genesis 35:17*
*Genesis 38:28*

**Migdol** (**mig**-dol)

"Fortress," name of a city in the northern part of Egypt. The Israelites stopped at Migdol on their way out of slavery. Hundreds of years later Jeremiah addressed some of his prophesies to the Jews who lived in Migdol.

*Exodus 14:2*
*Ezekiel 30:6*

**mighty men, David's** (**mye**-tee **men, day**-vidz)

A small group of warriors famous for their bravery, skill in combat, and devotion to David. These mighty men came from all over Israel and even *Philistia*. Some had been officers in Saul's army. They defended David while Saul was king and helped David establish his kingdom after Saul's death. The *Thirty* and the *Three* distinguished themselves as the best of the best among them.

*2 Samuel 23:8, 16-17*
*1 Chronicles 11:10*
*1 Chronicles 28:1*

**Mikneiah** (mik-**nee**-yuh)

A temple gatekeeper appointed to sing and play music during the return of the Ark to Jerusalem.

*1 Chronicles 15: 19-21*

**miktam** (**mik**-tam)
A term that appears in the title of Psalms 16 and 56-60. Its meaning is unknown.

*Genesis 11:29*
*Genesis 24:15*

**Milcah** (**mil**-kuh)

• *Nahor's* wife. Milcah was Abraham's niece. She had eight sons and became the grandmother of Rebekah. She had a sister named Iscah.

*Numbers 26:33*

• One of *Zelophehad's* daughters.

**Milcom** (**mil**-kuhm)
Another name for *Molech.*

*Acts 20:15, 17*
*2 Timothy 4:20*

**Miletus** (mye-**lee**-tuhss)
A port city in the Roman province of Asia about 50 kilometers south-southwest of Ephesus. Paul stopped at Miletus on his third missionary journey.

*Revelation 20:2-7*

**millennium** (muh-len-ee-uhm)
A term often used for the time described in Revelation 20:2-4. The millennium follows Christ's return and defeat of Satan, when he reigns over the whole earth. The word "millennium" means one thousand.

See also *day of his coming; return of Christ*

*2 Samuel 5:9*
*1 Kings 11:27*

**Millo** (**mil**-oh)
A portion of Jerusalem's defenses built by David and reinforced by Solomon. The word "millo" means "filled."

**millstone** (**mil**-stone)
A round stone used to grind wheat or grain into flour for baking bread.

*Job 41:24*
*Mark 9:42*
*Revelation 18:21*

**mina, minas** (**mye**-nuh, **mye**-nuhss)
A unit of weight equal to about 600 grams, or 20 ounces; 50 *shekels*. People used the mina in trade. Ezekiel described an exception to the common way of figuring the value of a mina.

*1 Kings 10:17*
*Ezekiel 45:12*
*Luke 19:24*



**minister** (**min**-i-stur)
A person who serves. The word "minister" means "servant."

*Exodus 28:43*
*Ephesians 3:7*
*Colossians 4:7*

**ministry** (**min**-i-stree)
Service.
See also *minister*

*1 Chronicles 25:1*
*Acts 6:2*

**Minni** (**min**-eye)
A small kingdom in the hills of northern Media mentioned in Jeremiah's prophesies against Babylonia.

*Jeremiah 51:27*

**minor prophets** (**mye**-nur **prof**-uhtz)

Twelve books of prophecy in the Old Testament: Hosea, Joel, Amos, Obadiah, Jonah, Micah, Nahum, Habakkuk, Zephaniah, Haggai, Zechariah, Malachi. They are called minor because they were written by prophets of lesser influence than the *major prophets*.

*Joel 1:1*
*Nahum 1:1*

*Nehemiah 9:17*
*Psalm 78:12*
*John 15:24*

**miracle** (**mihr**-uh-kuhl)

An act of God or a deed done by God's power; also called *signs*, *wonders*, and *miraculous signs*. Jesus said that the miracles he did showed that he was from God.

Miracles require God's power, but they can be faked. God warned the Israelites, and the apostle Paul warned the Thessalonians, to beware of false prophets who do miraculous signs.

*Exodus 8:23*
*2 Chronicles 32:24*
*John 10:41*

**miraculous sign** (mihr-**ak**-yoo-luhss **syne**)

A miracle or use of power meant to be an indication of *Deity*; a *wonder*. God did miraculous signs during the Exodus. Jesus did miraculous signs to show that he was the Son of God. And the beast does miraculous signs in an effort to make people worship him.

See also *sign*

*Exodus 15:20-21*
*Numbers 12:10-15*
*Micah 6:4*

**Miriam** (**mihr**-ee-uhm)

Moses' older sister. Miriam is famous for leading the victory song after the crossing of the Red Sea, and for getting leprosy after rebelling against Moses during the Exodus.

**mirror** (**mihr**-ur)
In Old and New Testament times, usually a sheet of polished metal.
*Job 37:18*
*1 Corinthians 13:12*
*James 1:23*

**Mishael** (**mish**-ay-el)
• *Meshach* — *Daniel 1:6-7*
• Aaron's cousin, mentioned in the story of *Nadab* and *Abihu*. — *Leviticus 10:4*
• One of those who stood with Ezra as he read the Law aloud. — *Nehemiah 8:4*

M

**Mishmannah** (mish-**man**-uh)
A skilled Israelite soldier from the tribe of Gad who defected to David at Ziklag; fourth in command under *Ezer*.
*1 Chronicles 12:10*

**Mithredath** (**mith**-ri-dath)
Two Persians:
• *Cyrus's* treasurer who helped Ezra prepare for his trip back to Jerusalem. — *Ezra 1:8*
• One of the Persian officials who urged *Artaxerxes* to stop the Jews from rebuilding Jerusalem. — *Ezra 4:7*

**mitre** (**mye**-tur)
A turban.
*Exodus 28:4*
*Leviticus 8:9*
*Zechariah 3:5*

**Mitylene** (mit-uh-**lee**-nee)
A city on the island of Lesbos in the Roman province of Asia. Paul stopped briefly at Mitylene
*Acts 20:14*

on his way back to Palestine during his third missionary journey.

**Mizar** (**miz**-ar)

*Psalm 42:6* A mountain mentioned only in Psalm 42. Mizar's location is unknown.

**Mizpah, Mizpeh** (**miz**-pah)

"Watch tower," the name given to several places:

*Genesis 31:48-49* • A city in Gilead. Jacob and Laban made an agreement here. This is probably also where the Israelite army set up camp to do battle with the Ammonites during the time of Jephthah.

*Jeremiah 40:6-8* • A fortified city in the territory of Benjamin. This is where *Gedaliah* lived.

*Joshua 15:38* • A town in the western low-lands of Judah.

*1 Samuel 22:3* • A hideout for David's parents in Moab.

*Joshua 11:3* • A place at the foothills of Mount Hermon that was home to the *Hivites*.

**Mizraim** (**miz**-ray-im)

*Genesis 10:6, 13* • *Ham's* second son and father of seven nations. The Philistines were descended from Mizraim.

*Genesis 50:11* • Another term for the people of northern Egypt (Lower Egypt).

**Mnason** (**nay**-suhn)

Paul's host in Jerusalem at the end of Paul's third missionary journey.

*Acts 21:16*

**Moab** (**moh**-ab)

One of Lot's sons and the people descended from him. The Moabites occupied the east side of the Dead Sea as far as the desert. The Israelites passed through this land on their way to the *promised land.*

See also *Eglon; Ehud*

*Genesis 19:37*
*Joshua 13:32*

**Moabites** (**moh**-uh-bites)

People who traced their roots to *Moab*; people from the land of Moab. Some of Israel's problems with *idolatry* came from mixing with the Moabites.

*2 Kings 3:21-22*

**Moladah** (**moh**-luh-duh)

A town near Beersheba in the land allotted to Simeon. Moladah's location is unknown.

*Joshua 15:21, 26*
*Joshua 19:1-2*

**Molech** (**moh**-lek)

Chief god of the *Ammonites*. Worship of Molech involved child sacrifice. Sadly, several kings of Judah became worshipers of Molech and sacrificed children in the valley of *Hinnom*. Even Solomon built a shrine to Molech in Jerusalem.

See also *idolatry; Chemosh*

*Leviticus 18:21*
*2 Kings 23:13*
*Acts 7:43*

**money** (**mun**-ee)
See *mina; shekel; talent*

*Exodus 12:2*
*Exodus 13:4*
*1 Kings 8:2*

**month** (**muhnth**)
One-twelfth of the year. The Israelites divided their year into these twelve months: *Abib*, *Ziv*, *Sivan*, Tammuz, Ab, *Elul*, *Ethanim*, *Bul*, *Kislev*, *Tebeth*, *Shebat*, *Adar*. Only Tammuz and Ab do not appear in the Bible.

*Esther 2:7*
*Esther 10:2-3*

**Mordecai** (**mor**-duh-kye)
Jewish man of the tribe of Benjamin taken captive to Babylon at the beginning of the Exile. Mordecai was *Esther's* cousin and adopted her into his family after her parents died. Mordecai became famous for persuading Esther to talk to King Ahasuerus about Haman's plot against the Jews. His story is told in the book of Esther.

*Judges 7:1*

**Moreh** (**mor**-uh)
A hill in the land of Issachar between Mount *Gilboa* and Mount Tabor, about one and a half kilometers south of *Endor*. Moreh overlooked the *Valley of Jezreel*.

*Jeremiah 26:18*
*Micah 1:1*
*Micah 1:14*

**Moresheth** (**mor**-uh-sheth)
The prophet Micah's hometown. Moresheth was in the lowlands of Judah, but its exact location is unknown.

**Moriah** (mor-**eye**-uh)
The hill where Abraham was to sacrifice Isaac and where Solomon built the temple.

Genesis 22:2
2 Chronicles 3:1

**morning star** (**mor**-ning **star**)
The planet Venus, so named because it looks like a bright star in the morning sky; also called "day star" or "shining star." The term "morning star" is used as a nickname in two different ways:

- A nickname given to the king of *Babylon* in Isaiah's prophecies against Babylon. Isaiah's passage mocks the king for setting himself up as a god, and condemns him for his pride. Many people believe that this passage describes the downfall of Satan.
- A nickname for *Jesus*.

Isaiah 14:12

2 Peter 1:19
Revelation 22:16

**Moses** (**moh**-zuhss)
*Kohathite* Hebrew *prophet* who led the nation of Israel out of slavery in Egypt. Moses is one of the most important people in the Bible and often considered the greatest prophet. He wrote most of the *Pentateuch*, gave the Israelites God's Law, got the priests and Levites started in their duties, and established

Exodus 2:10
Exodus 10:3
Hebrews 11:24

the worship of God at the *tabernacle*. Moses' older brother Aaron played a big part in all of these achievements; his older sister *Miriam* played a key part in his boyhood. Moses' story is told in the books of Exodus, Leviticus, Numbers, and Deuteronomy.

See also *Exodus, the; Pharaoh*

M

*Leviticus 16:1-34*
*2 Chronicles 3:8-14*
*Hebrews 9:1-28*

**Most Holy Place (most hoh**-lee **playss)**

The small space behind the curtain in the tabernacle and the *temple* where the presence of God stayed; sometimes called the *sanctuary*. The Ark of the Covenant was kept in the Most Holy Place. Only the *high priest* was allowed to enter this space, and then only once a year on the *Day of Atonement*. Jesus acted as the perfect high priest entering the Most Holy Place for the last time when he offered his own life for the sins of the world.

See also *holy; salvation; worship*

*1 Kings 18:19*
*2 Kings 4:25*

**Mount Carmel (mount kar**-muhl)

The main mountain peak in the *Carmel* range and the sight of the famous stand-off between Elijah and the prophets of Baal.

**Mount Ebal (mount ee**-bawl)

See *Ebal*

**Mount Gerizim (mount gair**-uh-zim)

See *Gerizim*

**Mount Gilboa** (**mount** gil-**boh**-uh)
See *Gilboa*

**Mount Hermon** (**mount hur**-muhn)
See *Hermon*

**Mount Horeb** (**mount hor**-eb)
See *Horeb*

**Mount Moriah** (**mount** mor-**eye**-uh)
See *Moriah*

**Mount of Olives** (**mount** uhv **awl**-ivz)
A small but important mountain on the east side of Jerusalem across from the *Kidron Valley*. Jesus taught from the Mount of Olives.

*2 Samuel 15:30*
*Matthew 24:3*
*Acts 1:12*

**Mount Paran** (**mount pair**-uhn)
See *Paran*

**Mount Sinai** (**mount sye**-nye)
The mountain peak in Sinai where Moses received the *Ten Commandments* from God. No one knows exactly where Mount Sinai was, but it was at least three days' journey from *Elim*, probably in the south of Sinai's rocky desert.
See also *Sinai*

*Exodus 19:18*
*Exodus 31:18*
*Acts 7:38*

**Mount Siyon** (**mount sye**-yon)
See *Siyon*

**Mount Tabor** (**mount tay**-bor)
See *Tabor*

M

**Mount Zion** (**mount zye**-uhn)
See *Zion*

**music** (**myoo**-zik)
See *harp; horn; lyre; Merarites*

*Esther 2:12*
*John 19:39*
*Matthew 2:11*

**myrrh** (**mur**)
Resin made from the sap of the *Commiphora myrrha* tree. The Israelites used myrrh as an incense because it had a strong, pleasant smell. The *magi* who visited Jesus brought a gift of myrrh.
See also *frankincense*

*Acts 16:7*

**Mysia** (**mish**-yuh)
A region of northwest Asia Minor directly north of *Lydia* and west of Bithynia and *Phrygia* in the Roman province of *Asia*. Assos and Troas were major cities in this region.

N

**Naaman** (**nay**-muhn)

• Commander of the Aramean army during the time of *Elisha*. Naaman was famous in Aram for his military leadership, and famous in Israel for being healed of leprosy by following Elisha's instructions. *2 Kings 5:1-6*

• One of *Benjamin's* sons and father of the Naamite *clan*. Naaman went to Egypt with Jacob and his family when Joseph invited them to come. *Genesis 46:21*

**Nabal** (**nay**-bahl)

Abigail's husband before she married David. Nabal was a rich sheep farmer in *Maon* before his death. His name means "fool." *1 Samuel 25:3, 25-26*

**Naboth** (**nay**-both)

Israelite man from Jezreel killed and robbed by *Ahab* and *Jezebel* during the time of *Elijah*. Naboth owned a vineyard that Ahab wanted. Jezebel arranged to have Naboth murdered so Ahab could have it. *1 Kings 21:1-16*

**Nadab** (**nay**-dab)

• Aaron's oldest son and brother of *Abihu*; one of the priests who died during the Exodus for disobeying God's laws for burning incense. *Exodus 6:23*

*1 Kings 15:25* • Son of *Jeroboam* I and second king of Israel after his father. Nadab reigned two years and then was assassinated by *Baasha*.

*1 Chronicles 2:28* • An Israelite in the tribe of Judah; son of Shammai in Jerahmeel's clan.

*1 Chronicles 8:29-30* • A man of Gibeon mentioned in Saul's genealogy.

**Nahash** (**nay**-hash)

*1 Samuel 11:1-2* • Amorite king who attacked *Jabesh-gilead* right after Saul became king.

*2 Samuel 17:25* • Abigail's father.

**Nahbi** (**nah**-bye)

*Numbers 13:3, 14* One of the 12 men chosen by Moses at *Kadesh Barnea* to spy out the land of Canaan during the Exodus; a leader of the tribe of Naphtali; son of Vophsi.

**Nahor** (**nay**-hor)

*Genesis 11:24-27* • *Terah's* father. This Nahor was Abram's grandfather.

*Genesis 11:24-27* • Terah's son. This Nahor was *Abram's* brother and father of Abram's nephew Lot. Twelve *Aramean* tribes descended from Nahor.

**Nahshon** (**nah**-shon)

*Exodus 6:23; Numbers 7:12; 10:14; Luke 3:23, 32* Leader of the tribe of Judah during the Exodus; son of Amminadab. Nahshon is mentioned in the genealogy of Jesus.

**Nahum** (**nay**-huhm)

Israelite prophet to Nineveh during the reign of Manasseh in Judah. Nahum was from Elkosh and wrote the *book of Nahum*. We know nothing else about him.

Jonah was also a prophet to Nineveh.

*Nahum 1:1, 7-8*

**Nahum, book of** (**nay**-huhm, **buk** uhv)

Thirty-fourth book of the Old Testament and seventh of the *minor prophets*. The prophecies of Nahum reaffirm God's love for Judah and explain why God was going to judge the people of Assyria (Nineveh).

See also *Nineveh; Jonah*

*Nahum 1:1*

**Nain** (**nayn**)

A town in Jezreel where Jesus raised a boy back to life. Nain is on a hill called Little Hermon, about 10 kilometers southeast of Nazareth.

*Luke 7:11-12*

**Naomi** (nay-**oh**-mee)

Israelite woman from the tribe of Judah who played a key part in *Ruth's* life. Naomi was Ruth's mother-in-law and a relative of *Boaz*. She was from Bethlehem.

See also *Ruth, book of*

*Ruth 1:1-6*

N

Genesis 25:13-15
1 Chronicles 1:31

**Naphish (nay-fish)**
Eleventh son of Abraham's son *Ishmael* and father of the tribe of Arabs named after him.

**Naphtali (naf-tuh-lee)**

Genesis 30:8
Numbers 1:42-43

• Jacob's son and the tribe of Israel named after him. *Rachel* was his mother.

Isaiah 9:1
Matthew 4:13

• The land allotted to the tribe of Naphtali.

Judges 4:6

Barak was from the tribe of Naphtali. It was also the first tribe to be taken captive by the *Assyrians*.

See also *tribes of Israel*

**Nathan (nay-thuhn)**
A common name among the Israelites:

2 Samuel 7:2-4
2 Samuel 12:5-7

• Prophet of Israel and counselor to King David.

Nathan is famous for bringing several messages of God directly to *David*, including messages about the temple, Bathsheba, *Uriah*, and Solomon.

2 Samuel 5:13-14
1 Chronicles 3:5

• One of David and *Bathsheba's* sons; brother of Solomon.

2 Samuel 23:36

• Father of *Igal*.

1 Chronicles 11:38

• Brother of David's mighty man *Joel*.

Ezra 8:16

• An Israelite leader who went to Jerusalem with Ezra.

1 Chronicles 2:36

• An Israelite in the tribe of Judah; son of Attai in Jerahmeel's clan.

• Several others who are hard to identify.

**Nathanael** (nuh-**than**-ee-uhl)
One of Jesus' Twelve disciples, possibly the same as *Bartholomew*. Nathanael first heard about Jesus from his friend *Philip* and is famous for saying, "Nazareth! Can anything good come from there?" (John 1:46). We know little else about him.

*John 1:45-49*
*John 21:2*



**Nazarene** (**naz**-uh-reen)
A person from the town of *Nazareth*. Many people called Jesus a Nazarene because Nazareth was his hometown. In the days of the early church, Christians were sometimes called Nazarenes or members of the Nazarene sect of Judaism. A Nazarene is not the same as a *Nazirite*.

*Matthew 2:23*
*Mark 14:67*
*Acts 24:5*

**Nazareth** (**naz**-uh-reth)
A town in Galilee among the southern hills of Lebanon, in the territory originally allotted to Zebulun. Jesus grew up in Nazareth after Joseph and Mary settled there. It was south of Cana.

*Matthew 26:71*
*John 18:7*
*Acts 3:6*

**Nazirite** (**naz**-uh-rite)
A person who took a Nazirite vow; a person who promised to devote his or her life to God's service and abide by certain rules. The Nazirite could not drink wine or cut his hair. Samson is the most famous Nazirite. *Amos* also mentions

*Numbers 6:4*
*Judges 13:5*
*Judges 16:17*

Nazirites. The rules for Nazirites are found in Numbers 6.

Numbers 6:2, 21

**Nazirite vow** (**naz**-uh-rite **vou**)
A promise to serve God as a *Nazirite*; a promise or vow to abide by the Nazirite rules. The rules for Nazirites are found in Numbers 6.
See also *Samson*

Acts 16:11

**Neapolis** (nee-**ah**-puh-liss)
"New city," the name of Philippi's port in the Roman province of Macedonia. The apostle Paul landed at Neapolis on his way to Philippi during his second missionary journey.

1 Chronicles 1:29
Isaiah 60:7

**Nebaioth** (nuh-**bye**-uhth)
Firstborn son of Abraham's son Ishmael and father of the tribe of Arabs named after him. This tribe became shepherds in northwestern Arabia.

1 Kings 12:2

**Nebat** (**nee**-bot)
Father of *Jeroboam* I.

**Nebo** (**nee**-boh)

Deuteronomy 32:49
- Mount Nebo, a high hill in the northern territory of Moab from which Moses saw the promised land and died.

Ezra 10:43
- Israelite priest and ancestor of some Jews who participated in *Ezra's reform*.

Isaiah 15:2
- A Babylonian god, the so-called son of *Bel*.

Numbers 32:37-38
- A city of Moab in the land allotted to Reuben.

Ezra 2:29
- A town in Judah.

**Nebuchadnezzar** (**neb**-uh-kuhd-**nez**-ur)

King of Babylonia who started the *Exile* of Judah. Nebuchadnezzar came to power during the reign of *Jehoiakim* in Jerusalem. His army besieged and captured the city and took many Jews to Babylon. *Jehoiachin* and *Zedekiah* ruled Judah under Nebuchadnezzar's control. Meanwhile, several important Jews served him in Babylon. Daniel and his friends are the most famous.

Nebuchadnezzar is mentioned 90 times in the Old Testament. He is best known for his part in the lives of *Shadrach*, Meshach, and Abednego; for his dreams, which Daniel interpreted; and for a bout of insanity. The prophets *Jeremiah*, Ezekiel, and Daniel wrote about Nebuchadnezzar many times. He reigned from 605-562 B.C.

See also *Habakkuk*

*2 Kings 24:1*
*Ezra 6:5*
*Daniel 1:1*

**Necho** (**nek**-oh)

See *Neco*

**Neco** (**nek**-oh)

Pharaoh of Egypt during the reign of Josiah king of Judah. Neco's forces killed Josiah in battle at Megiddo and made *Judah* subject to Egypt. To keep control of Judah, Neco made Jehoiakim king in place of Josiah's son *Jehoahaz*.

*2 Kings 23:33-35*
*Jeremiah 46:2*

**necromancer** (**nek**-roh-**man**-sur)
An older word for *medium*.

**Negeb** (**neg**-eb)
See *Negev*

Genesis 13:1
Joshua 11:16
Jeremiah 33:13

N

**Negev** (**neg**-ev)
"The dry," name of the area of wilderness between Kadesh Barnea and the region of *Beersheba*, including the land north of Beersheba. The Negev included the *Desert of Zin*.

Nehemiah 8:9

**Nehemiah** (**nee**-uh-**mye**-uh)
Jewish *cupbearer* to King Artaxerxes during the Exile. Nehemiah is most famous for returning to Jerusalem to lead his people in rebuilding the city walls. At that time he became governor of Judah. His story is told in the *book of Nehemiah*.

See also *Ezra; Sanballat; Tobiah; Zerubbabel*

Nehemiah 12:26

**Nehemiah, book of** (**nee**-uh-**mye**-uh, **buk** uhv)
Sixteenth book of the Old Testament and eleventh of the *books of history*. The book tells how Nehemiah returns to Jerusalem to rebuild the city walls, despite resistance from enemies. It also tells of *Ezra's reform*.
See also *Ezra; Sanballat; Tobiah; Zerubbabel*

**Nepheg** (**nee**-feg)

• Son of Izhar and brother of Korah and Zicri; a Levite; a Kohathite. *Exodus 6:20-21*

• One of David's sons. *2 Samuel 5:13-16*

**Nephilim** (**nef**-uh-lim)

A group of people famous for their large size. Ten of the Israelites who spied out Canaan were terrified of the Nephilim that they saw. *Genesis 6:4*; *Numbers 13:33*



**Ner** (**nur**)

A man mentioned in the genealogies of *Saul*. Ner was either Saul's uncle (father of Abner) or Saul's grandfather (father of Kish). *1 Samuel 14:50-51*; *1 Chronicles 26:28*

**Nergal** (**nur**-gahl)

The *idol* worshiped by the people of *Cuthah* who settled in Samaria after the destruction of Israel. *2 Kings 17:29-33*

**Nethanel** (nuh-**than**-uhl)

A common name among the Israelites:

• A leader of the tribe of *Issachar* during the Exodus; son of *Zuar*. *Numbers 1:4, 5, 8*

• One of David's brothers; fourth son of *Jesse*. *1 Chronicles 2:13-14*

• A Levite leader who gave generously to the Levites during *Josiah's* reforms. *2 Chronicles 35:7-9*

• An official sent by Jehoshaphat to teach in Judah. *2 Chronicles 17:7*

• One of Obed-Edom's sons; a temple *gate-keeper*. *1 Chronicles 26:1, 4*

• Several others mentioned only once.

**Nethaniah** (**neth**-uh-nye-uh)

A common name among the Israelites:

2 Chronicles 17:8 • A Levite sent by Jehoshaphat to teach in Judah.

2 King 25:25 • Father of Gedaliah's murderer *Ishmael*.

1 Chronicles 25:2 • One of the musicians appointed by David to serve in the choir; son of Asaph.

Jeremiah 36:13-14 • *Jehudi's* father.

N

Revelation 3:12
Revelation 21:2

**New Jerusalem** (**noo** juh-**roo**-suh-lem)

The city that God will create as part of the new heavens and the new earth. It is described in the *book of Revelation*.

See also *heaven*

Numbers 10:10
Psalm 81:3-5
Colossians 2:16

**New Moon festival** (**noo moon fess**-tuh-vuhl)

A celebration of the coming month and a dedication of it to God. It is called the New Moon festival because it took place at each New Moon—when the moon was not visible in the sky. The offerings for this festival are described in Numbers 28:11-15.

John 3:1-10
John 7:50
John 19:39

**Nicodemus** (**nik**-uh-**dee**-muhss)

A Pharisee, member of the *Sanhedrin*, and secret disciple of Jesus. Nicodemus is famous for coming to Jesus at night and asking, "How can an old man go back into his mother's womb and be born again?" (John 3:4). He also helped *Joseph* of Arimathea bury Jesus' body.

**Nicopolis** (nik-**ah**-puh-liss)
A city in the Roman province of Epirus on the western coast of Greece where the apostle Paul wanted to go. The name means "City of Victory" and was given to many cities of the Roman world.

*Titus 3:12*

**Nile** (**nye**-uhl)
The river of Egypt.

*Exodus 2:1-4*
*Exodus 8:3*
*Ezekiel 29:9*

**Nimrod** (**nim**-rod)
Son of Cush and therefore Noah's great-grandson; a famous hunter.

*Genesis 10:8*
*Micah 5:6*

**Nineveh** (**nin**-uh-vuh)
Capital city of Assyria, located in the north of Mesopotamia on the east bank of the *Tigris* River. Jonah and Nahum prophesied to the people of Nineveh.

*Jonah 1:1-3*
*Nahum 1:1, 8*

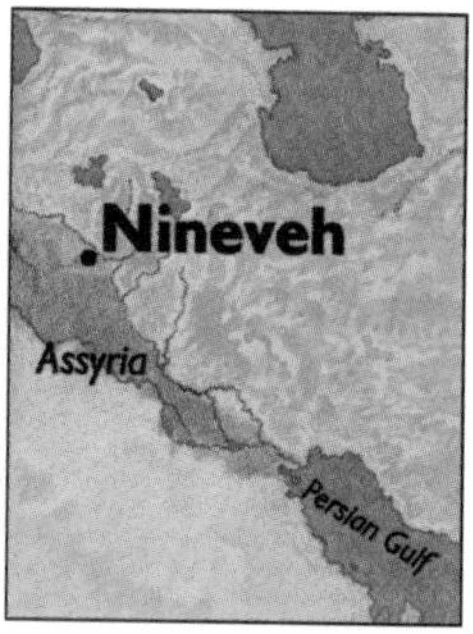


**Ninevites** (**nin**-uh-vites)
People who lived in *Nineveh*.

*Jonah 3:5*
*Luke 11:30*

**ninth hour** (**nynth our**)
Nine hours from sunrise; three o'clock.
See also *hour*

*Matthew 20:3-6*
*Mark 15:33-34*

Nehemiah 2:1
Esther 3:7

**Nisan** (**nee**-sahn)
First *month* of the Israelite year, overlapping March and April. Also called *Abib*.

2 Kings 19:37

**Nisroch** (**niss**-rok)
Assyrian god worshiped by *Sennacherib*.

Genesis 5:32
Genesis 7:1-5
1 Peter 3:18-21

**Noah** (**noh**-uh)
• "The only blameless man living on earth" ten generations after Adam and Eve; son of Lamech.

Noah is famous for building the ark that carried the only survivors of the *flood*. His sons Shem, Ham, and Japheth became the ancestors of every nation on earth. Noah's story is told in Genesis 6:1-10:32 and in Hebrews 11.

Numbers 26:33

• One of *Zelophehad's* daughters.

1 Samuel 21:1
1 Samuel 22:18-19

**Nob** (**nob**)
A town near Jerusalem, in the territory of Benjamin. David hid from Saul in Nob, and Saul murdered the 85 priests who helped him. Nob's exact location is unknown.

Numbers 32:42
Judges 8:11

**Nobah** (**noh**-buh)
An Israelite of Manasseh who captured *Kenath* during the conquest of Moab. Nobah named the city after himself. Gideon chased the army of Midian past this city.

**nomads** (**noh**-mads)

People who move their home from place to place; people who have no permanent home or homeland. Nomads of Old Testament times moved around because they depended on their animals for food, and their animals needed pasture land. As seasons changed, so did the pasture land, and the nomads had to move to new areas.

*Judges 8:11*
*Jeremiah 3:2*
*Jeremiah 35:7*

**North Gate** (**north gate**)

One of the gates in the walls of the *temple*. *Obed-Edom* was its *gatekeeper*.

See also *East Gate; South Gate; West Gate*

*1 Chronicles 26:14-19*

**northern kingdom** (**nor**-thurn **king**-duhm)

The ten tribes of *Israel* that split from Rehoboam and chose Jeroboam as their king after Solomon's death (the southern kingdom became *Judah*).

See also *kings of Israel; southern kingdom; prophets to Israel*

*1 Samuel 11:8*
*Jeremiah 3:12*

**Numbers, book of** (**nuhm**-burz, **buk** uhv)

Fourth book of the Old Testament and fourth of the *books of law*. The book is called Numbers because it includes two censuses and many other numbers. But it tells mainly about Israel's

*Numbers 2:3-8*
*Numbers 12:1-5*
*Numbers 26:63-64*

wanderings in the desert during the *Exodus*. Some of its most famous stories include *Korah's rebellion*, Miriam and Aaron's mutiny, the failure at *Kadesh Barnea*, Moses' failure at *Meribah*, *Balaam*, an explanation of *cities of refuge*, and *Zelophehad's* daughters. Numbers was written by Moses.

N

*Colossians 4:15*

**Nympha** (**nim**-fuh)
A Christian in *Laodicea* whose home was used as a church in New Testament times.

**Nymphas** (**nim**-fuhss)
See *Nympha*

**oath (ohth)**

A promise made in God's name; a solemn promise; a promise that a person asks God to witness. A true oath invites God's punishment if broken.

See also *vow*

*Genesis 14:22*
*Deuteronomy 29:14-15*
*Hebrews 6:16-17*

**Obadiah** (**oh**-buh-**dye**-uh)

A very common name among the Israelites:

• Israelite prophet of Judah who wrote the *book of Obadiah*. We know nothing else about him. *Obadiah 1:1*

• *Ahab's* palace manager and friend of Elijah. Obadiah became a hero for hiding 100 true prophets from Ahab and Jezebel's executioners. *1 Kings 18:2-4*

• A Levite musician who helped repair the temple during Josiah's reform. Obadiah served as foreman. *2 Chronicles 34:8-12*

• A skilled Israelite soldier from the tribe of Gad who defected to David at Ziklag; second in command under *Ezer*. *1 Chronicles 12:1-2, 9*

• An official sent by Jehoshaphat to teach in Judah. *2 Chronicles 17:7*

• A temple gatekeeper during the time of Nehemiah. *Nehemiah 12:25-26*

• Several others mentioned only once.

**Obadiah, book of** (**oh**-buh-**dye**-uh, **buk** uhv) *Obadiah 1:1, 18*

Thirty-first book of the Old Testament and fourth of the *minor prophets*. The book of

Obadiah records prophecies against Edom. It is the shortest book in the Old Testament.
See also *Obadiah*

**Obed** (**oh**-bed)

*Ruth 4:17*
*Luke 3:23, 32*
• Son of Ruth and Boaz; David's grandfather. Obed is mentioned in the genealogy of Jesus.

*1 Chronicles 11: 26, 47*
• One of David's *mighty men*.

*1 Chronicles 2:32, 37*
• An Israelite in the tribe of Judah; son of Ephlal in Jerahmeel's clan.

*1 Chronicles 26:7*
• One of Obed-Edom's grandsons and a leader in the clan of Korah; son of *Shemaiah*.

*2 Chronicles 23:1*
• Father of one of the two Azariahs who helped Jehoiada overthrow *Athaliah*.

**Obed-Edom** (**oh**-bed-**ee**-duhm)

*1 Chronicles 15: 17-18*
• A temple *gatekeeper* appointed to sing and play music during the return of the Ark to Jerusalem.

*2 Samuel 6:10-12*
• A *Gittite* who housed the Ark of the Covenant for three months during its journey back to Jerusalem from Philistia.

**obedience** (oh-**bee**-dee-uhnss)

*1 Chronicles 21:19*
*Romans 5:19*
*Hebrews 5:7-9*

Doing what God says; following God's commands and guidance. Obedience to God is an important Christian duty. God rejected Saul as king because he refused to obey God. Jesus died on the cross out of obedience to God the Father.

**obeisance** (oh-**bee**-uh-suhnss)
An older word for bowing. Bowing showed great respect, honor, or submission.

*Exodus 18:7*
*2 Chronicles 24:17*

**obey** (oh-**bay**)
See *obedience*

**Oded** (**oh**-ded)
• Prophet in Judah who inspired *Azariah*, *Amasa*, *Berekiah*, and *Jehizkiah* to protest the enslavement of 200,00 prisoners of war. This was during the reign of Ahaz. *2 Chronicles 28:9*
• Father of *Azariah* the prophet. *2 Chronicles 15:1*

**offering** (**awf**-ur-ing)
Another word for *sacrifice*; something a person gives up or presents to God, usually to *make atonement* for sin or to offer thanks. Some offerings required a person to kill an animal, but others involved the giving of grain or even praise. The rules for offerings are given in Leviticus 1:1–7:38.

See also *fellowship offering; grain offering; guilt offering; ordination offering; sin offering*

*Genesis 4:3-5*
*2 Chronicles 29:21*
*Ephesians 5:1-2*

**Og** (**og**)
Amorite king over *Bashan* during the Exodus. Moses and the Israelites defeated Og and gave Bashan to the tribe of Manasseh.

*Numbers 21:33*
*Joshua 13:12*

O

Ezekiel 23:4-5
Ezekiel 23:36-37

**Oholah** (oh-**hoh**-luh)
Another name for *Samaria*, or the northern kingdom of Israel, used in Ezekiel's prophesies. The prophesies describe Oholah as a prostitute, because Israel worshiped idols.
See also *Oholibah*

Exodus 31:1-6
Exodus 38:22-23

**Oholiab** (oh-**hoh**-lee-uhb)
Assistant to *Bezalel*. Oholiab was chosen for this job by God himself. Oholiab was the son of Ahisamach from the tribe of Dan.

Ezekiel 23:4
Ezekiel 23:44

**Oholibah** (oh-**hoh**-li-buh)
Another name for *Jerusalem*, or the southern kingdom of Judah, used in Ezekiel's prophesies. The prophesies describe Oholibah as a prostitute, because Judah worshiped idols.
See also *Oholah*

Genesis 36:2, 14
1 Chronicles 1:51-52

**Oholibamah** (oh-**hah**-li-**bay**-muh)
- One of *Esau's* wives.
- A clan chief in the tribe of Edom.

Genesis 28:18
Luke 10:34
James 5:14

**oil (oil)**
Usually olive oil, a very common food, medicine, and even currency mentioned often in the Bible. Olive oil was made from pressed olives. It was used as a fuel for *lamps*, as an ingredient in many kinds of *food*, and as the main ingredient in *anointing oil*.

**Olives, Mount of** (**awl**-ivz, **mount** uhv)
See *Mount of Olives*

**Omega** (oh-**meg**-uh)
See *Alpha and Omega*

**omer** (**oh**-mur)
A dry measure equal to about two liters, or two quarts; one-tenth of an *ephah*.
*Exodus 16:16-22*

**omnipotence** (om-**ni**-poh-tenss)
Unlimited power. The Bible often describes *God* as having omnipotence. It means he is omnipotent, or almighty.

See also *omnipresence; omniscience*
*Psalm 24:8*
*Jeremiah 32:27*

**omnipresence** (**om**-nee-**prez**-uhnss)

Being everywhere. The Bible often describes *God* as omnipresent, or everywhere at once.
See also *omnipotence; omniscience*
*Psalm 46:1*
*Proverbs 15:3*
*1 Peter 3:12*

**omniscience** (om-**ni**-shenss)
Knowledge of everything. The Bible often describes *God* as omniscient, or aware of everything.

See also *omnipotence; omnipresence*
*Psalm 94:11*
*Matthew 6:8*
*Luke 16:15*

**Omri** (**om**-ree)
• Sixth king of the northern kingdom of Israel. Omri was not the son of the king nor even one of the princes, but commander of the army.
*1 Kings 16:16*

Omri came to power by besieging Tirzah after *Zimri* assassinated *Elah*. When Zimri realized he was trapped, he set fire to the palace and died. Omri's men had already declared him king. The next three kings of Israel were sons or grandsons of Omri.

1 Chronicles 27:18
• Commander of the forces of *Issachar* in David's army; son of Michael.

1 Chronicles 7:8
1 Chronicles 9:4
• Two others mentioned only in the genealogies of 1 Chronicles.

**On** (**on**)

Genesis 41:45
• A city in *Egypt* where people worshiped the sun god Atum-Re; also called Heliopolis.

Numbers 16:1
• One of those who joined *Korah's rebellion*; son of Peleth.

Genesis 38:2-4, 8-9
**Onan** (**oh**-nan)

One of two sons of Judah who died for their wickedness (the other was *Er*).

Colossians 4:9
Philemon 1:10
**Onesimus** (oh-**nes**-i-muhss)

A slave who became a Christian while on the run from his master. The New Testament *book of Philemon* is about Onesimus.

2 Timothy 1:16
2 Timothy 4:19
**Onesiphorus** (**oh**-ne-**si**-for-uhss)

Christian who helped the apostle Paul in his ministry at Ephesus and who visited Paul in prison at *Rome*.

**only begotten** (**ohn**-lee bee-**got**-uhn)
A term used to describe Jesus in several translations of the New Testament (see John 3:16). It means "one and only," or "unique." Jesus is God's only Son.

*John 1:14*
*John 3:16*
*Hebrews 11:17*
*1 John 4:9*

**onycha** (**on**-i-kuh)
The curved piece of a mollusk shell. God told the Israelites to use this as an ingredient in holy *incense*.

*Exodus 30:34*

**Ophel** (**oh**-fel)
The name often given to the main *citadel* of a fortified city in Old Testament times. Jerusalem and Samaria both had an Ophel. The word means "swelling."

*2 Chronicles 33:14*
*Nehemiah 11:21*

**Ophir** (**oh**-fihr)
A region in south Arabia famous for its gold.

*1 Kings 9:28*
*Job 28:16*
*Isaiah 13:12*

**Ophrah** (**ohf**-ruh)
• A *Canaanite* city in the land allotted to Benjamin. Its exact location is unknown.

*Joshua 18:21-23*

• A Canaanite city in the land allotted to Manasseh west of the Jordan River. This Ophrah was Gideon's hometown. Its exact location is unknown.

*Judges 6:11*

**oracle** (**or**-uh-kuhl)
A *prophecy*; a message from God spoken by a prophet.

*Numbers 23:7*
*Isaiah 23:1*
*Malachi 1:1*

O

O

*Exodus 28:41*
*Leviticus 21:10*
*2 Kings 19:25*

**ordain** (or-**dayn**)
Set apart for a special duty, job, or purpose.

*Exodus 28:43*
*Psalm 81:3-4*

**ordinance** (**or**-di-nenss)
A *law*, rule, command, or statute.

*Leviticus 7:37*
*Leviticus 8:28*

**ordination offering**
(**or**-di-**nay**-shuhn **awf**-ur-ing)
A special *offering* done only once, when Aaron and his sons were first set aside as priests, during the Exodus.

*Judges 7:25*
*Psalm 83:11*

**Oreb** (**or**-uhb)
One of the Midianite generals defeated by Gideon's 300-man force.
See also *Zeeb*

*Ruth 1:4, 14*

**Orpah** (**or**-puh)

Ruth's sister-in-law; Midianite woman who married Naomi's son *Kilion*. Ruth married Kilion's brother *Mahlon*. Unlike Ruth, Orpah stayed in Midian and went back to her Midianite gods after Naomi left for Bethlehem.

*Exodus 22:22*
*John 14:15-18*
*James 1:27*

**orphan** (**or**-fuhn)
A child whose parents have died. God instructed his people always to provide for *widows* and orphans. *Esther* was an orphan.

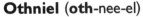

**osprey** (**os**-pri)
One of the birds that the Israelites were not allowed to eat. It was probably a vulture of some kinds, but its exact identity is unknown.

*Leviticus 11:13-18*
*Deuteronomy 14:11-17*

**Othni** (**oth**-nye)
One of Obed-Edom's grandsons and a leader in the clan of Korah; son of *Shemaiah*.

*1 Chronicles 26:7*

**Othniel** (**oth**-nee-el)
Son of Kenaz, younger brother of Caleb, and first judge of Israel. Othniel married his cousin Acsah, Caleb's daughter. He judged Israel 40 years.

*Joshua 15:16-17*
*Judges 3:9-11*

**Ovens, Tower of** (**uhv**-uhnz, **tou**-ur uhv)
See *Tower of Ovens*

**ox, oxen** (**oks, ok**-sen)
A male of cattle; a *bull* (plural: oxen). The Israelites and many other peoples of ancient times used oxen to pull plows.
See also *oxgoad*

*Exodus 21:33-34*
*Numbers 7:6*
*1 Corinthians 9:9*

**ox goad** (**oks** gode)
A long stick used to prod oxen while they were plowing. It had a flat piece of iron attached to it for scraping mud off the plow, and a point for poking the ox. The resurrected Jesus scolded *Saul* of Tarsus by comparing him with an ox that tries to kick the goad when poked.

*Judges 3:31*

Genesis 28:5-7
Genesis 31:18

**Paddan Aram (pad-en air-uhm)**

The area around *Haran* in upper Mesopotamia between the Euphrates River and the Habur River. Abram lived in Paddan Aram before moving to Canaan. *Rebekah* was from this area too. Isaac sent Jacob there to find a wife, and Rebekah sent him there to flee from Esau.

See also *Aram; Bethuel; Laban*

P

Matthew 18:17
Luke 12:29-31

2 Kings 23:5
Isaiah 57:8

**pagan (pay-guhn)**

• Noun: An unbeliever; a person who does not love or obey God.

• Adjective: Unbelieving; faithless; wicked.

See also *Gentile; Jew*

Numbers 7:72-77
Numbers 10:26

**Pagiel (pay-gee-el)**

Leader of the tribe of Asher during the Exodus; son of Ocran.

Genesis 17:8
2 Chronicles 9:26
Joel 3:4

**Palestine (pal-uh-styne)**

The land of the Philistines; *Philistia* and the land to the east of it. When the Canaanites lived in this land, it was known as *Canaan*. When the people of Israel lived there, it was known as the land of *Israel*. It includes the smaller areas known as *Edom*, *Moab*, *Judea*, *Gilead*, *Bashan*, *Ammon*, *Negev*, and *Galilee*, among others. It also includes *Lake Huleh*, the *Sea of Galilee*, the *Jordan River*, and the *Dead Sea*.

P

**Palti** (**pal**-tye)

- One of the 12 men chosen by Moses at Kadesh Barnea to spy out the land of Canaan; a leader of the tribe of Benjamin; son of Raphu. *Numbers 13:3, 9*
- *Paltiel.* *Numbers 34:17, 26*

**Paltiel** (**pal**-tih-uhl)

- The family leader of *Issachar* chosen by God to help divide up the land after the conquest of Canaan. *Numbers 34:26*
- The man from the tribe of Benjamin to whom Saul gave *Michal* after David fled Jerusalem; also called Palti; son of Laish. *1 Samuel 25:44*

**Pamphylia** (pam-**fil**-ee-uh)

*Acts 13:13*
*Acts 15:37-38*
*Acts 27:5*

Roman province directly south of *Galatia* along the Mediterranean coast of Asia Minor. Pamphylia was east of *Lycia* and west of *Cilicia*. Paul traveled through the Pamphylian cities of Attalia and *Perga* during his first missionary journey. This is also where *John Mark* deserted Paul and Barnabas.

**Paphos** (**pay**-fos)

*Acts 13:6*
*Acts 13:13*

A city and its port on the southwest coast of *Cyprus* during New Testament times. Paul sailed through the port city of Paphos during his first missionary journey.

*Exodus 2:3*
*Job 8:11*

**papyrus** (puh-**pye**-ruhss)
A plant native to the Nile delta of Egypt and *Lake Huleh* that grows in marshes and muddy soil; *Cyperus papyrus*. People of Old Testament times used papyrus to make paper, rope, sandals, mats, baskets, and even boats. Moses' mother hid her baby in a basket made of papyrus.

P

*Psalm 78:2-3*
*Ezekiel 20:49*
*Matthew 13:10-12*

**parable (pair**-uh-buhl)
A story with a special meaning. Jesus told many parables to teach his disciples.
See also *Gospels*

*Luke 23:32-43*
*2 Corinthians 12:2-4*
*Revelation 2:7*

**paradise (pair**-uh-dise)
Another word for *Heaven*.

*Genesis 21:17-21*
*Deuteronomy 33:2*
*1 Kings 11:17-18*

**Paran (pair**-uhn)
The region between *Negev* and *Sinai*. No clear boundaries marked Paran from the rest of the surrounding areas.
See also *Desert of Paran*

*2 Samuel 23:9*
*1 Chronicles 11:13*

**Pas-dammim (pas dam**-uhm)
Site of a great Israelite victory against the Philistines. Dodai's son *Eleazar* was responsible for the remarkable outcome. Pas-dammim is also called *Ephes-dammim*.

**Pashhur** (**pash**-ur)

• Chief priest during the reign of *Zedekiah* who had Jeremiah beaten and put in stocks; son of *Immer*. *Jeremiah 20:1-3*

• One of the four royal officials who put Jeremiah in a cistern; son of *Malkijah*; grandson of King *Zedekiah*. *Jeremiah 21:1*

• Father of *Gedaliah*. *Jeremiah 38:1-2*

• One of those who agreed to Nehemiah's reforms. *Nehemiah 10:1-3*

**Passover** (**pass**-oh-vur)

Part of the *Feast of Unleavened Bread* and one of the most important annual Jewish *festivals*. Passover celebrates the night God freed his people from Egypt. On that night, the death angel swept through the land but passed over each house of the Israelites. The *Last Supper* that Jesus ate with his disciples was a Passover meal.

*Exodus 12:11*
*John 18:28*
*1 Corinthians 5:7*

**Passover lamb** (**pass**-oh-vur **lam**)

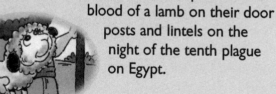

The lamb eaten at the *Passover* meal. A lamb is eaten because the Israelite slaves sprinkled the blood of a lamb on their door posts and lintels on the night of the tenth plague on Egypt.

*Exodus 12:21*
*2 Chronicles 35:1*
*1 Corinthians 5:7*

John 10:11-18
Hebrews 13:20
1 Peter 2:25

**pastor** (**pas**-tur)
"Shepherd," a word used for church leaders.
See also *elders*

1 Timothy 1:2-7
2 Timothy 2:1-2
Titus 1:4-9

**pastoral epistles** (**pas**-tur-uhl eh-**pis**-uhlz)
A term often used to describe the New Testament books of 1 Timothy, 2 Timothy, and Titus. A pastor is a church leader and an epistle is a letter; thus, "pastoral epistle" means "letter to a church leader." Each letter gives advice and instructions especially for leaders of a church. The apostle *Paul* wrote all three.
See also *Timothy; Titus*

Jeremiah 44:15
Ezekiel 29:13-14

**Pathros** (**path**-ros)
The land of *Upper Egypt*; the southern part of Egypt. In ancient times the region of Pathros was between the cities of Memphis and Syene. In modern Egypt, this would be the land between Cairo and Aswan.
See also *Pathrusites*

**Pathrusim** (path-roo-**seem**)
See *Pathrusites*

Genesis 10:13-14

**Pathrusites** (**path**-roo-sites)
People who lived in southern Egypt; Egyptians from *Pathros*.
See also *Mizraim*

**Patmos** (**pat**-muhss)

A small island about 55 kilometers off the southwestern coast of *Asia*, near *Cos*. The apostle John wrote the *book of Revelation* while on Patmos.

*Revelation 1:9*

**patriarch** (**pay**-tree-ark)

A forefather or ancestor. Abraham, Isaac, and Jacob were patriarchs of Israel.

*Acts 7:8*
*Hebrews 7:4*

P

**Paul** (**pawl**)

"Saul of Tarsus," the *apostle*, *evangelist*, and author of 13 New Testament books. Saul was his Hebrew name; his Greek name was Paul. Paul influenced the spread of Christianity more than any other person. He led three missionary journeys to many Roman provinces and cities before he was arrested and forced to go to Rome to stand trial. The famous story of his conversion is told in Acts 9. Acts 13:1–21:16 records his missionary journeys. Acts 22:17–28:31 records his journey to Rome.

*Acts 13:9*
*Acts 13:45-46*
*Colossians 1:23*

**Paulus, Sergius** (**pawl**-uhss, **sur**-jee-uhss)

See *Sergius Paulus*

**Peace Offering** (**peess awf**-ur-ing)

Another term for *Fellowship Offering*.

*Leviticus 3:1*
*Numbers 7:8*

P

Numbers 34:28

**Pedahel** (**ped**-uh-hel)

The family leader of *Naphtali* chosen by God to help divide up the land after the conquest of Canaan.

Nehemiah 3:22-26

**Pedaiah** (pe-**dye**-uh)

A common name among the Israelites:

- One of those who helped *Nehemiah* repair the walls of Jerusalem; son of Parosh.
- At least six others mentioned only by name.

2 Kings 15:25
Isaiah 7:1

**Pekah** (**pee**-kuh)

Son of Remaliah and nineteenth king of Israel after *Pekahiah*. Pekah was commander of the army under Pekahiah. Pekah came to power by assassinating the king and taking his place. He reigned 20 years and was remembered as an evil king.

2 Kings 15:22-25

**Pekahiah** (**pek**-uh-**hye**-uh)

Son of *Menahem* and eighteenth king of Israel after his father. Pekahiah reigned two years and was remembered as an evil king.

Jeremiah 50:21
Ezekiel 23:22-23

**Pekod** (**pee**-kod)

A tribe of Arameans living in Babylonia during the time of *Jeremiah*.

**Peleg** (**pel**-eg)

Son of Eber and therefore great-grandson of Noah. He was named Peleg, which means "division," because he was born during the time of *Babel*, when the people of the world first became divided.

*Genesis 10:25*
*Genesis 11:16*

**Pelet** (**pe**-let)

• An Israelite warrior from the tribe of Benjamin who defected to David at *Ziklag*; brother of *Jeziel* and son of Azmaveth.

*1 Chronicles 12:3*

• Father of his clan during the time of David; son of Jahdai; a descendant of Caleb.

*1 Chronicles 2: 46-47*

**Pelethites** (**pel**-uh-thytes)

A group of people that settled in the Negev across from the *Kerethites*. The Pelethites were among those who served as David's bodyguards under Benaiah's command.

*2 Samuel 20:7*
*1 Kings 1:38*

**Peloponnesus** (**pel**-uh-puh-**nee**-siss)

The south-most part of Greece. The word Peloponnesus does not appear in the Bible, but the biblical cities of *Cenchrea* and *Corinth* were located there.

*Acts 18:18*
*Romans 16:1*

**Peniel** (puh-**nye**-uhl)

The name *Jacob* gave to the place where he wrestled with God.

*Genesis 32:30*

P

P

1 Samuel 1:1-4

**Peninnah** (puh-**nin**-uh)

Wife of *Elkanah* who teased Hannah for having no children. Peninnah had several sons and daughters.

Deuteronomy 29:21
1 Corinthians 9:9

**Pentateuch** (**pen**-tuh-took)

The first five books of the Bible: *Genesis*, *Exodus*, *Leviticus*, *Numbers*, and *Deuteronomy*; also called the Law, the Books of Law, the Law of Moses, the *Book of the Law*, and the Book of the Law of God.

Acts 2:1
Acts 20:16
1 Corinthians 16:8

**Pentecost** (**pent**-uh-kost)

New Testament name for the *Feast of Weeks*, the fiftieth day after Passover. "Pentecost" means "fiftieth." The famous coming of the Holy Spirit at Jerusalem took place during a celebration of Pentecost.

**Penuel** (**pen**-yoo-uhl)

Genesis 32:30-31

- Another spelling for *Peniel*.

1 Chronicles 4:4
1 Chronicles 8:25

- Two clan leaders mentioned in the genealogies of First Chronicles.

Numbers 23:27-28
Numbers 31:16

**Peor** (**pee**-ohr)

A mountain in Moab whose exact location is unknown. *Balak* took *Balaam* to the top of this mountain in an effort to have Balaam curse Israel.

**perdition** (pur-**di**-shuhn)
An older word for eternal destruction. The term is used of those condemned to hell.

*John 17:12*
*2 Thessalonians 2:3*

**Perez** (**pair**-ez)
Son of Judah and Tamar; twin brother of *Zerah*; father of Hezron and Hamul; forefather of the *Perizzites*.

*Genesis 38:26-30*
*Ruth 4:12*

**Perga** (**pur**-guh)
A port city in the Roman province of *Pamphylia* visited by the apostle Paul during his first missionary journey. Perga, like Ephesus, had a temple of *Artemis*. The port city of *Attalia* was nearby to the west.

*Acts 13:13-14*
*Acts 14:24-25*

**Pergamum** (**pur**-guh-muhm)
A city in the Roman province of *Asia* and headquarters of Roman emperor worship. Jesus called Pergamum "the city where that great throne of Satan is located" (Revelation 2:13). The city was about 24 kilometers inland from the coast of the Aegean Sea, and 110 kilometers north of *Smyrna*.

*Revelation 1:10-11*
*Revelation 2:12-17*

**Perizzites** (**pair**-uh-zites)
People descended from *Perez*.

*Genesis 34:30*
*Joshua 17:15*
*Nehemiah 9:8*

P

Mark 4:16-17
Acts 8:1
1 Thessalonians 3:7

**persecution** (pur-si-**kyoo**-shuhn)
The abuse or torture of others because of their beliefs or devotion to God. Many people persecuted the prophets of Israel, especially *Jeremiah*. Saul of Tarsus persecuted Christians before he believed in Christ. The *book of First Peter* was written to help Christians deal with persecution.

2 Chronicles 36:20-23
Daniel 10:1

**Persia** (**pur**-zhuh)
The land directly east of Babylonia and Elam, and the people that lived there; modern Iran. The *Persians* ruled the kingdom of Babylonia after the Babylonians during the Exile. *Cyrus*, *Darius*, and *Artaxerxes* were Persian kings.
See also *Ahasuerus; Daniel; Esther; Ezra; Nehemiah; Zerubbabel*

Daniel 5:25-28
Daniel 6:12

**Persians** (**pur**-zhinz)
People of *Persia*.

Matthew 10:2
Mark 14:70-72
Acts 1:15-16

**Peter** (**pee**-tur)
*Simon* Peter.
See also *First Peter, Second Peter*

1 Peter 1:1-2

**Peter, First** (**pee**-tur, **furst**)
Twenty-first book of the New Testament, a letter written by the apostle Peter to the Christians who were driven out of Jerusalem and scattered throughout *Asia Minor*. Believers of Peter's day had been persecuted for their

faith and therefore had traveled from their homes to all parts of the Roman Empire, especially Asia Minor. Many churches had started there. Peter wrote this letter to them. Most of the letter encourages Christians to stay true to Christ as they suffer for their faith.
See also *Second Peter*

**Peter, Second** (**pee**-tur, **sek**-uhnd)
Twenty-second book of the New Testament, a letter written by the apostle Peter to all Christians everywhere. Peter wrote this letter to teach about Christian growth, and to warn about *false teachers*.
See also *First Peter*

*2 Peter 1:1-2*

**Pharaoh** (**fair**-oh)
The king or ruler of *Egypt*. "Pharaoh" was a title, like "President."
See also *Hophra; Neco; Shishak*

*Genesis 40:4-5*
*Exodus 1:15-18*
*Acts 7:17-18*

**Pharaoh Hophra** (**fair**-oh **hof**-ruh)
See *Hophra*

**Pharaoh Neco** (**fair**-oh **nek**-oh)
See *Neco*

**Pharisees** (**fair**-uh-seez)
A group of leaders among the Jews in New Testament times famous for their opposition to Jesus. Pharisees stressed strict obedience to the *law* and had a lot of extra rules, called "oral

*Matthew 5:20*
*Mark 8:11*
*Acts 23:6-8*

laws," to explain how. They challenged Jesus for doing what they thought illegal. Jesus said that

they applied the law too strictly and had lost sight of the law's intent. Pharisees were among those on the *Sanhedrin* who had Jesus arrested and tried for blasphemy. But not all Pharisees opposed him: *Joseph* of Arimathea and *Nicodemus* were secret disciples.

See also *Judaism; judaizer; Sadducees*

**Phicol** (**fye**-kohl)

*Genesis 21:22, 32*
- Commander of the *Philistine* army in Abraham's time.

*Genesis 26:25-27*
- Commander of the Philistine army in *Isaac's* time.

These two Phicols may have been the same man. It is also possible that "Phicol" was a title rather than a personal name.

See also *Abimelech*

*Revelation 1:10-11*
*Revelation 3:7*

**Philadelphia** (**fil**-uh-**del**-fee-uh)

A city in the heart of the Roman province of Asia, sixth of the seven mentioned in the letters of *Revelation*. The churches at Philadelphia and *Smyrna* were the only two that Jesus did not rebuke in these letters. Jesus commended the Christians at Philadelphia for being *faithful* to him. The city was located 32 kilometers east of Sardis.

**Philemon** (fye-**lee**-muhn)

Christian man named in the *book of Philemon*; Christian co-worker of Paul's, host of a church in his home, and owner of a slave named Onesimus. Philemon was probably from *Colosse*.

*Philemon 1:1, 8-11*

**Philemon, book of** (fye-**lee**-muhn, buk uhv)

Eighteenth book of the New Testament, a letter written by Paul to *Philemon*. Paul wrote this letter because Philemon's runaway slave Onesimus had become a Christian and was about to return. Paul wanted Philemon to forgive *Onesimus* and receive him as a brother.

*Philemon 1:1, 8-11*

**Philetus** (fye-**lee**-tuhss)

A false teacher at Ephesus who made the same mistakes as *Hymenaeus*.

*2 Timothy 2:16-18*

**Philip** (**fil**-ip)

A common name in New Testament times:

- *Tetrarch* of *Iturea* and *Traconitis* when John the Baptist started preaching. *Luke 3:1-3*

- *Herod Antipas*.
- One of Jesus' first disciples and the man who introduced Nathanael to him. Philip is always listed fifth among the Twelve. *John 1:44-46*
- One of seven *evangelists* sent by the church in Jerusalem to preach in the surrounding areas. This is the Philip who explained Isaiah 53 to the Ethiopian eunuch. *Acts 8:38-40; 21:7-8*

*Matthew 16:13*
*Acts 16:12*
*1 Thessalonians 2:2*

**Philippi** (**fil**-i-pye)
City in the Roman province of *Macedonia* 15 kilometers northwest of *Neapolis*. Paul visited Philippi during his second and third missionary journeys and started the church there.

See also *Philippians, book of*

P

*Philippians 4:15*

**Philippians** (fil-**ip**-ee-uhnz)
- People who lived in *Philippi* in New Testament times.
- Christians of the church in Philippi. Paul wrote the *book of Philippians* to these believers.

*Philippians 1:3-11*
*Philippians 4:15*

**Philippians, book of** (fil-**ip**-ee-uhnz, **buk** uhv)
Eleventh book of the New Testament, a letter by Paul to the Christians at *Philippi*. Paul wrote this letter while in prison in Rome, and it is one of the most personal letters in the New Testament. It has a lot of kind words for the Philippian Christians and the way they treated Paul while he was there. More than anything else, Paul urged his readers to be joyful.

*Exodus 15:14*
*Joel 3:4*

**Philistia** (fuh-**lis**-tee-uh)
The land of the *Philistines*, mainly the western strip of the Negev along the Mediterranean coast around the cities of *Ashkelon*, *Ashdod*, *Ekron*, *Gath*, and *Gaza*.

*Genesis 21:32*
*Judges 13:5*

**Philistines** (**fil**-i-steenz)
Descendants of the *Casluhites*, the people of Philistia and constant enemies of Israel. *Goliath* is

one of the most famous Philistines of all. Many of the judges fought against the Philistines.

**Phinehas** (**fin**-ee-uhss)
See *Hophni and Phinehas*

**Phoebe** (**fee**-bee)
Christian woman who was highly respected in the early church.
*Romans 16:1-2*

**Phoenicia** (fuh-**nee**-shuh)
Another name for the land of *Lebanon*, especially the coastal part between *Carmel* and the Orontes River. *Tyre* and *Sidon* were in Phoenicia.
*Isaiah 23:11*
*Mark 7:26*
*Acts 11:19; 15:3; 21:2*

**Phoenix** (**fee**-nikss)
A harbor on the southwestern side of the island of *Crete*. The ship carrying Paul and other prisoners to Rome was blown off course while en route to Phoenix after sailing from *Fair Havens*.
*Acts 27:12*

**Phrygia** (**frij**-ee-uh)
A mountainous region in the western center of Asia Minor, directly west of the region of *Galatia*. Phrygia overlapped the Roman provinces of Asia and Galatia.
*Acts 16:6*
*Acts 18:23*

**phylacteries** (fil-**ak**-tur-eez)
Small boxes containing verses of Scripture. Devout Jews and *Pharisees* would strap these to their foreheads in observance of Deuteronomy 6:8.
*Matthew 23:5*

P

Exodus 14:2
Exodus 14:9
Numbers 33:7-8

**Pi-hahiroth** (**pye** hah-**hye**-roth)
The place in the east of *Egypt* where the Egyptian chariots caught up with the fleeing Israelites, and where the Israelites entered the Red Sea after it had parted.

Genesis 15:9
Leviticus 1:14
Leviticus 12:6

**pigeon** (**pij**-uhn)
A medium-sized, plump bird closely related to the *dove* and one of the kinds of animals the Israelites were allowed to *sacrifice* for sin. Pigeons were darker in color than doves. Doves and pigeons were chosen by those who could not afford bulls, sheep, or goats.

See also *offering*

**Pilate** (**pye**-luht)
See *Pontius Pilate*

Numbers 23:14
Deuteronomy 3:17
Joshua 12:3

**Pisgah** (**piz**-guh)
A mountain or range of mountains in Moab near Mount *Nebo*. Its exact location is unknown.

Genesis 2:10-14

**Pishon** (**pye**-shon)
One of the four rivers that flowed out of the garden of *Eden*.

Acts 14:24

**Pisidia** (pi-**sid**-ee-uh)
A rugged, mountainous region directly south of *Phrygia* in the Roman province of Galatia. Pisidia

was sandwiched between *Phrygia*, *Lycia*, *Pamphylia*, and *Lycaonia*.

**Pisidian Antioch** (pi-**sid**-ee-uhn **an**-tee-ahk)

The city of Antioch that was located in *Pisidia*. (There was another *Antioch* in Syria.) Paul and Barnabas visited Pisidian Antioch on their first missionary journey. Their short stay proved to be one of the most important events in all of New Testament history, because the Jews of that city rejected Paul's message out of jealousy. Paul's response, "well, we will offer it to the Gentiles" (Acts 13:46), marked the start of Gentile Christianity. Paul and his companions probably returned to Antioch on his second and third missionary journeys.

*Acts 13:14*

**Pithom** (**pith**-uhm)

One of two cities built by the Hebrew slaves in Egypt before the *Exodus*. The other was *Rameses*.

*Exodus 1:11*

**Place of the Skull** (**playss** uhv the **skuhl**)

See *Golgotha*

**plague** (**playg**)

• Noun: Wide-spread disease or destruction; any intrusion that brings disease or harm to many people.

*Exodus 9:15*
*Psalm 78:50*
*Revelation 6:8*

*Exodus 8:2*
*Ezekiel 28:23*

• Verb: To cause wide-spread harm or destruction to life.

See also *plagues of Egypt*

*Exodus 5:3-4*
*Amos 4:10*

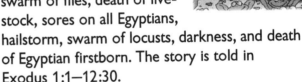

**plagues of Egypt** (**playgz** uhv **ee**-jipt)
Ten disasters that God brought on Egypt during the time of the Israelites' slavery in Egypt. God had sent Moses to lead the people of Israel across the wilderness to Canaan, but *Pharaoh* said no. Each time Pharaoh denied permission, God sent a plague. The ten plagues were: water to blood, swarm of frogs, swarm of gnats, swarm of flies, death of livestock, sores on all Egyptians, hailstorm, swarm of locusts, darkness, and death of Egyptian firstborn. The story is told in Exodus 1:1—12:30.

**plain, cities of the** (**plane, si**-teez uhv the)
See *cities of the plain*

*1 Samuel 13:20-21*
*Joel 3:10*

**plowshare** (**plou**-shair)
The blade of a plow.
See also *ox goad*

**pole, Asherah** (**pohl, ash**-ur-uh)
See *Asherah pole*
See also *high place; idolatry; shrine*

**Pollux** (**pol**-uhks)
See *Castor and Pollux*

**Pontius Pilate** (**pon**-shus **pye**-luht)

Roman *procurator* (governor) of Judea during the time of Jesus' arrest, trial, and crucifixion. Pilate is the one who sentenced Jesus to death.

Luke 3:1
Acts 4:27
1 Timothy 6:13

**Pontus** (**pon**-tuhss)

The middle portion of Asia Minor's Black Sea coast. The Romans administered Pontus together with *Bithynia* as a single province.

Acts 2:7-9
Acts 18:2
1 Peter 1:1

**Pool of Siloam** (**pool** uhv sye-**loh**-uhm)

A shallow pool at the south end of the city of Jerusalem supplied by fresh water from the spring *Gihon*. The water comes through Hezekiah's tunnel. The *Fountain Gate* is named for being right nearby this pool.

Nehemiah 3:15
John 9:7

**Porcius Festus** (**poor**-shuhss **fest**-uhss)
See *Festus*

**possessed by a demon**
(puh-**zesst** bye a **dee**-muhn)
See *demon-possessed*
See also *demon*

**Potiphar** (**pot**-uh-fur)

Officer in Pharaoh's service who bought *Joseph* as a slave. Potiphar's wife got Joseph thrown into prison.

Genesis 37:36
Genesis 39:1-5

P

*Genesis 41:45*
*Genesis 41:50*
*Genesis 46:20*

**Potiphera** (pah-**tif**-uh-ruh)
Egyptian priest of *On* when *Joseph* became a ruler in Egypt. Joseph married Potiphera's daughter *Asenath*.

*Psalm 22:15*
*Isaiah 45:9*
*Jeremiah 19:2*

**potsherd** (**pot**-shurd)
A piece of broken pottery.

*Matthew 27:27*
*Mark 15:16*

**Praetorium** (pray-**tohr**-ee-uhm)
The home of a Roman governor in New Testament times. A Praetorium usually had barracks and jail cells as well as living space.

*Psalm 111:10*
*Hebrews 13:15*
*1 Peter 1:7*

*Genesis 29:35*
*Psalm 9:1*
*1 Peter 4:16*

**praise** (**prayz**)
• Noun: Applause; approval; any word or gesture that declares the worth of something or someone. Praise is a key part of worshiping God.

• Verb: To applaud; to say or declare that something or someone is valuable, worthy, or important. Those who love God praise him.

Praise is not the same as flattery. Praise reflects a person's true attitude; flattery does not.

*Genesis 25:21*
*Psalm 61:1*
*Philippians 1:9*

**prayer** (**pray**-ur)
Talking to God, a very important Christian duty. Prayer plays a key part in the lives of God's people. Moses, David, Daniel, Nehemiah,

Paul, and many others relied on prayer. The *book of Psalms* is a collection of prayers set to music. Jesus prayed and taught his disciples to pray. Prayer can include *praise*, *confession*, thanks, and requests. Romans 12:12 says, "Always be prayerful."

See also *Lord's Prayer, the; worship*

**preach, preaching** (**preech**, **preech**-ing)

To exhort, advise, or warn others with a message.

See also *prophesy*

*Ezra 6:14*
*Luke 3:1-3*
*Galatians 1:8-9*

**precept** (**pree**-sept)

A command, *law*, or *ordinance*.

*Exodus 12:14*
*Psalm 119:104*
*Hebrews 9:19*

**predestinate** (pree-**dess**-ti-nate)

See *predestined*

**predestined** (pree-**dess**-tind)

Planned beforehand by God.

*Romans 8:29-30*
*Ephesians 1:11*

**prefect** (**pree**-fekt)

Governor of a city or province that had been taken over by the Persians. Daniel was in charge of all the prefects of Babylonia during the *Exile*.

*Daniel 3:2-3*
*Daniel 3:27*
*Daniel 6:7*

**Preparation Day** (prep-ur-**ay**-shuhn **day**)

The day before *Passover*. It was called Preparation Day because the Jews had to make so many preparations for this important *festival*. Jesus died and was buried on Preparation Day.

*Matthew 27:62-64*
*Mark 15:42-44*
*Luke 23:54-56*

P

1 Timothy 4:14

**presbytery** (prez-bi-**tair**-ee)
An older word for *elders* of a group of churches in one geographical location.

Leviticus 26:19
Proverbs 29:23
James 1:9-10

**pride (pride)**
Belief that you are better than you really are; conceit; arrogance. God condemned Pharaoh, Nebuchadnezzar, the Pharisees, and many others for their pride. Pride is one of the most dangerous sins because it makes people think they do not need God.

Exodus 3:1
Joshua 22:13
John 18:15-16

**priest, priesthood (preest, preest**-hud)
Person who serves as a mediator between God and others. In Israel, priests administered the *offerings* and supervised the *festivals*. Every priest had to be a descendant of *Aaron*, and every priest had to *consecrate* himself before serving. The priests worked together with the *Levites*. God first gave the priests their duties while the Israelites were camped in the desert during the Exodus. The *book of Leviticus* explains all the details.

See also *chief priest; high priest; Levite; tabernacle; temple; worship*

Ephesians 6:12
Colossians 1:16
Colossians 2:15

**principalities and powers**
(**prin**-si-**pal**-i-teez and **pou**-urz)
Supernatural forces. "Principalities" and "powers" can refer to either *angels* or *demons*.

**Priscilla** (pri-**sil**-uh)
See *Aquila and Priscilla*

**proconsul** (**proh**-kon-suhl)

The position and title given to governors of peaceful Roman provinces in New Testament times. Proconsuls answered to the Roman senate. *Sergius Paulus* and *Gallio* were proconsuls. A proconsul was not the same as a *procurator*.

*Acts 13:6-12*
*Acts 18:12*

**procurator** (**prok**-yuh-ray-tur)
The position and title given to governors of unruly Roman provinces in New Testament times. Procurators answered to the emperor. *Pontius Pilate*, *Felix*, and *Festus* were procurators. A procurator was not the same as a *proconsul*.

*Matthew 27:2, 15-26*
*Acts 23:23-35*
*Acts 24:27*

**prodigal** (**prah**-dig-uhl)
Reckless; wasteful; *wicked*.

*Luke 19:22*
*Matthew 13:49*

**profane** (proh-**fane**)
- Adjective: Unholy; wicked.
- Verb: To make unholy; to *desecrate*.

*Ezekiel 21:25*
*Leviticus 19:12*
*Ezekiel 22:26*

**promised land** (**pro**-misst **land**)
The land that God promised to Abraham and his descendants; the land of *Canaan*; *Palestine*.

*Hebrews 11:9*

**prophecy** (**prof**-uh-see)
Noun: A message from God. Sometimes the message predicted the future, and sometimes it

*2 Kings 9:25*
*Matthew 13:14*
*1 Corinthians 13:2*

merely told God's appraisal of what was happening. A person chosen by God to deliver a prophecy was called a *prophet*.

The verb form is *prophesy*.

See also *prophets to Israel; prophets to Judah*

Ezekiel 37:9
Matthew 7:22
1 Corinthians 14:39

P

**prophesy** (**prof**-uh-sye)

Verb: To speak *prophecy*; to deliver a message from God.

The noun form is *prophecy*.

See also *prophets to Israel; prophets to Judah*

Exodus 7:1
Matthew 27:9
1 Corinthians 14:37

**prophet** (**prof**-uht)

A person who speaks for God; a person who receives and delivers messages from God. Some prophets wrote down their prophecies, but others did not. Some of the most famous prophets were Moses, Elijah, Elisha, Isaiah, Jeremiah, Ezekiel, Daniel, and John the Baptist.

See also *false prophet; prophets to Israel; prophets to Judah*

**prophetess** (**prof**-uh-tess)

Exodus 15:20
Judges 4:4
Luke 2:36

• A female *prophet*. The Bible mentions five prophetesses: Miriam, Deborah, Huldah, Noadiah, and Anna. Noadiah was a false prophetess.

Isaiah 8:3

• A prophet's wife. Isaiah called his wife a prophetess.

**prophets to Israel** (**prof**-uhtz too **iz**-ree-uhl)
The prophets who brought God's messages to the northern kingdom of *Israel*: Ahijah, Elijah, Elisha, Jonah, Amos, and Hosea.

*1 Kings 20:13*
*Luke 4:27*

**prophets to Judah** (**prof**-uht too **joo**-duh)
The prophets who brought God's messages to the southern kingdom of *Judah*:
- Before the *Exile*: Obadiah, Elisha, Joel, Micah, Isaiah, Nahum, Zephaniah, Huldah, Jeremiah, and Habakkuk.
- During the Exile: Ezekiel and Daniel.
- After the Exile: Haggai, Zechariah, and Malachi.

*1 Kings 13:20-21*
*2 Chronicles 36:12*
*Matthew 24:15*
*Ezra 6:14*

**propitiation** (proh-**pi**-chee-**ay**-shuhn)
An older word for *atonement*.

*Romans 3:25*
*1 John 2:2*
*1 John 4:10*

**proselyte** (**pros**-uh-lite)
An older word for *convert* (noun).

*Acts 2:7-11*
*Acts 13:43*

**prostitute** (**pros**-ti-toot)
A person who gives sexual favors for money.

*Deuteronomy 23:17-18*
*Joshua 6:25*
*Hebrews 11:31*

**Proverbs, book of** (**prah**-vurbz)
Twentieth book of the Old Testament and third of the *books of poetry*. The word "proverb" means "rule"; the book of Proverbs is a collection of rules or principles for living. Solomon wrote most of them. Proverbs 1:5 says, "Let those who are wise listen to these proverbs and become even wiser."

*Proverbs 1:1*
*Proverbs 10:1*

P

Psalm 3:1
Psalm 47:1, 7

**Psalms, book of** (**sahlmz**, buk uhv)
Nineteenth book of the Old Testament and second of the *books of poetry*. The word "psalm" means "sacred song"; the book of Psalms is a collection of songs written by David, *Asaph*, Levites of the clan of Korah, Solomon, Moses, and others. Psalm 23 is one of the most famous passages in the Bible.

Acts 21:7

**Ptolemais** (**tahl**-uh-**may**-uhss)
Port city on the coast of Phoenicia across the bay from modern Haifa; also called Acco. Ptolemais was due north of *Mount Carmel*.

Matthew 10:3
Luke 18:10

**publican** (**pub**-li-kuhn)
An older word for *tax collector* that is found in some translations of the Bible.

2 Kings 15:19
1 Chronicles 5:26

**Pul** (**puhl**)
Another name for *Tiglath-Pileser*.

Numbers 33:42-43

**Punon** (**poo**-non)
One of the places in *Edom* where the Israelites stopped on their way to the promised land during the Exodus. Punon was between Zalmonah and Oboth, but its exact location is unknown.

**pur** (**poor**)
The Hebrew word for "lot." The term *Purim* comes from this word.
See also *cast lots*

Esther 3:7
Esther 9:24-26

**Purah** (**poo**-ruh)
Gideon's servant. Purah went with Gideon and his 300 men to the *Midianite* camp.

Judges 7:10-11

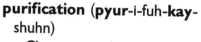

**purification** (**pyur**-i-fuh-**kay**-shuhn)
Cleansing; making *clean*.

Numbers 19:17
Luke 2:22
Acts 21:26

**purify** (**pyur**-i-fye)
To make *clean*.
See also *purification*

Leviticus 14:49
James 4:8

**Purim** (**poo**-rim)
A Jewish holiday that commemorates God's rescue of the Jews from *Haman's* plot to destroy them. The name means "lots," and comes from the fact that Haman *cast lots* to determine the day of the Jews' extermination. Purim is celebrated on the thirteenth, fourteenth, and fifteenth of day *Adar*.
See also *Esther; Mordecai*

Esther 9:26-32

**Puteoli** (pyoo-tee-**oh**-lee)
Port city on the southwestern shore of Italy where Paul's ship landed during his journey to Rome.

Acts 28:13

Romans 16:23

**Quartus** (**kwor**-tuhss)

One of those who sent greetings to the Roman Christians at the end of Paul's letter to the Romans.

1 Kings 1:11-21
Esther 1:12
Esther 5:2

Q

**queen** (**kween**)

Wife of the king. In the kingdoms of Israel and Judah, queens had little power or authority. Most had to share the king with other wives, and were not mentioned in genealogies. The most famous queens include *Bathsheba*, *Jezebel*, *Vashti*, *Esther*, and the *queen of Sheba*. *Athaliah* is the only queen of Israel or Judah who ever ruled in place of the king.

See also *queen mother; Queen of Heaven*

1 Kings 2:13-18
2 Chronicles 22:10-12

**queen mother** (**kween muh**-thur)

Mother of the king. In the kingdoms of Israel and Judah, the queen mother always had more power and authority than the king's wives, and her name was always listed in the genealogies. Many wives' names were left out of the genealogies. Two of the Bible's most notable queen mothers are *Bathsheba* and Rehoboam's wife *Maacah*. One of the most evil was *Athaliah*.

**Queen of Heaven** (**kween** uhv **hev**-en)
A name for the Mesopotamian goddess *Ishtar*.

*Jeremiah 7:18*
*Jeremiah 44:18*

**queen of Sheba** (**kween** uhv **shee**-buh)
Ruler of the land of *Sheba* who came to test Solomon "with hard questions" (1 Kings 10:2) and went away impressed by his wisdom. We do not know her name.

*1 Kings 10:1-13*

**Quirinius** (kwi-**rin**-ee-uhss)
Publius Sulpicius Quirinius, legate (governor) of *Syria* during Jesus' birth.

*Luke 2:2*

R

*Genesis 10:7*

**Raamah** (**ray**-uh-muh)
One of the sons of *Cush*.

**Raamses** (**ram**-uh-seez)
See *Rameses*

*Deuteronomy 3:11*
*Ezekiel 25:5*
*Joshua 15:20, 60*

**Rabbah** (**rab**-uh)
• Capital city of *Ammon*; modern Amman, Jordan. Rabbah was 35 kilometers east of the Jordan River.
• A Canaanite city in the territory allotted to Judah, near *Kiriath-jearim*.

*Mark 14:45*
*John 3:2*

**Rabbi** (**rab**-eye)
"My great one," a title given to teachers of the *law* among the Jews.

*2 Kings 18:17*
*Jeremiah 39:3*

**Rabsaris** (**rab**-sar-iss)
The chief officer of an Assyrian or Babylonian king. "Rabsaris" was a title, like "chief of staff."
See also *Rabshakeh; Tartan*

*2 Kings 18:17*
*Isaiah 36:2*

**Rabshakeh** (rab-**shay**-kuh)
High-ranking official of an Assyrian or Babylonian king; a field commander or governor of provinces. The Rabshakeh spoke to the men on the wall at the siege of Jerusalem during Hezekiah's reign.

See also *Rabsaris; Tartan*

**Raca** (**rah**-kuh)
A term of contempt or scorn; an insult. It means, "you fool."
*Matthew 5:22*

**Rachel** (**ray**-chuhl)
Daughter of *Laban* and younger sister of *Leah*. Rachel became famous for her part in the story of Jacob. Jacob agreed to work seven years for Rachel's hand in marriage but ended up having to work seven more years. Rachel became the mother of *Joseph* and *Benjamin*.
*Genesis 29:9-12*
*Genesis 35:24*

**Rahab** (**ray**-hab)
• A *prostitute* from *Jericho* who helped the Israelite spies and became a hero for her faith in God even though she lived among the Canaanites. Rahab was rescued from Jericho's destruction.
*Joshua 2:1-21*
*Joshua 6:22-23*
*Hebrews 11:31*

• A nickname for *Egypt*.
*Psalm 87:4*
*Isaiah 30:7*

• Name for a powerful being or force that God can easily defeat.
*Job 9:13*

**raiment** (**ray**-ment)
Clothing.
*Genesis 24:53*
*Matthew 6:25*

**rainbow** (**rayn**-boh)

*Genesis 9:16* — Sign of God's promise never to destroy all living things with a flood.

**ram** (**ram**)

*1 Chronicles 2:9* — • One of *Hezron's* sons; brother of Jerahmeel and Caleb.

*1 Chronicles 2:25* — • Firstborn son of *Jerahmeel.*

*Job 32:2* — • A clan of the Buzites to which Job's friend *Elihu* belonged.

*Genesis 22:13*, *Numbers 28:11* — • An adult male *sheep*. The Israelites used rams for meat, wool, and *offerings*.

**Ramah** (**rah**-muh)

*Joshua 18:25* — • A border city allotted to the tribe of Benjamin, near Bethel.

*1 Samuel 1:1*, *1 Samuel 7:17* — • *Ramathaim Zophim.*

*Joshua 19:29* — • A border city allotted to the tribe of Asher.

*Joshua 19:36* — • A fortified city in the land allotted to Naphtali.

• *Baalath Beer.*

*2 Kings 8:28-29* — • Another name for *Ramoth Gilead*.

**Ramath Lehi** (**ray**-muhth **lee**-hye)
The place in the lowlands of Judah where Samson killed a thousand Philistines with a jawbone; also called *Lehi* "Lehi" means "jawbone hill."

*Judges 15:17*

**Ramath-mizpah** (**ray**-muhth-**miz**-puh)
A border city in the land allotted to *Gad*.

*Joshua 13:24*

**Ramathaim** (**ray**-muh-**thay**-im)
*Ramathaim Zophim*

**Ramathaim Zophim**
(**ray**-muh-**thay**-im **zoh**-fum)
*Samuel's* hometown; also called *Ramah*. Its exact location is unknown.

*1 Samuel 1:1*

**Rameses** (**ram**-uh-seez)
- Another name for *Goshen*.
- One of two cities built by the Hebrew slaves in Egypt before the *Exodus*. The other city was *Pithom*.

*Genesis 47:11*
*Exodus 1:11*
*Exodus 12:37*

**Ramoth** (**ray**-moth)
- Alternate spelling for *Rehob*.
- "Ramah of the Negev," or *Baalath Beer*.
- *Ramoth Gilead*.

*Joshua 21:31*
*1 Samuel 30:27-31*
*Joshua 20:8*

**Ramoth Gilead** (**ray**-moth **gil**-ee-ad)
A city in the land allotted to Gad and one of the six *cities of refuge*. By the time of Solomon,

*Deuteronomy 4:43*
*2 Kings 9:14*

Ramoth Gilead was an important fortified city on the border with Syria.

1 Samuel 30:27

**Ramoth Negev** (**ray**-moth **neg**-ev)
"Ramah of the Negev," or *Baalath Beer.*

1 Thessalonians 4:13-17

**rapture** (**rap**-chur)
The time when all believers in Christ will be taken to be with Jesus at his *second coming*. The word "rapture" does not appear in the Bible; it is used to describe the event. Like the *return of Christ*, no one knows when the rapture will happen.
See also *day of his coming; last day*

Leviticus 23:22
1 Corinthians 9:11
2 Corinthians 9:6

**reap** (**reep**)
To harvest.

**Rebecca** (re-**bek**-uh)
See *Rebekah*

Genesis 24:64-67
Genesis 27:13-18

**Rebekah** (re-**bek**-uh)
Daughter of *Bethuel*, wife of *Isaac*, and mother of *Jacob* and *Esau*. Rebekah is famous for being a hard worker, but also for helping Jacob deceive Isaac. Rebekah is featured in the stories of Genesis 24–49.

Titus 3:4-5

**rebirth** (ree-**burth**)
Being *born again*.

**Recab** (**ree**-kab)

• A captain of Ishbosheth's raiding parties together with his brother *Baanah*; son of Rimmon. Recab and Baanah tried to win favor with David by killing *Ishbosheth*. *2 Samuel 4:1-12*

• Father of *Jonadab* and ancestor of the *Recabites*. We know nothing else about him. *2 Kings 10:15*

**Recabites** (**ree**-kuh-bites)

People who traced their roots to Jonadab's father *Recab*; members of the clan of *Recab*. The Recabites were famous for their devotion to God during the time of Jeremiah. *Jeremiah 35:1-19*

**Recah** (**ree**-kuh)

An unknown place in Judah. *1 Chronicles 4:12*

**Rechab** (**ree**-kab)

See *Recab*

**Rechabites** (**ree**-kuh-bites)

See *Recabites*

**reconciliation** (**rek**-uhn-**sil**-ee-**ay**-shuhn)

The making of peace between people; settlement of differences. Reconciliation is an important part of *salvation*. Christ came to bring reconciliation between people and God. *Romans 5:11*; *Romans 11:15*; *2 Corinthians 5:18-19*

R

**Red Sea (red see)**

Literally, "Sea of Reeds." The term refers to at least three bodies of water:

Exodus 13:18, 21-31

• A series of lakes in the northeast of Egypt directly west of *Shur* known as the Bitter Lakes. It is called the Sea of Reeds because of the huge numbers of *reeds* that grow there.

Numbers 33:10-11

• The narrow body of water between *Sinai* and the continent of Africa, known today as the Gulf of Suez.

Deuteronomy 2:1

• The narrow body of water between Sinai and the Arabian peninsula, known today as the Gulf of Aqabah.

Ruth 4:8, 14
Job 19:25

**redeemer** (ree-**dee**-mur)

A person who recovers, buys back, or ransoms something. *Boaz* was Ruth's redeemer because he bought back her widower's land. Jesus Christ is the redeemer of every Christian because he ransoms the person's life.

Ephesians 4:30
Hebrews 9:12

**redemption** (ree-**demp**-shuhn)

The Christian doctrine that Jesus Christ paid the

price so his people could go free; that Jesus Christ is our *redeemer*. Redemption is one of the key ideas mentioned in the *book of Romans*.

See also *propitiation*

**reed, reeds** (**reed, reedz**)

A reference to some species of tall grass that grow in marshes and shallow lakes. The most famous is *papyrus*, but the term also applied to cattails and other water grasses.

Exodus 2:3
Matthew 11:7
Revelation 11:1

**refuge, city of** (**ref**-yooj, **si**-tee uhv)
See *cities of refuge*

**regeneration** (ree-**jen**-ur-**ay**-shun)
See *rebirth*
See also *born again*

**Rehob** (**ree**-hob)

A *levitical city* in the land allotted to Issachar.

Joshua 21:31

**Rehoboam** (**ree**-huh-**boh**-uhm)

Son of *Solomon* and first king of the southern kingdom of *Judah*. Rehoboam's rule over only two tribes of Israel, Benjamin and Judah, resulted from Solomon's *idolatry*. The prophet *Ahijah* predicted that *Jeroboam* would rebel and take the other ten tribes away from Rehoboam, and that is exactly what happened. The tragic story is told in 1 Kings 11:26–12:24. Rehoboam reigned 17 years.

1 Kings 14:21-31
2 Chronicles 10:1–12:16

**Rehoboth** (ruh-**hoh**-buhth)

• "Room," the name that Isaac gave to a well he dug near *Gerar* after trying several other places that the herdsmen of Gerar did not like.

Genesis 26:22

• A city in *Edom*. Its exact location is unknown.

Genesis 26:22

*Ezra 4:8*

**Rehum** (**ree**-huhm)

Persian governor who tried to stop *Zerubbabel* from rebuilding the temple in Jerusalem.

See also *Shimshai*

*Matthew 26:28*
*Hebrews 9:22*

**remission** (ree-**mi**-shuhn)

An older word for *forgiveness.*

R

**remnant** (**rem**-nuhnt)

*2 Chronicles 36:20*

- Survivors; those who live through something awful.

*Isaiah 6:9-13*
*Romans 9:27-29*

- A small number of people who remain faithful to God while others turn away from him. The apostle Paul called Christians a remnant of believers among the *Jews.*

*Ezekiel 18:32*
*Matthew 3:2; 4:17*
*Acts 2:38*

**repent** (ree-**pent**)

To turn away from sin and turn back to God. *Repentance* is one of the most important themes in the Bible. Many of the *prophets* urged the Jews to repent. Both John the Baptist and Jesus said, "Turn from your sins and turn to God, because the Kingdom of Heaven is near." Following Christ and receiving God's *forgiveness* requires that a person repent.

See also *born again; salvation*

*Isaiah 30:15*
*Matthew 3:11*
*2 Corinthians 7:9*

**repentance** (ree-**pent**-uhnss)

The act of turning away from sin and turning to God; sorrow for sin and turning away from it; to *repent.*

**Rephael** (**ref**-uh-el)
One of *Obed-Edom's* grandsons and a leader in the clan of Korah; son of *Shemaiah*.
1 Chronicles 26:7

**Rephaiah** (ruh-**fay**-uh)
A common name among the Israelites:
- Ruler of a Jerusalem district who repaired part of the city wall during the time of Nehemiah; son of *Hur*. Nehemiah 3:9
- A clan chief in the tribe of *Issachar*; one of Issachar's grandsons; son of Tola. 1 Chronicles 7:2
- Three others mentioned only in the genealogies.

**Rephaim** (**ref**-ay-im)
See *Rephaites*
See also *Valley of Rephaim*

**Rephaites** (**ref**-uh-ites)
Another name for the *Emites* and the *Anakites*.
Deuteronomy 2:11

**Rephidim** (**ref**-i-dim)
Last place in the *Desert of Sin* where the

Israelites stopped before reaching Sinai. God did two miracles for the Israelites at Rephidim, one when God provided water, and another when he enabled them to defeat the Amalekites. The exact location of Rephidim is unknown.
See also *Massah; Meribah*
Exodus 17:1-13

**reprobate** (**rep**-roh-bate)
An older word for *depraved*.
Romans 1:28-29
2 Timothy 3:8

R

**resin droplets** (**rez**-in **drop**-letz)
See *stacte*

Exodus 22:5-6
Leviticus 5:16

**restitution** (**ress**-ti-**too**-shuhn)
Give back; restore. God's law requires criminals to make restitution to the victims.

Matthew 27:53
1 Peter 1:3

Matthew 22:30-31
Acts 23:6-8

**resurrection** (**re**-zur-**ek**-shuhn)

- The resurrection of Christ. Three days after Jesus died, he rose from the dead, and now he lives in heaven.
- The resurrection of all believers. When Christ returns, he will raise back to life all those who have died.

Matthew 24:33-44
1 Thessalonians 4: 14-18

**return of Christ** (**ree**-turn uhv **kryste**)
A time still in the future when *Jesus Christ* will come back, defeat Satan and all evil, judge all people, and set up his kingdom; Christ's *second coming*. Jesus told his disciples that he would return, and that his coming would surprise everyone.

Genesis 29:32

2 Kings 10:32-33

**Reuben** (**roo**-buhn)

- Jacob's oldest son and the tribe of Israel named after him. Reuben is famous for stopping his brothers from killing *Joseph*. *Leah* was his mother.
- The land allotted to the tribe of Reuben.

See also *twelve tribes of Israel*

**Reubenites** (**roo**-buhn-ites)
People who trace their roots to *Reuben*; people of the tribe of Reuben.
*Numbers 32:6*
*Joshua 13:23*

**Reumah** (**roo**-muh)
*Nahor's* wife; mother of *Maacah*.
*Genesis 22:23-24*

**Revelation of Jesus Christ, the**
(**rev**-uh-**lay**-shuhn uhv **jee**-zuhss **kriste**, the)
See *Revelation, book of*

**Revelation, book of**
(**rev**-uh-**lay**-shuhn, **buk** uhv)
Twenty-seventh and last book of the New Testament, and the New Testament's only book of *prophecy*; also called the *Apocalypse*. The book is called "Revelation" because it "is a revelation from Jesus Christ" (1:1) to the apostle John. The book is famous for its detailed descriptions of *heaven*, the *last day*, the return of Christ, the defeat of Satan, the final *day of judgment*, and the *New Jerusalem*.
*Revelation 1:1*
*Revelation 21:2*

**Rezeph** (**ree**-zef)
One of the cities mentioned in *Sennacherib's* threat of Hezekiah at the siege of Jerusalem.
*Isaiah 37:9-12*

**Rezin** (**ree**-zin)
- King of Aram in Damascus who allied with *Pekah* of Israel during the reign of *Ahaz* in Judah. *2 Kings 16:5-6*; *Isaiah 7:1*
- Head of one of the families of temple servants who returned to Jerusalem with Ezra. *Nehemiah 7:46, 50*

R

1 Kings 11:23-25

**Rezon** (**ree**-zon)
Survivor of David's attacks on *Zobah* who fled to Damascus and became a powerful enemy of Solomon. Rezon ruled in Damascus for a long time. His grandson *Ben Hadad* I also gave Israel a lot of trouble.

Acts 28:13

**Rhegium** (**ree**-jee-uhm)
Port city in the Roman province of Italy at the "toe" of the Italian boot. Sailing from Rhegium was hazardous because of rocks and a dangerous whirlpool. It took a proper south wind to get past safely. This is what delayed Paul's ship for one day during his journey to Rome.

Acts 12:13-17

**Rhoda** (**roh**-duh)
Servant girl who answered the door at John Mark's house when Peter was freed from prison.

Ezekiel 27:15
Acts 21:1

**Rhodes** (**rohdz**)
An island just off the southwest coast of Asia Minor and also the island's capital city. Paul passed through Rhodes on his way back to Jerusalem during his third missionary journey.

2 Kings 23:31-34
Jeremiah 52:26-27

**Riblah** (**rib**-luh)
City on the Orontes River in *Aram* about 16 kilometers southwest of *Kadesh*. Pharaoh Neco exiled Jehoahaz to Riblah, and Nebuchadnezzar had Zedekiah tortured there.

**right hand (rite hand)**

A term sometimes used as a figure of speech:

- Skill, power, or authority. *Exodus 15:6; Psalm 20:6*
- Close association; the place of honor next to someone. *Psalm 16:8; Mark 16:19*

**righteous (rye-chuhss)**

- Adjective: Good; perfect; upright; blameless; without fault. *Genesis 7:1; Romans 2:13*

- Noun: "the righteous"; people who love God and act to please him; people who are good, perfect, blameless, upright, or without fault. *Genesis 18:25; 1 Peter 3:12*

**righteousness (rye-chuhss-ness)**

Harmony with God, his will, and with others; goodness; perfection. *Deuteronomy 6:25; Galatians 2:21*

**Rimmon (rim-uhn)**

- The god that *Naaman* worshiped in Damascus until God cured his leprosy. The name means "thunderer." *2 Kings 5:17-18*
- Father of *Ishbosheth's* assassins *Baanah* and *Recab*. *2 Samuel 4:2*
- One of the cities in the territory of Judah that was given to the tribe of Simeon. *1 Chronicles 6:64-77*
- One of the border cities of Zebulun. *Joshua 19:10-13*

R

Judges 20:43-47

• A rocky area near *Gibeah* where 600 Benjamites stayed in hiding for four months. Its location is unknown.

Numbers 33:19-20

**Rimmon Perez** (**rim**-uhn pair-ez)
A place in Sinai between Rithmah and Libnah where the Israelites stopped during the Exodus. Its exact location is unknown.

Numbers 33:21-22

**Rissah** (**riss**-uh)
A place in Sinai between Libnah and Kehelathah where the Israelites stopped during the Exodus. Its exact location is unknown.

Numbers 33:18-19

**Rithmah** (**rith**-muh)
A place in Sinai between Hazeroth and Rimmon Perez where the Israelites stopped during the *Exodus*. Its exact location is unknown.

**River Jordan** (**riv**-ur **jor**-duhn)
*See Jordan*

2 Samuel 3:7

**Rizpah** (**riz**-puh)
One of Saul's *concubines*, and mother of *Armoni* and *Mephibosheth*. Rizpah suffered greatly as David and Saul's sons competed for control of Israel.

Genesis 10:1-5

**Rodanim** (**roh**-duh-nim)
People from *Rhodes*.

Luke 2:1
Acts 11:28

**Roman world** (**roh**-muhn **wurld**)
The Roman Empire; the land and people ruled from *Rome* during the time of Christ. This

included much of Europe and the entire coast of the Mediterranean Sea.

**Romans** (**roh**-muhnz)

• People who lived in *Rome* or citizens of the Roman Empire in New Testament times. The apostle *Paul* was a Roman citizen. *John 11:48*

• Christians of the church in Rome. Paul never visited Rome, but he did write the *book of Romans* to them. *Romans 1:7, 15*

**Romans, book of** (**roh**-muhnz, **buk** uhv)

Sixth book of the New Testament, a letter written by the apostle Paul to the churches of *Rome*. Paul wrote the letter because he planned to go to Rome on his way to Spain and he wanted to prepare the believers there for his visit. The letter explains Christianity in more detail than any other single book. It explains *sin*, the *law*, and *salvation*. It explains why God created the *church* and how the church relates to *Israel*. It also explains spiritual gifts and many Christian duties. The letter was written in A.D. 57.

*Romans 1:7, 15*
*Romans 13:11*
*Romans 3:25*

See also *atonement; glorification; justification; redemption; sanctification*

**Rome** (**rohm**)

Important city in Italy and capital of the Roman Empire in New Testament times. Rome had over a million citizens when Jesus was on earth.

*Acts 23:11*
*2 Timothy 1:16-18*

The apostle Paul wrote the *book of Romans* to the Christians of this city.

Ruth 1:3-5

**Ruth (rooth)**

*Moabite* widow who traveled with her mother-in-law Naomi to Bethlehem and married Boaz; mother of *Obed*; grandmother of *Jesse*; great-grandmother of *David*. Ruth was *Mahlon's* widow before leaving Moab. She is most famous for her devotion to Naomi and for saying to her, "I will go wherever you go and live wherever you live. Your people will be my people, and your God will be my God" (Ruth 1:16). Her story is told in the *book of Ruth*.

Ruth 1:16-18

**Ruth, book of (rooth, buk** uhv)

Eighth book of the Old Testament and third of the *books of history*. The book of Ruth tells how God restored *Naomi's* hope and faith through the loyalty of her daughter-in-law *Ruth*. It was written during the time of the *judges*.

**sabachthani** (suh-**bak**-thah-nee)

Part of Jesus' cry of anguish on the cross, taken from Psalm 22:1. The word is Hebrew or *Aramaic*, but its exact meaning is unknown.

*Psalm 22:1*
*Mark 15:34*

**Sabaoth, Lord of** (**sab**-ay-oth, **lord** uhv)

See *Lord of Sabaoth*

**Sabbath** (**sab**-uhth)

Rest; a time when a person does no work. The fourth of the *Ten Commandments* tells people to do no work every seventh day, because God rested on the seventh day of creation. This was called the Sabbath day. God also required the Israelites to stop planting and harvesting one year out of every seven. The year of *Jubilee* was a Sabbath year. The term comes from the Hebrew word for "cease."

Jesus had several conflicts with the Pharisees because of the Sabbath day. The Pharisees said no one could do any work of any kind on the Sabbath. Jesus said it was permitted to heal people and to rejoice on the Sabbath.

*Exodus 20:8-11*
*Leviticus 25:2*
*John 5:1-15*

**Sabbath day's journey** (**sab**-uhth **dayz jur**-nee)

A distance of two thousand *cubits*.

*Acts 1:12*

**Sabbath day's walk** (**sab**-uhth **dayz wok**)
See *Sabbath day's journey*

*Leviticus 25:1-7*
*2 Chronicles 36:21*

**Sabbath Year** (**sab**-uhth **yihr**)
A time of *Sabbath* for the land. The Israelites were to observe this by not planting or harvesting any food once every seven years. The Exile made up for their failure to obey this command.

*Job 1:15*

**Sabeans** (suh-**bee**-uhnz)
A tribe of people that lived in south Arabia and also Ethiopia across the Red Sea from Sheba. They were one of the groups that raided Job's home and killed his farm workers.

*Genesis 10:7*
*1 Chronicles 1:9*

**Sabta, Sabtah** (**sab**-tuh)
Third son of *Cush* and the tribe descended from him.

*Genesis 10:7*
*1 Chronicles 1:9*

**Sabteca** (sab-**tee**-kuh)
Fifth son of *Cush* and the tribe descended from him.

*Genesis 37:34*
*Jonah 3:8*

**sackcloth** (**sak**-kloth)
A rough cloth usually made from black goats' hair. It was called sackcloth because it was often used to make sacks, being too rough for clothing. People wore sackcloth to show mourning, sadness, or *repentance*.

**sacrament** (**sak**-ruh-ment)

A ceremony or ritual that has a *sacred* purpose or meaning. *Baptism* and the *Lord's Supper* are examples of sacraments. The term does not appear in the Bible.

*Matthew 3:13-16*
*Luke 22:19*

**sacred** (**say**-krid)

*Holy*; set apart to God's use; devoted to God.

*Exodus 28:2*
*1 Corinthians 3:17*

**sacrifice** (**sak**-ri-fise)

• Noun: Something that is destroyed or given up, usually as an act of worship. The *offerings* that God required of the Israelites were sacrifices of animals, food, money, or time. In place of those sacrifices, Jesus gave his life as a once-for-all sacrifice for the sins of the world. God condemned all sacrifices to *idols*.

*Proverbs 15:8*
*Hebrews 9:26*

• Verb: To destroy or give up something, usually as an act of *worship*.

*Exodus 20:24*
*Hebrews 11:17*

See also *bull; fellowship offering; freewill offering; grain offering; guilt offering; idolatry; lamb; sin offering; temple*

**Sadducees** (**sa**-joo-seez)

A group of religious leaders who lived during the time of Jesus. The Sadducees believed only in the law of Moses; they ignored the *Pharisees'*

*Matthew 16:1*
*Acts 23:6-8*

oral law. Many Sadducees were priests, and many members of the *Sanhedrin* were Sadducees. They were very unpopular because they concerned themselves mostly with political power. Jesus criticized the Sadducees for not believing in the *resurrection*.

2 Chronicles 6:41
Philippians 4:21-22

**saints (saynts)**
The people of God; God's people.

Acts 13:5

**Salamis (sal-uh-miss)**
A large port city on the east coast of *Cyprus* in New Testament times. Paul and his friends landed at Salamis at the start of Paul's first missionary journey. They preached in the *synagogues* there before traveling to Paphos.

Deuteronomy 3:10
Joshua 13:11-12

**Salecah (sal-uh-kuh)**
A city on the eastern boundary of *Bashan* allotted to the tribe of Gad. Its location is unknown.
See also *Og*

Hebrews 7:1-2

**Salem (say-luhm)**
Another name for *Jerusalem*.

John 3:23

**Salim (say-lim)**
A place on the west bank of the Jordan River near *John the Baptist's* place of ministry. Its exact location is unknown.
See also *Aenon*

**Salmon** (**sal**-muhn)

• Husband of *Rahab* and father of *Boaz*; son of Nahshon; great-great-grandfather of David. Salmon is mentioned in the genealogy of Jesus. — *Ruth 4:20-22*, *Matthew 1:5*

• Another spelling for Salma; an ancestor of several clans of Caleb; son of Hur. — *1 Chronicles 2:51, 54*

**Salmone** (sal-**moh**-nee) — *Acts 27:7*

A place in the Mediterranean Sea, not to be confused with *Salome*:

Cape Salmone, a narrow strip of land at the east end of *Crete*, now called Cape Sidero. The ship carrying Paul to Rome sailed past this landmark.

**Salome** (suh-**loh**-mee)

Two women, not to be confused with *Salmone*:

• One of the women who saw Jesus crucified. — *Mark 15:40*

• Possibly the daughter of *Herodias* who danced before Herod. Herodias had a daughter named Salmone, but she is not mentioned in the *Gospels*. — *Mark 6:22*

**Salt Sea** (**sahlt see**) — *Numbers 34:3*, *Joshua 18:19*

Another name for the *Dead Sea*.

**Salt, Valley of** (**sahlt**, **val**-ee uhv)

See *Valley of Salt*

S

**salvation** (sal-**vay**-shuhn)

*Psalm 51:12*
*Hebrews 2:3-4*
*Revelation 7:10*

• *Forgiveness* of sins; God's gift of *eternal life*. This doctrine is called salvation because God saves us from *death*, sin's penalty. Salvation involves four details: (1) All people have sinned. (2) The penalty for sin is death. (3) Jesus died for sin. (4) To be saved, people must believe in Christ and confess that Jesus is Lord. Salvation is explained in Romans 3:23; 6:23; 5:8; 10:8-10.

*Exodus 15:2*

• Deliverance; rescue; source of safety.

*See also born again; saved; Savior*

**Samaria** (suh-**mair**-ee-uh)

*1 Kings 16:23-24*
*John 4:4-5*

• A fortified city in the territory of Manasseh that served as the capital of the northern kingdom of Israel. *Omri* built the city after reigning at *Tirzah* for seven years. The city was on a high hill directly northwest of Mount *Ebal*.

*2 Kings 17:24*
*Acts 9:31*

• The whole area of Palestine between *Judea* and *Galilee* in New Testament times. The city of Samaria had been renamed to Sebaste by this time. The region of Samaria was part of the kingdom of *Herod the Great*. People who lived in this area were called *Samaritans*.

**Samaritans** (suh-**mair**-i-tuhnz)

People who lived in *Samaria* and held to the religion of that area in New Testament times. The Samaritans believed that they were descended from the Israelite tribes of Ephraim and Manasseh. They also believed they had a more pure version of the *Pentateuch* than the Jews. The Jews believed that the Samaritans were descended from the Assyrians and changed the Pentateuch to say what they wanted it to say. This is why Jews and Samaritans disliked each and did not get along.

*Matthew 10:5*
*Luke 10:30-36*
*John 4:7-9*

**Samlah** (**sam**-luh)

A king of *Edom* during the time of the *patriarchs*. He ruled from the city of Masrekah.

*Genesis 36:36-37*

**Samos** (**say**-muhss)

A mountainous island about 1.5 kilometers off the coast of Asia Minor southwest of *Ephesus*. Samos was north of *Patmos* and *Cos*.

*Acts 20:15*

**Samothrace** (**sam**-oh-thrayss)

A mountainous island about 30 kilometers off the coast of *Thrace* where Paul stopped during his second missionary journey. Samothrace was famous for being a center of cult worship. It has the highest peak in the Aegean Sea islands.

*Acts 16:11*

Judges 14:19
Judges 16:4-31
Hebrews 11:32

**Samson** (**sam**-suhn)

Son of Manoah and twelfth judge of Israel after *Abdon*. Samson became famous for his great strength and many victories over the Philistines. Samson was a *Nazirite* from the day he was born, and this is the reason he was not supposed to cut his hair. Samson judged Israel 20 years. His story is told in Judges 13:1–16:31.

See also *Delilah*

1 Samuel 1:20
Jeremiah 15:1
Acts 13:20

**Samuel** (**sam**-yoo-uhl)

• Israelite prophet who anointed Saul and David as kings; son of Elkanah and Hannah reared by *Eli* in the tabernacle. Samuel was leader of Israel when the *elders* of Israel demanded a king. Samuel's story is told in *First Samuel* 1–28.

1 Chronicles 7:2

• One of Issachar's grandsons and head of his clan; son of *Tola*.

1 Samuel 3:19-21

**Samuel, books of** (**sam**-yoo-uhl, **buks** uhv)

Two books of the Old Testament, *First Samuel* and *Second Samuel*. These books tell about the rise of the monarchy in Israel under Saul and David. They are named after the prophet *Samuel*.

**Samuel, First** (**sam**-yoo-el, **furst**)

Ninth book of the Old Testament and fourth of the *books of history*. First Samuel tells how Saul became king over Israel, and about his troubled reign. It begins in the days of the prophet Samuel and continues through Saul's tragic death at Gilboa. The book is also famous for the account of David and Goliath.

See also *Second Samuel*

*1 Samuel 8:1-22*

**Samuel, Second** (**sek**-uhnd **sam**-yoo-el)

Tenth book of the Old Testament and fifth of the *books of history*. Second Samuel tells about David's deeds as king, including his mistakes and the many problems that resulted.

See also *First Samuel*

*2 Samuel 5:1-3*

**Sanballat** (san-**bal**-uht)

"Sanballat the Horonite," one of those who tried to stop *Nehemiah* from rebuilding the walls of Jerusalem. Sanballat had an important family connection in Jerusalem: his daughter was married to the high priest's son.

See also *Geshem; Tobiah*

*Nehemiah 4:1-9*
*Nehemiah 6:1-19*
*Nehemiah 13:28-30*

**sanctification** (**sangk**-ti-fi-**kay**-shuhn)

The Christian doctrine that God works to make a believer more and more like Christ, or more and more *holy*. The term comes from the verb *sanctify*.

*Romans 15:16*

**sanctify, sanctified** (**sangk**-ti-fye, **sangk**-ti-fide)

To make holy; to set apart as holy.

*John 17:17*
*1 Corinthians 1:2*

Exodus 36:3-4
Hebrews 9:24

**sanctuary** (**sangk**-choo-**air**-ee)
Any place of God's presence. The term is often used to refer to the temple, and sometimes to the *Most Holy Place*.

Matthew 26:59
Acts 6:12

**Sanhedrin** (san-**hee**-druhn)
The official group of ruling *priests* and *Levites* among the Jews during New Testament times. The Sanhedrin held the highest authority over all religious matters and could try offenders for religious crimes such as blasphemy. Jesus was tried by the Sanhedrin for calling himself God. This is why they stirred up the crowd to demand that Jesus be crucified.

Acts 5:1-2

**Sapphira** (suh-**fye**-ruh)
Wife of *Ananias* who lied to church leaders about the money she and her husband gave. Ananias and Sapphira were struck down for their sin.

Genesis 17:15
Genesis 21:1-3

**Sarah** (**sair**-uh)
Wife and half-sister of *Abraham*; mother of *Isaac*. Her name means "princess"; God changed it from *Sarai*. She is famous for her part in God's plan to create a nation through her and Abraham.

**Sarai** (**sair**-eye)

The name that *Sarah* had before God changed it; the name Sarah had when God first called Abram out of *Ur*.

Genesis 17:15-16

**Sardis** (**sar**-diss)

A city 80 kilometers west of *Smyrna* in the Roman province of *Asia*. Jesus addressed one of the letters in the book of Revelation to this church. The city was the ancient capital of *Lydia* in Asia Minor.

Revelation 1:11
Revelation 3:1-6

**Sargon** (**sar**-gon)

Sargon II, king of *Assyria* after *Shalmaneser* mentioned in the prophesies of Isaiah. He reigned 722-705 B.C.

Isaiah 20:1

**Saron** (**sair**-uhn)

See *Sharon*

**Satan** (**say**-tuhn)

Literally, "adversary," or enemy. Satan is God's enemy and the enemy of all God's people. Jesus called Satan the father of lies. Satan hates God and tries to stop God's work in the world. But his power is subject to God's, and in the end he will be thrown into the *lake of fire*. He is also called the devil.

See also *beast; demon; demon-possessed; false prophet; hell*

Job 1:6-9
1 Timothy 5:15

Ezra 8:36
Daniel 6:1-9

**satrap** (**say**-trap)

The title given Persian governors over each province during the time of the *Exile*.

See also *Daniel*

Isaiah 13:21
Isaiah 34:14

**satyr** (**say**-tur)

An older word for wild *goat*.

**Saul** (**sawl**)

Two of the Bible's most important people:

1 Samuel 9:15–10:1
1 Chronicles 10:4-6

• Saul son of Kish: First king of Israel. God chose Saul to be Israel's king after the *elders* of Israel insisted that Samuel give them one. But Saul quickly became famous for his short temper, extreme jealousy of David, and lack of concern for obedience to God. He ruled from *Gibeah* for 40 years.

Saul was from the tribe of Benjamin. He killed himself after being defeated by the Philistines at Mount *Gilboa*. He had several sons, the most famous being *Jonathan* and *Ishbosheth*.

Acts 9:1-9
Acts 13:9

• Saul of Tarsus: Hebrew name of the apostle *Paul*.

John 10:9
Ephesians. 2:4-5

**saved** (**sayvd**)

Short for: saved from sin, saved from spiritual death, or saved from hell; forgiven of all sin; *born again*.

**Savior** (**sayv**-yor)
The one who saves people from their sins; *Jesus Christ*.

Psalm 25:5
2 Timothy 1:10

**scapegoat** (**skape**-goht)
A goat used to *make atonement* for the people of Israel on the Day of Atonement. The scapegoat, or "goat of removal," was sent out into the wilderness as a picture of the removal of sin.

Leviticus 16:8, 10, 26

S

**scarlet** (**skar**-let)
Another word for crimson, or deep red. The word often described richly dyed cloth or cloth worn by royalty. Scarlet thread and cloth, therefore, were signs of wealth.

Exodus 28:15
Joshua 2:21
Isaiah 1:18

**Sceva** (**see**-vuh)
Father or group name of a band of Jewish exorcists rebuked by Paul.

Acts 19:13-14

**scourge** (**skurj**)
A barbed leather strap attached to a stiff rod, used by the Romans to beat criminals before execution; a barbed whip.

2 Chronicles 10:11,14
John 2:15

**scribe** (**skribe**)
• A person who wrote and copied important documents. In Old Testament times, kings often had scribes write letters, record histories, and take notes on legal matters. Scribes also copied the *Scriptures*.
• An older word for *teacher of the law*.
See also *Pharisees*

Jeremiah 36:32

Nehemiah 8:13

**Scripture, Scriptures** (**skrip**-chur)

Written words of God. In the New Testament, the term usually refers to the books of the Old Testament. Peter referred to Paul's letters as Scripture.

Daniel 9:2
Luke 24:25-27
2 Peter 3:16

See also *books of law; books of history; books of poetry; major prophets; minor prophets.*

**scroll** (**skrohl**)

A piece of paper rolled into a cylinder and used for writing. Scrolls were read from side to side, with individual "pages" marked off with lines.

1 Samuel 10:25
Luke 4:16-20

**Scythian** (**sith**-ee-uhn)

A person of the Scythian tribe, a tribe of horse-riding nomads from southern Russia that once lived in north Persia.

Colossians 3:11

**Sea of Chinnereth, Chinneroth**
(**see** uhv **kin**-uh-reth, **kin**-uh-roth)

See *Sea of Galilee*

**Sea of Galilee** (**see** uhv **gal**-i-lee)

The freshwater lake in the northern end of Palestine between Lake Huleh and the Dead Sea. In Old Testament times the Israelites called it the Sea of Kinnereth. In New Testament times the Romans called it the Sea of Tiberias.

Mark 1:16
Mark 7:31
John 6:1

Jesus spent a lot of time in the region of Galilee and did several *miracles* involving the sea. He provided a miraculous catch of fish; he walked on the water; he calmed a storm.

The Sea of Galilee is fed by the Jordan River at the north end, and it empties into the Jordan River at the south end. Sudden storms affect the lake whenever strong winds come from the east off the Golan Heights.

**Sea of Kinnereth** (**see** uhv **kin**-uh-reth)
An older name for the *Sea of Galilee.*

*Numbers 34:11*
*Joshua 13:27*

**Sea of Tiberias** (**see** uhv tye-**bihr**-ee-uhss)
Roman name for the *Sea of Galilee.*

*John 6:1*
*John 21:1*

**Sea, Red** (**see, red**)
See *Red Sea*

**seah** (**see**-uh)
A dry measure equal to about seven-and-a-third liters, or seven quarts; one-third of an *ephah.*

*2 Kings 7:1*
*2 Kings 7:16-18*

**seal** (**seel**)
• Noun: An engraved picture or image used to make an impression in soft material. A seal could be round or flat. In Old Testament and New Testament times, people would stamp things with a metal seal to show that those things belonged to them or were authentic.

*Exodus 28:11*
*Matthew 27:66*
*Revelation 5:5*

S

*Esther 8:8*
*Ephesians 4:30*

• Verb: To stamp with a seal. The Bible says that the Holy Spirit seals his people.

*Genesis 10:7*

**Seba** (**see**-buh)
Firstborn son of *Cush*; also the people of south Arabia descended from Seba.

*Numbers 32:3, 38*

S

**Sebam** (**see**-buhm)
Another name for *Sibmah*, probably the name the Israelites gave to this Moabite city after taking it over.

*1 Thessalonians 4:16*

**second coming** (**sek**-uhnd **kum**-ing)

A reference to the *return of Christ*. See also *day of his coming*

**second death** (**sek**-uhnd **deth**)
See *death*

*Acts 20:4-5*

**Secundus** (suh-**kuhn**-duhss)
A Christian from Thessalonica who went with *Sopater*, *Aristarchus*, *Gaius*, *Timothy*, *Tychicus*, and *Trophimus* to await Paul at *Troas* during Paul's third missionary journey.

*1 Samuel 9:9*
*1 Chronicles 26:28*

**seer** (**sih**r)
A *prophet*.

**Seir** (**see**-ur)
• *Horite* descendant of Esau who settled in Edom, the tribe descended from Seir, and the land settled by Seir's clans. *Genesis 36:20-21*
• A mountain on the northern boundary of Judah. Its exact location is unknown. *Joshua 15:10*

S

**Sela** (**see**-luh)
"Cliff," name given to at least two places:
• A city of Edom in the *Valley of Salt* captured by *Amaziah* and renamed Joktheel. *2 Kings 14:7*
• A location on the Amorite border. *Judges 1:36*

**Selah** (**see**-luh) *Psalm 48:8* *Psalm 84:4*
A term that appears 71 times in the *Psalms* and three times in *Habakkuk*. It may be a musical rest or an instruction for worship, but its meaning is unknown.

**Seleucia** (suh-**loo**-shee-uh) *Acts 13:4*
Port city of Syria on the Orontes River eight kilometers inland from the Mediterranean coast. *Antioch* was 26 kilometers to the east of Seleucia.

**self-control** (**self-kuhn**-trohl) *Proverbs 25:28* *Galatians 5:22-23* *2 Peter 1:5-7*
Rule of oneself; choosing how to behave despite feelings or desires. Self-control is one of the nine *fruit of the Spirit* and therefore a result of surrender to God.

Deuteronomy 3:8
1 Chronicles 5:23

**Senir** (**see**-nihr)
Another name for Mount *Hermon*.

2 Kings 18:13
Isaiah 37:21

**Sennacherib** (suh-**nak**-uh-rib)
King of *Assyria* who succeeded *Sargon* and laid siege to Jerusalem during the reign of Hezekiah. The prophet Isaiah predicted Sennacherib's defeat and death. He reigned 705-681 B.C.

S

Genesis 10:30

**Sephar** (**see**-far)
A place somewhere in south Arabia settled by *Joktan's* clans.

Obadiah 1:20

**Sepharad** (**sef**-uh-rad)
One of the places where Israelites from Jerusalem were exiled. Its location is unknown.

2 Kings 17:24-25

**Sepharvaim** (**sef**-ur-**vay**-im)
A city in *Syria* whose inhabitants were sent to live in Samaria after the Assyrians took away the Israelites of Samaria. Its exact location is unknown.

Genesis 23:6
Luke 11:47

**sepulchre** (**sep**-uhl-kur)
An older word for grave or *tomb*.

Genesis 46:17
1 Chronicles 7:30

**Serah** (**seer**-uh)
Daughter of *Asher* and the clan named after her.

**Seraiah** (suh-**rye**-uh)
A very comman name among the Israelites:

2 Samuel 8:17

• David's court secretary; also called Sheva, Shisha, and Shavsha.

• *Othniel's* brother and *Joab's* father; son of *Caleb*. — *1 Chronicles 4:14*

• Leader of his clan in Simeon; son of Asiel. — *1 Chronicles 4:35*

• Son of Azriel ordered by Zedekiah to arrest Baruch and Jeremiah. — *Jeremiah 36:26*

• Son of Neriah and brother of *Baruch* who went with Zedekiah to Babylon with a scroll of prophesy from Jeremiah. Seraiah was Zedekiah's staff officer. — *Jeremiah 51:59*

• Israelite army officer who served during the time of *Gedaliah*; son of Tanhumeth. — *2 Kings 25:23*, *Jeremiah 40:8*

• *Chief priest* during the fall of Jerusalem; son of Azariah; father of Jehozadak; grandfather of the *Jeshua* who helped Zerubbabel rebuild the temple. Seraiah was executed at *Riblah*. He is also named as *Ezra's* "father," or ancestor. — *1 Chronicles 6:14*, *Ezra 7:1*, *Jeremiah 52:24-27*

• Several others who are hard to identify.

**seraphims** (**ser**-uh-fim)
See *seraphs*

**seraphs** (**sair**-uhfs)
Spiritual beings mentioned only in the *book of Isaiah*. Isaiah saw seraphs in his vision of God's throne. They sang praise to God and therefore may have been *angels*. — *Isaiah 6:2-6*

See also *cherub*

S

S

*Acts 13:6-7*

**Sergius Paulus** (**sur**-jee-uhss **pawl**-uhss)
Roman *proconsul* (governor) of Cyprus during Paul's shipwreck there.

*Matthew 5:1-7:29*

**Sermon on the Mount** (**sur**-muhn on thuh **mount**)
The name given to the teachings of Jesus recorded in Matthew 5:1–7:29, one of the most important collections of commands in the Bible.

The Sermon on the Mount includes the *Beatitudes*; instructions on keeping the law; teachings on anger, lust, and hatred; teaching on prayer, giving, and fasting.

See also *fruit of the Spirit; Jesus Christ; Ten Commandments*

*Genesis 3:1-4*
*Revelation 12:9*

**serpent** (**sur**-pent)
A snake.

**servant** (**sur**-vuhnt)

*Exodus 21:2-6*
• A slave; a person forced to work against his or her will.

*Genesis 18:7*
• A hired worker; a person who works for another person for pay.

*Romans 16:1*
• A person who chooses to serve or help another person.

*Joshua 1:13*
*Psalm 18:1*

**servant of the Lord** (**sur**-vuhnt uhv thuh **lord**)
A term used in the Bible to describe *Moses*, *Joshua*, and *David*.

**set apart for destruction**
(**set** uh-**part** for di-**struhk**-shuhn)
See *devoted to destruction*

**Seth** (**seth**)
Third son of Adam and Eve. Seth was an ancestor of Noah.
*Genesis 4:25-26*
*Luke 3:23, 38*

**Sethur** (**see**-thur)
One of the 12 men chosen by Moses at Kadesh Barnea to spy out the land of Canaan; a leader of the tribe of *Asher*; son of Michael.
*Numbers 13:3, 13*

**sexual immorality**
(**sek**-shoo-uhl **im**-mor-**al**-i-tee)
Any sexual act between two people who are not married to each other; either *fornication* or *adultery*.
*Numbers 25:1*
*Matthew 15:19*
*Romans 13:13*

**Shaalbim** (shay-**ahl**-bim)
An Amorite town in the territory allotted to Dan. The Amorites of Shaalbim and *Aijalon* stayed and became slaves of the Israelites rather than leave.
*Judges 1:35*

**Shaalbonite** (shay-**ahl**-buhn-ite)
A person who lived in *Shaalbim*.
*2 Samuel 23:23-24, 32*

**Shaalim** (shay-**ahl**-im)
One of the places *Saul* searched for his father's donkeys. Its exact location is unknown, but it was probably in *Benjamin*.
See also *Gibeah; Ramah; Zuph*
*1 Samuel 9:4*

S

Esther 2:14

**Shaashgaz** (shay-**ahsh**-gahz)
One of the *eunuchs* in charge of *Esther's* harem.

**Shaddai** (shuh-**dye**)
See *El Shaddai*

Daniel 1:7
Daniel 3:26-30

**Shadrach** (**shad**-rak)
Babylonian name given to *Hananiah*, a Hebrew exile in the service of King *Nebuchadnezzar*. Shadrach was one of the three men thrown into the fiery furnace for refusing to bow down to an idol of gold.

See also *Meshach; Abednego*

1 Chronicles 8:8

**Shaharaim** (**shay**-huh-**ray**-im)
A family leader mentioned in the genealogy of Saul; father of nine clan leaders in the tribe of *Benjamin*.

1 Samuel 9:4

**Shalisha** (shuh-**lye**-shuh)
One of the places *Saul* searched for his father's donkeys. Its exact location is unknown, but it was probably in *Benjamin*.
See also *Gibeah; Ramah; Zuph*

1 Chronicles 26:16

**Shalleketh Gate** (**shal**-i-keth **gate**)
A gate in the wall of Solomon's temple near the *West Gate*. Both gates were assigned to the gatekeepers Shuppim and Hosah.

**Shallum** (**shal**-uhm)

A very common name among the Israelites:

• Son of Jabesh and sixteenth king of Israel after *Zechariah*. Shallum came to power by assassinating the king. He reigned only one month—*Menahem* assassinated him. *2 Kings 15:13-14*

• Another name for *Jehoahaz*, king of Judah. *Jeremiah 22:11, 18*

• Ruler of a Jerusalem district who, with the help of his daughters, repaired part of the city wall during the time of Nehemiah; son of Hallohesh. *Nehemiah 3:12*

• Ruler of a Jerusalem district who repaired the *Fountain Gate* and the *Pool of Siloam* during the time of Nehemiah; son of Col-Hozeh. *Nehemiah 3:15*

• *Huldah's* husband. *2 Chronicles 34:22*

• At least ten others mentioned only by name or only in passing.

**Shalmaneser** (**shal**-muh-**nee**-zur) *2 Kings 17:3-4* *2 Kings 18:9*

Shalmaneser V, king of Assyria who besieged Samaria during the reign of *Hoshea*. Shalmaneser was the son of *Tiglath-Pileser*. He reigned 727-722 B.C. and was succeeded by *Sargon*.

**Shama** (**shah**-mah) *1 Chronicles 11:44*

One of David's *mighty men*; brother of Jeiel; son of Hotham.

**Shamgar** (**sham**-gar)

Judges 3:31
Judges 5:6

Son of Anath and third judge of Israel after *Ehud*. Shamgar used a most unusual weapon against the Philistines: an *ox goad*. The Bible does not say how long he served as a judge.

**Shammah** (**sham**-uh)

S

- 1 Samuel 16:9 — Third son of *Jesse* and big brother to David; also called Shimeah and Shimei.

- 2 Samuel 23:11-12 — One of David's *three* mighty men; son of Agee; a Hararite. Shammah became a hero for defending a field singlehandedly against the Philistines.
- 2 Samuel 23:24-25 — One of David's *thirty* mighty men; a Harodite; also called Shammoth and Shamhuth.
- Genesis 36:13 — An *Edomite* who was head of his clan, one of Reuel's sons; grandson of Esau and Basemath.

**Shammua** (shuh-**moo**-uh)

- Numbers 13:3-4 — One of the 12 men chosen by Moses at Kadesh Barnea to spy out the land of Canaan; a leader of the tribe of Reuben; son of Zaccur.

- 2 Samuel 5:13-14 — One of David and Bathsheba's sons; brother of *Solomon*; also called Shimea.
- Two others mentioned only by name.

**Shaphan** (**shay**-fuhn)

• King *Josiah's* court secretary; son of Azaliah. Shaphan is the one to whom *Hilkiah* reported finding the lost book of the law. He was a *scribe*.

• *Jaazaniah's* father. *Ezekiel 8:11*

**Shaphat** (**shay**-fat)

A common name among the Israelites:

• One of the 12 men chosen by Moses at Kadesh Barnea to spy out the land of Canaan; a leader of the tribe of Simeon; son of Hori. *Numbers 13:3, 5*

• *Elisha's* father. *1 Kings 19:16*

• Several others mentioned only once.

**Shaphir** (**shay**-fur) *Micah 1:11*

"Pleasant" or "Beautiful," name of a town in *Judah* condemned in the prophecies of Micah. Its location is unknown.

**Sharezer** (shuh-**ree**-zur)

• Son of *Sennachrib* and brother of *Adrammelech*. Sharezer and Adrammelech murdered their father just as *Isaiah* predicted. *2 Kings 19:36-37*; *Isaiah 37:7, 38*

• One of those sent by the people of Bethel to ask the prophet Zechariah about God's will during the rebuilding of the temple under Zerubbabel. *Zechariah 7:2*

**Sharon** (**shair**-uhn)

The plain in the middle of Palestine along the Mediterranean coast bounded on all sides by the hills. The northern and northeastern boundary *1 Chronicles 5:16*; *1 Chronicles 27:29*

S

was at *Carmel*. Sharon was and is a very fertile tract of land.

1 Chronicles 27:29

**Sharonite** (**shair**-uhn-ite)
A person who lived in *Sharon*.

**Shaul** (**shawl**)

Genesis 36:37-38

• A king of *Edom* during the time of the *patriarchs*. He ruled from the city of *Rehoboth*.

Genesis 46:10

• One of *Simeon's* sons who went to Egypt with the family of Jacob.

1 Chronicles 6:24

• Head of his clan in the tribe of Kohath; son of Uzziah.

Numbers 26:13

**Shaulite** (**shawl**-ite)
People in *Shaul's* clan.

Genesis 14:5

**Shaveh Kiriathaim**
(**shay**-vuh **kihr**-ee-uh-**thay**-im)
The *Emite* city attacked and defeated by *Kedorlaomer* shortly before his attack on Sodom in the days of Abram and Lot. Its location is not known.

1 Chronicles 18:14-17

**Shavsha** (**shav**-shuh)
Another name for David's scribe *Seraiah*.

**Shealtiel** (shee-**ahl**-tee-el)

1 Chronicles 3:17-18

• Firstborn son of King *Jehoiachin*.

Ezra 3:2

• *Zerubbabel's* father.

**Shear-Jashub** (**shee**-ar-**jay**-shuhb)
Isaiah's firstborn son. Shear-Jashub's name means "a remnant will return." God told Isaiah to take his son with him as a message of hope to King Ahaz as Jerusalem was about to be attacked. *Isaiah 7:3*

S

**Sheba** (**shee**-buh)
• A land and people in southwestern Arabia. The *queen of Sheba* is famous for coming to visit Solomon. *1 Kings 10:1-13*
• One of the cities in the territory allotted to *Simeon*. *Joshua 19:1-2*
• Leader of a serious revolt against David some time after Absalom's rebellion; son of Bicri. Sheba had the backing of ten tribes of Israel, but only until Joab stopped him at *Abel Beth Maacah*. *2 Samuel 20:1-22*
• Leader of his clan in *Gad*; son of Abihail. *1 Chronicles 5:13*

**Sheba, queen of** (**shee**-buh, **kween** uhv)
See *queen of Sheba; Sheba*

**Shebat** (**shee**-bat)
The eleventh *month* of the Israelite year, overlapping January and February. *Zechariah 1:7*

**Shebna** (**sheb**-nuh)
Hezekiah's court secretary during the siege of Jerusalem; a *scribe*. The prophet *Isaiah* had harsh words for Shebna. *2 Kings 18:18* *Isaiah 37:2*

*Joshua 21:21*

**Shechem** (**shek**-uhm)

One of the six *cities of refuge*, a city in the territory allotted to Manasseh but also near Ephraim and often described as being in the hill country of Ephraim. Shechem was between Mount Ebal and Mount Gerizim. The city played a big part in Abimelech's power struggle. After the split of the kingdom, *Jeroboam* I fortified it.

S

*Numbers 26:31*

**Shechemite** (**shek**-uhm-ite)

A person from the town of *Shechem*.

*Exodus 20:24*
*Psalm 119:176*
*John 10:14-15*

**sheep** (**sheep**)

A animal that chews the cud and has cloven hooves and a coat of wool, one of the kinds of

animals the Israelites were allowed to sacrifice for sin. Sheep are closely related to *goats*. People who could not afford sheep or goats were allowed to sacrifice *doves* or *pigeons* instead.

In some parts of the Bible, sheep are used as a symbol of those who love God. Psalm 23 is one famous example.

See also *offering*

*Nehemiah 3:1*

**Sheep Gate** (**sheep gate**)

One of the gates in the north wall of Jerusalem repaired by the high priest Eliashib and other priests during the time of Nehemiah.

**Sheerah** (**she**-uh-ruh)

The daughter of Ephraim who built both towns of *Beth Horon*.

1 Chronicles 7:24

**shekel** (**shek**-uhl)

A unit of weight equal to about eleven-and-a-half grams, or two-fifths of an ounce; two *bekas*. Like the *mina* and the *talent*, the shekel could be used as a standard unit of money in trade.

Exodus 30:13
2 Kings 7:16

**Shem** (**shem**)

Firstborn son of *Noah*. Shem and his family rode on the ark and therefore survived the flood. His descendants became nations that settled north and east of Canaan.

Genesis 5:32
1 Chronicles 1:17

**Shemaiah** (shuh-**mye**-uh)

A very common name among the Israelites:

- The son of *Shecaniah* who served as guard at the East Gate of Jerusalem and made repairs to it during the time of Nehemiah. (Nehemiah 3:28-29)
- "Shemaiah the Nehelamite," the Israelite man who called Jeremiah crazy and an impostor. Shemaiah demanded that the high priest Zephaniah lock Jeremiah in stocks and leg irons. (Jeremiah 29:24-32)
- "Shemaiah son of Delaiah," one of those hired by Tobiah and Sanballat to stop Nehemiah from (Nehemiah 6:10-14)

rebuilding the walls of Jerusalem. Shemaiah tried to scare Nehemiah into hiding in the temple. Nehemiah was not allowed in the temple because he was a *eunuch* and not a priest or a Levite.

1 Kings 12:22-23
• "Shemaiah the man of God," whose prophecy told *Rehoboam* not to go to war against *Jeroboam* I.

2 Chronicles 17:7-9
• One of the Levites sent by Jehoshaphat to teach the law of Moses in Judah.

• A Levite leader who gave generously to the Levites during Josiah's reforms.

1 Chronicles 26:6
• *Obed-Edom's* oldest son.

• Many others mentioned only once, most of whom lived during or after the *Exile*.

**Shemariah**
(**shem**-uh-**rye**-uh)

1 Chronicles 12:5
• An Israelite warrior from the tribe of Benjamin who defected to David at Ziklag.

2 Chronicles 11:18-19
• One of Rehoboam's sons.

Ezra 10:17, 25, 32, 41
• Two men who submitted to Ezra's reform.

**Shemer** (**shee**-mur)

1 Kings 16:24
• Owner of the hill that *Omri* bought and called *Samaria*. Shemer was probably a clan as well as an individual.

1 Chronicles 6:46
• One of the Levite musicians appointed by David.

**Shemiramoth** (shuh-**mir**-uh-moth)

- A temple *gatekeeper* appointed to sing and play music during the return of the Ark to Jerusalem. — *1 Chronicles 15:16-20*
- One of the Levites sent by Jehoshaphat to teach the law of Moses in Judah. — *2 Chronicles 17:7-9*

**Shemuel** (**shem**-oo-el)

The family leader from the tribe of *Simeon* chosen by God to help divide up the land after the conquest of Canaan. — *Numbers 34:20*

**Sheol** (**shee**-ohl)

The Old Testament word for the place of the dead; death. — *Genesis 42:38; Psalm 49:14-15; Psalm 89:48*

*See also Abyss; Hades; lake of fire; Gehenna; hell*

**Shephatiah** (**shef**-uh-**tye**-uh)

A common name among the Israelites:

- An Israelite warrior from the tribe of Benjamin who defected to David at Ziklag; the Haruphite. — *1 Chronicles 12:5*

- Commander of the forces of Simeon in David's army; son of Maacah. — *1 Chronicles 27:17*
- One of the four royal officials who put Jeremiah in a cistern; son of *Mattan*. — *Jeremiah 38:1-6*
- One of David and Abital's sons. — *1 Chronicles 3:1-3*
- One of King *Jehoshaphat's* sons. — *2 Chronicles 21:2*
- Several others mentioned only once.

S

1 Kings 10:27
Jeremiah 17:26
Obadiah 1:19

**shephelah** (shuh-**fee**-lah)
Lowlands; foothills; land between the coastal plains and the mountains or hilly areas. A person traveling from Jerusalem to Joppa would go from *hill country* to *shephelah* to *Sharon*.

Isaiah 40:10-11
John 10:1-18
Hebrews 13:20-21

**shepherd** (**shep**-urd)
A person who tended sheep. A shepherd's duties included leading the sheep to good pasture, providing water for the sheep, keeping sheep close by, protecting sheep from wild animals, tending to sheeps' cuts and wounds, giving rest to birthing mothers and lambs, and doing anything else necessary to care for the flock. These duties often required shepherds to spend weeks away from home at a time, so they had to live in tents and walk wherever needed to find pasture for the flock.

Shepherds had to be skilled and resourceful. They used a rod or staff to guide sheep and to protect them. Many, like *David*, were also skilled with a sling as a weapon against wild animals and other intruders. When David was a shepherd, he passed the time by playing his *harp*.

The Bible refers to shepherds well over 100 times because of their importance. Many people depended on sheep for food and wool, and sheep were a key part of Israel's sacrifices and *offerings*. Shepherds also cared for sheep much the way God cares for people, and this led many of the prophets and writers of Psalms to speak of God as a shepherd. Psalm 23 is one of the Bible's most famous passages about shepherds. Jesus called himself "the Good Shepherd."

**Sheshbazzar** (shesh-**baz**-ur)

Prince of Judah during the *Exile* appointed governor of Judah by Cyrus after the first return of Jews to Jerusalem. "Sheshbazzar" may be a Persian name for *Zerubbabel*.

*Ezra 1:8*
*Ezra 5:16*

**Sheva** (**shee**-vuh)

- Another name for David's scribe *Seraiah*. *2 Samuel 20:23-26*
- Leader of his clan in the tribe of Judah; son of Caleb and *Maacah*. *1 Chronicles 2:49*

**shewbread** (**shoh**-bred)

An older term for showbread, or *bread of the presence*.

*Exodus 25:30*
*1 Samuel 21:6*

**Shibah** (**shib**-uh)

*Genesis 26:32-33*

"Oath," the name that Isaac gave to the well that his servants dug in *Beersheba*. Isaac and Abimelech had just settled a dispute over the land by swearing an oath of peace.

S

Judges 12:4-6

**Shibboleth** (**shib**-oh-leth)

A password used by *Jephthah's* Gileadite forces. Their enemies could not say "Shibboleth" right, and this enabled them to tell friend from foe. Forty-two thousand men died for failing the test.

**Shibmah** (**shib**-muh)
See *Sibmah*

**Shichron** (**shik**-ron)
See *Shikkeron*

Psalm 7:1

**shiggaion** (shi-**gay**-on)

A term used in the title of Psalm 7. The meaning of "shiggaion" is not known.

Habakkuk 3:1

**shigionoth** (shi-**gee**-oh-noth)

A term used to describe the prayer of Habakkuk in the *book of Habakkuk*. Its meaning is unknown.

1 Chronicles 13:5
Isaiah 23:3

**Shihor** (**shye**-hor)

A river in Egypt that marked its eastern boundary with the wilderness and Israel's southern boundary during David's reign. No one is quite sure where Shihor was.

Joshua 19:26

**Shihor Libnath** (**shye**-hor **lib**-nath)

A place in the land allotted to Asher, at the intersection of its southern border with Manasseh and Zebulun. Shihor Libnath was in the Carmel range.

**Shikkeron** (**shik**-ur-on)
A city on the northern border of Judah, just south of Dan. Shikkeron was between *Ekron* and Baalah, but its exact location is unknown.
*Joshua 15:11*

**Shiloah** (shye-**loh**-uh)
See *Siloam*

**Shiloh** (**shye**-loh)
City in the hill country of Ephraim where the Israelites set up the *tabernacle* right after the conquest of Canaan. Shiloh served as Israel's capital and center of worship all during the time of the *judges*. Young Samuel grew up in the tabernacle at Shiloh.
*Joshua 18:1*
*Judges 18:31*

**Shilonites** (**shye**-luh-nites)
People from *Shiloh*.
*1 Chronicles 9:5*

**Shimea** (**shim**-ee-uh)
- Another name for David's son *Shammua*. *1 Chronicles 3:5*
- Another name for David's brother *Shammah*. *1 Chronicles 2:13*
- Two Levites. *1 Chronicles 6:30, 39*

**Shimeah** (**shim**-ee-uh)

*2 Samuel 13:3* • Another spelling of Shimea, who was David's brother *Shammah*.

*1 Chronicles 8:32* • Head of his clan in the tribe of Benjamin; son of Mikloth.

**Shimei** (**shim**-ee-eye)

A very common name among the Israelites:

*2 Samuel 16:5-14*
*2 Samuel 19:14-23*
*1 Kings 2:36-46* • Israelite of Saul's clan famous for opposing David and welcoming *Absalom's rebellion*. Shimei threw rocks at David and cursed him; then he later asked David to forgive him. The king granted his request, but Solomon had him executed.

*1 Chronicles 6:17* • Son of Gershon and head of the clan named after him, the *Shimeites*; grandson of Levi.

*2 Samuel 21:21* • Another name for David's brother *Shammah*; father of *Jonathan*.

*1 Kings 1:7-8* • One of the palace officials who stayed loyal to Solomon during *Adonijah's* revolt.

• Many others mentioned only once.

*Numbers 3:21* **Shimeites** (**shim**-ee-ites)

An important clan of *Levites* in Israel throughout Old Testament times. The *Gershonites* were part of this larger clan.

*Ezra 4:1-23* **Shimshai** (**shim**-shye)

Court secretary under *Artaxerxes* and one of those who tried to stop the Jews from rebuilding the temple during the time of Zerubbabel.

See also *Rehum*

**Shinar** (**shye**-nar)
An older name for Babylonia, the region of Mesopotamia settled by the descendants of *Nimrod*.
*Genesis 10:9-12*
*Genesis 10:32–11:2*

**Shisha** (**shye**-shuh)
Another name for David's scribe *Seraiah*.
*1 Kings 4:2-3*

**Shishak** (**shye**-shak)
King of Egypt during the later years of Solomon's reign and at the beginning of Rehoboam's; pharaoh Sheshonq I. Shishak did a lot of damage to the cities of Judah that *Rehoboam* had spent years fortifying.
*1 Kings 11:40*
*2 Chronicles 12:9*

**Shittim** (**shit**-im)
- A town in Moab across the Jordan River from Jericho; site of the *Baal Peor* rebellion. *Joshua 2:1*
- A valley in or near Jerusalem mentioned in the prophecies of Micah. *Micah 6:5*

**Shoa** (**shoh**-uh)
A group of people in Mesopotamia.
*Ezekiel 23:23*

**Shobab** (**shoh**-bab)
- One of David and Bathsheba's sons; brother of *Solomon*. *2 Samuel 5:14*
- One of *Caleb* and Azubah's sons; grandson of Hezron. *1 Chronicles 2:18*

**Shobi** (**shoh**-bye)
One of those who brought provisions to David at *Mahanaim* during Absalom's
*2 Samuel 17:27-29*

rebellion; son of Nahash. Shobi was an Ammonite. Unlike his brother *Hanun*, Shobi stayed loyal to David.

**showbread** (**shoh**-bred)
See *bread of the presence*

Judges 17:5
2 Kings 10:25

**shrine** (**shrine**)
A place of *idol* worship, usually a small building or shelter.
See also *high place; temple*

Genesis 38:22
Deuteronomy 23:17

**shrine prostitute** (**shrine pros**-ti-toot)
A person who gave sexual favors as a part of idol worship at a Canaanite *high place* or *shrine*.

Genesis 25:1-2

**Shuah** (**shoo**-uh)
One of Abraham and Keturah's sons.

Job 2:11

**Shuhite** (**shoo**-hite)
The tribe or clan of *Shuah*. *Bildad* was a Shuhite.

Song of Songs 6:13

**Shulammite** (**shoo**-luhm-ite)
A term used of Solomon's bride in the *Song of Songs*. "Shulammite" probably means that the woman was from a town or place called Shulam. Shulam can also be spelled *Shunem*.
See also *Shunammite*

**Shunammite** (**shoo**-nuhm-ite)
A person from *Shunem*. *Abishag* was a Shunammite.
*1 Kings 1:3*
*2 Kings 4:25*

**Shunem** (**shoo**-nuhm)
A Canaanite city in the territory allotted to Issachar. *Elisha* did a famous miracle while in Shunem. It was located at the southwestern foot of *Moreh* and overlooked the *Valley of Jezreel*.
*Joshua 19:18*
*2 Kings 4:8-37*

**Shur** (**shoor**)
A desert area in the northwest region of the *Sinai* peninsula.
See also *Desert of Shur*
*Genesis 20:1*
*Genesis 25:18*

**Sibmah** (**sib**-muh)
A *Moabite* town in the territory allotted to Reuben and noted for its vineyards; also called *Sebam*. *Sibmah* was close to *Nebo* and *Heshbon*.
*Numbers 32:3, 38*
*Joshua 13:15, 19*

**Siddim** (**sid**-im)
See *Valley of Siddim*

**Sidon** (**sye**-don)
• Firstborn son of *Canaan*. The descendants of Sidon became the Sidonians.
*Genesis 10:15*
• A major fortified city on the Mediterranean coast 40 kilometers north of *Tyre*. Sidon marked the northern border of Canaan.
*Genesis 49:13*
*Mark 7:31-37*
*Acts 27:3*

**Sidonians** (sye-**dohn**-ee-uhnz)
People from the city of *Sidon*.
*Joshua 13:6*

Genesis 9:12-13
Luke 2:11-13

**sign (syne)**
A deed or event that indicates *Deity*; a *wonder*; a *miracle* or *miraculous sign*.

S

Genesis 41:42
Daniel 6:17

**signet ring (sig-net ring)**
A ring with a *seal* on it.

**signs and wonders (sinze and wuhn-durz)**
See *signs*

Numbers 21:23
Deuteronomy 3:2

**Sihon (sye-hon)**
Amorite king in *Heshbon* when the Israelites were on their way to the *promised land*. The Israelites defeated Sihon's forces after he said no to their offer of peace.

**Sihor (sye-hor)**
See *Shihor*

Acts 15:22-35
1 Thessalonians 1:1
1 Peter 5:12

**Silas (sye-luhss)**
Jewish Christian and leader in the church at Jerusalem during the early days of Christianity; also called Silvanus. Silas went with Paul on his second missionary journey and helped with the ministry at *Corinth*. He also helped with the writing of First Peter.
See also *Barnabas; John Mark; Timothy*

**Siloah** (si-**loh**-uh)
See *Siloam*

**Siloam** (sye-**loh**-uhm) *Nehemiah 3:15; John 9:11*
The *Pool of Siloam* in Jerusalem.

**Silvanus** (sil-**vay**-nuhss)
See *Silas*

S

**Simeon** (**sim**-ee-uhn)
A common name among the Israelites:
- Jacob's son, the tribe of Israel named after him, and the land allotted to that tribe. *Leah* was Simeon's mother. The land of Judah surrounded the land of Simeon. *Genesis 29:33; Joshua 19:1*

- Another spelling for *Simon*. *Acts 15:14*
- Jewish prophet who recognized the infant Jesus as the Messiah. *Luke 2:25-35*
- "Simeon called Niger," one of the Christian leaders at *Antioch* when God sent Paul on his first missionary journey. *Acts 13:1-2*
- One of the people mentioned in the genealogy of Jesus. *Luke 3:30*

See also *tribes of Israel*

**Simeonites** (**sim**-ee-uhn-**ites**) *Joshua 19:8-9*
Members of the tribe of Simeon; Israelites who traced their roots to Jacob's son Simeon.

**Simon** (**sye**-muhn)
A common name among the Israelites:
- Simon Peter: son of John and disciple of Jesus. Jesus gave him the name Peter as a nickname *Matthew 10:2*

(the Greek form of *Cephas*). He was the first disciple to express belief in Jesus as the Son of God and one of the most important of Jesus' twelve disciples. He wrote *First Peter* and *Second Peter*.

*Matthew 10:2-4* • Simon the Zealot: Jewish man who became one of the *Twelve* disciples of Jesus.

*Matthew 13:55* • One of Jesus' half-brothers.

*John 6:71* • *Judas Iscariot's* father.

*Matthew 26:6* • Leper from Bethany who welcomed Jesus into his home; possibly related to Mary, Martha, and Lazarus.

*Luke 7:36-50* • A Pharisee who invited Jesus to dinner.

*Mark 15:21* • A passerby from Cyrene forced to carry Jesus' cross.

*Acts 8:9-24* • Simon Magus: A *sorcerer* who clashed with *Peter* while he was in Samaria shortly after the stoning of Stephen.

*Acts 9:43* • Simon the tanner: leatherworker who gave lodging to Peter while he was in Joppa.

**Simon Magus** (**sye**-muhn **may**-guhss)
*See Simon*

**Simon Peter** (**sye**-muhn **pee**-tur)
*See Simon*

**Simon son of John** (**sye**-muhn **suhn** uhv **jon**)
*See Simon*

**Simon the sorcerer** (**sye-**muhn the **sor**-sur-ur)
*Simon* Magus.

**Simon the tanner** (**sye-**muhn the **tan**-ur)
*See Simon*

**Simon the Zealot** (**sye-**muhn the **zel**-uht)
*See Simon*

**sin** (**sin**)

• Noun: Any act of wrongdoing; any violation of God's law; missing the mark. Sin brings *death*; this is sin's penalty. In Old Testament times, God allowed the Israelites to *make atonement* for their sins through the *offerings*. Today God allows a person to *make atonement* by receiving the atonement that Jesus Christ provides.

Second, sin is a part of human nature that cannot be removed. Every person is a sinner. God seeks to change that in us by *sanctification*.

*Leviticus 5:5-6*
*John 3:16-21*
*Romans 6:23*
*2 Corinthians 5:21*
*1 John 1:7-9*

• Verb: To do wrong; to break God's commands; to do what God says not to do. All people sin. But Christians have the benefit of *sanctification*.

*2 Chronicles 6:36-39*
*Romans 3:23*
*Ephesians 4:26*

See also *born again; Desert of Sin; forgiveness; salvation; sin offering*

**sin offering** (**sin awf**-ur-ing)
One of three kinds of sacrifices that the Israelites made to pay for *sin*. The sin offering was required of anyone who broke God's commands accidentally or without meaning to. It involved the slaughter of a perfect *bull*, goat,

*Leviticus 4:1–5:13*
*Leviticus 6:24-30*

S

lamb, pair of *doves*, or pair of pigeons, depending on what the person could afford. A very poor person could bring fine flour instead. The rules for sin offerings can be found in Leviticus 4:1—5:13 and 6:24-30.

See also *offering*

S

**Sin, Wilderness of** (**sin**, **wil**-dur-ness uhv)
See *Desert of Sin*

**Sinai** (**sye**-nye)

Deuteronomy 33:2
• The V-shaped portion of land between Egypt and the land of Palestine, bounded on the southwest and southeast by the Red Sea.

Exodus 19:1
• A region of rocky desert in the south of the Sinai peninsula. Sinai is home to *Mount Sinai* and the *Desert of Sinai*. The Israelites traveled through this area during the Exodus.

Colossians 2:19
**sinews** (**sin**-yooz)
Tendons; tissue that connects muscle to bone or cartilage.

Deuteronomy 9:21
Proverbs 12:13
**sinful** (**sin**-fuhl)
*Wicked*; evil; bad.
See also *sin; sinful nature*

Romans 7:18
Galatians 5:16-17
**sinful nature** (**sin**-fuhl **nay**-chur)
The part of human nature that loves wrongdoing; evil or wicked desires. All people have a sinful nature. God enables his people to resist and overcome it through *sanctification*.

**Sinites** (**sye**-nites)
A tribe of people that settled in or near Canaan.
*Genesis 10:17*

**sinner** (**sin**-ur)
• A person who is hostile to God's will; an unbeliever; a *wicked* person. *Psalm 1:1*

• A person such as a prostitute or murderer who is guilty of gross or obvious *sins*. *Luke 7:37-39; Mark 14:41*
• A person who has sinned even once; any person who has a *sinful nature*. Every person is a sinner in this sense. *Romans 5:8*
See also *born again; salvation*

**Sion** (**sye**-uhn)
See *Zion*

**Sirion** (**sihr**-ee-on)
The name given to Mount *Hermon* by the people of *Sidon*.
*Deuteronomy 3:9*

**Sisera** (**sis**-ur-uh)
• Commander of *Jabin's* army defeated in battle by Barak and Deborah, and killed in his tent by *Jael*. *Judges 4:2, 17-22*

• A temple servant during the time of Nehemiah. *Nehemiah 7:55*

**sistrum** (**sis**-truhm)
A musical instrument much like a castanet, a U-shaped piece of metal with other pieces of metal attached across the U and made for rattling.
*2 Samuel 6:5*

S

*Esther 8:9*

**Sivan (sye**-van)
The third *month* of the Israelite year, overlapping May and June.

*Matthew 20:5*
*John 4:6*

**sixth hour (siksth our**)
Six *hours* from sunrise, or six twelfths of the day after sunrise; halfway between sunrise and sundown; noon.

*Deuteronomy 4:48*

**Siyon, Sirion (sye**-yon, **sihr**-ee-uhn)
Another name for *Hermon*.

**Skull, Place of the (skuhl, playss** uhv the)
See *Golgotha*

*Exodus 1:11*
*Genesis 39:17*
*Philemon 1:16*

**slave (slayv**)
A person who is owned by another. Joseph was

a slave of Potiphar. Onesimus was a slave of Philemon. The *Exodus* came about because of God's desire to free the Israelites from slavery in Egypt.

**sling (sling**)

*1 Samuel 17:40-50*

• Noun: A long, narrow strip of leather with a wide portion in the middle used for throwing stones. David used a sling to kill *Goliath*.

*Judges 20:16*

• Verb: To throw a stone with a sling. The warriors of Benjamin were once famous for their slinging skills.

**slingstone** (**sling**-stohn)
A stone thrown from a *sling*.
*1 Samuel 17:49*

**slothful** (**sloth**-fuhl)
Lazy.
*Proverbs 12:27*
*Matthew 25:26*

**Smyrna** (**smur**-nuh)
A port city north of *Ephesus* and south of *Pergamum* in the Roman province of *Asia*. Jesus addressed one of the letters in the book of Revelation to this church.
*Revelation 1:11*
*Revelation 2:8-11*

**Soco** (**soh**-koh)
See *Socoh*

**Socoh** (**soh**-koh)
- A town in the *shephelah* of western Judah where the Philistines assembled for war against the Israelites right before the battle between David and Goliath. *1 Samuel 17:1*
- A town in the *hill country* of Judah. *Joshua 15:48*
- A town in the *Sharon* near Hepher. *1 Kings 4:10*

**Sodom** (**sod**-uhm)
One of the five *cities of the plain* and the home *Lot* chose for his family. The city is famous for being destroyed by God in a hail of fire for its terrible wickedness.
*Genesis 13:10*
*Genesis 18:26*

**Sodoma** (**sod**-uhm-uh)
An older word for *Sodom*.

S

*Judges 17:7-8*
*Acts 7:6*

**sojourn** (**soh**-jurn)
To stay for a while; to visit.

*Genesis 23:4*
*Psalm 39:12*

**sojourner** (**soh**-jurn-ur)
A person who stays or settles in a particular area that is not his home; a stranger or alien.

**solace** (**sol**-iss)
Comfort.

*2 Samuel 5:13-14*
*1 Kings 1:38-39*
*1 Kings 7:1*

**Solomon** (**sol**-uh-muhn)
Son of David and third king of the united kingdom of Israel after his father. Solomon was famous for his wisdom, but he also had hundreds of foreign wives and *concubines* who turned him away from God. Solomon wrote the books of Proverbs and Ecclesiastes.
See also *Rehoboam*

*Luke 18:38*

**Son of David** (**suhn** uhv **day**-vid)
A title of *Jesus Christ*. It means that Jesus is descended from David. The *messianic prophecies* say that the Messiah would be a descendant of David.

*Matthew 27:54*
*Galatians 2:20*

**Son of God** (**suhn** uhv **god**)
A title of *Jesus Christ*. It means that Jesus is the second person of the *Trinity*.
See also *sons of God*

**son of man, Son of Man**
(**suhn** uhv **man**)
- "son of man": A human being; a person.
- "Son of Man": A title of *Jesus Christ*. It means that Jesus is a human being; a man.

*Numbers 23:19*
*Psalm 144:3*
*Mark 10:45*
*John 8:28*

S

**song of ascents** (**song** uhv uh-**sents**)
One of fifteen *Psalms* (120–134) that are also called "Pilgrim Psalms." These Psalms were sung by worshipers going to Jerusalem for one of the three annual feasts (the *Feast of Unleavened Bread*, the *Feast of Weeks*, or the *Feast of Booths*).

*Psalm 121:1*
*Psalm 128:1*

**Song of Solomon** (**song** uhv **sol**-uh-muhn)
See *Song of Songs*

**Song of Songs** (**song** uhv **songz**)
Twenty-second book of the Old Testament and fifth of the *books of poetry*. Solomon wrote the Song of Songs for his bride, a *Shulammite* woman. The book celebrates marriage.

*Song of Songs 1:1*

**sons of God** (**suhnz** uhv **god**)
- Angels.
- God's people; also called "children of God."
- People who act like God.

*Job 1:6*
*Deuteronomy 14:1-2*
*Romans 8:14-19*
*1 John 3:1-2*
*Matthew 5:9*

**sons of men** (**suhnz** uhv **men**)
See *son of man*

*Isaiah 3:1-2*

**soothsayer** (**sooth**-say-ur)
A fortune-teller; a *diviner*.

*John 13:26*

**sop** (**sop**)
A piece of bread used to soak up soup.

*Acts 20:4-6*
*Romans 16:21*

**Sopater** (**soh**-puh-tur)

A Christian from *Berea* who went with Paul to *Troas* during Paul's third missionary journey; son of Pyrrhus. This may be the man named Sosipater who greeted the Romans in Paul's letter.

*Jeremiah 27:9-10*
*Malachi 3:5*
*Acts 13:6*

**sorcerer** (**sor**-sur-ur)
A person who uses or controls supernatural forces through *magic* or *sorcery*; a *diviner*; a *magician*.

*Leviticus 19:26*
*Deuteronomy 18: 9-16*

**sorcery, sorceries** (**sor**-sur-ee, **sor**-sur-eez)
Control use or of supernatural powers; *magic*.

**Sosipater** (soh-**sip**-uh-tur)
See *Sopater*

*Acts 18:14-17*

**Sosthenes** (**sos**-thuh-neez)

The synagogue ruler in *Corinth* during Paul's second missionary journey who was beaten by an angry mob. Certain Jews did not like Paul's preaching about Jesus and wanted Gallio to try him. *Gallio* refused, and Sosthenes paid.

**soul (sohl)**
The essense of a person; the emotions, personality, and *spiritual* part of a person. God creates every soul, and the soul lives on after the body dies.

*Deuteronomy 11:13*
*Hebrews 4:12*

**South Gate (south gate)**
One of the gates in the walls of Solomon's temple. *Obed-Edom* was its *gatekeeper*. Ezekiel also mentioned a south gate in the temple he saw in his vision.

See also *East Gate; North Gate; West Gate*

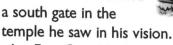

*1 Chronicles 26:14-19*

**southern kingdom (suh-thurn king-duhm)**
The kingdom known as *Judah* that was formed after the split between *Rehoboam* and *Jeroboam* I. The southern kingdom became known as Judah because only the tribes of Judah and Benjamin stayed loyal to Rehoboam, and Judah was the larger of the two. Over the years, this kingdom had 18 kings and one queen.
See also *kings of Judah; northern kingdom; prophets to Judah*

*2 Chronicles 11:1-4*

**Sovereign LORD (sov-rin lord)**
Literally, "*Lord Yahweh*," a name for God.
See also *Jehovah; lord*

*Deuteronomy 3:24*
*Judges 6:22*

S

Exodus 23:10
Luke 8:5

**sow (soh)**
To plant.
See also *sower*

Isaiah 55:10
John 4:36

**sower (soh-ur)**
A person who plants; a farmer.
See also *sow*

Romans 15:24

**Spain (spane)**
The same people and land of Spain in western Europe today. Paul wanted to go to Spain, but never made it.

Psalm 39:5
Ezekiel 43:13

**span (span)**
A measure of distance used in Old Testament times: The distance from the tip of the little finger to the tip of the thumb of a spread-out hand. The *Israelites* used the span as a standard unit of length. It was equal to about twenty-three centimeters, or nine inches; one-half a *cubit*; three *handbreadths*.

1 Samuel 19:9-10
1 Samuel 26:5-25
John 19:34

**spear (spihr)**
A pole with a sharp point or blade at one end, a very common stabbing weapon used in Old Testament times. Spears were used in hand-to-hand combat, like swords. Spears were longer than *javelins* but shorter than lances.

**spell** (**spel**)
Another word for *sorcery* or *magic*.
Revelation 18:23

**spirit, Spirit** (**spihr**-it)
• Human emotions and attitudes.
Psalm 51:12, 17
Haggai 1:14
Luke 9:37-43

• Any supernatural being, such as an *angel* or *demon*.

• The *Holy Spirit*.
Psalm 51:11
Joel 2:28-29

See also *flesh; soul*

**spiritist** (**spihr**-it-**ist**)
A *medium*.
Leviticus 20:27
Deuteronomy 18:10-12

**spiritual** (**spihr**-i-choo-uhl)
• Having to do with the *spirit* or *soul*. The spiritual is always invisible because the spirit and soul are invisible.
1 Corinthians 2:13
Ephesians 1:3

• Another word for *godly*.
Galatians 6:1

**spiritual gift** (**spihr**-i-choo-uhl **gift**)
A special talent or ability that God gives to a Christian so he or she can help God's people. Every Christian has spiritual gifts. The *Holy Spirit* gives the ability to use the gifts.
1 Corinthians 1:7
1 Corinthians 12:4-11
Ephesians 4:4-13

**spotless** (**spot**-less)
Without spot in behavior or attitude, that is, *blameless*.
Daniel 12:10
2 Peter 3:14

S

*Exodus 30:34*

**stacte** (**stak**-ti)
One of four ingredients that the Israelites used to make holy *incense*. It was either the same as the *balm of Gilead*, or sap from the storax tree. It is also sometimes called *resin droplets* or *gum resin*.

*Revelation 14:20*
*Revelation 21:16*

**stadia** (**stay**-dee-uh)
Plural of stade or stadium, a unit of length equal to about 185 meters.

*Exodus 4:2-4*
*Mark 6:8*
*Mark 15:19*

**staff** (**staf**)
A stick or rod used to guide *sheep*, to steady a person while walking, or as a crude weapon.

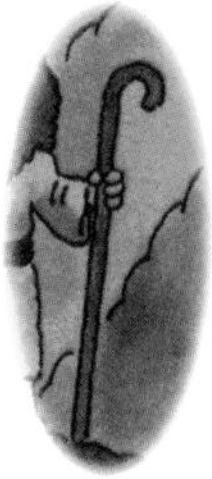

*1 Kings 11:34*
*Psalm 119:168*

**statute** (**stach**-oot)
A *law*, *decree*, or *commandment*.

*Isaiah 26:3*
*1 Peter 5:10*

**steadfast** (**sted**-fast)
Loyal; firm; constant; *faithful*.

*1 Corinthians 1:16*
*1 Corinthians 16:15-18*

**Stephanas** (**stef**-uh-nuhss)
First person to become a Christian in Greece, a *Corinthian*. Stephanas and his family were well-known for their service in the church at *Corinth*.

*Acts 6:1-15*
*Acts 7:54-60*

**Stephen** (**steev**-uhn)
Jewish Christian noted for his spiritual wisdom and also the first Christian *martyr*. Stephen was stoned to death by an angry mob after he preached about Jesus.

**steward** (**stoo**-urd)
A manager.

*Genesis 43:16*
*2 Samuel 19:17*

**stiff-necked** (**stif**-nekt)
Stubborn.

*Exodus 33:5*
*Acts 7:51*

**Stoic** (**stoh**-ik)
A person who believes in the philosophy of Stoicism. Stoics of New Testament times believed that happiness came from accepting the way things are and not fighting against them. The apostle Paul debated with Stoics at *Athens* during his second missionary journey.
See also *Epicurean*

*Acts 17:18*

**stone** (**stohn**)
• Noun: A rock.

*Genesis 28:20-22*
*Exodus 24:4*

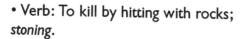

• Verb: To kill by hitting with rocks; *stoning*.

*Deuteronomy 17:5*
*John 8:5-7*
*Acts 7:58*

**stoning** (**stohn**-ing)
The standard method of execution used in Old Testament times. Several violations of the law, including child sacrifice and *idolatry*, were punishable by stoning. *Mediums* were also to be stoned. Crowds tried to stone Jesus because they believed him to be guilty of blasphemy.

*Leviticus 20:2, 27*
*Deuteronomy 13:6-11*
*John 10:31-39*

**stronghold** (**strong**-hohld)
A fortification, *fortified city*, or *fortress*.

*1 Samuel 22:5*
*Psalm 144:2*

S

Leviticus 26:37
Psalm 119:165

**stumble** (**stuhm**-buhl)
To fall down. The word is sometimes used as a synonym for *sin*.

Genesis 33:17
Judges 8:4-6

Exodus 12:37
Exodus 13:20

**Succoth** (**sook**-oth)
- A town near the *Jabbok* River and east of the *Jordan* in the territory allotted to Gad. Jacob named the place after setting up shelters for his animals there. "Succoth" means "booths" or "shelters."
- A city in Egypt on the eastern border with Sinai and first place the Israelites stopped after leaving.

2 Kings 17:29-33

**Succoth Benoth** (**sook**-oth **bee**-noth)
The *idol* worshiped by the people of *Babylon* who settled in Samaria after the destruction of Israel.

**Sukkiim** (**suhk**-ee-im)
See *Sukkites*

2 Chronicles 12:3-4

**Sukkites** (**suhk**-ites)
Mercenaries from a region of Lybia who helped *Shishak* ransack Judah during the reign of Rehoboam.

Deuteronomy 1:1

**Suph** (**soof**)
A place that was "opposite" where Moses spoke to the Israelites. Its location is unknown.

1 Kings 8:30
Psalm 119:170

**supplication** (**suhp**-li-**kay**-shuhn)
Request.

**surety** (**shur**-i-tee)
An older word for a guarantee or pledge of collateral.

*Genesis 43:9*
*Hebrews 7:22*

**Susa** (**soo**-suh)
Capital city of *Elam* and of Persia during the time of Esther. Susa was about 80 kilometers north of the Persian Gulf.

*Nehemiah 1:1*
*Esther 2:3*

**Susanna** (soo-**zan**-uh)
One of the women who gave money to help support Jesus' ministry.

*Luke 8:1-3*

**Sychar** (**sye**-kar)
A town in Samaria on the east slope of Mount *Ebal* and one kilometer north of Jacob's well, where Jesus once talked with a Samaritan woman.

*John 4:5*

**synagogue** (**sin**-uh-**gog**)
A place of worship and learning for a local *congregation* of Jews. Synagogues were not part of the tabernacle or temple worship; they arose during the *Exile* in Babylonia among Jews who loved God but could not worship at the *temple* in Jerusalem. Both Jesus and the apostle Paul preached in synagogues.

*Matthew 13:54*
*Mark 5:38*

**Syntyche** (**sin**-ti-kee)
A Christian woman who had a dispute with another Christian at Philippi, *Eudia*. In the *book of Philippians*,

*Philippians 4:2*

Paul pleaded with the two women to settle their differences.

Acts 28:12

**Syracuse** (**sihr**-uh-kyooss)
A large port city on the east coast of Sicily in New Testament times. Paul stopped there on his way to Rome.

S

Matthew 4:24

**Syria** (**sihr**-ee-uh)
Another word for the land of *Aram*, used mainly in New Testament times.

Luke 4:27

**Syrian** (**sihr**-ee-uhn)
A person from *Syria*.

Mark 7:26

**Syrian Phoenicia** (**sihr**-ee-uhn fuh-**nee**-shuh)
The region of *Phoenicia* that was in Syria.

**Syropheonician** (**sye**-roh-fuh-**nish**-uhn)
See *Syrian Phoenicia*

Acts 27:17

**Syrtis** (**sur**-tuhss)
A very shallow gulf off the coast of Lybia in the Mediterranean Sea. Syrtis was famous for being hazardous to ships.

**Taanach** (**tay**-uh-nak)
A Canaanite city eight kilometers southeast of *Megiddo* in the territory allotted to *Manasseh*.

*Joshua 17:11*

**Tabbath** (**tab**-uhth)
A place somewhere east of the *Jordan* River. Its exact location is unknown.

*Judges 7:22*

**Taberah** (**tab**-ur-uh)
"Burning," the name given to the place in the wilderness where the Israelites once complained about their situation during the *Exodus*. Its location is unknown.

*Numbers 11:1-3*

**tabernacle** (**tab**-ur-**nak**-uhl)
The Israelites' portable place of worship during the Exodus; a tent *sanctuary*. The tabernacle was made of lightweight parts that could easily be put together and taken down. God put *Bezalel* and *Oholiab* in charge of making it. Hundreds of Israelites carried the pieces as they traveled. Exodus 25:1–31:11 and 35:4–40:38 give detailed instructions for every piece of it. When the Israelites got to Canaan, they placed the tabernacle in *Shiloh*. The *temple* replaced it.

See also *Ark of the Covenant; mercy seat; Most Holy Place*

*Exodus 26:1-37*
*Exodus 40:1-38*
*Hebrews 8:1-6*

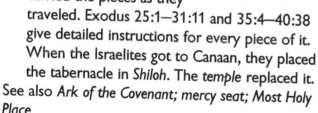

**Tabernacles, Feast of**
(**tab**-ur-**nak**-uhlz, **feest** uhv)
See *Feast of Booths*

*Acts 9:36-41*

**Tabitha** (**tab**-i-thuh)
Another name for *Dorcas*.

*Exodus 32:15-16*

**tablets** (**tab**-lets)
A piece of stone used for writing.

**Tabor** (**tay**-bor)

*Judges 4:6-14*

• Mount Tabor:
A mountain in Galilee 10 kilometers east of Nazareth.

*1 Chronicles 6:77*

• A *Levitical city* in the territory allotted to Zebulun, possibly on or near Mount Tabor.

*2 Chronicles 8:4*

**Tadmor** (**tad**-mor)
A city in *Aram* between Damascus and the Euphrates River that Solomon fortified.

*Jeremiah 43:4-13*

**Tahpanhes** (**top**-uh-neez)
A city in northeast Egypt, east of *Rameses* near Egypt's border with the *Desert of Shur*.

*2 Samuel 12:30*
*2 Chronicles 3:8*
*Matthew 25:14-30*

**talent** (**tal**-ent)
A unit of weight equal to about 34 kilograms, or 75 pounds; 60 *minas*; 3,000 *shekels*. Like the *mina* and the *shekel*, the talent could be used as a standard unit in trade. One talent was a huge sum of money.
See also *money*

**Talmai** (**tal**-mye)

King of *Geshur* and father of David's wife *Maacah*. Talmai let his grandson Absalom hide out in Geshur after the murder of *Amnon*.

2 Samuel 3:3
2 Samuel 13:35-39

**Tamar** (**tay**-mar)

- Daughter of David; sister of *Absalom*; half-sister of *Amnon*. Tamar was so beautiful that Amnon raped her, a crime that Absalom avenged by killing Amnon. — 2 Samuel 13:1-32
- Wife of Judah's son *Er*. After Er died, Tamar married Judah's son *Onan*. — Genesis 38:6-11
- Absalom's only daughter. — 2 Samuel 14:27
- An unknown place along Israel's border with Edom in the Arabah south-southwest of the Dead Sea. — Ezekiel 47:18-19

**tamarisk tree** (**tam**-uh-risk **tree**)

A large desert shrub with thin leaves that stays green most of the year and therefore provides much—needed shade.

Genesis 21:33

**tambourine** (tam-bor-**een**)

In Israel, a hand-held drum with jingles attached that was usually played by women during celebrations and parades. Tambourines were not allowed in the *temple*.

Exodus 15:20
Psalm 81:2

T

**Tammuz** (**tam**-uhz)
The fourth *month* of the Israelite year, overlapping June and July.

1 Kings 4:11
**Taphath** (**tay**-fath)
One of Solomon's daughters.

**Tappuah** (**tap**-oo-uh)
Joshua 15:34
• A city in the lowlands of Judah.
Joshua 17:8
• A border city of Ephraim that was originally given to Manasseh.
2 Kings 15:16
• A city in Samaria near Tirzah that suffered terribly for Menahem's evil ways.

**Tarshish** (**tar**-shish)
2 Chronicles 20:36
• A port city in Arabia near *Sheba*.
Ezekiel 38:13
Jonah 1:3
Jonah 4:2
• A port city somewhere in the Mediterranean Sea. The prophet *Jonah* tried to run away to Tarshish.
Esther 1:13-22
• One of the advisors who agreed with *Memucan's* recommendation that King Ahasuerus replace *Vashti*.
Genesis 10:4
• One of *Javan's* sons.
1 Chronicles 7:10
• Head of his clan in the tribe of Benjamin; son of Bilhan.

Acts 9:30
**Tarsus** (**tar**-suhss)
Capital city of *Cilicia* and the apostle Paul's hometown. Tarsus was in southeast Asia Minor.

**Tartan** (**tar**-tan)

2 Kings 18:17
Isaiah 20:1

Commander of the army of an Assyrian or Babylonian king. The Tartan was the highest-ranking Assyrian officer at the siege of *Jerusalem* during Hezekiah's reign.

See also *Rabsaris; Rabshakeh*

T

**tassel** (**tass**-uhl)

Numbers 15:37-41

A set of threads that hang down from a piece of cloth. God told the Israelites to make tassels, each with one blue cord, to remind them of the commandments. Modern Jews use the prayer shawl for this purpose.

**Tattenai** (**tat**-uh-nye)

Ezra 5:3
Ezra 6:6

Governor of *Trans-Euphrates* who tried to stop *Zerubbabel* and the Jews from rebuilding the temple during the time of Ezra.

See also *Haggai; Zechariah*

**tax collector** (**takss** cuh-**lek**-tur)

Matthew 10:3
Mark 2:15

In New Testament times, a person who collected money from citizens and paid a portion of it to the Roman government. The Jews hated tax collectors because they worked for the Romans, took money for themselves, and did business with *Gentiles*. Jesus' disciple *Matthew* was a tax collector.

T

Matthew 5:20
Mark 12:28-34

**teacher of the law** (**teech**-ur uhv the **law**)

A *scribe* during the time of Jesus. Some translations of the Bible refer to them as lawyers, but these teachers of the law were experts in the law of Moses and the Pharisees' oral law, not civil law. Some of the members of the Sanhedrin were teachers of the law. Many of them challenged Jesus' authority.

Genesis 22:24

**Tebah** (**tee**-buh)

One of *Nahor* and Reumah's sons; Abraham's nephew.

Esther 2:16-17

**Tebeth** (**tee**-beth)

The tenth *month* of the Israelite year, overlapping December and January.

**tekel** (**tek**-uhl)

See *mene, mene, tekel, upharsin*

2 Chronicles 20: 20-23
Nehemiah 3:27
Amos 1:1

**Tekoa** (te-**koh**-uh)

A city in the territory of Judah about 16 kilometers south of Jerusalem. Tekoa was the prophet Amos's hometown.

1 Chronicles 27:9

**Tekoite** (te-**koh**-ite)

A person from *Tekoa*.

**Tel Abib** (**tel** uh-**beeb**)
A city in Babylonia near the *Kebar* River where some of Judah's exiles lived during the time of Ezekiel.
*Ezekiel 3:15*

**Tel Assar** (**tel ass**-ur)
A city in *Aram* destroyed by *Sennacherib*. Sennacherib tried to scare Hezekiah by mentioning the destruction of this city.
*2 Kings 19:12*
*Isaiah 37:12*

**Tel Harsha** (**tel har**-shuh)
One of the towns near Nippur in Babylonia occupied by Jewish exiles. Its exact location is unknown.
*Ezra 2:59*

**Tel Melah** (**tel mee**-luh)
One of the towns near Nippur in Babylonia occupied by Jewish exiles. Its exact location is unknown.
*Ezra 2:59*

**Tema** (**tee**-muh)
Son of *Ishmael* and the tribe named after him; grandson of Abraham. Tema's people settled in northern Arabia and were the target of some of Jeremiah's prophecies.
*Isaiah 21:13-17*
*Jeremiah 25:23-29*

**Teman** (**tee**-muhn)
Son of Esau's son *Eliphaz* and the clan of *Edomites* named after him; grandson of Esau.
*Genesis 36:11, 15-16*

**Temanite** (**tee**-muhn-ite)
A member of the clan of Teman; an *Edomite* descended from *Teman*.
*Genesis 36:34*
*Job 2:11*

*Galatians 5:23*

**temperance** (**tem**-pur-enss)
An older word for *self-control* that is found in some translations of the Bible.

*1 Kings 5:1-6*
*1 Kings 6:37-38*
*Ezra 1:1-8*
*John 2:13-22*
*2 Kings 1:2*
*Acts 14:13*
*Acts 19:27, 35*

**temple** (**tem**-puhl)
God's "house"; a place of *worship*; a *sanctuary* that is used for worship.
• The temple built by *Solomon*: The Bible's most famous temple, a grand building of stone and wood built in Jerusalem over a period of seven years.
• The temple rebuilt by *Zerubbabel*: Shortly after the exiles returned to Jerusalem, Zerubbabel and others rebuilt the temple that had been destroyed by Nebuchadnezzar's invading army. The prophets *Haggai* and *Zechariah* wrote about this temple.
• The temple built by *Herod*: King Herod invaded Jerusalem in 37 b.c. and damaged the temple walls, but he returned to repair and rebuild it 17 years later. This project doubled the temple's size. This is the temple that was in place when Jesus taught.
• Other temples: The Canaanites, Philistines, Assyrians, Babylonians, Persians, Egyptians, Ephesians, and many other peoples of Bible times built temples for their gods. Samson destroyed the temple of *Dagon*.
See also *Ezekiel, book of; high place; shrine*

T

**tempt** (**tempt**)
To lure, entice, or coax someone into *temptation*; to try to make a person want to sin. The *devil* is called the tempter, but God never tempts anyone.

*Matthew 4:1-11*
*1 Corinthians 10:13*
*James 1:13-15*

**temptation** (temp-**tay**-shuhn)
Wanting to *sin*; the desire to sin; any time of wanting to sin. Jesus taught his disciples to pray that God will lead them away from temptation.

*Matthew 6:13*
*Luke 22:40*
*1 Corinthians 10:13*

**Ten Commandments** (**ten** cuh-**mand**-ments)
The 10 laws given by God to Moses at Mount Sinai during the Exodus. The Ten Commandments form the core of God's *law* and the heart of God's *covenant* with Israel. God himself wrote the commandments on two stone tablets. They are recorded in Exodus 20:1-17 and Deuteronomy 5:4-21.

*Exodus 20:1-17*
*Deuteronomy 5:4-21*

**tent of meeting** (**tent** uhv **meet**-ing)
- The tent where God met with Moses before the Israelites built the tabernacle. *Exodus 33:7-11*
- Another term for the *tabernacle*. *Exodus 35:20-21*

**tenth hour** (**tenth our**)
Ten-twelfths of daylight after sunrise; two-twelfths of daylight before sundown.
See also *hour*

*John 1:39*

T

Acts 18:3

**tentmaker** (**tent-**may-kur)
A person who makes tents. The apostle Paul earned his living as a tentmaker.

Genesis 11:24-32

**Terah** (**tair**-uh)
Father of *Abram*, Nahor, and Haran; son of Nahor.

Esther 2:21-23

**Teresh** (**tair**-esh)
One of the *eunuchs* who plotted to assassinate *Ahasuerus* but was caught by *Mordecai*.
See also *Bigthana; Esther*

Romans 16:22

**Tertius** (**tur**-shuhss)
Christian man who took dictation for Paul in writing the *book of Romans*.

Acts 24:1-8

**Tertullus** (**tur**-tuhl-uhss)
Lawyer who presented the case against Paul to *Felix* at Caesarea on behalf of Ananias.

Matthew 14:1

**tetrarch** (**tet**-rark)
A title sometimes given to Roman rulers who had less power than a king. *Herod Antipas* was a tetrarch.

Matthew 10:3
Mark 3:18

**Thaddaeus** (**thad**-ee-uhss)
One of Jesus' *Twelve* disciples; son of James. We know little about him besides what we know about all of the Twelve.

**thank offering** (**thangk awf**-ur-ing)
One of three kinds of *fellowship offerings*; a sacrifice that a person offers to God as an expression of gratitude to him. The rules about thank *offerings* are in Leviticus 7:11-15.

*Leviticus 7:11-15*

**Thebes** (**theebz**)
A city in *Upper Egypt*.

*Nahum 3:8-10*

**Thebez** (**thee**-bez)
A fortified city attacked by *Abimelech*. The location of Thebez is unknown.

*Judges 9:50-53*

**Theophilus** (thee-**ah**-fil-uhss)
The person to whom Luke wrote the *book of Luke* and the *book of Acts*. The name "Theophilus" means "friend of God."

*Luke 1:1-4*
*Acts 1:1-3*

**Thessalonians** (**thess**-uh-**loh**-nee-uhnz)
• People who lived in *Thessalonica*.

• Christians of the church in Thessalonica.
• Two books of the New Testament: *First Thessalonians and Second Thessalonians*.

*1 Thessalonians 1:1*

**Thessalonians, First**
(**thess**-uh-**loh**-nee-uhnz, **furst**)
Thirteenth book of the New Testament, a letter written by the apostle Paul to the Christians at the church in *Thessalonica*. Paul wrote this letter to teach the believers of this young church and

*1 Thessalonians 1:1-3*

to encourage them with the promise of Christ's return.

See also *Second Thessalonians*

2 Thessalonians 2:1-3

**Thessalonians, Second** (**thess**-uh-**loh**-nee-uhnz, **sek**-uhnd)

Fourteenth book of the New Testament, a letter written by the apostle Paul to the Christians at the church in *Thessalonica*. Paul wrote this letter to clear up some confusion they had about Christ's return.

See also *First Thessalonians*

Acts 17:1, 11-13
Philippians 4:16
1 Thessalonians 1:1

**Thessalonica** (**thess**-uh-loh-**nye**-kuh)

A major port city in the Roman province of *Macedonia* in New Testament times. Thessalonica was located about 60 kilometers east-northeast of *Berea*. Paul visited the city during his second and third missionary journeys and started a church there that received two of his many New Testament letters. The city survives today as one of the largest in Greece.

See also *First Thessalonians; Second Thessalonians*

**third hour** (**thurd our**)

Three-twelfths of daylight after sunrise.

See also *hour*

2 Samuel 23:24-39

**Thirty, the** (**thur**-tee, the)

An elite corps of David's mighty men. The Thirty are listed in 2 Samuel 23:24-39.

See also *Three*

**Thomas** (**tom**-uhss)

One of Jesus' twelve disciples. Thomas is the one who doubted Jesus' resurrection after all the others had seen Jesus alive. In the Gospel of John, Thomas is called *Didymus*.

*Luke 6:15*
*John 11:16*
*John 20:24-29*

**Three, the** (**three**, the)

An elite corps of David's mighty men: *Jashobeam*, *Eleazar*, and *Shammah*. Chief among them was Jashobeam. Another of David's mighty men, Abishai, commanded the Three in David's army. Their story is told in 2 Samuel 23:8-19.

See also *Thirty*

*2 Samuel 23:8-19*

**threshing floor** (**thresh**-ing **flor**)

A space of flat rock or ground used for separating the seeds of *grain* from their shells.

*1 Samuel 23:1-2*
*2 Samuel 24:18-25*

**Thummim** (thuhm-im)

See *Urim and Thummim*

**Thyatira** (**thye**-uh-**tye**-ruh)

A city about 40 kilometers north of *Sardis* in the Roman province of *Asia*. Jesus addressed one of the letters in the book of Revelation to this church. Thyatira was famous for its red dye.

See also *Lydia*

*Acts 16:14*
*Revelation 1:11*
*Revelation 2:18-29*

T

*John 6:23*

**Tiberias** (tye-**bihr**-ee-uhss)
A city on the southwest coast of the Sea of Galilee in New Testament times. Herod Antipas built Tiberias shortly before Jesus began his ministry, to serve as the capital of his *tetrarchy*. It was named after the emperor *Tiberius Caesar*.

*Luke 3:1*

**Tiberius Caesar** (tye-**bihr**-ee-uhss **see**-zur)
Second Roman emperor after Caesar Augustus.

Tiberius Caesar came to power on September 17, A.D. 14 and was still in power when *John the Baptist* started preaching and when Jesus died on the cross.

*1 Kings 16:21-22*

**Tibni** (**tib**-nye)
Israelite who fought against *Omri* for control of Israel after Zimri's death; son of Ginath. Omri defeated Tibni's forces after a short civil war.

*Genesis 14:1*

**Tidal** (**tye-**dal)
King of *Goiim* during the time of Abram and Lot. Nothing else is known about him.

*2 Kings 15:19*

**Tiglath-Pileser** (**tig**-lath pil-**ee**-zur)
King of Assyria during the reigns of Menahem, Pekahiah, and Pekah in Israel. Tiglath-Pileser was responsible for the exile of many Israelites from the northern kingdom.

**Tigris** (**tye**-griss)
One of the two main rivers of Mesopotamia, opposite the *Euphrates*.

Genesis 2:14
Psalm 89:25

**Tilgathpilneser** (**til**-gath-pil-**nee**-zur)
See *Tiglath-Pileser*

**Timnah** (**tim**-nuh)
One or more towns in the territory allotted to Judah. *Samson* stirred up trouble in Timnah.
See also *Timnite*

Judges 14:1-20

T

**Timnite** (**tim**-nite)
A person from *Timnah*.

Judges 15:6

**Timothy** (**tim**-uh-thee)
Jewish Christian leader who worked closely with Paul in his ministry from the time of Paul's second missionary journey. Paul wrote the letters of First Timothy and Second Timothy to this second-generation believer. Timothy became such a close student of Paul that the apostle called Timothy "my dear son."
See also *First Timothy; Second Timothy*

Acts 16:1-3
1 Corinthians 16:10-11
2 Timothy 1:3-4

**Timothy, First** (**furst tim**-uh-thee)
Fifteenth book of the New Testament and first of three *pastoral epistles*, a letter written by the apostle Paul to *Timothy*. Paul wrote this letter to teach and guide Timothy in his duties as a church leader.
See also *Second Timothy; Titus, book of*

1 Timothy 1:1-5

T

2 Timothy 2:15

**Timothy, Second** (**sek**-uhnd **tim**-uh-thee)

Sixteenth book of the New Testament and second of three *pastoral epistles*, a letter written by the apostle Paul to *Timothy*. Paul wrote this letter to give Timothy some final instructions. Timothy was pastor of the church at *Ephesus*; Paul was in prison awaiting execution.

See also *First Timothy; Titus, book of*

1 Kings 4:24

**Tiphsah** (**tif**-suh)

A city on the western bank of the *Euphrates* River that marked the northern extent of Solomon's kingdom.

2 Kings 19:9
Isaiah 37:9

**Tirhakah** (tur-**hay**-kuh)

King of Egypt who distracted Sennacherib from the siege of Jerusalem during the reign of Hezekiah.

**Tirzah** (tihr-zuh)

Joshua 12:7-8, 24
1 Kings 16:6, 8, 15, 23

• A Canaanite city in the territory allotted to Manasseh. Tirzah served as the capital of the northern kingdom of Israel until *Omri* moved the capital to *Samaria*.

Numbers 26:33

• One of Zelophehad's daughters.

1 Kings 17:1

**Tishbe** (tish-bee)

A town in *Gilead*. Its location is unknown.

See also *Tishbite*

1 Kings 21:17

**Tishbite** (tish-bite)

A person from *Tishbe*. Elijah was a Tishbite.

**tithe** (tythe)

"Tenth," a standard amount given to God by God's people. The tithe is taken from the goods or income produced. God required the Israelites to give tithes to the priests, Levites, aliens, widows, and orphans. The apostle Paul urged God's people to give generously and cheerfully.

See also *firstfruits*

*Deuteronomy 14:22-29*
*Nehemiah 10:35-39*
*Hebrews 7:4-10*

**Titius Justus** (tye-tee-uhss juhst-uhss)

A *Gentile* convert to *Judaism* who let Paul stay at his house in Corinth during Paul's second missionary journey.

*Acts 18:7*

**Titus** (tye-tuss)

A Gentile Christian who worked with the apostle Paul in his ministry and who received the New Testament *book of Titus*. Titus spent some time in Jerusalem with Paul and Barnabas during the early days of Christianity. He also got the very difficult job of straightening out some of the problems in the church at Corinth, a job Paul gave him because he was so capable. When he received the book of Titus, he was a church leader in *Crete*.

*2 Corinthians 7:13-16*
*2 Corinthians 8:16-24*
*Galatians 2:1-3*
*Titus 1:4-5*

**Titus, book of** (tye-tuss, buk uhv)

*Titus 1:4-5*

Seventeenth book of the New Testament and third of the three *pastoral epistles*, a letter written by the apostle Paul to *Titus*. Titus was on *Crete* at the time and giving leadership to several churches there. Paul wanted to give Titus specific instructions on what to do next.

See also *First Timothy; Second Timothy*

**Tobiah** (toh-bye-uh)

*Nehemiah 2:10*
*Nehemiah 4:1-9*
*Nehemiah 6:1-19*

• "Tobiah the Ammonite official," one of those who tried to stop *Nehemiah* from rebuilding the walls of Jerusalem. "Ammonite" can mean either that he was in charge of the territories of *Ammon*, or that he was one of the *Ammonite* people. Tobiah is a Hebrew name, and both his children had Hebrew names, so he may have been half-Jewish.

*Ezra 2:59-60, 62-63*

• A clan of Jews that lost their family records while exiled in Babylonia.

See also *Geshem; Sanballat*

**Tola** (**toh**-luh)

*Judges 10:1-2*

• Son of *Puah* and sixth judge of Israel after *Gideon*. Tola judged Israel 23 years.

*1 Chronicles 7:1-2*

• Firstborn son of *Issachar*.

**tomb (toom)**

*2 Chronicles 16:13-14*
*Luke 24:1-7*

A place where a dead body is buried. Sometimes caves were used as tombs.

**Topheth** (**toh**-feth)
The *high place* in the *Valley of Hinnom* where people sacrificed their children to *Molech*.

*Jeremiah 7:30-34*

**Torah** (**tor**-uh)
The Hebrew word for *law*, often used in the Old Testament for God's law.

**Tou, Toi** (**toh**-oo)
King of *Hamath* during the reign of David.

*1 Chronicles 18:9-11*

**tower** (**tou**-ur)
Usually a tall stone structure in the walls of a *fortified city* used for lookout.
See also *fortress*

*Psalm 144:2*

**tower of Babel** (**tou**-ur uhv **bay**-buhl)
See *Babel*

**Tower of Hananel** (**tou**-ur uhv **han**-uh-nel)
A tower in the city walls of Jerusalem mentioned in the *book of Nehemiah* and always in connection with the *Tower of the Hundred*. The Tower of Hananel was between the Fish Gate and the Sheep Gate. *Jeremiah* and *Zechariah* mentioned this tower in their prophecies about Jerusalem's reconstruction.

*Nehemiah 3:1; 12:38-39*
*Jeremiah 31:38-40*
*Zechariah 14:10-11*

T

*Nehemiah 3:1*
*Nehemiah 12:38-39*

**Tower of the Hundred**
(**tou**-ur uhv the **huhn**-druhd)
A tower in the city walls of Jerusalem mentioned only in the *book of Nehemiah* and always in connection with the *Tower of Hananel*. The Tower of the Hundred was between the Fish Gate and the Sheep Gate, but no one is sure why it was called Hundred.

*Nehemiah 3:11*
*Nehemiah 12:38-40*

**Tower of the Ovens** (**tou**-ur uhv the **uhv**-uhnz)
A tower in the city walls of Jerusalem mentioned only in the *book of Nehemiah*.

**Trachonitis** (**trak**-oh-**nye**-tis)
See *Traconitis*

*Luke 3:1*

**Traconitis** (**trak**-oh-**nye**-tis)
A region northeast of the Sea of Galilee in the *tetrarchy* of Philip.

*Ezra 4:11*
*Ezra 5:6*
*Nehemiah 2:7-10*

**Trans-Euphrates** (**tranz**-yoo-**fray**-teez)
A province of the Persian Empire during the time of Ezra and Zerubbabel. Trans-Euphrates included all the land west of the *Euphrates* River. Tattenai was governor.

*Matthew 17:2*
*Mark 9:2*

**Transfiguration, the** (tranz-**fig**-yur-**ay**-shuhn)
Name given to the time when *Peter*, *James*, and *John* saw Jesus in his glory.

**transgression** (tranz-**gre**-shuhn)
An older word for *sin*, *lawlessness*, or wrongdoing; violation of God's *law*.

*Psalm 19:13*
*Romans 11:11-12*

**tree of life** (**tree** uhv **life**)
Something that brings life or makes life go on. The word "tree" means "source." In the Bible, the term refers to two kinds of life:

- Eternal life in God's presence—the kind of life that Adam and Eve gave up, and the kind that all God's people will enjoy in heaven.
- Ongoing, joyful, successful life on earth.

*Genesis 2:9*
*Genesis 3:22-24*
*Revelation 22: 14, 19*

*Proverbs 11:30*
*Proverbs 13:12*
*Proverbs 15:4*

**trespass** (**tress**-pass)
An older word for *sin*.

*Matthew 6:12*
*Romans 5:15*

**tribe** (**tribe**)

A group of people who all trace their roots to the same person; a family unit larger than a *clan* but smaller than a nation. One tribe can have more than one clan. Many of the genealogies in *First Chronicles* and other Bible books list the clans within each of the twelve *tribes of Israel*.

*Genesis 36:20-21*

**tribes of Israel** (**tribes** uhv iz-**ree**-uhl)
Twelve family units that traced their roots to ten of Jacob's sons and two of Joseph's. Sons of

*Genesis 49:28*
*Matthew 19:28-30*
*Revelation 21:12*

*Jacob*: *Reuben*, *Simeon*, *Judah*, *Issachar*, *Zebulun*, *Benjamin*, *Dan*, *Naphtali*, *Gad*, and *Asher*. Sons of *Joseph*: *Ephraim* and *Manasseh*.

See also *clan*

Revelation 7:14-17

**tribulation, the great** (**trib**-yoo-**lay**-shuhn, the **grate**)

A time of suffering described in the *book of Revelation* when God's people are persecuted and martyred. The account in Revelation tells how all of those who come through this time will praise God as God welcomes them into *heaven*. Some people believe the great tribulation is the suffering that all Christians have gone through ever since the time of Christ. Other people believe that the great tribulation is one big event still to come in the future.

2 Kings 17:3-4

**tribute** (**trib**-yoot)

Payment made to a king or ruler in recognition of his or her authority.

John 10:30-38
John 16:5-11
Colossians 2:9

**Trinity, the** (**tri**-ni-tee)

The Christian doctrine that one God exists in three persons: *Father*, Son, and *Holy Spirit*. The term "Trinity" does not appear in the Bible, but the concept does.

See also *Son of God*

**Triumphal Entry** (trye-**uhm**-ful **en**-tree)
The time when Jesus rode into *Jerusalem* on a donkey and was greeted by a cheering crowd. The people made a path for Jesus with their cloaks, waved palm branches in the air, and shouted "Hosanna!" The Christian holiday known as Palm Sunday celebrates this occasion.

See also *Jesus Christ; Kingdom of Heaven; Messiah*

*Matthew 21:1-11*
*Luke 19:28-44*
*John 12:12-19*

**Troas** (**troh**-az)
A large port city about 85 kilometers northwest of *Assos* in the Roman province of Asia. Troas was in the region of Asia Minor known as *Mysia*.

*Acts 16:6-11*
*2 Timothy 4:13*

**Trophimus** (**troh**-fim-uhss)
One of the Gentile Christians who traveled with Paul during his third missionary journey. The Jews arrested Paul in Jerusalem partly because of his association with Trophimus.

*Acts 20:4*
*Acts 21:27-29*

**trumpet** (**truhm**-pet)
A wind instrument usually made from a ram's horn, bone, or metal. The trumpets of Old and New Testament times had no moving parts.

*Psalm 150:3*

Romans 16:12

**Tryphena and Tryphosa**
(trye-**fee**-nuh, trye-**foh**-suh)
Two Christian women greeted in the conclusion of Paul's letter to the Romans.

Genesis 10:2
Isaiah 66:19

**Tubal** (**too**-buhl)
One of Japheth's sons, the nation descended from him, and the land they settled.

T

Genesis 4:22

**Tubal-Cain** (**too**-buhl-**kane**)
Son of Lamech and Zillah who invented metal-working.

**twelve tribes of Israel**
(**twelv tribes** uhv iz-**ree**-uhl)
See *tribes of Israel*

Mark 3:16-19
Matthew 17:1; 26:37

**Twelve, the** (**twelv**)
The twelve men Jesus chose to follow him and travel with him throughout his three-year ministry; also called *apostles*. The most prominent were Peter, James, and John. The others were Andrew, Philip, Bartholomew, Matthew, Thomas, James son of Alphaeus, Thaddaeus, Simon the Zealot, and Judas Iscariot. Judas is always named last.

See also *prophet*

**twenty-four elders** (**twen**-tee-**for el**-derz)
See *elders*

**Tychicus** (**tik**-i-kuhss)

One of the Gentile Christians who traveled with Paul during his third missionary journey. Tychicus also carried some of Paul's letters from place to place.

See also *Trophimus*

*Acts 20:4*
*Ephesians 6:21-22*
*Colossians 4:7*

**Tyrannus** (tye-**ran**-uhss)

Name given to the lecture hall in Ephesus where Paul preached for two years.

*Acts 19:9*

**Tyre** (**tire**)

A city in *Phoenicia* on the Mediterranean coast often mentioned together with *Sidon*. *Hiram* ruled Tyre during the reigns of David and Solomon.

*1 Kings 5:1*
*Matthew 11:20-22*
*Acts 21:3*

**Tyrians** (**tihr**-ee-uhnz)

People of *Tyre*.

*1 Chronicles 22:4*

Daniel 8:2, 16

**Ulai** (**yoo**-lye)

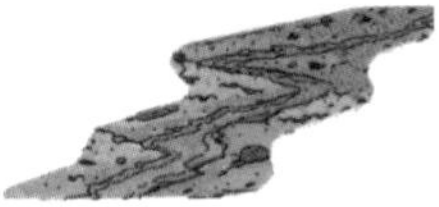

A wide stream in *Elam* near *Susa* that Daniel saw in one of his visions.

Romans 11:23
Hebrews 3:19

**unbelief** (uhn-bee-**leef**)

A refusal to believe God or his word; hostility to God and what he wants. Unbelief is the opposite of *faith*.

See also *foolishness; unbeliever*

U

2 Corinthians 6: 14-15

**unbeliever** (uhn-bee-**leev**-ur)

A person who refuses to believe God or his word; a person who is hostile to God; a person who does not believe in or worship God; a person who is not *devout*.

**uncircumcised** (uhn-**sur**-kuhm-sized)

Not circumcised. This adjective can have two different shades of meaning:

1 Samuel 17:26

- Pagan or wicked; unbelieving; not of God's people. David used the word this way in his confrontation with Goliath.

Galatians 2:9
Galatians 6:14-15

- Not Jewish; *Gentile*. After Christ, God's people did not need to be circumcised, so even believers could be uncircumcised.

See also *circumcision*

Leviticus 5:2
2 Chronicles 23:19

**unclean** (uhn-**kleen**)

Unholy; impure; the opposite of *clean*. This word was often used to describe a person who had disobeyed rules about what to eat or

touch. An unclean person was not allowed to *worship* with others in the temple.
See also *clean*

**unfaithful** (uhn-**fayth**-fuhl)
The opposite of *faithful*; not faithful; disloyal.

*2 Chronicles 12:2*
*2 Timothy 2:13*

**ungodly, ungodliness**
(uhn-**god**-lee, uhn-**god**-lee-ness)
• Adjective: Not *godly*; not *devout*; evil; *wicked*.
• Noun: A person who does not act like God; a person who is not godly or devout; a person who is evil or wicked.

*Ephesians 5:12*

*Psalm 7:9*
*Ephesians 4:17*

**unlawful** (uhn-**law**-fuhl)
The opposite of lawful; against the *law*.

*Matthew 12:2*

**unleavened bread** (uhn-**lev**-end **bred**)

Bread that has not had any *leaven* added. Unleavened bread is an important part of the *Passover* meal.
See also *Feast of Unleavened Bread*

*Exodus 12:17-20*
*Leviticus 8:26*

**Unleavened Bread, Feast of**
(uhn-**lev**-uhnd **bred, feest** uhv)
See *Feast of Unleavened Bread*

**Unni** (**uhn**-eye)
One of those who sang and played the harp to celebrate the return of the *Ark of the Covenant* to Jerusalem.

*1 Chronicles 15:17-20*

1 Peter 3:18

**unrighteous** (uhn-**rye**-chuhss)
Noun: People who are not *righteous*; *sinners*; people who are *wicked* or *evil*; the opposite of *righteous*.

Romans 7:14
James 3:15

**unspiritual** (uhn-**spihr**-i-choo-uhl)
The opposite of *spiritual*; *ungodly*.

2 Corinthians 3:18

**unveiled face** (uhn-**vaild fayss**)
A face that is not covered with a *veil*.

Deuteronomy 3:5

**unwalled** (un-**wald**)
Not protected by a wall. The term is used to describe a city that has no walls.
See also *fortified city; tower*

**upharsin** (oo-**par**-sin)
An older spelling for parsin.
See *mene, mene, tekel, parsin*

Jeremiah 44:15
Ezekiel 29:13-14

**Upper Egypt** (**up**-ur **ee**-jipt)
The southern part of *Egypt*, often called *Pathros* in the Bible. It is called Upper Egypt because it lies at a higher elevation than the rest of Egypt.
See also *Pathrusites*

Luke 22:10-13

**upper room** (**up**-ur **room**)
The room in Jerusalem where Jesus and his disciples had the *Last Supper*. It is called "upper" because it was on the second story of a two-story house.

**upright** (**up**-rite)

- Adjective: Honest; fair and open in dealing with others. *Proverbs 11:11*
- Noun: A person who is honest, or fair and open in dealing with others. *Proverbs 29:10*

**Ur of the Chaldeans** (**ur** uhv the kal-**dee**-uhnz)
A major city on the west bank of the Euphrates River in *Chaldea* during the time of Abram. Ur was *Abram* and *Terah's* home when God called Abram to leave and "go to a land that I will show you." The land of Ur today is dry and barren.
*Genesis 11:27-12:4*
*Genesis 15:7*
*Hebrews 11:8-10*

**Ur of the Chaldees** (**ur** uhv the **kal**-deez)
See *Ur of the Chaldeans*

**Uriah** (yur-**eye**-uh)
A *Hittite* commander in David's army. Uriah was besieging Rabbah, the capital of Ammon, when David committed *adultery* with Uriah's wife Bathsheba. David sent Uriah to the front lines, knowing that he would die, leaving Bathsheba to himself.
*2 Samuel 11:1-27*

**Uriel** (yur-**ee**-el)

- Head of the clan of *Kohath* during the time of David. David put Uriel in charge of getting the *Ark of the Covenant* into Jerusalem after *Uzzah* and Ahio failed to do it right.
*1 Chronicles 15:1-15*
*2 Samuel 6:1-11*

2 Chronicles 13:2

• An Israelite from Gibeah who became the father of Maacah and therefore grandfather of King *Abijah*.

*Exodus 28:30*
*Numbers 27:21*
*Deuteronomy 33:8*

**Urim and Thummim** (**oo**-rim and **thuhm**-im)
An object or several objects used by leaders of Israel to determine God's will in some situations. The Urim and Thummim were kept in the high priest's *ephod*. They were first given to Levi and used throughout the Exodus, the time of the judges, and the time of David. After that, either the objects were lost or the Israelites stopped using them. The Bible does not say what the Urim and Thummim were, how many there were, or exactly how they were used.
See also *cast lots*

**Uz** (**uhz**)

*Job 1:1*

• An unknown land and its people in Old Testament times, the land where *Job* lived.

*Genesis 22:21*

• Firstborn son of Nahor and Milcah; nephew of Abram.

*Genesis 10:23*

• Son of *Aram* and the tribe descended from him; grandson of *Shem*.

*2 Samuel 6:1-11*

**Uzzah** (**uz**-uh)
Israelite who died trying to bring the *Ark of the Covenant* into Jerusalem; son of Abinadab. Uzzah and his brother Ahio were moving the ark on a cart instead of by carrying it with poles as instructed in the law.

**Uzziah** (uh-**zye**-uh)

A common name among the Israelites:

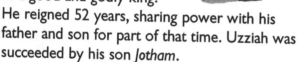

• Son of *Amaziah* and tenth king of Judah after his father. Uzziah was a strong and able king who improved life for farmers and built up Judah's military strength. Except for a bout of pride, he was also known as a good and godly king. He reigned 52 years, sharing power with his father and son for part of that time. Uzziah was succeeded by his son *Jotham*. *2 Kings 14:21-15:1-7; 2 Chronicles 26:1-23*

• Several others named only once.

**Uzziel** (**uhz**-ee-el)

A common name among the Israelites:

• Moses and Aaron's uncle; son of *Kohath*; father of Mishael, Elzaphan, and Sithri. *Uzziel* became head of his clan of *Levites*, the *Uzzielites*. *Exodus 6:18; Numbers 3:19*

• Five others mentioned only once or only by name.

**Uzzielites** (**uhz**-ee-uhl-ites)

The clan of Levites descended from *Uzziel*. *Numbers 3:27*

V

Genesis 4:12-14

**vagabond** (**vag**-uh-bond)
An older word for wanderer.

2 Chronicles 26:9
Nehemiah 2:13-15

**Valley Gate** (**val**-ee **gate**)
One of the gates in the walls of Jerusalem. It was probably named for being near the *Kidron Valley*.

Joshua 7:16-26

**Valley of Achor** (**val**-ee uhv **ay**-kor)
A valley on the northwest side of the Dead Sea and south of Jericho, where Qumran is today. The name means "Valley of Trouble," given because *Achan* was stoned there for his sin.

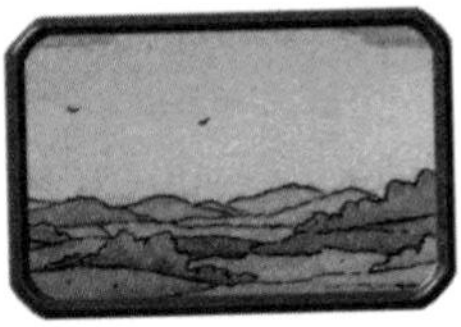

Joshua 10:12

**Valley of Aijalon** (**val**-ee uhv **ay**-juh-lon)
The valley surrounding the city of *Aijalon* and scene of the battle of *Gibeon* where the moon stood still.

Amos 1:5

**Valley of Aven** (**val**-ee uhv **ay**-ven)
A valley somewhere between the mountains of *Lebanon* and the mountains of western *Aram*. "Aven" means "wickedness."

Psalm 84:6

**Valley of Baca** (**val**-ee uhv **bay**-kuh)
"Valley of Weeping."

**Valley of Ben Hinnom**
(**val**-ee uhv **ben hin**-uhm)
See *Valley of Hinnom*

**Valley of Beracah** (**val**-ee uhv **bair**-uh-kah)

"Valley of Blessing," the place where *Jehoshaphat* and his people celebrated their victory over Moab, Ammon, and Edom. It is a valley near *Tekoa* on the road to Hebron from Jerusalem.

*2 Chronicles 20:20-26*

**Valley of Elah** (**val**-ee uhv **ee**-luh)

Scene of the battle between David and Goliath, a valley in the foothills of western Judah east of *Ashdod*.

*1 Samuel 17:2*

**Valley of Eshcol** (**val**-ee uhv **ess**-kohl)

A valley about three kilometers north of *Hebron* famous for its grapes. "Eschol" means "cluster."

*Numbers 13:23-24*

**Valley of Gerar** (**val**-ee uhv guh-**rar**)

The valley in the region of *Gerar*; also called Gerar Valley.

*Genesis 26:17-19*

**Valley of Hinnom** (**val**-ee uhv **hin**-uhm)
See *Hinnom*

V

Joshua 19:14-15

**Valley of Iphtah El** (**val**-ee uhv **if**-tuh **el**)
A valley along the north and western border of the territory of Zebulun near *Bethlehem*.

Joel 3:12

**Valley of Jehoshaphat**
(**val**-ee uhv juh-**hoh**-shuh-fat)
Another name for the *Kidron Valley*.

1 Chronicles 10:7
Hosea 1:5

**Valley of Jezreel** (**val**-ee uhv jez-**ree**-el)
The large plain that lies between the mountains of *Galilee* and the *Carmel* range; also called the Jezreel Valley. The Valley of Jezreel stretches all the way from *Megiddo* to the Jordan River.

Joshua 11:17
Joshua 12:7

**Valley of Lebanon** (**val**-ee uhv **leb**-uh-non)

The valley between Mount Hermon and the mountains of *Lebanon*.

Joshua 15:8
2 Samuel 5:18-19

**Valley of Rephaim** (**val**-ee uhv **ref**-ay-im)
The valley that lies immediately southwest of *Jerusalem*, named for the giant *Rephaites* that lived in the land long ago.

2 Samuel 8:13-14
2 Kings 14:7
1 Chronicles 18:12-13

**Valley of Salt** (**val**-ee uhv **sahlt**)
A valley somewhere between the territories of *Judah* and *Edom* south of the Dead Sea. David, Abishai, and *Amaziah* defeated the Edomites several

times in the Valley of Salt. Its exact location is unknown.

**Valley of Shaveh** (**val**-ee uhv **shay**-veh)
An unknown location in the land of Canaan.

*Genesis 14:17*

**Valley of Siddim** (**val**-ee uhv sid-im)
A valley near the Dead Sea where the five *cities of the plain* were located. Kedorlaomer defeated his enemies in the Valley of Siddim. It was riddled with tar pits. The valley's exact location is unknown, but it was probably at the Dead Sea's southern end, where evidence of tar pits can still be found.

*Genesis 14:1-16*

**Valley of Slaughter** (**val**-ee uhv **slaw**-tur)
A name given to the Valley of *Hinnom* in the prophecies of Jeremiah because of the evil killing that went on there.

See also *idolatry; Molech*

*Jeremiah 7:30-32*
*Jeremiah 19:4-6*

**Valley of Sorek** (**val**-ee uhv sor-ek)
Delilah's home, a valley in the lowlands of Judah along the northern boundary of Judah. *Ekron* and *Timnah* were major cities in this valley.

*Judges 16:4*

V

Isaiah 22:1, 5

**Valley of Vision** (**val**-ee uhv vizh-uhn)
A name for Jerusalem used by Isaiah.

2 Chronicles 14:10

**Valley of Zephathah** (**val**-ee uhv zef-uh-thuh)
A valley near *Mareshah*.

V

**Valley, Kidron** (**val**-ee kid-ruhn)
See *Kidron Valley*

**Valley, King's** (**val**-ee kingz)
See *Valley of Shaveh*

Ecclesiastes 1:2

**vanity** (**van**-i-tee)
An older word for meaningless, futile, or pointless.

Esther 1:10-12
Esther 2:17

**Vashti** (**vash**-tee)
The queen of Persia whom *Esther* replaced.

Job 22:14
2 Corinthians 3:13-16

**veil** (**vale**)
A piece of cloth used as a covering.

Deuteronomy 32:43
Micah 5:15

**vengeance** (**ven**-juhnss)
Revenge.

Leviticus 19:10
Matthew 21:33

**vineyard** (**vin**-yurd)
A grape farm; a place where grapes are grown and harvested. Vineyards provided an important source of food and drink and were a symbol of fruitfulness.

**virgin** (**vur**-jin)

A person who has never had sex. Mary was a virgin when she gave birth to Jesus because God, not Joseph, was his father. This is what Isaiah said would happen when the *Messiah* came.

*Isaiah 7:14*
*Matthew 1:18-25*
*Luke 1:26-35*

**vision** (**vizh**-uhn)

A prophecy or revelation in which a person sees something that God wants him or her to see. Many of the prophets received their messages through visions.

*Genesis 15:1*
*Acts 12:9*

**vow** (**vou**)

• Noun: A promise to give God a gift or serve God in some specific way if he will grant a request.

*Genesis 28:20-22*
*Acts 18:18*

• Verb: To promise to give God a gift or serve God in some specific way if he will grant a request.

*Numbers 29:39*
*Ecclesiastes 5:4-6*

**vow offering** (**vou awf**-ur-ing)

One of three kinds of *fellowship offerings*; a sacrifice that a person offers to God to fulfill a vow. The rules about vow offerings are the same as for freewill offerings and appear in Leviticus 7:16-18.

See also *offering*

*Leviticus 7:16*
*Acts 21:22-26*

W

1 Kings 8:65
Ezekiel 48:28

**wadi** (**wah**-dee)
A dry river bed.

**Wadi Zered** (**wah**-dee **zair**-ed)
See *Zered Valley*

Exodus 29:2

**wafer** (**way**-fur)
A thin cake of bread.

**walls** (**wahlz**)
See *fortified city*

2 Samuel 13:34
Ezekiel 3:16-17

**watchman** (**woch**-muhn)
A lookout; a person who watches for enemies or other dangers. Shepherds that guarded flocks of sheep were called watchmen. Many fortified cities stationed a watchman at the top of a city wall, *tower*, or *citadel*. Israel's prophets served as watchmen over Israel's spiritual condition.

Joshua 11:1-9

**Waters of Merom** (**wah**-turz uhv **mee**-rom)
Place where Jabin formed an alliance of armies against Joshua during the conquest of Canaan. Jabin's alliance lost.

**weights and measures** (**waytss** and **mehz**-urz)
See *bath; beka; cab; cubit; ephah; gerah; handbreadth; hin; homer; lethek; log; mina; omer; seah; shekel; span; talent*
See *also money*

**well** (wel)

A hole dug down to a source of underground water. A well was not the same as a *cistern*.

*Genesis 21:25*
*John 4:6*
*Luke 14:5*

**West Gate** (**west gate**)

One of the gates in the walls of Solomon's *temple*.

See also *East Gate; North Gate; South Gate*

*1 Chronicles 26:16*

**wicked** (**wik**-id)

• Bad; evil; sinful; corrupt; hostile to God.

*Genesis 13:13*
*Acts 2:23*

• People who are bad or evil; people who are hostile to God. The Psalms and Proverbs say a lot about "the wicked" and "wicked people."

*Proverbs 29:27*
*Luke 6:35*

**widow** (**wid**-oh)

A woman whose husband has died. Many widows of Old Testament times had no way to support themselves, making life for widows and their children very difficult.

*Exodus 22:22*
*Mark 12:42*

**wilderness** (**wil**-dur-ness)

Another word for *desert*.

*Isaiah 35:6*
*Jeremiah 2:6*

**Wilderness of Sin** (**wil**-dur-ness uhv **sin**)

See *Desert of Sin*

Judges 6:11
Mark 12:1

**winepress** (**wine**-press)
A vat where grapes are placed and crushed with bare feet so the juice can be squeezed out.

Joshua 9:13
Luke 5:37-38

**wineskin** (**wine**-skin)
An animal skin used to hold wine, much the way a bottle is used for the same purpose today. Most wineskins were made of goat hides.

W

Proverbs 1:7
Proverbs 3:5-7
James 1:5

**wisdom** (**wiz**-duhm)
Good sense; insight; understanding. The Bible says that wisdom is important to have, but that only God can make a person *wise*.

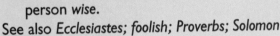

See also *Ecclesiastes; foolish; Proverbs; Solomon*

James 3:13-16

**wise** (**wyze**)
Having good sense or insight; prudent; sensible. A wise person has *wisdom*.
See also *foolish; Solomon*

**wise men** (**wyze men**)
See *magi*

1 Samuel 28:7

**witch of Endor** (**wich** uhv **en**-dor)
A *medium* from Endor hired by King Saul to call up the spirit of Samuel. Saul wanted advice.

**wonders** (**wuhn**-durz)
Great deeds or acts of God, or deeds meant to look like acts of God.
See also *miracles; miraculous signs; signs*

Exodus 4:21
John 4:48

**word of God** (**word** uhv **god**)
• Any message from God.
• The messages of God's prophets; the Old Testament.

Luke 3:21-22
1 Chronicles 17:3
Mark 7:13
Acts 18:11

**world** (**world**)
• The planet earth.
• All people.
• The ways of people who do not know God; life apart from God.

Genesis 41:57
1 Samuel 17:46
Matthew 13:38

**worldly** (**world**-lee)
Like the *world*; sinful; *ungodly*.

Luke 16:9
2 Corinthians 1:12

**worship** (wur-ship)
To serve; to revere, honor, or *praise* as master; to be devoted to. Worshiping God is a very important part of the Christian life, because it motivates us to obey him. The first and second of the *Ten Commandments* are about worship.
See also *glorify; idolatry*

Deuteronomy 5:7
Psalm 29:2
Hebrews 12:28

W

X

*Esther 1:1*
*Esther 8:1-8*

**Xerxes** (**zurk**-seez)

Persian name of *Ahasuerus*; son of Darius the Great.

See also *Cyrus; Darius*

**Yahweh (yah-way)**
The Hebrew word for God's name, YHWH with vowels added. Most English Bibles use LORD, with small capitals for the *o*, *r*, and *d*, instead of Yahweh. This is because *God* is also called *Lord*.

*Genesis 2:8-9*
*Jonah 1:9*

**Year of Jubilee (yeer** uhv **joo**-buh-lee)
*See Jubilee*

**yearling (yeer**-ling)
An animal that is between one and two years old.

*Isaiah 11:6*

**yeast (yeest)**
A fungus used to *leaven* bread dough.

*Exodus 12:15*
*Luke 13:21*

**yoke (yohk)**
• Noun: A beam or wooden frame that is placed over the necks of two *oxen* and attached by straps to a plow behind them. The yoke holds the animals together and transfers the weight of the plow to their shoulders as they walk forward.

*Leviticus 26:13*
*Acts 15:10*

• Noun: Synonym for pair; team of two.

*Job 1:3*

• Verb: To fasten a yoke to two oxen; to bind one ox to another with a yoke.

*Numbers 19:2*

Deuteronomy 22:10
2 Corinthians 6:14

**yoked (yohkt)**
Bound together with a *yoke*.

Philippians 4:3

**yokefellow (yohk**-fel-oh)
A partner, spouse, teammate, or comrade.

Genesis 16:6
2 Kings 4:16
Luke 2:29

**your servant (yor sur**-vuhnt)
A formal way of saying "me." People of Bible times would call themselves "your servant" to show respect to elders, rulers, or others more powerful than themselves.

**Zacchaeus** (zuh-**kee**-uhss)
Chief *tax collector* in *Jericho* who welcomed Jesus into his home and promised to return money he had stolen. — *Luke 19:1-10*

**Zachariah** (zek-uh-**rye**-uh)
See *Zechariah*

**Zacharias** (zek-uh-**rye**-uhss)
See *Zechariah*

**Zadok** (**zay**-dok)
A common name among the Israelites:

- High priest at the time of David; son of *Ahitub*. — *2 Samuel 8:17*, *Ezekiel 40:46*
- Two of those who helped repair the walls of Jerusalem; son of Baana and son of Immer. — *Nehemiah 3:4*, *Nehemiah 3:29*
- One of those named in the genealogy of Jesus; son of Azor. — *Matthew 1:14*
- Several others who are hard to identify.

**Zadokites** (**zay**-dok-ites)
Descendants of Zadok the priest; Levites in the clan of Zadok. — *Ezekiel 44:15-16*

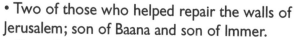

**Zalmon** (**zal**-muhn)
- One of David's *mighty men*; also called Ilai; an Ahohite. — *2 Samuel 23:28*
- An unknown mountain near *Shechem*. — *Judges 9:48*
- An unknown mountain mentioned in Psalm 68:14. — *Psalm 68:14*

**Zalmonah** (zal-**moh**-nuh)

Numbers 33:41-42

One of the places in Edom where the Israelites stopped on their way to the *promised land* during the *Exodus*. Zalmonah was between Mount Hor and *Punon*.

**Zalmunna** (zal-**muhn**-uh)

Judges 8:1-21

One of two Midianite kings (the other was *Zebah*) whose army *Gideon* defeated with only 300 men.

Z

**Zanoah** (zuh-**noh**-ah)

Two towns:

Joshua 15:33-36
Nehemiah 11:30

• A town in the northern part of Judah's lowlands, near Zorah. The people of Zanoah helped *Nehemiah*.

Joshua 15:56

• A town near *Hebron* whose exact location is unknown.

**Zaphon** (**zay**-fon)

Joshua 13:27-28
Judges 12:1-4

• A town east of the Jordan River in the territory allotted to Gad where *Jephthah* attacked the men of Ephraim.

Isaiah 14:13
Psalm 48:2

• A mountain in the north that became a synonym for "north" and for places high up.

**Zarephath** (**zair**-uh-fath)

1 Kings 17:8-16
Luke 4:24-26

A small port city in Lebanon about 13 kilometers south of *Sidon*. Elijah stayed in Zarephath during a drought in Israel and did several miracles there.

**Zarethan** (**zair**-uh-than)
A city on the banks of the Jordan River near and somewhere north of *Adam*. Its exact location is unknown.
*Joshua 3:14-17*

**zeal** (**zeel**)
Extreme devotion to a person or cause.
*See also Zealot*
*Galatians 1:14*
*Philippians 3:6*

**Zealot** (**zel**-uht)
Name of a group of Jews who were very devoted to Israel in New Testament times. One of the two Simons among Jesus' *Twelve* disciples was a Zealot.
*Luke 6:15*

**Zebadiah** (**zeb**-uh-**dye**-uh)
A common name among the Israelites:

- An Israelite warrior from the tribe of Benjamin who defected to David at *Ziklag*; son of Jeroham and brother of *Joelah*. *1 Chronicles 12:1-7*
- A temple gatekeeper in the time of David; son of Meshelemiah. *1 Chronicles 26:1-2*
- Governor of Judah appointed by *Jehoshaphat* to serve as a judge in Jerusalem; son of Ishmael. *2 Chronicles 19:8-11*
- Several others mentioned only once.

Z

*Judges 8:1-21*

**Zebah** (**zee**-buh)

One of two *Midianite* kings (the other was *Zalmunna*) whose army Gideon defeated with only 300 men.

*Luke 5:10*

**Zebedee** (**zeb**-uh-dee)

Father of James and John, two of Jesus' disciples. Zebedee was a fisherman from *Galilee*.

*Genesis 10:19*

**Zeboiim** (zuh-**boi**-im)

One of the five *cities of the plain* during the time of Abram.

**Zeboim** (zuh-**boh**-im)

*Nehemiah 11:31-35*

- A town in the territory of Benjamin settled by Jews returning from the *Exile*.

*1 Samuel 13:18*

- A valley in Benjamin northeast of Jerusalem, probably the modern "Ravine of the Hyenas."

*Judges 9:28*

**Zebul** (**zee**-buhl)

*Abimelech's* lieutenant.

**Zebulun** (**zeb**-yoo-luhn)

*Genesis 30:19-20*

- Jacob's son and the tribe of Israel named after him. *Leah* was his mother.

*Joshua 19:10-16*

- The land allotted to the tribe of Zebulun.

See also *tribes of Israel*

**Zebulunite** (**zeb**-yoo-luhn-**ite**)

A person descended from Jacob's son *Zebulun*; member of the tribe of Zebulun. *Numbers 26:27*

**Zechariah** (**zek**-uh-**rye**-uh)

A very common name among the Israelites:

- Son of *Jeroboam* II and fourteenth king of Israel after his father. Zechariah is known only for continuing in the evil ways of his father. He reigned for six months and was assassinated by *Shallum*. *2 Kings 15:8-12*
- Meshelemiah's firstborn son, a wise counselor and temple *gatekeeper* with charge of the temple's north side. *1 Chronicles 26: 1-2, 14*
- A temple *gatekeeper* appointed to sing and play music during the return of the Ark to Jerusalem from Kiriath Jearim. *2 Chronicles 15: 18-20*
- An official in Josiah's service and temple supervisor who gave generously to the priests and Levites during Josiah's reforms. *2 Chronicles 35:8*

- An official sent by *Jehoshaphat* to teach in the cities of Judah. *2 Chronicles 17:7-9*
- King *Jehoshaphat's* fourth son. *2 Chronicles 21:2*
- Israelite prophet during the time of *Joash* who was stoned for prophesying against the people; son of *Jehoiada* the priest. *2 Chronicles 24: 20-22*

Z

2 Chronicles 26:5

• Prophet and counselor to King Uzziah.

• Israelite prophet during the time of *Zerubbabel* who wrote the *book of Zechariah*; son of Berechiah.

Luke 1:5-25

• *John the Baptist's* father, a priest in Jerusalem who doubted the angel's message that his wife Elizabeth would have a baby.



• Many, many others mentioned only once or only in passing.

Zechariah 9:9-10

**Zechariah, book of** (**zek**-uh-**rye**-uh, **buk** uhv)
Thirty-eighth book of the Old Testament and eleventh of the *minor prophets*. The prophecies in the book of Zechariah encourage the Jews who had returned from Exile with visions of the temple and news of the *Messiah*. The book is famous for its many *messianic prophecies*. It predicts both the first and second comings of *Jesus Christ*.

See also *Haggai; Zerubbabel*

**Zedekiah** (**zed**-uh-**kye**-uh)

A common name among the Israelites:

2 Kings 24:18–25:21
1 Chronicles 3:15
Jeremiah 27:1; 32:1; 34:1-7

• Third son of *Josiah* and last king of Judah before the Exile. Zedekiah reigned 11 years. He is named in many of Jeremiah's prophecies.

1 Kings 22:5-36

• A false prophet during the reign of Ahab and a bitter enemy of the prophet *Micaiah*; son of

Chenaanah. Zedekiah slapped Micaiah in the face.

• One of two false prophets (the other was *Ahab*) who spread lies about *Jeremiah*; son of Maaseiah. *Jeremiah 29:21-23*

**Zeeb** (**zee**-eb) *Judges 7:25; Psalm 83:11*

One of the Midianite generals defeated by Gideon's 300-man force.

*See also Oreb*

**Zelophehad** (zuh-**loh**-fuh-hod) *Numbers 27:1-11; Numbers 36:1-13*

Father of five daughters who received an inheritance because Zelophehad had no sons; son of *Hepher*. Their case set an important precedent in Israel. Until then, inheritances had always passed only to sons by law. God told Moses to change the law so that Zelophehad's daughters would receive justice. Zelophehad lived during the *Exodus*.

**Zemarites** (**zem**-uh-rites) *Genesis 10:15-19*

A *Canaanite* tribe that settled on the coast of *Phoenicia*.

**Zephaniah** (**zef**-uh-**nye**-uh)

• A priest in Jerusalem at the time of Jeremiah; son of Maaseiah. *Jeremiah 21:1; 37:3*

*Zephaniah 1:1* • Prophet who wrote the *book of Zephaniah* during the reign of *Josiah*; son of Cushi.

• Two others mentioned only once.

*Zephaniah 1:1*
*Zephaniah 2:1-3*

**Zephaniah, book of** (**zef**-uh-**nye**-uh, **buk** uhv)
Thirty-sixth book of the Old Testament and ninth of the *minor prophets*. This book was the last to be written before the *Exile* of Jews to Babylonia. It urges the people of Judah to return to God and give up the evil ways that *Manasseh* and *Amon* had encouraged. *Josiah's* reform happened at about this time.
See *also Huldah; Jeremiah*

**Zephath** (**zee**-fath)
See *Hormah*

**Zephathah** (**zef**-uh-thuh)
See *Valley of Zephathah*

**Zerah** (**zee**-ruh)

*Genesis 38:27-30* • Son of Judah and Tamar; twin brother of *Perez*.

*2 Chronicles 14: 9-15* • An Ethiopian ruler who attacked Asa's forces and lost.

*Numbers 26:13* • Head of his clan in the tribe of Simeon; a son of Simeon; also called Zohar.

• Several other minor characters.

*Deuteronomy 2: 13-15*

**Zered Valley** (**zair**-ed **val**-ee)
A *wadi* at the southeast corner of the Dead Sea; also called Zered Brook. The Israelites crossed it on their way to the *promised land*.

**Zerubbabel** (zuh-**ruh**-buh-buhl)
Israelite governor of Judah after the Exile; son of *Shealtiel*; grandson of *Jehoiachin*. Zerubbabel was a descendant of David from the tribe of Judah. He returned to Jerusalem to rebuild the temple. His story is told in the books of Ezra, Nehemiah, Haggai, and Zechariah.

*Ezra 2:1-2; 3:2, 8*
*Haggai 1:1-2*
*Zechariah 4:6-10*

**Zeruiah** (zair-oo-**eye**-uh)
Mother of *Joab*, *Abishai*, and *Asahel*, three of David's most valiant warriors.

**Zeus** (**zooss**)
One of the main gods of Greek religion.

*Acts 14:11-13*

**Ziba** (**zye**-buh)
A servant of King Saul who also served David. Ziba himself had 20 servants. David appointed him to care for *Mephibosheth* and his family.

*2 Samuel 9:1-13*
*2 Samuel 19:15-18*
*2 Samuel 19:24-30*

**Ziklag** (**zik**-lag)
A *Canaanite* town in the *Negev* on the border of *Edom*. Ziklag was allotted to Simeon, then later became part of Judah. David and his men stayed in this town for over a year while raiding towns in Judah still held by Canaanites. Many Israelites of Benjamin, Gad, Judah, and Manasseh deserted Saul and joined David while he was there. He avoided trouble with the Philistines by telling *Achish* that he was actually raiding Israelites. The location of Ziklag is unknown.

*1 Samuel 27:1-12*
*1 Chronicles 12:1-22*

1 Chronicles 12: 20-22

**Zillethai** (**zil**-uh-thye)

A commander in Saul's army who defected to David at *Ziklag* along with several others from the tribe of Manasseh. Zillethai became a commander in David's army.



Genesis 30:9-13
Genesis 35:26

**Zilpah** (**zil**-puh)

Leah's *maidservant*, whom Leah gave to her husband Jacob as a *concubine*. Zilpah was the mother of *Gad* and *Asher*.

Genesis 25:1-4

**Zimran** (**zim**-ruhn)

One of Abraham and Keturah's sons.

**Zimri** (**zim**-rye)

Numbers 25:1-14

• An Israelite clan leader who boldly committed adultery with a woman from Moab during the Exodus, causing a plague among the people; son of Salu.

1 Kings 16:15-20

• Fifth king of Israel after *Elah*. Zimri came to power by assassinating Elah. But as soon as *Omri* heard of it and besieged *Tirzah*, Zimri burned the palace to the ground and died in the fire. He reigned just seven days.

**Zin, Desert of** (**zin**, **dez**-urt uhv)

See *Desert of Zin*

**Zin, Wilderness of** (**zin**, **wil**-dur-ness uhv)

See *Desert of Zin*

**Zion** (**zye**-uhn)
The term is used of three parts of Jerusalem:

- The original fortress or *citadel* of *Jebus*; the City of David. 2 Samuel 5:7 1 Kings 8:1
- The temple mount in Jerusalem; the place where God lives. Psalm 9:11 Psalm 68:16
- The entire city of *Jerusalem*. Isaiah 52:1-3

**Ziph** (**zif**)

- A town in the hill country of Judah where David tried to hide from Saul. 1 Samuel 23:13-29
- A descendant of Caleb. 1 Chronicles 2:42
- A clan chief in the tribe of Judah (with a brother named Ziphah). 1 Chronicles 4:16

**Ziphites** (**zif**-ites) 1 Samuel 23:19-29
People from the town of *Ziph* who betrayed David to Saul.

**Zipporah** (**zip**-or-uh) Exodus 2:15-22 Exodus 18:1-6
Daughter of Jethro and Reuel who married Moses; mother of *Gershom* and *Eliezer*. Zipporah was *Midianite*. Moses met her while on the run from pharaoh. Zipporah did not return to Egypt with Moses, but did rejoin him during the Exodus.

Z

Daniel 3:5

**zither** (**zith**-ur)

A musical instrument, possibly a ten-stringed *harp*.

1 Kings 6:1, 37

**Ziv** (**ziv**)

The second *month* of the Israelite year, overlapping April and May. Also known as Iyyar.

Numbers 13:22
Isaiah 19:11-15

**Zoan** (**zoh**-on)

A city in the northeastern part of Egypt's *Nile* delta; also called Tanis.

Genesis 19:18-22, 30
Deuteronomy 34:3

**Zoar** (**zoh**-ar)

"Little," name of one of the five *cities of the plain*, the only one not destroyed by fire when Lot fled from Sodom. Zoar marked the southern extent of the promised land that Moses saw.

1 Chronicles 18:3-4, 9-11

**Zobah** (**zoh**-buh)

A major fortified city of *Aram* in the north of Lebanon ruled by *Hadadezer*.

Job 2:11
Job 11:1-6

**Zophar** (**zoh**-far)

One of *Job's* friends. Zophar believed that Job suffered because he had sinned, and that Job deserved to suffer even more than he already had. See also *Elihu; Eliphaz; Zophar*

**Zorah** (**zor**-uh)
*Manoah's* hometown, a city in the lowlands of Dan almost three kilometers west of *Eshtaol*.
*Judges 13:2*

**Zorathites** (**zor**-uh-thites)
People who lived in *Zorah*.
*1 Chronicles 2:53; 4:2*

**Zuzim** (**zoo**-zim)
See *Zuzites*

**Zuzites** (**zoo**-zites)
One of the groups defeated by *Kedorlaomer*. Exactly who they were and where they lived is unknown.
See also *Emites; Horites; Rephaites*
*Genesis 14:5-6*